HILL *of*
SECRETS

HILL *of* SECRETS

A NOVEL

GALINA VROMEN

LAKE UNION
PUBLISHING

Published by Lake Union Publishing, Seattle

www.apub.com

Amazon, the Amazon logo, and Lake Union Publishing are trademarks of Amazon.com, Inc., or its affiliates.

ISBN-13: 9781662520792 (paperback)
ISBN-13: 9781662520808 (digital)

Cover design by Faceout Studio, Elisha Zepeda
Cover images: © Marie Carr / ArcAngel; © Oleksiichik, © BlackCat Imaging, © Ismael Khalifa, © Melanie Hobson, © Dimitris Leonidas, © Kaiskynet Studio, © Radoslaw Lecyk / Shutterstock; © EThamPhoto, © KenWiedemann, © Matthias Clamer / Getty

Printed in the United States of America

To those who believed in me long before I believed in myself and led me to somewhere I have never traveled, gladly beyond

Man is not what he thinks he is. He is what he hides.
—André Malraux

CHAPTER 1
CHRISTINE

July 1943

The new white pumps Christine had bought for the trip were instantly caked with dust when Thomas threw their baggage down onto the platform, ruining the first impression she hoped to make—although she didn't know on whom. The farther she and Thomas had traveled from New York, the more numerous the cacti were and the scanter the signs of human life. They had finally arrived. But *where?* The sun was so blinding she could barely read the sign plastered on the white station house: LAMY. She lingered on the platform, considering how to pronounce the name of the town, and longed to flee with the train as it chugged away.

Thomas was already striding toward the station house, a suitcase in each hand and various packages jammed under each arm. Christine stuffed the piece she had been writing into her purse, grabbed the remaining two duffel bags, and rushed to join her husband. Ever since he told her they were heading west, she had been trying to keep up with him, to match his enthusiasm for this mysterious adventure. Her shoes hurt her as she walked, her feet swelling and chafing from the heat. She'd need to buy a larger size for this place.

A soldier with curly black hair, unruly under a felt side cap, approached and saluted. "Professor and Mrs. Star!"

"Sharp," Thomas corrected him. "The name is Sharp."

The soldier lowered his voice, his blue eyes earnest. "Sir, we do not use real names in public for security reasons."

The station was deserted—no one to overhear their names. In other circumstances, Christine would have been amused by a rule so clearly irrelevant, but the soldier's insistence unnerved her.

"I'm Corporal James Campbell," he said, saluting for a moment before dropping his hand and smiling. "But you can call me Jimmy."

He grabbed the largest suitcases, leaving Thomas and Christine to pick up what was left, and led them to a 1942 Chevy sedan so coated in dust it was the same shade as the otherwise empty dirt lot. While the men loaded the luggage, Christine cleaned the sand off the back seat with her handkerchief, a Christmas present from her mother. Trimmed with lace, it was fancier than anything her mother would use in rural Maine. She must have thought it would be suitable for Christine's sophisticated life in New York City. Christine had loved exploring the city with Thomas, who introduced her to the magic of walking across the Brooklyn Bridge at midnight and the pleasure of smooching in the gardens of the Cloisters on Sunday afternoons. How ironic that Christine now reluctantly used the handkerchief as a cleaning rag in some godforsaken place neither she nor her mother could have ever imagined.

Following the instructions Thomas received, Christine hadn't told her mother—or anyone else—where they were moving. She wasn't even allowed to express her exasperation that she didn't know the details, only that it was somewhere in the West. She'd told her parents and business partner, Samantha Lewis, what she could—that Thomas was being stationed far from New York and she was going with him. She'd have to leave her job as deputy curator at Samantha's gallery and abandon the subsidiary business in art-and-antique restoration they'd recently launched together. Sorry to see her go, Samantha suggested that Christine continue to write the catalogs for the gallery's exhibits. Christine accepted enthusiastically. She had finished the catalog copy on the gallery's upcoming show of pointillist artists on the train ride and needed only to type the final text and mail it off.

The car zoomed across an infinity of flatness, the monotony broken only by hills on the horizon. This was where Thomas told her he had been offered "the opportunity of a lifetime"? It seemed more like an opportunity for a lizard than for a man as brilliant as Thomas. There must be a post office here, somewhere.

Christine's eyes burned from the dust squalls, but closing the car window was so stifling, she immediately opened it again. They passed a village of abandoned clapboard houses and, a few miles later, a cluster of mud huts. Thomas always seemed to know what he was doing. Was this what he had expected? Overcome by the heat, Christine dozed off until the Chevy jolted to a stop on a street lined with adobe houses. They were set back by covered porches, which were anchored by posts near the road, creating a shaded arcade along the sidewalk.

"Our first stop, folks. Administration Headquarters." Jimmy pulled up in front of a wrought iron gate. Behind it lay a courtyard of raked pebbles surrounded by low buildings.

Leaving Jimmy with the luggage, Christine and Thomas walked up to a one-story house with a thick wooden door, marked **109** in big black letters. Finally, she might learn why they were here. 109 East Palace Avenue, Santa Fe, New Mexico, was the return address on the letters Thomas had received regularly at their apartment in New York before their departure. The arrival of each letter had filled her with trepidation. He had ordered her never to open them and would dash into the bedroom to read each new missive. He was so secretive, she imagined him eating them to ensure they were destroyed once read. Then he would emerge from the bedroom to launch the next phase of his war to wear her down and win her agreement to the move. In their final battle, she had accused him of being selfish. He'd insisted he was doing what was best for them both.

"What's best for you and what's best for me are not the same," she'd shot back.

"How can you say that?"

She'd reminded him then—hating her angry, whining tone—that she had scrapped her PhD studies to join him in London for his postdoc in chemistry. And how, soon after she had parlayed her knowledge of chemistry into an apprenticeship as an art restorer at the National Portrait Gallery, they had moved back to New York so Thomas could take a new job. And after flailing for a year, she had met Samantha and started the joint restoration business, which she was loving more than anything she'd ever done before.

"And now, you're taking me somewhere you can't even tell me, and I'm supposed to land like a cat on my feet—and purr about it."

"That's what I love about you. How you always make it work. We'll be together. And, honestly, your business isn't going gangbusters, what with the war and all. Maybe it's time to kick up your heels. Relaxing might help—you know—with what we both want, with having a kid. Maybe you're working too hard, and that's why you haven't . . ."

They had been trying for three years already, and just that morning, she had gotten her monthly cramps and would disappoint him yet again. She crumbled at the thought, and tears welled in her eyes. Noticing them, Thomas had taken her into his arms and held her close and kissed her until she wiped them away.

He had sat her down on their sofa and brought her a glass of water. "We live in a time of unknowns. The only thing I do know is that I have to do whatever I can to help win this war. And so do you."

He'd said it almost as a reprimand. They had had their differences over the war. She was, at first, opposed to the United States getting embroiled in a European war, sacrificing American boys, especially after Hitler invaded Russia. Fascists, Communists—they were all equally abhorrent. Why not just let them destroy each other? It had taken the attack on Pearl Harbor and England's desperation to turn her around, but even then, she felt American lives were being wasted.

"This job means I won't get drafted. Not everyone gets a chance to be exempted and yet fight the good fight. I know this is hard for you. I'll try and make it up to you someday, somehow."

That had ended the discussion. Thomas knew she was terrified that he would be called up and become part of the slaughter. So often, she had watched him as he slept next to her and wondered how long she would have him by her side. She loved how, from their first date, when he learned she was studying for a PhD in chemistry, he'd been thrilled that she grasped problems in his experiments most people found obtuse, and how their intense conversations unfailingly morphed into even more passionate lust. The realization that this mysterious opportunity ensured Thomas would stay with her, far from the front, consoled her.

So, she had sipped the water he had handed her and blown her nose.

Now they were here in this sweltering courtyard of cacti and pale-purple flowers in front of a screen door that would reveal their future. For the first time since she had packed their bags in New York, curiosity trumped her misgivings.

"Come in, the door is open," came the singsong response to Thomas's knock.

A woman with wavy brown hair flecked with gray sat alone at a desk in the middle of a large room with beamed ceilings. She looked up from her typewriter and smiled.

"Thomas and Christine Sharp, I presume." She rose to greet them.

The alias had been dropped. A secure place. The woman seemed kind.

"I'm Dorothy McKibbin." She held out her hand to shake theirs. "I'm here to help you get settled. Have a seat." Dorothy pointed to two chairs, offered them cherry sodas—gratefully accepted—and opened an information packet on her tidy desk.

"You'll be living in a restricted military area with several hundred other families, about thirty miles from here. Corporal Campbell will take you there shortly."

Christine looked at Thomas. "A closed military area? Did you know this?"

Dorothy reached across the desk and patted Christine's hand.

"It must be a shock. No one is told where they're going or why until they get here. But the secrecy is necessary. We do want to win this war, don't we?" She held Christine's eyes.

"Yes, of course." Christine managed a meek smile.

"'Standing by and making do.' That's what we women here say." Dorothy sifted through papers on her desk and pulled out a photograph of a two-story barrack-like clapboard building.

"This is where you will be living. In one of the Sundt units. Sundt's a local contractor, done a lot of building for us. You're lucky there's still one available. They've just been completed, so the yard is still a bit of a mess. But the units have hardwood floors, two bedrooms, and a larger kitchen than any others on the site. Two sinks, plenty of storage space, and a big new stove. That's considered luxury around here." She handed over the packet. "I hope you will find the answers to your questions in this material. If not, you can send a message from the director's office. Or ask around. You will find people very friendly on the Hill—that's what we call Los Alamos. You'll be old-timers before you know it."

"Is there a post office?" asked Christine.

"Yes, of course, although your letters will have to go through censorship."

"Censorship?"

"If you stick to your knitting, it shouldn't be a problem. You wouldn't want to inadvertently harm the war effort, would you, dear? There's an army commissary for most things. You'll find it exceptionally well stocked with food and sundries. Lots of things rationed elsewhere are available. You can thank General Groves in DC for that. He's always looking after his scientists, only the best for them." Dorothy smiled brightly. "And then there are buses taking you down here to Santa Fe, for shopping and whatnot. You can do that about once a month if you care to."

As Christine was wondering how long these shopping-trip rides would take, the phone on the desk rang. Dorothy excused herself to answer. "Yes, Oppie, they've arrived. Everything's fine. Yes, I'll send him right up." She hung up.

"Well, Dr. Oppenheimer is delighted you're here," she said, addressing Thomas. "He asks that you report to the Tech Area as soon as you get to the Hill. It seems he has a problem that he's waiting to discuss with you. It's so like Oppie. I mean Dr. Oppenheimer—we all call him Oppie." She chuckled and shook her head. "It wouldn't occur to him that you might want to unpack before reporting to work." She peered at Christine. "The unpacking, I'm afraid, will be left to you, deary."

Dorothy turned her attention to typing up their passes.

It struck Christine that already this new place was tearing her husband away from her. To flick away the unpleasant thought, she joined Thomas in studying the information packet, which described Fuller Lodge social and dining hall and contained a list of hobby clubs—singing, theater, stamp collecting, chess, folk dancing, a chamber music ensemble—and the schedule on the Hill: six workdays a week. Only Sundays off.

Christine knew the packet did not contain the answers to the questions racing through her mind . . . how long they would stay, what she would do with herself, and whether she'd be the only married woman without a child.

She glanced at Thomas, who was absorbed in reading the information sheets, and felt a surge of affection, rare in past weeks, for her dapper, lanky husband, so enthralled to be here.

"You will need these to enter and leave the Hill." Dorothy handed them passes. "They are good for a month at a time. Best not to lose them if you want to avoid fuss and feathers."

Thomas squeezed Christine's hand as they left the building. "Dorothy seems nice enough," he said. "So far, so good, don't you think?"

"Sounds like one big, happy summer camp." Her sarcasm was lost on Thomas, who beamed at Jimmy, leaning on the parked Chevy and waiting for them at the curb.

"You'll be fine," Thomas murmured as he opened the back door for her.

"Sure," she answered, not sure at all, as she settled into the seat. Even cats with nine lives, if forced to leap too far, were not guaranteed to land on their feet.

The car growled as it climbed curve after hairpin curve from the Valle Grande to the mesas above. The sand and scrub stretched to the horizon, punctuated by rock ridges that looked like gnarled arms ending in fingerlike formations that gripped the bottom of the crater. Other than an occasional pine tree, there was little discernable vegetation. Christine felt diminished by the landscape.

In the front seat, Jimmy nattered on about their surroundings. She heard snippets: "Valle Grande, the biggest crater around here . . . created when a volcano collapsed on itself . . . the light-colored rock around the top is called Bandelier Tuff . . . highest peak rises eleven thousand feet . . . Los Alamos is Spanish for the cottonwoods in these parts . . ."

Christine had worked hard to escape the drudgery of small rural life in her native Maine for the excitement of New York, reshelving books at a public library by day and waitressing by night to earn the money for college. But it seemed that she had just switched the foggy, cold denseness of her Maine for hot, sparse New Mexico.

Well, at least she had the work she agreed to do for Samantha. She rummaged in her bag and pulled out the twenty handwritten pages as if they were a good luck charm. She sifted through the papers and felt a momentary satisfaction, sure that Samantha would love how she had insightfully explained the historical context of the pointillist works on exhibit.

Suddenly, the car swerved on a hairpin curve, throwing her off balance. She was hurled to the other side of the back seat, and the papers fluttered out the window.

"Stop! My work!"

The papers whirled into the crater below.

"I can't stop, it's steep. There's no shoulder," Jimmy shouted back to her.

"Stop, please stop!"

"There's no point, hon," Thomas said as his gaze followed the spiraling papers.

"I have to get them!"

"They're gone."

"Oh God, what am I going to do? I promised to mail them to Samantha this week."

"You didn't lose everything, did you?" Thomas turned around to look at the sheaves scattered on the back seat and floor. "You'll rewrite what's missing while it's fresh in your mind. It'll probably turn out even better the next time. It usually does, doesn't it?"

He was right. But she didn't want him to be. She wanted him to sympathize. It was all too much, this wretched place and this crazy, dangerous road that could send them plunging into the crater, like her papers, at any moment. And her work, the one thing that had kept her mind calm during the exhausting four-day trip to this confounding place, was now mostly gone. What had she agreed to by coming here?

Christine was jerked out of her internal agitation when the sedan bumped over a pothole and she hit her head on the car's roof. Up ahead was a row of white security booths. This must be the Hill. Jimmy drove up to one of the booths and handed over the Sharps' passes. The grim duty officer inspected the documents, glared at Thomas and Christine, and then handed the papers back to Jimmy reluctantly, as if disappointed he had not found some kind of fault. He waved the car through.

Jimmy brought the car to a lurching halt at another security booth. Beyond, Christine could see a complex of low-slung buildings fenced off with two rows of barbed wire.

"First stop, Site Y, otherwise known as the Tech Area," Jimmy said. "Off you go, Dr. Sharp. The officers in that booth there will want to see your security pass again and will direct you to Oppie's office. I'll make sure the missus is okay." He took a hand off the steering wheel to salute, then extended it to shake Thomas's hand. "It's been a pleasure, sir."

Thomas threw a glance back at Christine. "You'll be okay?"

"Sure." She smiled bravely. "Will you know the way home?"

"A good question." Thomas laughed.

"Don't worry," said Jimmy. "Anyone can direct you to the Sundt units. They're walking distance. And at the Sundts, people will know your apartment. Only one unit was empty, and everyone's been waiting to see who gets it."

Thomas hopped out of the car and stopped a moment at the back window to give Christine a peck on the cheek. He squeezed her hand. "Wish me luck," he said.

With a start, Christine realized that Thomas was nervous, intimidated even—something she had never seen before. *Brilliant* was the adjective normally used in conjunction with her husband. Although he was not arrogant, she knew he did not consider it inaccurate.

"I guess this is big," she said. She was still as baffled as she had been since those letters started arriving in New York as to why his expertise in developing highly resilient coatings could be of such importance to the war effort.

A flicker of uncertainty crossed his face, and he shrugged. "I think it is."

She realized suddenly that maybe even he didn't know exactly why he had been summoned here. "Good luck." She squeezed his hand and let him go, proud to see him walk purposefully toward the security booth and into the inner sanctum of the exceptional, brought together to try to win this horrid war.

Jimmy stepped on the gas, and Christine tried to memorize the route as they turned right, down one unpaved road and left on another. All around, she saw construction sites and flimsy houses scattered like a trail of shoeboxes, their fresh green paint and corrugated tin roofs already dusty. She had never noticed before that dust had a smell. She wondered if there were as many varieties of dust smell as there were of natural Maine mulch. Would she learn to discern them?

Women with strollers struggled to push their charges through deep-rutted roads. Others trudged along, looking defeated by the heat, loaded down with net bags of groceries in each hand. The women were all dressed in dungarees and sported neck bandannas, apparently high fashion in these parts. They wore workmen's boots, sneakers, or sandals; none wore pumps like hers.

On a balcony, a cluster of women chatted, laughing over tea or coffee, and Christine was surprised at the flash of longing she felt. Could they be future friends? In her experience with small, remote places, chattiness was cattiness. What were the chances things would be different here?

The sound of nails being pounded into clapboard created a sense of bustle and newness. It felt as if, when she awoke the next day, she might find herself in a town constructed overnight by leprechauns.

There were telephone poles on the side of the road, but she noticed that no lines ran between them.

"Anybody have a phone in this place?" she asked.

"Only the director, and only in his office. The poles were put in place, but then the security guys decided it was better not to let folks have phones."

Christine didn't like these security guys, whoever they were.

Jimmy stopped in front of a two-story unit with small windows and front balconies bordered with slat-wood balustrades.

"You're in the apartment upstairs," he said, opening the door of the Chevy for her.

While she stared at the steep wooden stairs, Jimmy pulled out the suitcases, duffel bags, and packages from the trunk. He nodded to her to lead the way, but she let him go first. She was curious to see her new home, but as long as she stayed in the street, maybe she could still drive away to New York, to Samantha, to restoring antique furniture and old paintings, to new exhibitions by upcoming artists, to Broadway plays and walks in Central Park.

Jimmy made his way down and up with more luggage, sweat pouring from his brow. This time she followed him up the stairs. Standing on the landing balcony before the door of the apartment, she looked around at the tangle of children's bicycles in the lot between the buildings. The clothesline across the way fluttered with T-shirts of every color and size. Another line displayed only diapers. Did *everyone* here have children? Sand scratched her throat.

"Let me get you some water," she said to Jimmy as he walked past her into the unit.

She followed him in and headed into the sunny kitchen. After opening and shutting the white cabinets until she found glasses, Christine turned on the cold-water tap at the sink. The water was warm, slightly brown. She let it run.

"Don't do that," said Jimmy. "No wasting water!"

"But it's brown."

"That water takes too long to run clear to waste it that way. You probably want to be boiling the water you drink until your body gets used to it."

"How long does it take a body to get used to the water, to this place?"

"Everyone's different." He gulped the murky water she offered him.

"Do you like it here?"

"I do." He set the empty glass on the counter. "People try to do right by each other. Respectful even if they're famous. And some of them are world famous, even. It's an honor." He wiped his sweaty brow. "There's not much to miss about my dad's fish business on Cape Cod. Don't miss that one little bit."

She smiled. "So, you're from New England, like me—I grew up in Maine. I was glad to leave too. But this place feels like the end of the world."

12

"A lot of people come to like it here, or at least get used to it." He seemed to be chiding her, although not unkindly. "If you're all set, I'll be getting on now."

"Sure." She sighed and looked around the room at its bare white walls. "All set." Her ruefulness earned her an apologetic smile from Jimmy. But by the time she thought to say thank you, he was already bounding down the stairs, too far away to hear.

She turned on the tap and defiantly ran the water until it was clear. Her skin felt stretched and tight. Her lips were cracking. She found a pitcher in the closet, filled it to the brim. She plugged in the refrigerator and put the pitcher inside. Soon there would be cold, clear water to drink. It was a start.

The kitchen was flooded with light, a pleasure after their dark one-bedroom apartment in New York. It was roomier, too, and had all the basics. A pine dining table, four matching chairs, and dishes. The living room had an olive green sofa, which looked as if it had been upholstered with army surplus left over from soldiers' winter coats. A bare light bulb hung overhead. She opened the linen closet in the hall. There was nothing in it. She was glad she had brought her own sheets and towels, disregarding Thomas's assurances that everything would be provided. In the bedroom, she put her bag on the one side of the bed that had a reading light, then decided against it, moving the bag to the other side, conceding the light to Thomas. She would buy a lamp for herself on one of those shopping trips to Santa Fe that Dorothy had mentioned. If she were asked to give a name to the style of their new home, she would call it "authentic flimsy." But it was like an empty canvas, something she could work with and upgrade with a few rugs, cushions, and lampshades.

She unpacked Thomas's clothes and placed his slacks and T-shirts in the chest of drawers, then slammed shut the drawers with difficulty and moved on to the bathroom to put away toiletries. She peered at her gaunt face in the medicine cabinet mirror.

What was his once-in-a-lifetime opportunity going to be for her? In her wildest dreams, she could not have imagined that Thomas would land her in a place like this. He had grown up with all the refinements of a family listed for generations in the *Social Register*, that index of high-society lineage she had never even heard of before she knew him.

She had moved to New York as soon as she finished high school, graduating at the top of her class, desperate to leave behind the fumes of her father's gas station, to escape his temper and the sight of her mother slinking into the bathroom for a nip of booze. New York had been daunting, intoxicating, as unexpectedly friendly as it could be brusque—and oblivious to any reality but its own. She was thrilled that no one cared where she came from or what she had been before she got there and had grabbed the opportunity to reinvent herself, first by enrolling in the undergraduate and then the graduate chemistry department at New York University. Later, the revamp of her life included Thomas, not the sort of man she would have ever met growing up nor the sort of man she would have expected to notice her, never mind love her.

He had been astounded when she told him that she planned to continue all the way to a doctorate—and delighted. He called her his "woman of substance and beauty." He seemed entranced with the idea that she had come from nothing and believed in becoming a "someone." He reveled in her unabashed enthusiasm to see art, hear music of all kinds, taste whatever he and the city might offer. She had been overcome with gratitude that he didn't mind the long hours she put in at the lab and how he boasted to friends and family that they would one day be Dr. and Dr. Sharp. She had thrilled at the incisive way they could talk about each other's research. A year after the wedding, he received a three-year fellowship in London. They both agreed she should abandon her PhD for the "European adventure." She told herself it would be a wonderful chance to immerse herself in the world of art to which Thomas had introduced her. She took classes in restoration and art history, lapping up a new world of beauty, which led to her business in art restoration and curating.

Now she was back to zero, she thought, as she plunked her lipstick on a shelf in the bathroom and unpacked their toothbrushes. Done in the bathroom, Christine decided it was time to think about making her way to the commissary to buy food and prepare dinner.

Tomorrow she would look through what remained of the catalog copy she had been writing, see what was missing, and rewrite what she remembered, as Thomas suggested. Type it all up and send it off to Samantha. What had Dorothy said? Standing by and making do. How exactly? She doubted even Dorothy knew the answer.

CHAPTER 2
GERTIE

September 1943

Clay oozed between Gertie's toes as she waded into the swimming hole near the Tech Area, guarded by concertina wire that spooled like crazy scribbles against the afternoon sky. The pond was peaceful, rippling gently, the breeze swaying the tall grasses at the far edge.

Gertie plunged into the tepid water, washing away the sand lodged in every crevice of her body, then flipped onto her back. She floated and gazed at the blue above. In water, her body seemed to extend into liquid and sky. Papa said that matter was continuous, atoms flowing into each other. She could almost feel those connections in the water, even if she couldn't see them. Los Alamos, too, was real even if invisible to most, a military secret. No one, not even Papa—especially Papa, the renowned physicist Professor Kurt Koppel—was willing to explain to her what was so important about Los Alamos that her family had had to move here from Boston two months ago, just after her sixteenth birthday.

There was so much she wanted to know, so much to unravel. To extract the truth, to hold it to the light, made life pure and intense, like the awe in knowing the world was made of atoms. Yet so much was secret, forbidden. *Verboten.* She muttered it in her native German.

Even German was banned. Ever since America entered the war, Papa had forbidden Mama to speak German in public. And one did not disobey Papa.

But that didn't mean Gertie stopped arguing with him. She sputtered at Papa every time he refused to tell her what thousands of people were doing here, in this ugly, sprawling place called the Hill, its very existence concealed from the rest of the world.

"You've always told me to be curious, but when I am, you get mad at me," Gertie had fumed at him a week ago. Papa fumed back, furrowing his brow, sucking hard on his pipe, sweat forming on his bald head. She retreated to her room and he to the master bedroom. Mama had flitted between the two, as she so often did when Gertie and Papa fought, hoping to placate them with a pat on the arm or a cup of tea. Her efforts only added to their fury until, defeated, she settled in the living room with her knitting. Aside from such attempts, Mama was mostly numb, too anxious to even express her worry over the unknown fate of relatives left behind in Germany.

Gertie pounded the water in a swift backstroke, still seething from the most recent fight with her parents the previous day. They'd refused to let her hold on to her pass—the identity paper she needed to get out of Los Alamos.

"Sometimes kids at school borrow a car and drive to Santa Fe. I want to go with them. I want my pass."

This need for a pass was theoretical, since she had yet to make any real friends in school. There was no way she'd admit that to her parents. She also couldn't tell them how much she felt like a prisoner here. In Boston, protective as her parents were, they had at least allowed her to go to the library on her own and to movies with her best friend, Wilhelmina.

"We'll keep the pass. You might lose it. If you need it, we will give it to you," Papa had said.

"I won't lose it."

"It is best this way," Mama chimed in.

"Stop treating me like a child."

"Who are these young people who drive? Do they even have licenses? You could get hurt. Do we know their parents?" Papa asked.

"None of the people you work with have children my age. They're all young. Not like you. You must be the oldest, most old-fashioned people here!"

"Young lady, I will not tolerate your tone!" Papa had walked away. And kept her pass.

Her only escape was the pond, a ten-minute walk from the house. It was always blessedly deserted in the late afternoon.

Gertie lifted one arm after the other, stretching each as far as she could up and then back behind her head as she swam. Frogs croaked as if cheering her on. She felt the sinewy movement of her torso and could imagine her body merging with the clouds, pink and lavender in the fading light.

She flipped onto her stomach and sliced the water with long strokes. As she swam, she thought about Wilhelmina back in Boston. Papa said she could write now to her best friend but added that censors read every letter before it went out. Creepy. How could you write your true thoughts when you knew a stranger would read them? And she was not to mention where they lived or anything about their surroundings. What did it leave to write about? How lonely she was? How hard it was to go to a new school where she did not know anyone? She sighed. There was no point writing about the war. Wilhelmina followed Allied movements as much as Gertie did, as closely as everyone they knew did. How could one not, considering all that was at stake? She would write about peanut butter–and–jelly sandwiches, the disgusting new lunch rage that was too sweet and made your mouth stick to itself.

Gertie swam across the middle of the pond, her arms rotating like propellers, feet kicking.

Papa suggested she tell Wilhelmina they had moved to the West because they had come to visit relatives and found it so beautiful that they decided to stay. But Wilhelmina, who came from a Jewish refugee family like Gertie's, would never believe this. Neither Wilhelmina's parents nor Gertie's skipped into the future on a whim. No, they darted through an obstacle course of fear, real and imagined, holding their breath and hoping to reach safe shores. Would Wilhelmina figure out that Gertie had moved because Papa had a new job that had something to do with the war? Not that Gertie herself knew more than that, although she planned to find out. In fact, she was bent on unearthing all those truths adults tried to protect her from—about Europe, about life, about love. Her father was a scientist. He believed in knowing. But not in telling.

Gertie flipped onto her back, kicking her legs like a frog. Homework would have to be confronted—but first, just a few more minutes of water. She wondered if she would ever feel as good on land or with people as she felt floating in the pond.

Suddenly, a scream penetrated the stillness. Gertie stood up in the slimy mud and scanned the shore for its source. A second shriek focused her attention on a woman running on the beach.

"Are you okay?" Gertie called and immediately chided herself. The woman wouldn't be screaming and flapping her arms if she were okay. Gertie broke into a fast front crawl, stopped a few yards from shore, and stood.

"Don't come out of the water!" the woman shouted.

"Why not?" The mud sluiced through Gertie's toes, stirring up who knew what from the bottom.

"A snake, there's a snake! At least I think it's a snake." The woman skirted away from the water and flicked long strands of red hair from her face.

"Did it make a rattling sound?" Not long ago, Gertie, too, would have panicked at a snake.

"What? A sound? I don't think so."

"Probably harmless." Gertie walked closer to shore.

"Stay in the water!" The woman hopped forward and backward, as if she could not decide whether it was more important to stop Gertie from coming out of the water or to get as far away from the snake as possible.

"I can't stay in the water all night." Gertie laughed and advanced. She had learned in the first weeks of school that snakes in these parts were mostly harmless, except for rattlesnakes. She was close enough now to see that the woman was slim and tall. Her long red hair was slightly darker than the orange sun setting behind her. She would be pretty if she didn't look so scared.

"Don't move! I'll go get help," the woman commanded.

"Honest, I know what I'm talking about. There is nothing to be afraid of." Gertie's measured tone surprised even herself and was apparently reassuring enough to make the woman's eyes shift from fear to surprise to admiration by the time Gertie reached the bank.

"We'd better leave. It can't be safe here," the woman said.

"It's so beautiful at this hour. Don't let a harmless garter snake chase you away." Gertie wrapped herself in a towel and smiled.

The woman cocked her head. "How do you know it's a garter snake?"

For the first time in the six years since she came to this country, Gertie didn't feel like a foreigner around an American. "There are always snakes about. You must be new here if you're afraid of them."

"Not that new, since July."

"Same as me, in time for school," said Gertie.

"I don't know what I came in time for," the woman said wistfully, then seemed to catch herself and smiled brightly. "I'm Christine, Christine Sharp."

Gertie introduced herself and tried to gauge Christine's age, always difficult with adults. Lots older than Gertie in any case, and lots younger than Mama or Papa.

"Where are you from?" Christine asked, sitting down and tapping her hand on the sand for Gertie to join her.

Gertie, pleasantly cooled from her swim, sat down beside Christine and sighed. "Germany, Rochester, Syracuse, Boston. All of them, none of them. Where are you from?"

Christine laughed. "From almost as many places as you. Most recently from New York City. But I grew up in Maine."

"I've been to New York. For my sixteenth birthday, with my Papa, just before we came here. We had a grand time. Never been to Maine."

"Well, I've never been to Germany, or Rochester or Syracuse."

They were silent for a few minutes, but it was a comfortable lull, the air gentle and warm. They listened for a few moments to the birds and crickets in the nearby trees.

Gertie broke their silence. "Do you like peanut butter–and-jelly sandwiches?"

"Excuse me?"

"Peanut butter and jelly. Do you like them?"

Christine looked puzzled and answered slowly. "I like peanut butter, and I like jelly. Never had them together, though I understand it's popular with soldiers these days."

"With kids in school too," said Gertie.

"Sounds pretty awful to me."

"It is." Gertie smiled. Maybe she had found an ally. She couldn't think of anything else to ask Christine, who, unlike most adults, seemed in no rush to fill the stillness with chatter. They watched the water ripple in the breeze of the dying day.

"It's beautiful here, isn't it?" said Christine.

"Yes. It can make you forget how ugly the rest of the Hill is."

"True." Christine laughed. Her eyes settled on Gertie as if she had just discovered an alluring creature.

They gazed to the distance, where the Tech Area was lit up, looking less forbidding in the twilight, its barbed wire fence now hidden by the dark.

"Do you know what they do there?" Gertie asked.

"No, of course not. No one who's not supposed to know does," said Christine.

"Do you wonder about it, though?"

"You know we're not supposed to talk about it." There was no scolding in Christine's voice, just a statement of fact.

"Still, don't you wonder?"

"Of course. But I can more or less guess—I mean it's something to help end the war," said Christine.

"You mean 'the gadget' people talk about. But what is it, really?"

"Do the details beyond that matter, as long as it ends this awful war?"

"Yes, details always matter." Gertie spoke slowly, casting around for words to express herself. "They make things more real, more wonderful, or more awful. You can look at the setting sun and think it's beautiful, but when you know how the universe works, how everything orbits around and what makes the sun set, the beauty is more, more . . . wonderful. Take the war. It seems so abstract here, but when you know the details, when you live with the details, it makes it more real, and more awful, don't you think?"

"I never thought about it that way." Christine gazed at Gertie in that way adults did whenever she said something they wouldn't expect from a kid. But unusually for a grown-up, Christine didn't ask Gertie how old she was or what grade she was in. She seemed to accept that someone Gertie's age might have thoughts worth considering. They sat in silence, listening to the swamp grass at the edge of the swimming hole rustle like gossips passing secrets. With darkness coming, neither had a reason to stay, yet neither seemed eager to leave.

"You're a good swimmer," said Christine.

"My father gave me lessons when I was four. He didn't want me to drown, said it was very important to know how to swim. So, he threw me in a pool. That's how they teach children in Germany."

"That sounds absolutely awful!"

"Amazing thing is, it works. I learned really fast."

"I don't know how to swim."

"Really?"

"I guess my father never worried I would drown." Christine's eyes, suddenly harsh, focused on the water in the distance.

Gertie wanted to erase the look on her face. "I could teach you."

Christine looked at Gertie and smiled wistfully. "You make it look easy. It's hard to learn new things sometimes."

"Not if you try. And I'm very patient. I won't get angry or anything if you don't do it right the first time."

"It's getting dark. I should go make dinner." Christine rose to leave.

"We could meet tomorrow. And I could show you. Like I said, I'm pretty patient."

"I was thinking of going into town. Not sure when I'll be back."

"You'll be good at swimming. I can just tell. We could have a nice time, me teaching you to swim. And we could talk, too, and I could tell you more about snakes and other things about the wildlife here that we learn about at school. So let's meet, okay?"

Christine looked out onto the water and said nothing.

Gertie hoped it didn't sound as if she were pleading. She liked this woman and wanted a friend, or at least someone she found comfortable to talk to. And she really could teach her to swim.

"You are a very serious and frank young lady," Christine said gently.

"I could be here around four o'clock."

"And very determined." Christine smiled.

Gertie looked at Christine's delicate features, her warm eyes, slim nose, and high cheekbones, splashed with freckles. She could imagine learning grown-up things from Christine that her parents thought she shouldn't know and American things her parents couldn't know.

"I'll see if I can make it back in time."

"Good. I'll be here." Gertie slipped a shift over her bathing suit. As they headed in opposite directions, their calls of "good night" were muffled by the generator in the Tech Area.

CHAPTER 3
CHRISTINE

September 1943

Christine answered the knock on her door to find her neighbor, Martha McPherson, flapping a letter in front of her face.

"I have something for you," Martha sang. Her small brown eyes were a little too close together and darted around as if she were eager to find something to gnaw.

"It's such a lovely day, I went to the post office first thing, noticed there was a letter in your cubby, so figured I'd bring it. Save you the trouble." Martha waved the letter again.

"Oh, you needn't have," Christine said. Privacy was such a rare commodity around here.

"It was no trouble," Martha sang gaily.

"Honestly, I'd rather go myself. Gets me out of the house." Christine hoped she was being clear.

"From New York, I see." Martha craned her neck at the return address as she handed over the letter. "An art gallery . . . ," she noted with unconcealed curiosity.

Samantha! Finally, a response to the catalog copy sent two months ago, just a few days after they'd first arrived. God, the mail was slow! Christine clasped the letter.

"Come over for a cup of coffee." Martha flashed a broad, toothy smile. Christine looked down at her morning gown, as shapeless as the day ahead. Since she wasn't dressed yet, it was obvious that Martha was hoping for an invitation to come in. Martha's husband, Ed, held a senior position in Thomas's lab, so it would be diplomatic to accept. But Christine had no inclination to spend time gossiping with Martha.

"Another time maybe. I've been putting off errands for far too long."

"No harm in putting errands off a little while longer," Martha cooed.

Would her neighbor never go away? If anyone could kill you with kindness, it was Martha. Always chipper, her blonde curls perfectly in place with a Rosie the Riveter bandanna—today's was white with black polka dots.

"Not this morning, Martha. Thanks." Christine's fingers itched to open Samantha's letter.

"Well, if you change your mind, the kettle's always ready."

Christine barely managed to beam a false smile and a "thanks" at Martha before she closed the door on her and ripped open the envelope. She sat down at the breakfast table and read:

> "The catalog copy you wrote for the show is wonderful, but it arrived so late, I was forced to commission someone else at the last minute to write something suitable instead. I was worried about you. It's so unlike you to miss a deadline! When your letter finally arrived, I saw that it was dated in July, but it didn't get to me for more than a month! And a lot was blacked out. Censored? Why? Where are you?!!! In any case, I don't think our plan for you to write catalog material

is going to work out. I do hope you and Thomas are
doing well . . ."

All the work she had put into that piece: the hours of research, the
feverish writing, the all-nighter she had pulled to type it up. The damn
censors must have held it up. Why had they blacked out an article on
pointillist artists? It was crazy. Infuriating. Like everything else here.

When Samantha suggested that Christine keep her hand in the
New York art world by writing catalog articles, they hadn't considered
censors and slow mail. Besides, it was impossible to write insightfully
about up-and-coming artists she couldn't speak to and whose work she
could see only in photographs. Samantha was right. This was not going
to work.

She folded the letter and slipped it back in the envelope, tucking
away that part of her life. How she missed the gallery and the back-office
studio. Christine had organized it all: the tinctures in neat rows, the oils
for furniture separated from the oils for picture restoration, the reference
books she perused over her coffee breaks. Restoring art required empathy
to appreciate the logic and beauty of each piece, so that even without
knowing what had been destroyed, it was possible to imagine what it
must have looked like. She had a gift for appreciating and adapting to the
quirks of each craftsman, understanding the vision of the artist, restoring
each item according to its essence.

Life without all that seemed meaningless. She had to find something to do here, anything. Maybe she should take up Gertie's offer
yesterday of swimming lessons. Christine found herself considering
Gertie as she might a portrait: Dark unruly eyebrows, too thick and
clearly never plucked, rendered her big green-brown eyes disconcert-
ingly intense, unmitigated by her olive skin and dominant mouth. Yet
the features worked well together, conveying openness, mettle, and vul-
nerability. The girl's lack of guile, the way she wore loneliness on her
sleeve, made her seem like a work in progress, unaware of all the ways
she might yet develop into someone poised and beautiful.

She might make herself useful by befriending Gertie—and ease her own loneliness. Besides, it was high time to get over her fear of water. Learning to swim would be something new. If only the mere thought of the slimy pond bottom didn't make her queasy.

Christine set her empty coffee cup in the sink and turned on the radio, swept along with Bing Crosby's latest hit, "Sunday, Monday, or Always." She finished the dishes as the news came on. Mussolini was back in power, rescued from imprisonment by the Nazis. The next item—Christine wagered it was calibrated to boost morale—was about the US developing an improved bazooka antitank missile, demonstrated this week for reporters at Fort Benning, Georgia. *It's so simple and yet so powerful that any foot soldier using it can stand his ground with the certain knowledge that he is the master of any tank that may attack him.*

Christine turned off the radio and headed to the bathroom for a shower, wondering, not for the first time, what sort of weapon her own husband and the rest of the scientists here were developing. She couldn't figure out how Thomas's expertise fit in. His field wasn't explosives or radar or anything else particularly useful to the war effort, as far as she understood. His coatings were used for laboratory equipment. So, she suspected it had to do with that. She didn't have Gertie's burning desire to know all the details, but it nettled her that Thomas shared nothing about his work. Of course, she understood he wasn't allowed to talk about his days spent in the Tech Area, but it felt unfair, especially since she didn't have much going on in her life to contribute to a conversation—none of the art-world gossip or her impressions of the many exhibits they used to attend together in New York. Not that he would have had much energy to listen if she had something interesting to tell him; he was so often exhausted when he came home from work.

The water that cascaded down on her was brackish, lukewarm, and only marginally refreshing. She closed her eyes and let it flow, feeling deliciously criminal at defying the regulation to soap up with the faucet shut off. From the moment Jimmy had told her not to waste water by letting it run clear, she had felt goaded to flout the rules of Los Alamos. She hated the noise here, the arid air, the fact that everything smelled of dust—even the water, which she now let stream full blast down on her shampooed hair. How pathetic that she took pleasure in such a petty act of defiance.

Defiance was new to her. She could remember when she had cared, perhaps even too much, about being proper. So much so that she had been reading Emily Post's *Etiquette* on a bus on her way to NYU when she first met Thomas.

He sat down next to her, his pinewood aftershave prompting her to glance from her book to see who wore it. She caught him reading over her shoulder. He smiled sheepishly, as if shy; she doubted even then that he really was.

"Interesting?" he asked.

"Oh yes!" she answered.

"Really?"

"It explains how to behave," she said.

"Is that important?"

"I think so. Don't you?"

"Don't you know how to behave?" His tone hinted that he was not averse to improper behavior.

"I hope I do," she said earnestly. "I'm just never sure."

"So, what does the book say about first dates? How are you supposed to behave?"

"I haven't gotten to that chapter yet." She laughed.

"Hmm, maybe you should skip ahead to that chapter really soon."

No one had ever flirted so overtly with her before. "I'm not sure there even is such a chapter," she said.

"Can I see the book a moment?"

While he flipped through the table of contents, she took him in. He was good looking in a boyish sort of way, everything about him coordinated beige and blue: his hair, his suit, his skin, his straw fedora hat, all shades of beige; his eyes, his bow tie, the band on his hat, all blue. The colors were soft, the lines of his body sharp, economical.

"I need to get off at the next stop," she said.

He handed the book back. "You're right. There's no chapter on first dates. But if there was one, it would surely say they start by giving a very proper young man, one eager to teach you the intricacies of proper behavior, your phone number."

"Really?" She smiled, amused.

"No doubt about it," he said, fumbling until he produced a piece of paper from his pants pocket and the pen from his jacket pocket. As he handed both to her, he dropped his bravado for a quiet earnestness. "Please? Please give me your number."

She hesitated a moment, glanced up at his encouraging smile, and succumbed to his charm offensive. She scribbled her number, grabbed her book, and rushed from the bus. She was sure Emily Post would not have approved. She didn't even know his name.

She smiled at the memory as she closed the shower faucet and then dressed. While donning a pair of dungarees and a black-and-white gingham blouse, she let her eyes drift to the wedding picture perched atop the dresser. Theirs had been a whirlwind romance. Thomas had introduced her to all that was fine and refined about New York, easing her gallantly into a world of fine dining, museum exhibits, and high-society parties. She had been dazzled by his knowledge of the good things in life but even more impressed at his insistence on getting ahead on his own, eschewing his family's wealth.

They had fallen in love in front of a Cézanne painting, *The House with the Cracked Walls*, at the Metropolitan Museum of Art. He had already surveyed all the paintings in the room and returned to where she was, still at that first painting, staring at it. She did not have the knowledge of art to explain technically what moved her so deeply about this particular work. But noticing him staring at her, she had smiled and remarked, "It is so beautiful. So peaceful and so restless at the same time."

"Like you," he commented.

In a flash, she understood that what he said about her might possibly be true, although she had never thought of herself in this way.

"Maybe that is why I love it so much," she said.

"And maybe why I love you so much," he replied.

They had smiled and kissed lightly, then gone to a coffee shop for tea and blueberry muffins. But something had been settled between them in that moment, and within six months they were married.

Now, thinking of her marriage, she felt a need to open a window but immediately closed it again, the heat already intense even at nine o'clock in the morning. She tied her long wavy hair back at the nape. These days she felt distinctly more restless than peaceful. Maybe that was what drew her to Gertie, who seemed audacious for her age. At the same time, there was a sadness about the girl that made Christine want to hug her and assure her that all would be well.

But there was still the matter of swimming. She shuddered, imagining how the water grass would brush her unexpectedly, or worse, a fish might slither between her legs, or there might be more snakes. Of course, it was ridiculous, but she could imagine the water swelling and swirling her into the muddy bottom. The alternative was to drown in boredom.

CHAPTER 4
GERTIE

September 1943

When the bell finally rang at the end of the school day, Gertie bolted out the door, past the post office, the commissary, and Fuller Lodge. Out of breath, she slowed to a walk as she approached home.

Mama had set out freshly baked linzer cookies on the kitchen table. As usual, she was napping in the bedroom but had left the radio on in the kitchen, as if to ensure she didn't miss a single news bulletin, even while sleeping. But if Mama was hoping for some miraculous broadcast with a glimmer of information about the family in Hamburg, the news today would disappoint her.

"President Roosevelt's rubber investigating committee has recommended gasoline rationing as a way of conserving rubber from tires."

Gertie grabbed some milk and munched the cookies, noting they were underbaked and gooey as usual. Mama complained that the high altitude threw off all her recipes, and they had been eating food that was either undercooked or overcooked since their move. Mama obviously had still not gotten the knack of adjusting the temperature. Or the knack of much of anything else around here.

"How was school, *liebchen*?" Mama tied the belt of her dressing gown and rubbed her eyes, entering the kitchen just as Gertie was finishing the last cookie.

"Fine." There was no point in going into how horrible school was, how Enrique had tried to scare her by throwing a lizard at her face during recess. Refusing to let him or his smirking friends see her horror, she had walked calmly back into the school building, her head held high, bursting into tears only when she reached the washroom.

She hated her class. There were just ten kids, and she was the only girl. The boys ignored her after they discovered she didn't know the first thing about football or Captain Marvel. Most of their parents were plumbers, electricians, and construction workers who had moved to Los Alamos to service the Hill. They came from places she had heard about only in fifth-grade geography—Oklahoma, Utah, Nevada, Iowa—and lived in trailer parks just outside the base. Other students came in by bus from surrounding villages and spoke more Spanish than English.

"You have homework, yes?" Mama asked.

"Not much."

"Better it be done sooner than later."

"I'm going swimming first."

"Homework should be first."

"Oh, Mama, please!" There was no point in trying to explain—again—that schoolwork here was simple—tedious, really. She could do it in a cinch. And there was no time to explain if she was to get to the pond by four o'clock. "I've got to go." She pushed past Mama to change her clothes.

"Gertie, you know Papa says studies come first."

Gertie rolled her eyes, ignoring her mother, who was distracted by the radio, which was reporting on Russian advances in the Ukraine and Britain's RAF bombings of Hannover and other German cities.

Gertie wiggled into her red-and-white-striped suit, swished the swing skirt into place, and glanced in the mirror approvingly at how she filled the puckered bra part. She slipped on a sundress, donned her wedge sandals, and grabbed a towel.

As she raced through the living room to the front door, Mama grabbed her arm.

"You should stay home. Homework."

Gertie shook her arm free.

"Why don't you go back to sleep!" She felt horrible even as she said it, more so when she saw her mother's shocked, hurt face. On her way out, Gertie noticed the hands on the gilded mantel clock read 3:55 p.m.

She ran as fast as she could to the pond, concentrating on her breath and trying not to think about her cruel words. But Mama understood nothing. Not about Gertie, not about life here, not about how her constant preoccupation with what had become of the family in Germany made it awful to be at home. Of course, Gertie was worried about their family too. She missed making cookies with her grandmother and the smell of the tobacco of her grandfather's pipe. But what was the point of obsessing? Maybe Christine would understand.

Gertie scanned not only the narrow beach but also the water, in case Christine had ventured in on her own, tired of waiting. Although Gertie longed to plunge into the pond, she settled down on her towel to wait. Maybe Christine would come after all. Christine seemed different, but maybe she wasn't. Adults were so confounding. One never knew where one stood with them.

Especially Papa. He had tricked her into moving here, and she still couldn't forgive him.

He had promised her a sweet-sixteen birthday weekend in New York. Just the two of them, since he had been so busy and they had so little special time together, and Mama had said she wanted to stay home to prepare for their upcoming vacation in California.

The weekend had been spectacular. The first day, they fed the ducks in Central Park and wandered through Chinatown. The city was glorious at night, even with the nightly dimouts against naval and air raids. She tried to imagine what the street would be like if it were fully lit.

As it was, the crowds were so glamorous, the restaurants bustling and full of laughter. They went to see *Oklahoma!* on Broadway, which led Papa to reminisce, most unusually, about his youth back in Germany. He told her how he had acted in theater clubs during high school and university. The rage in Germany back then was cabarets, he explained. Momentarily forgetting his own rule against speaking German in public, he burst into a song from a high school cabaret as they walked down Broadway. He even danced a little jig as he sang. Had Gertie not been so surprised, she would have been embarrassed. She was able to make out the words but not the sense. Something about Papa being a swindler, Mother being a swindler, everyone being dishonest. The moment passed quickly, and Papa became his serious self again.

"Cabaret songs were political, a way of protesting, rebelling against corruption, high prices, hard times," he told her.

It was hard to imagine Papa as a rebel, and she hadn't heard him sing since she was very young, when he sometimes sang her a song before bedtime.

The enchantment of the weekend didn't end then. The next day they went to a Sunday matinee of *The Magic Flute* and afterward for dinner to the Rainbow Room. She hadn't understood half the menu but didn't want to ask Papa for an explanation, so she settled quickly on mallard (whatever that was) and wild rice with white asparagus sauce (it seemed exotic) and a Shirley Temple, which the waiter placed before her with a sweep of his arm.

"Here's to my wonderful daughter—happy birthday!" Papa lifted his glass of Riesling and clinked it against her ginger ale–and–grenadine drink. "What did you think of the opera?"

She tried to think of something clever to answer, the pounding of her heart competing with the din and tinkling glasses from nearby tables. It had been her first time at an opera. Although she had loved the stage setting and costumes, she didn't want to admit that the plot had confused her. Far more than by the performance, she had been enthralled at how the opera excited Papa, as if he were greeting a dear old friend. He smiled the whole time, his head swaying with the music. She could not remember ever seeing him enjoy himself so much. She had suddenly been able to imagine that once he might have been more carefree, less burdened than he had been for as far back as she could remember.

"I don't think I've ever seen anything so beautiful."

He smiled. "You used to think spiderwebs were beautiful. Do you remember?"

She shook her head.

"That's when I knew you had the mind of a scientist."

"Because I liked spiderwebs?"

"Because you were filled with awe when you discovered them. That's the secret to good science. To want to see and to have a capacity for awe. You must have been about three years old. And you started searching for spiderwebs everywhere. You would beg to go out and look for them. This was not an activity Mama liked. So it was something you and I did every Sunday. The two of us would go to the park and look for webs. And every time we found one, you would stare at it for the longest time. But I didn't mind. I was fascinated by how long you could look at them. Don't you remember?"

He reached across the table and squeezed her hand, and she felt his love wash over her.

It was the best moment of her life: that fancy restaurant; the women smelling of perfume, the men of cigars; the food of garlic and rosemary; the orchestra playing in the corner; and her father smiling at her.

But it had been a ruse. Even now, as she sat waiting for Christine, her stomach churned in anger at how, at the end of that weekend—when they'd stood in Grand Central Terminal and she'd thought they were about to head home to Boston—Papa had told her the truth: they were meeting Mama and moving out west.

"I have been meaning to tell you. Now there is no time. We must go."

"We're not going home to Boston?"

"No. While you and I have been having a nice time, your mother has been working very hard to pack everything up. She will meet us on the train. I have our compartment number." She hated his know-it-all tone and his calm self-assurance.

"What about our vacation in California?"

"There is no vacation in California. We are moving. Permanently. To the West."

"What? How can that be? I want to see Wilhelmina."

"We thought it would be less upsetting for you this way."

"You're taking me away from home, from my friends, from my things, and you didn't think this would upset me?"

"Mama's packed all your things up," he said in a smooth voice, obviously pleased all was under control.

"I want to go home!"

"You will have your things. You can write to Wilhelmina. We must go." He turned toward the tracks.

"Where are we going to live?"

"You will see when we get there."

"But, but, but what . . ." She was jostled by people passing her, cutting her off from Papa. She rushed to catch up, afraid of losing him in the cavernous, dim station. He trotted ahead of her, making his way down the platform, the steam rising from the train, swallowing them in its vapors. They spotted Mama's white-gloved hand waving from a compartment window. They made their way to her past duffel bags scattered at the feet of soldiers, who were smooching with their girlfriends or getting hugged to death by their mothers.

Mama opened her arms to hug Gertie. "Did you have a good time?"

Gertie stepped back. Oh, how she wanted to make a fuss. But she didn't. Her parents didn't tolerate such things. *Verboten.*

"Does it matter? Do I matter?" Gertie asked. She felt like a caged animal in the confines of the dark wood compartment, its overhead racks bursting with their suitcases.

"Oh, *liebchen*, I'm sorry. Papa has told you, yes?"

Gertie's eyes teared.

"We wanted you to have a good time." Mama rummaged in her large brown handbag, producing a handkerchief. "Be brave. We must all be brave. Please, *liebchen*, don't make a fuss."

They had no idea how furious she was.

She still felt angry, months later, sitting by the pond. She wanted to scream and pound her fists at them. Instead, she listened to the frog thrumming in the water. A flock of birds cawed overhead, streaming toward the dipping sun. It was getting late, already 4:35 p.m. Gertie rose to enter the water alone, but taking one last glance back after the trilling birds, she saw Christine's head crest the embankment that led down to the pond. Her lithe figure came into view, graceful in a floral sundress that rippled in the breeze, her red hair fluttering behind her. She'd come after all! Gertie plopped back down on her towel.

"Sorry I'm late," Christine said as she approached.

"That's okay."

"It's not. I shouldn't have kept you waiting." Christine pulled out her towel from a beach bag.

Gertie stared at Christine, unsure how to respond. An adult was apologizing to her. "Well, you're here now. That's what matters."

Christine put down her towel and was about to sit on it just as Gertie rose.

"Aren't we going in?" Gertie asked.

"We could sit a moment, couldn't we?"

Gertie shrugged. "I guess, if you want."

"Come sit." Christine patted Gertie's towel. "It's so nice out here. And we've hardly had a chance to get to know each other."

Gertie sat down. "What do you want to know?"

"Everything!" Christine laughed. "What it's been like for you. How did your family end up here?"

Could Christine really want to know? And where to begin? With that horrible train ride from New York? How Papa had sat across from her, his head buried in newspapers, ignoring her glares. Mama had spent the ride knitting, the click of her needles syncopating with the chugging train wheels. She had knitted all four days on the train, as if she could insulate them from their changing lives by working the wool hard enough. The stiff velvet upholstery had felt itchy against the back of Gertie's legs. The stench of the soldiers' cigarettes across from them had mixed nauseatingly with the salami Mama had brought along, their staple for the trip. Gertie wouldn't eat salami again—ever.

"It's a long story. We don't have time if I'm going to teach you to swim today."

"That can wait a bit. How long have you been in America? You don't have an accent."

"Don't you want to go in the water?"

"That's a long story too," said Christine.

"It is?" What could be more straightforward than plunging into the water when it was so hot outside? Gertie looked out at the pond, at the grass swaying in the breeze at its far end. She would have gone in earlier while waiting for Christine if she'd known she wasn't serious about learning to swim.

"It's silly, I know, not to go into the water." Christine's eyes darted around, unsettled.

"Are you okay?"

Christine laughed. "I'm fine. I'm being a silly dilly."

"What's the matter?"

"Oh nothing. I don't know how to say it."

"What?"

Christine looked up to the sky, and Gertie followed her gaze to the clouds that were wisping into ever-changing forms. Christine was silent for a moment, then let her gaze fall. "I'm scared of the water."

"You are? How could anyone be afraid of water?"

"When I was a kid, a wave knocked me out at the seashore. I almost drowned. My parents didn't notice. Some stranger rescued me from the water. Gave me artificial respiration. Left as soon as I came through. I never had a chance to thank him. I just got up and found my parents.

They were drinking. I didn't tell them what happened. I was seven at the time." Christine told the story without emotion, her eyes on the water. "Since then, I've never gone into water deeper than a bathtub."

There was so much sadness in what Christine had just divulged, and yet her even tone seemed like a plea against pity. Gertie didn't know what to say, so she joined Christine in looking at the pond, and they both watched the roadrunners skimming along the sand in front of them.

"Aren't you going to say that's stupid of me? That there's nothing to be afraid of?" Christine asked.

"Not unless you want me to. Everyone's afraid of something." Gertie wanted to say she couldn't imagine having parents who drank so much they didn't bother to watch their child in the water or notice her gone.

Christine turned to Gertie. "You don't seem afraid. You swim so well. You aren't even afraid of snakes. And you're sixteen, and I'm supposed to be the adult. It's so silly."

Gertie had never met an adult who made her feel so grown up. Someone who admitted things that were hard to admit.

"I'm afraid of different things—of not having friends or not knowing how to make them, of not being liked, of being kept in the dark about things, of why my mother seems sad all the time, and why that makes me mean to her."

"Those are serious matters. Not something silly like being afraid of water."

Gertie nodded. Wouldn't it be something if she could get Christine to like water?

"I have an idea." She stood up, took Christine's hand, and pulled her up.

"What?"

"Come to the edge of the water. Just splash me. I want to get wet, so splash me as hard as you can. With as much water as you can."

"Really?" Christine laughed nervously.

Gertie was already running toward the waterline and continued until she was up to her knees. She would have loved to plunge in but instead turned to Christine. "Come on now. Splash me. As hard as you can."

Christine started to back away.

"Come back. Just to the edge of the water. You don't have to go in."

Christine moved forward until the water covered her toes. She bent down and flicked the water as if it was a fly she was trying to shoo away.

"That wasn't much of a splash."

Christine flicked a few more times.

"That's better. But I'm not wet yet," Gertie taunted.

Christine moved forward to knee deep to better splash Gertie. The roadrunners stopped their dashing and stood still at a distance, their crested heads darting from Christine to Gertie. Gertie advanced until her hips were in the water, making it harder for Christine to reach her.

"Get me soaked. You can do it. I've been waiting all day to get in the water. You've got to do this for me. Come on, you can get me better than that."

Christine was laughing. She was beating the water now, harder and harder. Moving forward and swinging both arms around her, splashing herself as well as Gertie.

"I feel like I'm about three years old." Christine giggled.

Gertie joined her. "It's fun. You want to try another fun thing?"

Christine stopped, noticing for the first time that she was waist deep in the water. "Oh my God! I'm in deep water!"

"And look how okay you are. Totally in control. Doesn't it feel great?"

"I need to get out."

"No, wait. Let me show you something else fun. Stay just where you are. I'm going to make bubbles. See, I just hold my nose. You hold yours. And hold your breath."

"I can't go underwater!"

"No, of course not. Just hold your breath while I go under. The whole time I'm under the water, you hold your breath above. Okay? One, two, three . . ." Gertie plunged under and made bubbles for a few seconds, then popped up. "I love making bubbles. Bet you can't make them."

"Are you daring me, young lady?"

"I am."

Christine looked at Gertie hard. "Did you say you were afraid of not being liked?"

"Don't change the topic."

"I'm not. You have nothing to be afraid of."

"So maybe neither do you."

Christine laughed. "You've actually tricked me into getting into the water. You made me forget to be scared."

"So, are you going to try and blow bubbles, or aren't you? It's really fun."

"Okay, okay. I'll try."

CHAPTER 5
JIMMY

October 1943

Jimmy was alone when he awoke. He stretched and glanced at his watch: 2:05 p.m. A full eight hours of sleep after his night shift. Not bad. He reveled in the silence. The dorm smelled of dirty socks, butane gas, and burnt popcorn. For the umpteenth time, the guys had ignored the ban on food and snuck in a Bunsen burner to make popcorn at night. Lying in his bottom bunk, he peered down the row at the unkempt beds of his buddies from the army's Special Engineer Detachment. Sheets and blankets were strewn on bare mattresses. Only two beds—his and Owen's—were kept neat every day, not only for weekly inspections. Jimmy tended to tuck in his sheets in tight military style. Owen kept his looser, sheets and blanket draped and smoothed but still tidy. They both believed in taking care of things properly, one of the things that had drawn them to each other. They'd been roommates since their first semester at Northeastern University.

Everyone was off at work. The quiet let him go step by step through last night's experiment with the new supply of isotope, but he couldn't come up with anything he'd missed. So why had the calculations not yielded the desired results? A drip from a faucet distracted him.

Annoyed both at the squandered water and his inability to figure out his lab mistake, he kicked off his blanket, stepped over a trail of boxer shorts to the communal bathroom, and closed the offending tap.

He glanced at his face in the mirror above the row of sinks. He was putting on weight; he could use a horseback ride. Well, he had the rest of the day off. He'd shower, then saddle up a horse and head for the mountains.

Crap! He'd promised to tutor Professor Koppel's daughter at 3:30 p.m. Instead of a ride in the desert, there would be an annoying kid to deal with. He showered according to regulations, letting the thin stream flow for only a minute, then turned off the water while he soaped himself.

He had no experience teaching children. He sure hoped he'd figure out how to help this kid. He owed the professor; he was learning so much from him. Jimmy loved the way his boss would race through a new idea, leaving everyone in the lab breathless. And it certainly wouldn't hurt his future career to be on Koppel's good side. If that took tutoring the professor's daughter, so be it. Jimmy found it touching how Koppel worried about his daughter doing enough advanced math to get into a top college and how eagerly he had accepted when Jimmy suggested he tutor her. No one had cared about whether Jimmy went to college or ever thought of getting him a tutor.

He shaved, patted on cologne, and combed his wet, curly hair. He had his mother's light skin and coiled black locks and his father's blue eyes, which he narrowed, trying to look suave in the mirror. Who was he kidding? All bravado, no action when it came to women, even those in the Women's Army Corps who served at Los Alamos. There were so few WACs, the competition for their attention was fierce. Owen never missed a chance to flirt and joke. But Jimmy found it daunting to talk to the WACs, let alone ask one out for a drink or movie at Fuller Lodge.

He stuffed some cheese crackers he had stashed away into his pocket and rushed out to reach the Koppels' on time.

On his way, he passed maids in colorful ponchos headed to buses already lined up to take them home to the surrounding Pueblo villages. Women pushed baby carriages, too busy cooing at their little ones to notice him. Overhead, a flock of birds flew by in noisy argument over the best route south.

From the opposite direction, Christine Sharp approached, a net bag of groceries in each hand. From the moment he'd picked her up with her husband at Lamy station, she'd reminded him of Katharine Hepburn. Not just the red hair, which she wore today in a disheveled French twist, but also a sort of resilience about her, despite her palpable unhappiness that first day.

"How you doing?" He smiled at her.

She seemed startled.

"Gotten used to the brown water yet?"

"Oh, Corporal Campbell. Jimmy. I didn't recognize you without your uniform."

"One of the pleasures of the Hill. Most of the time, don't have to wear one. Sometimes seems like I'm not even in the army."

"Where are you off to? The Tech Area is in the other direction."

"I worked the night shift, so I have a few hours to myself now. Off to do the boss a favor, tutoring his daughter."

"Oppie doesn't have a daughter, does he?"

"Not Oppie. My direct boss, Kurt Koppel." Jimmy looked at his watch. "Got to run. Hope you and the mister are settling in okay." He rushed on without waiting for her answer.

The yard of the Koppels' home was grassless—the Los Alamos sandbox look. There appeared to be a victory garden in one of the flower beds off to the side, but the plants were so withered he couldn't even tell what they were—maybe tomatoes and peppers? It was not like the professor to let anything within his realm wilt for lack of care.

There was no doorbell, so he knocked.

Mrs. Koppel opened the door. She was short like her husband and had probably once been pretty in a round, pale sort of way.

47

"You are Jimmy, yes?" Mrs. Koppel's eyes were as nervous as a squirrel's as she wiped her hands on a white apron and patted her hair to tamp any stray strand that might have escaped her bun. None had.

"Pleased to meet you, ma'am." Jimmy extended his hand.

She looked at it in surprise, as if she did not expect anyone would want to shake hers.

When she responded, her fingers and palm felt limp in his grip. "Come in."

"Gertie," she called out in an anxious singsong as she led Jimmy to the dining table.

It took a moment for his eyes to adjust to the dark room, shielded from the day by burgundy velvet curtains. Mrs. Koppel switched on the crystal chandelier. "I hope this will do," she said, her eyes flitting around as if ascertaining that everything was in place.

"It's fine, Mama," said the young woman who breezed in, hips swaying her skirt. Tall, angular, with shoulder-length brown hair held back by a green headband, she was as brash as her mother was diffident. Her olive skin contrasted with her starched white blouse, its short, puffed sleeves accentuating her sturdy arms as she thumped her books on the dining room table. She flashed a smile. "Hi, I'm Gertie. I guess you already know that."

He nodded but she thrust out her hand and locked him in her gaze. She wasn't pretty in the usual sense—her mouth took up too much of her face—but when she smiled, it was the intense sparkle in her eyes that snagged all the attention.

He coughed and shook her hand. "Nice to meet you."

"You will be studying, yes?" Mrs. Koppel asked.

"Mama, don't you have some cookies we could serve our guest?" Gertie kept her eyes and smile on Jimmy while addressing her mother.

"That's not necessary. We'll be fine," said Jimmy.

"Nonsense." Gertie's life-thirsty eyes did not waver from his face.

Mrs. Koppel looked nervously from one to the other.

"Yes, of course. Cookies and milk." She walked out, mumbling as if castigating herself for forgetting the rudiments of hospitality.

Jimmy sat down and motioned for Gertie to do the same, then moved the books to the side. He was not sure how to start.

"So, I understand you want to skip ahead in math," he ventured.

"Not really. Papa thinks I should. He worries that the level in class isn't good enough for getting into a top college. So, he got me an algebra textbook. His idea of a present." She rolled her eyes.

"Do you like math? Algebra?"

"It's okay, I guess." Her tone belied her answer. "I understood the first chapter on my own. But now it's getting hard."

"What I like about algebra is that there's always one right answer. It's clear and definite."

"I suppose," said Gertie. "But there are lots of different ways to get to that right answer."

"Exactly. That's the beauty. There are simple ways, elegant ways, and complicated, circular ways. You can tell a lot about a person by the way they answer a complex equation."

"What's your way?" asked Gertie.

"Oh I don't know. Sometimes one way, sometimes another. I guess that says something about me. But we should get going here. Show me the book."

Gertie opened the textbook on the table to the questions at the end of the second chapter and slid the book over to him. He flipped through the section.

"It must be fun, living in the dorms," she said, watching him.

He looked up from the text. "It's not all it's cracked up to be."

"Sure beats living here." Her head roved the living room. "I mean, you must have friends, people to talk to. What's it like?"

"We're thirty guys in each dorm. That's a lot of smelly socks."

To his surprise, Gertie laughed. She was hanging on to his every word, which was rather pleasant. As Gertie's laugh trailed off, Mrs. Koppel entered the room.

"For your studying," she said in a firm voice, placing the tray on the table carefully as if cookies and milk were necessary offerings to assure the success of the tutoring session.

"Thanks, Mama. I can tell Jimmy is going to be an excellent teacher." Gertie beamed at them both.

"You have taught algebra before, yes?" Mrs. Koppel set a perfectly ironed pink napkin, trimmed with lace, beside Jimmy.

"Not really, ma'am. But I have, have of course, s-s-studied it," he stammered uncharacteristically.

"And you are how old?"

"Twenty-three, ma'am." He felt her inspecting him. He wished he had put on something fancier than the wrinkled khaki shirt he was wearing.

Mrs. Koppel nodded, taking in the information. Jimmy couldn't tell whether his answers had allayed her obvious suspicions that he had come under false pretenses or whether she disapproved of him but was too polite to show it. He suspected the latter.

"Mama, please. There's no need to interrogate Jimmy. Let us get on with my math."

Mrs. Koppel looked from one to the other, still uneasy. "I will be in the kitchen, yes?" She picked up the empty tray and left.

Jimmy resumed leafing through the pages of the textbook, then pushed the book aside. "Okay, how do you go about solving the problem?" he asked, pointing to the first exercise in the chapter.

Gertie bent over the book. "Four plus parenthesis $2y$ times $4z$ . . ."

"Hold on. You have to solve what's in parentheses first, and you have to figure out what the values of y and z are before you start adding things up."

"You want some milk?" Gertie asked.

"It sure looks good. It's been a while. We never get any; it's saved for the babies, then for families like yours. There's rarely any left for us single guys in the dorms."

She poured him some, and he gulped it down.

"There's plenty. Have some more."

"Thanks. I'm fine. Let's get back to those parentheses." He intercepted her before she could ask another question.

"Okay." Gertie sighed. "So $2y$ times $4z$ . . ."

She bent her head, stopped, and frowned, then chewed the pencil for a minute or so.

Jimmy wasn't sure whether to step in. Just as he was about to offer to help, she started to write and then swiftly worked her way through the problem.

"You have a lot of parties?" she asked while he checked her answer.

He looked up from her notebook. "What? Yeah, some, only on weekends. Most of the time, we're too beat after work. And there's stuff we have to read, scientific papers, that sort of thing. The pressure's fierce to keep up with everything, with everyone." He stopped; he was supposed to be teaching the girl math. "We should go through the rest of the problems," he said.

"I guess." She shrugged. "Have some cookies."

"Thanks." He cupped a hand under one to avoid making crumbs. "They're swell."

"My grandmother's recipe, from Germany," said Gertie. "I miss her."

"I guess a lot of people here miss someone," said Jimmy.

"Who do you miss, your parents? A girlfriend?"

Jimmy looked at Gertie, who was gazing at him with a captivating shyness, as if she had hesitated to ask about a girlfriend. He smiled and tried to think if, in fact, there was someone in his life to miss. "I guess I'm the exception. I don't miss anyone much. My college buddy, Owen, is here, and I'm not that close to my parents." He left the issue of a girlfriend unanswered. He'd never had one to miss.

She looked as if she was about to launch another question.

"We should get back to the problems here," Jimmy said.

"I guess," said Gertie listlessly.

Jimmy sat back in his chair. He had to try to infuse Gertie with his enthusiasm for algebra.

"Think about the big picture a minute. Algebra is about values that are initially unknown and their relationship to each other. It's all about trying to figure out the unknown by considering first the values that can be known."

"Kind of like figuring out people," said Gertie thoughtfully.

"Like people?"

"People don't know much about each other at first, and then they figure each other out from what can be known, from how a person acts, or what a person says."

"I suppose," Jimmy said. He'd never thought about people that way. "Let's get back to the equation."

Gertie sighed and turned her attention to the next problem. She hunched over the book, her thick hair falling on the page. Jimmy tried to remember if he had been as philosophical when he was her age. It wasn't that long ago—just seven years, if she was a junior in high school, which he figured she was. He had not been as self-confident as Gertie, although he had been curious, especially about science. At her age, he had finagled a job cleaning up the high school's labs for a chance to ask his teacher questions while he swept the floor and rinsed out tubes.

Jimmy helped Gertie work her way through problems with two unknown variables, showing her how to simplify the equation. He was surprised—and relieved—at how quickly she caught on.

"You're a better teacher than Papa. He likes everything complex. You noticed?"

"Your father's a genius. Different people solve things different ways. What I want to see now is how you solve these questions." He tried to sound stern.

"Okay, okay." She squirmed in her chair. While she scratched away with her pencil, working out the answers, he considered how she rattled him with her odd observations and yet how easy she was to talk to. No artifice about her. And so full of questions. It occurred to him, with a pleased jolt, that most of her questions were about him.

"There, I'm done!" she said.

He looked over the answers. "Good, yes. You got it. Simply, elegantly done."

"I like that—simply, elegantly," she repeated, her eyes dancing. "How would you have solved them?"

"Same way you did."

"Really? Good!"

Jimmy glanced at his watch. The hour was up, more than up. He should go.

"My father told me you got recruited here from MIT," Gertie said.

"Yup. No one was more surprised than me that I went there, believe me. My folks didn't want me to go to college. My high school chem teacher made me apply to Northeastern University. Helped with the application. And my profs there thought I should try for MIT for grad school. My folks still think it was a mistake, a big waste of time, especially grad school. They think I should be at the front, like the sons of everyone else they know."

"I can't imagine Papa not wanting me to go to college."

"My dad's a fisherman. Been working since he was fourteen. Wanted me to join him."

"And you didn't want to?" Gertie searched his face without judgment in her gaze.

"I hate fishing," Jimmy said.

Her eyes, which seemed one moment green and the next brown, were all sympathy.

"I get seasick," he explained.

Gertie nodded, absorbing the information. "I got seasick a lot on the boat from Germany. I was a little kid then, ten years old, but I still remember how it felt. Awful!"

"To my dad's way of thinking, being seasick is as sissy as it gets." Jimmy couldn't believe he was telling Gertie this, but it felt like a floodgate had opened, and now he couldn't stop. "In summer, he'd make me go out with him every day, sure that if I went out often enough, I'd get over the nausea. But I never did; it only got worse. And the sicker I got, the angrier he got."

"Is he still angry at you?"

Jimmy shrugged. "Disappointed, I guess."

"How can he be? Papa says you're the best assistant he's ever had. You're going to invent something really important someday, aren't you?"

It was good to know that Kurt Koppel thought well of him. He was not the sort of boss to mete out praise.

"I hope I invent something important someday. But my folks just know that I'm not in combat. If I'm not fighting, they think I'm shirking my duty. They don't care much about my inventing anything."

"Excuse me for saying so, but they sound kind of dumb."

"They're not stupid at all!" How could he explain to Gertie that his parents weren't sophisticated and fancy like hers? But they were good people. And they did their best to make a decent living, which left them with little energy or time for coddling him.

"They didn't grow up with much. Always took good care of me. I'm grateful for that."

"Being grateful, it's kind of a bore, don't you think? I'm not good at it at all. There's so much I want—do you know what I mean?"

"It's not that I don't want things, but I know I've got it good."

"Maybe you should give me lessons in how to be grateful." Gertie smiled.

"Algebra first, okay?" he said. "Same time next week?"

By their third lesson, Jimmy realized that Gertie was doing fine in algebra. She had not fully understood a few basic axioms at the beginning but was now proceeding through the textbook at a fast clip. He spent a few minutes explaining what she needed to know in the chapter on solving linear and quadratic equations by graphing and the rest of the time telling her about growing up on the Cape. He boasted, just a little, about how he'd won a scholarship to Exeter boarding school but stayed only for a year, confounded by the highfalutin manners of his wealthy classmates. He didn't tell her how Exeter's all-male atmosphere perturbed him deeply, stirring impulses that he fled by leaving. Instead, he told her about the sea.

"When I first learned about the concept of infinity, I used to think of the ocean." He munched one of the cookies, slightly underdone but still tasty, which Mrs. Koppel now regularly provided at the start of the lessons. "I like the froth. I think of it as the earth's brew on tap."

Gertie poured him milk without asking.

He liked how comfortable, domestic, that felt.

"The sea as a pub, waiting for the world to party," she said, pouring herself a glass too. "What a way of looking at it! I wish I had your lightness."

Jimmy didn't understand what she meant but didn't ask. At hand was the task of algebra, which Gertie was expert at dodging. He had to get her in line—and himself, too, if he were to be honest. It was so easy to get distracted by her.

"Come, let me look at the exercises you've done this week."

As he checked her answers, he felt her staring at him. This was not unpleasant. Finished, he looked up. "You're not going to need help with math much longer. It's one hundred percent correct again, and you're almost through with the book."

"Oh no!" Gertie sounded dismayed.

Jimmy looked at her, puzzled.

"I mean, I don't think I'm nearly ready to stop with lessons," she stammered, smoothing her hair back and straightening her headband. "Papa will want me to continue, I'm sure. You know what he's like." Pointing her index finger into the air in the emphatic way Kurt Koppel did and throwing her eyes to the ceiling, she imitated her father: "My daughter must be ze best!"

Jimmy laughed. Her imitation of her father was spot on. Gertie was trying hard to entertain him. That made him chuckle even more. She wanted him to like her.

"Maybe you can join some of us when we go riding on Sundays, instead of us both being cooped up over algebra." He smiled.

Gertie looked down at the textbook before her on the table. "I don't know how to ride."

"I could teach you." He was surprised at how smoothly this came out, as if he invited girls to go riding all the time. Of course, Gertie was a child almost, although the way she talked, Jimmy thought she'd figured out more about life than he had.

"Would you?"

Horses were his turf. As a teenager, he'd learned to ride and earned pocket money cleaning out stables. By the last year of high school, he'd worked his way up to tourist trail guide.

"Let's make a deal. You get through the rest of the book, and we'll convince your father you need horseback riding lessons more than math lessons." He stuck out his hand for her to shake. "Is it a deal?"

"Deal!" She seized his hand with both of hers, fear and excitement mixing in those bright eyes.

He extracted his hand from her grasp. What was he getting himself into?

CHAPTER 6
CHRISTINE

November 1943

Christine hooked her arm around Thomas's as they strode to the Oppenheimers' home. She would have liked to stroll leisurely and take in the cool evening air, but Thomas was walking quickly, glancing at his watch, and she struggled in her high-heeled pumps to keep up with him.

"Are we late?"

"Who cares?" He sighed. "These parties are always the same. Everyone pretending to get along. Too much alcohol. I already know I'll have a hangover tomorrow."

She thought only she had been uncomfortable at the parties on Saturday nights at one or another home on the Hill. Thomas usually glided through social gatherings, unlike her. At least he always had before their move to Los Alamos.

"Are you okay?" she asked.

"You know I can't talk about things. Why are you pressing me?"

"I'm not asking you to tell me what you're doing. Just how you're feeling."

"It's not easy to joke around and make nice with people that I've been arguing with all week, disagreeing about the best way to move forward, fighting over who gets the limited material we all need." The leaves rustled in the large trees as they made their way along Bathtub Row, so named because its stone and log houses, built when Los Alamos was still a boys' boarding school, were the only homes on the Hill with the luxury of bathtubs.

Christine patted his arm. "Maybe the party will help smooth things over." Approaching the house, they heard the din of voices, the clinking of glasses, and singing. They exchanged nods with the two military guards at the entrance and let themselves in through the open door.

"So glad you've come." Oppie loped toward them, gangly and graceful as a giraffe. "Let me take your jacket."

"You're looking lovely this evening," Oppie said, his intense blue eyes taking in Christine's off-the-shoulder satin dress, its close-fitting skirt hugging her hips.

"Why, thank you." She smiled. There were so few occasions to get dolled up; it was nice to have her efforts appreciated.

"Can I get you drinks? One of my martinis, perhaps?"

"Sure," Thomas said. "Wouldn't miss one of your famous martinis for the world." He twisted his neck as if it was constricted by a too-tight tie, even though, like Oppie, he wasn't wearing one.

"Why don't you join the crowd singing with Owen?" Oppie gestured toward a young man playing a ukulele. "He's with the Special Engineer Detachment. Seems to know all the latest hits, so I invited him to play for us this evening."

They made their way over to the group, nodding and smiling at the many people they knew. Owen, a strapping fellow with dark-blond hair slicked back with pomade and a dimple on his chin, was crooning a song Christine immediately recognized as the Mills Brothers's latest hit, "Paper Doll."

She leaned into Thomas and swayed to the music, wondering if her husband, like the lyricist, wanted a paper doll instead of a real live girl. Once, she had been sure he wanted a spirited, independent wife. As Thomas and others joined Owen in the song's refrain, she hoped he still did.

Oppie brought over their drinks, a martini in each hand. Christine took a sip. Thomas was right about the free-flowing alcohol: the drink had an overly generous amount of gin. She looked around the room, at the wood beams elegantly embedded in the high white plaster walls, the built-in and well-stocked bookshelves. Her eyes wandered to the chimney, its mantel decorated with a striking black vase. She stepped away from the group to take a closer look.

Oppie joined her. "I see you appreciate beautiful things."

She smiled at him. His fragile lankiness reminded her of the saints in medieval paintings. His penetrating eyes were like theirs, at once distant and comforting.

"I used to work as a restorer—paintings, furniture, porcelain, that sort of thing."

"Really?" He sucked her in with his gaze.

"The last project I worked on before we left New York were pointillist paintings. Seurat, Lemmen, if you know them."

"I do. Lemmen's and Signac's landscapes have always struck me as fine. Personally, I prefer Signac over Seurat. Do you like pointillist art in particular?" She had met Oppie at numerous parties, but their exchanges had been no more than perfunctory before. Now she found his erudition and affable curiosity made talking to him surprisingly easy and pleasant.

"I'm fascinated by them. Actually, I wrote a long article for the catalog to a show in New York. All about how pointillists deconstructed color to its most essential elements, influenced, of course, by advancements in science at the time—our understanding of atoms, the discovery of electrons, et cetera, et cetera." She ended with a laugh, afraid that she may have gone on too long.

"Never thought of pointillism that way. Very interesting." He seemed genuinely intrigued, ignoring the gleeful shrieks from across the room and the singing, which had grown louder. "I'd love to see that catalog."

"Unfortunately, the article never made it in. Arrived too late to be included, apparently delayed by the censors. And censored so much, it was unreadable. Imagine! An article about art!"

Oppie combed her face with his eyes for a moment before answering. "It can be hard to understand the censors, but sometimes they do make sense." His lips quivered as if he were trying to suppress a mischievous grin.

She could tell that he had been a good professor, forcing students to think for themselves rather than immediately revealing what was to him an obvious answer.

Then it struck her. "You mean atoms, electrons? That's what bothered them?"

He didn't look at her and instead busied himself with taking down the vase from the mantel, deliberately inspecting it for a few moments.

He held up the piece. "I got this from Maria Martinez, a potter from San Ildefonso. Met her more than a decade ago, when I lived here."

It took Christine a moment to focus again on the pot; she was trying to absorb what Oppie had said—actually, not said—about her censored article. He was looking at her expectantly, obviously waiting for her to respond to the change in topic.

"You lived here?"

"I was sickly as a teenager. I always liked horseback riding. My parents sent me out here to recover from dysentery. The air here was good for me, and ever since, I've come whenever I could, just to ride and camp out."

Christine tried to imagine the energetic man standing before her as sickly.

"When I was asked to find a remote place for our little project, naturally I looked here. In a way, everyone in this room is here because of my dysentery." Oppie laughed, then continued wistfully. "I guess a part of me was hoping to relive that magical past." He took a generous sip of his martini, and she took a small one of hers, unsure what to say.

"I even got myself a horse," he continued.

"Really?"

"Odysseus. White gelding, but frisky."

"I rode a lot growing up in Maine. Always loved it."

"Me, too, but I never have time now. Feel free to take Odysseus out whenever you want."

"I couldn't."

"You'd be doing me—and him—a favor. He needs the exercise."

"That's very generous of you." Her heart skipped at the thought of being able to ride out into the desert any time she wanted, and he must have seen the excitement in her eyes.

"Great. It's a deal then," he said, smiling at her.

Just then, Kitty teetered up on high heels. She was as petite as Oppie was tall. She nodded a hello at Christine, her eyes sweeping her with suspicion, before looking up at her husband and tossing her curly dark hair. "I need your help getting Peter to sleep." She patted his arm possessively. "Come, now."

"Two-year-olds." Oppie smiled ruefully at Christine as if she surely understood the difficulty of getting his son to sleep. He handed her the vase before going off with his wife, who grabbed his arm, unsteady on her feet.

Christine was glad to be left on her own to marvel at the vase with its fine design—part matte, part shiny. As she gazed at it, she heard Enrico Fermi, a few feet away, animatedly explaining recent events in his native Italy to a few colleagues.

"I always believed my countrymen would come to their senses and break with Hitler. They're really not Fascists at heart. It's only a pity it took them so long," he said.

"But we hear it is terrible now, with the Nazis taking over Rome. They say Jews are being deported. It's most troubling," his wife, Laura, added.

Christine listened to the assenting murmurs of the group around the Fermis as she inspected the vase. It struck her how many people at Los Alamos lived with bifocal vision—here and now but simultaneously with another distant world in view where unspeakable things were happening. The Fermis, the Koppels, and so many others had relatives and friends in Europe whose lives were in danger, their fates unknown. Knowing that, feeling their anguish, Christine found the war made more sense to her now than it had before she'd come here. And yet, the war still felt so remote.

But this vase, that was immediate. She traced the animallike design on the surface with a finger, trying to determine what it was meant to be.

Suddenly something jabbed her waist. She jumped. The vase dropped. It shattered on the flagstone floor before the chimney. Owen's singing and the guests accompanying him masked the sound of the crash. She looked down in horror, then turned to find Thomas beside her.

"What have you done?" he said.

"You startled me! Why did you poke me like that?"

"I just came to see how you were doing!"

"I was doing just fine!" She crouched down and started picking up the pieces. What would Oppie say?

Oppie, now back in the living room, saw the shattered vase and approached them.

"I'm so sorry." Christine held out the pieces of the vase in her hand.

"Don't worry about it. It's just a pot." His wistful eyes belied a weak smile.

"It was an accident," Thomas said.

"Of course," Oppie said.

"Maybe I can fix it." Christine rose and placed some pieces on the mantel.

"Some things can't be fixed." Oppie stood, fingering the gathered shards.

"Let me try. It's the least I can do."

"Sure," Oppie answered, but without conviction. He got her a paper bag, left her with Thomas to collect the pieces, and went back to pressing martinis on the crowd.

"Let's go," Thomas said after they had picked everything up.

"It's awkward to leave so soon."

"Breaking the vase is awkward. You've done enough damage." He went to fetch her jacket.

Waiting for him to bring it, she gazed at the room of lively people. Martha McPherson, her neighbor in the Sundt unit, waved at her from across the room to come join the singing. The last thing she needed was for busybody Martha to know she'd broken Oppie's vase. Christine smiled but shook her head. Thomas returned, jacket in hand, as Martha approached them.

"Leaving already?"

Thomas coughed in annoyance and thrust the jacket at her.

"I have a headache." Christine took it and slipped it on. "I shouldn't have come."

"That's too bad. The party's just getting started." Martha put a hand on Christine's arm. "If you're not better tomorrow, need me to pick up anything, you know where to find me."

Christine nodded her thanks as Thomas opened the door. On the walk home, he was silent. She did not link her arm in his nor did he in hers. As they left Bathtub Row, the silence of the desert engulfed them.

"It wasn't entirely my fault," she said into the dark.

"Well, it certainly wasn't mine."

"But when you jab me like that, it startles me."

"You dropped the vase."

"Yes, I did."

"Oppie could hold it against us, against me."

"He doesn't seem like the sort of person who would."

"How would you know what kind of person he is, Christine?"

Thomas seemed to take pleasure in making sure she was aware that there was so much that she must remain in the dark about. Her heart howled in frustration, like the coyotes now filling the night air with their cries. She turned up the collar of her jacket against the breeze.

Despite being upset about the pot, she could not help mulling over her conversation with Oppie about the censors. She thought back to graduate school, to other students working in her field of food preservatives. There had been one working on irradiating food to preserve it with x-rays and electron beams. It hadn't been her field, but she did understand the fundamentals. Electron beams had energy. Her article must have touched too closely on something to do with that here, although what, she had no idea.

"There's so much you don't know about how hard the work is and how competitive. Sure, we're a team here, but everyone wants to be Oppie's favorite," Thomas said.

"I know more than you might think. I know you are tenser than you've ever been. It isn't bringing out the best in you. Maybe, on a theoretical level, you could tell me a bit about the kinds of problems you are working on, what everyone around here calls the gadget. After all, I was a chemist once, or going to be one, if you remember."

He thrust his hands deeper in his pockets and scowled. "It's not allowed."

She decided to venture a guess, not a wild one, given Oppie's telling silence. "It has to do with atoms, right?"

He looked at her in shock. "Where'd you get that idea?"

She noticed he did not say she was wrong. Now she knew why so much of her article was censored. And suddenly Thomas's specialization made sense. If the work here had to do with electron beams, with unstable atoms, with the energy they generated, the environment emitting the beams and the receptacle receiving the beams would need to be contained in something especially resilient, unalterable—something with a very special coating.

"You're trying to trick me into telling you things I'm not supposed to talk about."

"I'm not. I just want to have the sort of discussions we used to have."

"That was then. These are different times."

"Too different." She sighed. They said nothing more the rest of the way home.

CHAPTER 7
CHRISTINE

November 1943

Riding the white gelding out of the base, Christine surrendered to the beauty around her and shed the gloom of the silent treatment Thomas had meted out the rest of the weekend after the party. The formations in the crater below looked like meringue peaks lavished by a whimsical god on a sunken pie.

After breaking Oppie's prized pot, Christine figured the least she could do was make good on her promise to exercise his horse. Furthermore, she realized she could ride Odysseus to San Ildefonso, about ten miles east, where Oppie had bought the pot, maybe find the potter who made black ceramics and buy a replacement.

As Christine followed the same dirt route the bus took to fetch the maids from San Ildefonso, she could see why Oppie loved this desert and had brought them all here. In Maine, a view above the tree line was the prize after a long climb; sunny days were rare and treasured. Here, the sun and horizon were ever present. The war and its hundreds of thousands of dying soldiers were unfathomable in this piercing silence, under this cloudless sky.

Odysseus snorted for attention, and Christine gave him an appreciative pat on the mane followed by a light kick to prompt him to keep up his pace. Up ahead were adobe huts, first widely scattered and then clustered as she entered San Ildefonso. She crossed the central square, dominated by an adobe church. To the north was an imposing mesa that seemed to guard the town. At a trading post, she stopped to ask the way to Maria Martinez, the potter. She passed a group of children. They waved and ran after her, clambering so close she feared the horse would kick them. She pressed her heels into his side to nudge him into a trot, leaving the children in a cloud of dust.

She rode on, bearing left past a water pump to a house where a solidly built woman squatted, coiling a pot.

"Good day," Christine called.

"Blessed day, indeed." The woman smiled and nodded, her knotty, large hands continuing to pinch the coils in place. Her black hair was cut in a bob with bangs, but when she bent over the pot, Christine noticed that longer hair was gathered at her nape in a chignon held together with purple yarn.

Christine dismounted, introduced herself, and confirmed that the woman was, indeed, Maria. "I saw a vase you made. I loved it."

She felt Maria eye her intently.

"I used to restore bone china."

"You from up there?" Maria nodded in the direction of Los Alamos, her hands still smoothing the coils.

"Yes, well, at least recently."

"A friend of Robert's, then." It was less a question than a statement.

"Robert?"

"The professor, from California." Maria said it matter of factly while inspecting her handiwork.

"Oh, you mean Oppie." Christine had never heard anyone call him by his first name. "Ummm, yes." Hopefully she was not violating some military rule by admitting this.

"Don't look so surprised. I see that you ride Robert's horse. He's a good man. Any friend of his is a friend of ours. He used to come out here a couple times a year." Maria looked up from her work, inspecting Christine with the same care she had previously given to the pot. "But now, seems he likes it so much in these parts, he brought half the world to live with him here to make merry. He doesn't bother with us anymore." Maria looked at Christine expectantly, as if she might provide an explanation.

"Oh, I know he'd love to come out more. It's just that he's busy."

"Busy? Folks say there's lots of party cleanup to do when they go up there on Mondays." Maria's hands resumed working the clay.

Christine laughed weakly. "I guess it looks like all we do is party, but that's not true. Just sometimes, on weekends. Frankly, I don't know what we're all doing there. My husband, he's one of those friends of Oppie's, of Robert's, but no one tells us wives anything."

Maria seemed to take this in but said nothing, her attention focused on the pot before her.

Christine watched Maria's long, thick fingers deftly pinch and smooth the clay. Maria didn't seem to mind being observed, and for a few minutes neither woman spoke. Odysseus neighed, breaking the silence.

"Could I see your pots?"

"Sure." Maria stood up and motioned for Christine to follow her. Until then, Christine had guessed Maria to be about forty by her skin, weatherworn yet smooth. But noticing Maria's belabored tread as they walked toward a wood shack in the yard, Christine added another twenty years.

In the shed stood a heap covered by burlap, which Maria pulled back to reveal stacks of black pots. Christine crouched to take a closer look.

"I don't sell much. Just make 'em and keep 'em mostly," Maria said.

Christine was entranced by the shiny onyx-like buff of the pots, by the inlaid matte designs. Black on black. She traced the curves of one of the creatures etched into a piece with a finger. The incisions were clean and precise, from tail to tongue. "This is beautiful."

Christine meant the pot, but Maria thought she meant the etched creature. "It's Avanyu, the serpent that gives birth to waterways. Its tongue is lightning, and its voice is thunder. Avanyu brings good luck and good health."

Christine ran her fingers along the etched creature appreciatively.

"My husband, he's the one that decorates the pots. Used to decorate them."

"Oh?"

"He passed away a few months ago."

Christine looked up and saw pain cross Maria's face. "This must be a hard time for you."

Maria nodded. "We were married for almost forty years. Worked together most times. He helped me with everything."

Christine did not know what to say other than that she was sorry. "He was clearly very talented, both of you."

Maria seemed to rouse herself. "Well, it was his time, I suppose. I'm lucky I have my family, others who help, also good at making pots."

Christine inspected more pieces. "The work is really wonderful."

Wonderful was an understatement. She had never seen anything like this work. Before she had fully formulated the thought, she blurted out, "Would you want me to try and sell these for you?"

"I don't know." Maria shrugged.

"I used to do that. Sell art. Nothing like this, but paintings mostly."

Christine considered elaborating, then thought the better of it, not wanting to overwhelm Maria with her enthusiasm. As it was, Maria seemed suddenly uncomfortable; she was nervously fingering her skirt, her eyes darting around the shed before flitting again on Christine, who smiled warmly at her, giving Maria time to get used to the idea.

Holding her eyes, Maria nodded slowly, then motioned for Christine to follow her. She walked a few steps to another pile and drew back a tarp to reveal additional pottery. The two women were quiet for a few moments while Christine worked her way through one of the stacks, inspecting each piece. She didn't know how she could go about selling them, but she wanted to try.

"How much do you want for this one?" Christine pointed to a plate with Avanyu, feeling her pulse quickening as it had when she found treasures while trolling through thrift shops on weekends in the country with Thomas during those years in England. He had always admired how she could ferret out the one valuable piece from piles of junk at flea markets.

"Ten dollars," said Maria.

"How about eight?" asked Christine, continuing to peruse. She picked up a vase with wind-like swirls about the size of the vase she had broken at Oppie's. "Let's say fifteen dollars for both, if you can attach them to the saddle so they won't break. Do you want to pick out five other pieces that you can lend me until I either sell them or bring them back?"

Maria looked Christine up and down, then nodded slowly, her face impassive. "Nothing to lose, I guess, you being a friend of Robert's."

Maria picked out some pieces without hesitation. "How much you gonna pay for these?"

Christine smiled to herself. Maria clearly had a sense for business.

"Five dollars for the small ones, eight for the bigger ones. If I sell them. Does that sound reasonable?" Christine replied.

Maria nodded her agreement and bundled the pieces in a blanket. She plodded back to her hut to pack them while Christine pushed away cobwebs curtaining the heap and continued to inspect the works, flicking away spiders scurrying up her arm.

She held a vase in her hand, noting its delicate proportions, its burnished finish, cool and warm like a soothing kiss. It radiated perfection, stunning her the way the first ancient Greek pot she ever held had, back in London during a museum tour with an art-restoration class when the curator had opened a case to let them touch the artifacts. While the curator had droned on about Greek motifs, Christine had been consumed by the object's beauty.

Now, too, all her senses were immediately attuned. Focusing on the beauty of the piece paradoxically also made her more aware of her surroundings. She smelled the earth of the shed floor and the wood chopped and ready for winter in the corner. She heard the *pat-pat-pat* of someone slapping tortillas somewhere in the village. The vase's perfect self-contained proportions made her feel at peace. What made the pieces feel perfect? It pained her to think that such beauty should be hidden from view. Displayed at the right height and angle, under proper lighting, it was sure to enrapture.

For the first time in months, she felt optimism trill through her. She would make a business of selling these pots. Even though she was not allowed to travel, she would figure out a way to sell Maria's work. Could people at Los Alamos become buyers, collectors, even? That would be a start. And she would try to drum up interest further afield. Maria had so many pots just lying in piles. She'd learn more about the motifs from Maria. Over time she was sure she could attract attention to these magnificent pieces.

Maria returned with two gunnysacks rimmed with rope at the top to close them. She laid them beside Christine, who paid her. Maria stuffed the money into the pocket of her apron without counting it. Just as Christine was wondering if this was out of indifference or trust, Maria took Christine's hand and held it in both of hers. It wasn't really a handshake—more as if she was feeling Christine as she might a piece of clay, as if she was learning her.

Christine squeezed Maria's hand back. "I'll take good care of your work."

Maria nodded and let Christine's hand go.

"I'd better be getting on," said Christine, although she had no place in particular to be getting on to.

Maria nodded again and stepped back.

As she rode back to the Hill, Christine's mind raced with ideas: she would research the pots, create a catalog, talk to Samantha about the right place to exhibit them in an exclusive showing.

Preoccupied with her thoughts, she barely noticed the landscape and was surprised when the white inspection booths at the entrance of Los Alamos appeared in the distance.

She couldn't wait to tell Thomas about all this—if he came home while she was still awake. They had sparred at breakfast about his endless hours at the lab. As she had cleared the kitchen dishes that morning, he told her casually that he would be back late.

"It's that time of the month, Thomas. I can't make a baby by myself." She hated herself for pleading.

He responded with a sigh, and she wondered whether it was prompted by the specter of obligatory sex or lost hope that they would ever have a child.

"Isn't there some new theater group getting together tonight? I saw something posted about auditions. I think Ed McPherson's wife—Martha, that's her name, right?—is in charge of it. You should go. It would do you good," Thomas said.

"Why are you changing the subject?"

"I'm not."

"I wish you'd stop thinking you're such an expert on what's good for me."

"It was just a suggestion."

"You thought coming out here would do me good. It hasn't." When had she become such a griper? But join a troupe with Martha? Martha was so annoyingly peppy, like a piece of bread perpetually popping out of a toaster.

"Christine, I don't have time for useless arguments. I have to get to work."

He was right. They were stuck here. There was no use arguing about it. And she felt bad for making him feel bad. If only she weren't so bored, especially in the evenings when Thomas was working. A theater troupe would at least keep her busy.

"Try to be home if you can. And I'll think about joining the troupe," she said.

Thomas rose from the table and kissed her on the nose. "That's my girl."

She smiled weakly and accompanied him to the door, reluctant to see him go. Smelling faintly of aftershave, he turned around, stroked her cheek, and tousled her hair. "The best thing you could do is to let me get on with the work here," he had said before closing the door.

Now Christine dismounted, unsaddled Odysseus, and gave him a vigorous brushing before returning him to his stable. She untied the two bundles of pots, loaded one over her shoulder, and carried the second in her other hand. Although they were heavy, she thrilled at the weight. For the first time in months, she, too, had work to get on with.

CHAPTER 8
GERTIE

November 1943

Jimmy was cradling a saddle in his arms when Gertie reached the barn. The smell of dung, hay, and horse tickled her nose. She sneezed. A horse snorted, startling her.

"It smells funny in here."

"You'll get used to it. Come and meet Pinto." Jimmy nodded toward a dappled brown-and-white horse tied to a post outside.

He strapped on the saddle, smooth talking the horse as he worked. She loved how gentle he was, as if Pinto were a cat, not this huge beast. Pinto seemed almost human, the way he nuzzled Jimmy as she would have liked to if he talked to her so softly. Jimmy mounted and dismounted a few times to show Gertie how, then lowered the stirrup for her.

The saddle seemed so high up. She touched the horse's flank gingerly and let her hand slide up his side. It was so tall. Nothing like the ponies she had seen at a park back in Germany. And even then, she had been too afraid to take the kiddie ride offered on them. How would she ever get up on this monster of a horse? She grasped the horn and clenched her eyes shut out of fear. Ridiculous. She had to open them to stick her left foot into the stirrup. She felt the horse move forward. What if he took off and her foot got stuck?

"I'm holding him, don't worry. He's not going anywhere." It was as if Jimmy was reading her mind. "Just hop up."

"Just?"

"You can do it."

She tried but almost toppled. God, she was such a klutz. There was no way an hour would be enough time for Jimmy to show her the basics before his friends came.

"Almost." Jimmy smiled. "Try again. Use the horn more to lift yourself."

The second time she managed, gracelessly, and settled into the saddle. She was so far off the ground. Pinto neighed, prancing in place. Surely the next thing he'd do was buck. But Jimmy was still holding him. He smiled, so she tried to smile back. "What's next?"

Jimmy showed her how to hold her legs and arms, then mounted his horse and led them to the ring. Pinto sped up, and she jiggled like a marionette. Panic rose with each bounce. What if she lost her grip and fell? Got kicked in the head and was paralyzed for life? Why was she thinking like this? She was with Jimmy, who was now in the middle of the ring, watching her circle the edge. He would make sure she was okay, wouldn't he?

"Squeeze your knees into the horse's ribs. Move with the horse," Jimmy called out.

She could barely breathe. Squeeze her knees? Okay, she could do that. Did she look as uncoordinated as she felt?

Jimmy was so calm. He thought she could do this. She *was* doing it. The horse was smooth under her. She was becoming one with Pinto. She smiled at Jimmy.

"You're doing fine, cowgirl."

"Really?"

"You're a natural. Come, it's time to get back." He prodded his horse and led the way to the nearby stables.

She swayed with the horse, enjoying the rolling movement. Pinto was sweating lightly, and she was too. The day might not turn out to be a disaster after all. Ahead of her, Jimmy's broad shoulders relaxed even while he sat up straight on his horse. His rear and lower back swayed gently, almost hypnotically. He had an ease with his body she'd never seen in him before. The diffidence he'd shown at her parents' house was gone.

Jimmy's friends were waiting when they arrived. Gertie was glad he introduced her without suggesting she dismount. There were half a dozen technicians, including Owen, the best friend Jimmy had told her about, and four women from the Women's Army Corps, all blonde and pretty. As Jimmy rattled off their names, which she instantly forgot, Gertie felt Owen looking her over. She tried especially hard to seem confident and carefree, smiling and laughing. Owen was handsome in a classic sort of way—pronounced jawbone, dimpled chin, tall and broad, straight honey-colored hair that skimmed his forehead. He acted as if he knew he was good looking and expected her to return his smile with an admiring gaze. Instead, she tossed her hair, as if shaking away his attentions, and watched the WACs giggling and mounting their horses with ease. Gertie wished Christine was with them. Christine had assured her that horseback riding was easier to learn than swimming and had raved about her own foray on Oppie's horse two weeks ago.

As they headed toward Bandelier National Monument in single file, Gertie hoped she would conquer her fear of Pinto as successfully as Christine had overcome her fear of water. Owen took the lead, then the WACs, then Gertie, then Jimmy and the rest of the guys. Due to the war and gas rationing, the park had been closed for more than a year, but the trails were still intact. Gertie remembered Jimmy's instructions and sat up straight in the saddle. She felt his eyes on her back as they rode and sat up still taller, hoping this made her look regal and grown up. The day was crisp and cloudless, unusually warm for November, the sky so all-encompassing it felt as if it might swallow them. The rhythm of the hooves, the squeak of leather against leather, the neighing of the horses, and the birdcalls lulled them all into a pleasant silence.

An hour later, the burbling of the Frijoles River signaled they were approaching their destination. The path was shaded by the cottonwoods along the riverbank.

At a flat embankment, perfect for a picnic, Owen dismounted.

Gertie stared at the WACs in front of her following his lead, smoothly throwing a leg over the saddle, and easing themselves off their horses.

She froze. Pinto neighed. Yes, of course, he wanted her off his back. But how was she going to reach the ground? Pinto tossed his head and snorted. Was he about to throw her? Suddenly Jimmy was at Pinto's side.

He winked at her reassuringly. "Don't worry. I'll hold him. You get down."

"How?"

With the same calm he had when teaching her algebra, he explained, and she let herself be guided by his voice. She hoped he couldn't tell how relieved she was to have her feet back on the ground, that he took her smile to be solely gratitude for his attentiveness.

When they unpacked lunch, the WACs sat along the bank with their sandwiches while the men ventured out to the rocks in the water. One of the women, Betsy, patted a place next to her for Gertie to join them. Gertie had nothing to add to their talk of secretarial pool shifts and nostalgia for nylon stockings, which she couldn't very well miss since Mama forbade her to wear them. After wolfing down her egg-salad sandwich, she grew even more bored as the conversation meandered to the birthday party the WACs were planning for a friend. She walked out to a rock on the river, threw some pebbles into the water, then decided to join the guys, who were deep in a conversation sprinkled with the words *Vemork, Norway, heavy water*. Something about an Allied attack.

"That should set the Germans back and then some," said Owen.

"But it means they are seriously moving ahead. It surely isn't the only facility," added another technician.

They grew silent when she approached.

"Pretty here, isn't it," Jimmy said, breaking the silence. The water sparkled, flowing around rocks in various shades of gray, most dark and shiny. The flat slabs, where the guys sat, were lighter and dry.

"Don't let me disturb you. Can I just sit here?"

"Sure," said Owen, but the atmosphere changed. There was no more talk of Norway. The guys turned silent. Her presence clearly made them uncomfortable, but she couldn't think of a polite way to move away, or, having abandoned the WACs, where to go sit if she did.

Finally, Owen coughed. "This your first time here?"

She nodded. "Is this where you always ride?"

"Often," said Jimmy. "But the best is yet to come. There are caves nearby with Indian drawings." The conversation stilled. Some of the guys lay back on the rocks, eyes closed, warming themselves in the sun. All except Jimmy. "Wanna see?" he asked.

She nodded, glad to get away from the others and curious about the caves. They trekked a short distance in silence. It was so beautiful here, so romantic. She could hardly believe this was happening as she followed him, just the two of them, up a wood and rope ladder to the entrance of a cave. He waited for her at the top and gave her a hand from the top rung, pulling her in.

She didn't want him to let her hand go, but he did. It took her a moment to adjust to the dark. He switched on a flashlight to show her the images of animals on the wall.

"How old are these?" She traced the image with her finger.

"No one knows. Maybe two thousand years."

"So, people really lived here? Indians? I thought Indians lived in tepees."

Jimmy cast his light at the soot on the ceiling from the fires that once lit the cave. "Not if they could live in a cave. Much better protection."

"And a nice view." She looked past the opening to the treetops camouflaging the Frijoles River below. "I'm glad you brought me here."

"Me too."

"Are you?" She turned to him. "I'm sorry if I interrupted something before, your conversation with the guys."

"Don't worry." He squeezed her hand. Again, to her regret, he let it go.

"What's heavy water?"

"What?"

"Heavy water. You guys mentioned it when you were talking about some attack in Norway. What is it?"

"Not something you should worry your pretty head over."

"Jimmy, I'm not worried. But you must know by now that I want to know everything about everything. Don't you?"

"Well, there are some things I'm curious about and some I'm not. You're curious about things you can't possibly expect to understand."

"Try me." Her eyes challenged him. "What's heavy water?"

He scratched his head at her expectant face. Silence filled the cave. She didn't care. She could be patient.

"I don't want to talk about it," he said.

"But I want to understand. What harm could there be in that?"

"You're too curious."

"I can't help it. I just am."

"It's dangerous to talk," he said.

"Among friends, it is dangerous not to talk."

He looked at her, confused.

"We are friends, aren't we? We could be, couldn't we?" she asked, almost in a whisper.

He coughed. "Well, water is made of hydrogen and oxygen. H_2O. You know that, right?" He played absentmindedly with a strand of her hair and looked at her earnestly.

Gertie gazed back and nodded. Her heart raced. He was confiding in her, trusting her, treating her like a grown-up. One he talked to while touching her hair. Could she, might she, become his girlfriend?

"So heavy water is made up of a different kind of hydrogen, an isotope that is a form of hydrogen that is heavier than most hydrogen, and the result is that the hydrogen and oxygen are bound up even more tightly to each other, and so the water acts differently than other water."

Gertie nodded, although she barely grasped what Jimmy said. But she liked the idea of water that was special, where the hydrogen and oxygen were more tightly bonded than in regular water. That's the way she wanted to be with Jimmy. More tightly bound—acting differently together than with everyone else.

"I get the idea, but what does it have to do with the war?"

"The heavy water is used to create some kinds of weapons that the Germans are developing," Jimmy said. "That's why the Allies bombing a heavy water facility in Norway was important. It makes it more difficult for the Germans to produce their weapons."

"What kind of weapons could one possibly make with water?"

"Gertie, you know I cannot talk about these things. I've already said way more than I should. You must promise not to tell anyone about this conversation. It could get me into terrible trouble. Please. I don't want to think about the Germans." He pulled her to him clumsily. "Much better to think about you." He aimed a kiss at her forehead but missed, grazing her hairline.

She had never known what it felt like to have her heart plummet to her feet, but now she did. How could a fleeting kiss, barely a peck, do something like that? She touched his cheek, then kissed it to see what that would do to her. There was a softening deep inside her. Pleasant. No, much more than that. Wonderful. Her nose touched Jimmy's. He kissed her lips a few times lightly. Their moistness on her mouth made her feel like she was melting from the inside. So this was the big deal about kissing. All those times in films when the screen went into a swirl when couples kissed. She never wanted this to stop, but Jimmy pulled away.

"I'm sorry. I didn't mean to. I shouldn't have." He coughed and looked at the ground.

Her body felt like warm taffy stopped in midpull. "I'm not sorry you did."

"But still, I shouldn't have."

"Why? Don't you like me?"

From the tender way he looked at her, she did not need to hear his answer to know.

"Gertie, you're an amazing girl. I can never guess what you are going to say. And I feel good when I am around you. Really good."

The melting intensified, molten taffy, flooding her with relief that he felt for her what she felt for him.

"But your father. He trusts me with you."

"He trusts you not to hurt me. That doesn't mean you can't kiss me."

"Yes, it does. For him, it's the same thing."

"Well, then he's wrong."

"Your father is never wrong."

"Everyone's wrong sometimes."

Jimmy bussed her on the forehead. "Maybe," he allowed and pulled away again. "Still. We should get down. The others are probably ready to head back."

He moved toward the entrance of the cave, but she grabbed his arm. "No, not yet," she said.

He looked at her like a trapped animal.

"Please, kiss me again."

"I shouldn't have brought you up here. This is all wrong. I'm going down."

She watched him descend, closed her eyes until the melting at her core, this new sensation flooding her body, subsided enough for her to follow him down the ladder. She was in a daze, oblivious to the conversation as they mounted their horses again, as if there was a glass wall between her and the others. This time, Jimmy took the lead, and Owen fell in line behind her as they wound back to the Hill.

Letting the horse find its way along the path, she replayed the conversation with Jimmy. Each time she thought about his kisses, her stomach lurched. He felt both near and out of reach, a yo-yo pulling away and back, away and back.

CHAPTER 9
CHRISTINE

November 1943

Christine hummed to herself as she returned home from Fuller Lodge after rehearsal. She'd been pleased when Martha offered her the lead in *You Can't Take It with You* a week ago. She'd never tried acting before and had gone to the audition out of boredom and to please Thomas but found herself swept away when she tried out the role. She'd learned the part of lovestruck Alice in two days. Now, she walked briskly, shivering. Her light wool jacket was no match for the wind that whipped the last of the autumn leaves along the road. The rehearsal had gone well. She hadn't flubbed any lines, and neither had Kurt Koppel in their small scene together.

Kurt, so formal and stiff at the occasional parties where they had met in the past, was an unexpectedly good actor. During the improv warm-up before rehearsal, they'd all pretended to be awakened by burglars. Kurt was "it," in the middle of the circle, curled up in a ball like a child. The fear on his face had been palpable; he'd been shaking, and his eyes darted seemingly uncontrollably from one person to another. Now he was up ahead of her, hands in the pockets of his long overcoat, shoulders hunched against the cold. She quickened her pace to catch up with him.

"Lovely evening, isn't it?" she greeted him.

"Indeed."

"You gave me quite a scare earlier," she said.

"Me?"

"During the improv, your frightened look was, well . . . really frightening."

"Ah," he said.

"Ah? Ah what?" She laughed, cocking her face at him.

"Ah, and why should I be really frightened?"

"I don't know. Are you?"

"You look cold," he said. "Would you like my gloves?"

"Gloves? Well, yes, it is chilly. Sure."

He pulled out rabbit-lined brown leather gloves from his pockets—her size although they were for a man—gave them to her, and kept on walking.

"Wait!" She put them on while simultaneously trying to catch up to him.

He stopped as if given an order but kept his back to her. As she came closer, he looked as if he was going to walk away, as if he did not want to wait. Then he turned abruptly to face her.

"Are you frightened?" she asked again.

He looked down at the ground.

She was as taken aback by her intrusive question as he seemed to be. She did not know him well. Barely at all, except for what Gertie had told her. But she wasn't sorry she had asked. She wanted to know.

He stared up at her coldly.

She met his gaze.

Suddenly, his coldness melted, and his eyes welled. He dabbed them clumsily. "How does one explain what it is like to go to bed frightened, and to awake frightened, and not to sleep in between?"

He turned and began to walk away, but she kept pace with him. "Try me," she said, touching his shoulder so that he turned back toward her.

He snorted. "I am a Jew. My wife, Sarah, she is Jewish too. In Germany we left behind four siblings and their spouses and children, and our parents. Let me be more precise: twenty-three relatives. We have heard from none of them for fifteen months and nine days now, despite many inquiries to the Red Cross. We do not know where they are or if they are alive. That is enough fear to give one sleepless nights, don't you think?" His voice was soft and bitter. He strode away. Christine struggled to keep up with him.

"I'm so sorry," said Christine.

"Sorry? It is not your fault, certainly."

"I mean sorry about all that has happened."

"In that case, sorry does not even begin to help. That kind of sorry is no solace at all."

Christine wanted to apologize now for saying she was sorry, but it would only make her sound even sillier than Kurt obviously already thought she was. So she was silent, expressing solidarity by keeping pace with him.

He cleared his throat. "On the professional front, there are also fears: that the gadget we are all working on may be at a much more advanced stage of development in Germany. I tried out for this play because I will lose my mind if I do not get away from the lab occasionally. Acting is something I used to enjoy when I was young. But every moment that I am not working, I feel terrible—guilty that the Germans will win, will murder my family, and many of my friends. This, too, is not, you will admit, conducive to dispelling fright."

It was the most honest utterance Christine had heard since coming to Los Alamos. She grabbed his arm; she did not know if to stop him— he was frightening her—or to comfort the man who lay curled up in the circle earlier in the evening. She turned him toward her.

"This war will end. You do know that. We will win it," she said. She did not know where her optimism came from.

His sad eyes searched hers as if to discern whether she was genuinely so hopeful. He patted her hand, still on his arm, with his, as if indulging her sweet but naive thought, then pulled his arm away and shoved his hands in his pockets. But he didn't walk away, and so they continued in silence, the tread of their feet restoring normal boundaries, until they reached Kurt's home, two streets before hers.

"I will walk you home," Kurt said.

"There's no need."

"I know, for you there is no need, but it is good for me, this walk, this brisk air."

The silence as they walked to her house was comfortable and comforting, punctured by the distant putter of jeeps patrolling the perimeter road and the howl of coyotes.

Her house was dark. She had forgotten to leave on a light, and Thomas was not yet home.

"Thanks for walking me home—and for the gloves," said Christine, handing them back.

"Thank you," said Kurt.

"For what?" She shrugged dismissively.

"Your optimism. Your silence. I am grateful." He kissed her hand, which made her laugh. He looked offended.

"No one's ever kissed my hand before."

"No one has made me feel better for a long time," he answered.

CHAPTER 10
SARAH

November 1943

The wind whipped Sarah's face as she walked to the bus stop past clapboard houses that seemed to shudder at the coming winter. At the stop, a few women stood in a cluster, chatting and laughing.

"Hi, come join us," one said.

Sarah recognized her. Christine Sharp, whom Gertie mentioned all the time. It seemed this woman and her daughter were friends. It was odd. What did they talk about? Sarah found Gertie so difficult to talk to these days. She didn't know how to respond to this woman, casual and yet so in control that even the freckles on her nose and cheeks seemed sprinkled there deliberately. To refuse to join them would be rude.

Saved by the approaching bus, Sarah answered, "The bus, it comes," then felt her face redden in frustration. She knew English grammar from high school, but when she spoke, the words came out wrong.

"It is coming. I think the bus is coming." She corrected herself, but by then the bus had rolled into the stop, and the women formed a line behind her to board, oblivious to her perfected sentence.

The door opened, emitting the smell of warm tortillas even before a dozen domestics disembarked, their ponchos fluttering, their lunch pails swaying as they headed toward the administration building for the day's work assignments.

Sarah stepped forward, handed her pass to the military policeman at the foot of the bus, and held her breath while he inspected it. She must stop being so scared. This was America. She must try to smile the way the other women did when the policeman handed them back their passes. But she managed only a nod before climbing aboard and sitting in an aisle seat at the back to discourage anyone from joining her. As the bus drove off, she watched the maids, bending into the cold in the distance. In Germany, she'd had a live-in maid. Here she was not entitled to domestic help. That was only for women who worked on the Hill or who had young children. During the first weeks at Los Alamos, she'd wiped the chandelier every week. But it had been too much work. Only she cared if the crystal shone. No one else noticed her impeccable cleanliness any more than they noticed whether she got dressed or combed her hair. At first, neighbors had invited her for tea, but she found their cheerfulness enervating and could not follow their rapid conversation. So she'd made excuses a few times, and now they left her alone.

The bus took curve after hairpin curve. Sarah's ears popped from the change in elevation. They passed road signs to Taos, Española, Santa Clara, each in a different direction. America was like its landscape. Despite road signs, one got lost in its vastness.

Yet people here did try to make matters efficient and convenient. The identity passes were easy to renew. She only had to remember to ask before the old one expired. But she trembled each time, remembering how onerous bureaucracy had been in Germany. Especially the police clearance certification and tax confirmation receipt they needed before they could apply for a visa to the United States or anywhere. They could have gotten them easily if only she had acted differently.

When she thought of that day, seven years ago, she could still smell the single rose on the big oak desk and the fresh polish on the black boots of Jurgen Hartmann, a former high school classmate in charge of German certificates and receipts in Hamburg.

She'd asked to see Jurgen when she arrived at the Department of Internal Affairs.

Back in twelfth grade, he had once put a dead rabbit on her desk. She had screamed, and he'd laughed. But a week later, when she'd lost a necklace with a gold coin pendant, a gift from her grandmother, he had helped her search the school grounds until he found it. She had given him a spontaneous hug of thanks. A month later, they'd graduated from high school, and she had not seen him since but later heard that he had joined the Nazi Party and held an important position at the Department of Internal Affairs.

The clerk led her past people pleading their business to blank-faced bureaucrats and into Jurgen's office. The pounding of documents being stamped penetrated the room even after the clerk closed the door behind him. She stood before Jurgen's desk as he scratched his signature on a pile of documents, ignoring her presence.

She coughed timidly, and he raised his head and smiled.

"Sarah Weiner, it really is you. I didn't believe it when they told me a Sarah Weiner wanted to see me." He came out from behind the desk and clasped her hands.

"Sarah Koppel, actually. That's my married name."

"To me, you will always be Sarah Weiner. So good to see you!"

"You look well. Still doing all your sports?"

"Only when I can escape the office. So much work. Aggravating. You still have that lovely blonde hair I could never resist. You're as delicious as ever."

"Thank you." She blushed and looked down.

"So what brings you here?"

"These are not easy times."

"Indeed. A difficult time for the fatherland."

He invited her to sit on the overstuffed beige chintz sofa at the end of the room. The abundant cerise satin pillows left little room for human occupancy. Jurgen ordered tea and was so congenial at first that she was sure he would help.

Sarah was jerked out of her reverie by the screech of the bus braking to a halt when a bighorn sheep leaped across the dirt road. The beast dashed for a higher cliff. Jurgen would probably have loved to kill it. She felt nauseated from gasoline fumes, the lurching of the bus, and the memory of that horrendous day.

Sarah opened her purse and took out a letter from her brother-in-law, Bernard, which was always with her. It was dated November 9, 1941. Although she knew the contents by heart, she unfolded it and read:

"Dearest Kurt and Sarah, I hope you are well. I wish I could say all is well with us. Unfortunately, I must inform you that Sarah's Mama, Tata, and Hanneleh, and our own dear Mama and Tata have all been sent to reeducation camp in Dachau as have cousins Hubert, Henrietta, Sonya, Charlotte, and their families. After an initial postcard confirming their arrival, we have heard from none of them. Annamarie and the children are well. Annamarie continues to work at the hospital; business could be better for me. Hoping for better times. Love, Bernard."

Why hadn't she insisted the rest of her family come with them to America? Her mind reeled back to the day she fought with her father over the matter while her sister, Hannah, played the piano and mother watered the violets, pinching away the dead leaves.

"We will only be a burden," her father insisted. "Here we have our newspapers, and our schnapps, our bridge, and our friends. And Hannah has a piano teacher she loves. The situation is worrisome, but we are too harmless and too old for anyone to bother with."

Kurt had said her family must make their own decision. Indeed, he did not prevail upon his own brothers and parents to join them, although they all agreed that no good would come to Jews from the Nazis. In the end, at Kurt's insistence, he, Sarah, and Gertie alone left— in 1937. Only Kurt's older brother, Bernard, married to a Catholic, was optimistic. And this letter she kept with her always, sent more than two years ago, was the last she had heard from any of them.

What did Bernard mean by a reeducation camp? The question invaded her sleep nightly. In her dreams, the family wore dunce caps and sat in a classroom on plain wood benches, their feet in ice water— that was how she envisioned the camp. She would wake in a sweat, usually to find Kurt staring at the ceiling beside her.

"You have been talking in your sleep again," Kurt told her last night.

"It's that same terrible dream."

"You should take something for your nerves."

"You too," she said. "To help you sleep."

"If I sleep, I will have dreams like yours," he answered.

"We owe it to them, to worry about them, even if it means we cannot sleep," she said.

"We owe it to ourselves to keep going," he replied.

"But wouldn't that be forgetting them? Pills will make me forget a bit, won't they? I want to remember everything about them."

"I remember them. *Oft.*"

He hadn't said the English "often" but used "*oft*"—in German, a language he usually took pains to avoid, even in their private conversations. She wriggled to his side of the bed, hoping he would reach for her. But he only took her hand, patted it, and let it go. They lay in the dark separately then, afraid of disturbing each other.

The bus picked up speed as it approached Santa Fe, the road now level and straight. The terra-cotta houses had one or two stories. None of the curlicues, leaf and flower motifs, or faux Greek columns of houses in Europe.

The bus came to a halt in Santa Fe's main plaza, across from Saint Francis Cathedral.

Sarah looked out the window and saw two men with fedora hats and leather, wing tip shoes across the street. She knew now these were G-2 security detail who followed the women from the Hill while they shopped.

No one had warned her about them her first time in Santa Fe. When she'd sensed she was being followed, she had told herself not to panic as she turned back to Dorothy's office, so scared she could barely recall the way. She had forced herself to act normal until she reached the administration building, then had burst through the door and dived under a desk. "The Nazis, they found me," she'd gasped. "Please, let me hide here. Please."

Dorothy had explained they were security agents who routinely followed Los Alamos personnel to assure everyone watched what they said.

"The Hill is not even supposed to exist. You know that," Dorothy had explained. "There is only 109 East Palace Avenue as far as the world knows. And we want to keep it that way. You are safe, really. You can come out now."

Since then, Sarah had tried to ignore the security men. She walked past Pueblo women, selling jewelry in the shade of the cathedral, and headed for the office. Dorothy always took a break from her paperwork to hear how Sarah was faring, as she did now, her eyes sparkling as she stood up from behind her desk.

"How are you, my dear?" Dorothy asked, warmly shaking Sarah's hand and offering her a seat.

"I wish I could be better," Sarah admitted, remaining standing.

"The news from Europe must be a worry." Dorothy walked around her desk, put a hand on Sarah's shoulder, and looked deep into her eyes.

"It is." Tears welled. She usually did not come apart this way in front of people. It must be the freedom of getting away from the Hill. Or just that Dorothy was her own age—in her forties, older by a decade or two than most of the women at Los Alamos—and seemed to take a genuine interest in her.

"Dear, let me get you a cup of coffee."

"No time. I must do shopping. You can make for me a new pass?"

"Of course. Enjoy yourself." Dorothy shooed Sarah out the door.

Sarah headed for Woolworth's, her favorite store. So many things, all in one place, no one asking questions. She could feel the fabrics and read the labels, and no one disturbed her. Although it was too early for lunch, she treated herself to a hot dog, remembering how she and Gertie used to stop and eat sausages from street stands when they shopped in Hamburg. Gertie would insist on putting on all the relishes, most of the mixture ending up on her face. Sarah was always appalled by the mess but also amused, even proud, of her daughter's single-mindedness in consuming all she deemed tasty with such enthusiasm. Life had felt perfect, familiar, safe.

Now, even buying shoelaces was fraught. Fortifying herself to find the laces, she polished off the hot dog, bland compared to Hamburg sausages. She walked up and down the aisles without finding what she needed. Asking a shop clerk could not be avoided. Sarah explained she needed string for shoes until the woman finally understood she meant laces.

Her mission accomplished, she wandered to the clothing section; the fabrics were so shabby, the clothes so poorly cut. They simply would not do for Gertie. She would try elsewhere. She paid for the laces and went back out to the cold. As she walked down the street, about to enter Dress Shoppe Supreme, she heard someone call her.

"Sarah Koppel. Is that really you?"

She turned to find her former Boston neighbor, Eleanor Bell.

"What a surprise!" Sarah's astonishment was genuine; her anxiety at being recognized pinned her in place like a rabbit paralyzed in the searchlights of G-2. She tried to add joy to her voice. "My goodness, imagine!"

"What are you doing here?" Eleanor asked.

Sarah laughed nervously as she scrambled for a response. "What are *you* doing here?"

"Out here to visit my sister who's been hospitalized in Albuquerque with a broken leg. I took a break today to see some of the spectacular Indian ruins—Pooh Cliff or something like that. Wanted to wander around Santa Fe and shop. And you? I thought you'd dropped off the end of the earth. Moving away without so much as a goodbye!"

"We went on vacation and decided to stay in the West," Sarah said, realizing how unlikely her explanation sounded. She had, after all, packed up all their things.

"So you live here?"

"Yes, well no, well not exactly." She sounded stupid to herself.

"Come, tell me all about it." Eleanor slipped her arm into Sarah's in a manner much more familiar than when they were neighbors. "I'd much rather catch up with you than see some old church or buy trinkets I don't need. Let's get a cup of coffee."

"I can't." G-2 warnings to not reveal the Hill rose in Sarah's mind.

"Why not?"

Any reason Sarah might offer for not having coffee would give away more than if she sat down with Eleanor. Why hadn't G-2 instructed her on how to avoid a situation like this, or what the consequences would be if she made a mistake? She had to think quickly. She had an hour until the bus left for Los Alamos. Maybe this was a test. Had the security men planted Eleanor here, all the way from Boston, to see whether Sarah would keep their secrets? Or maybe Eleanor worked for the Nazis and was going to abduct Sarah and use her as ransom in exchange for Kurt. Sarah stumbled, almost fell. Eleanor caught her.

"Are you okay? You look like you're going to faint. Come. Let's get that coffee."

"It's just that I don't have much time, and I must get shopping done today." Who did Eleanor work for? But suddenly it didn't matter. Anger overcame fear. Whoever they were, Eleanor's bosses would not trick her. Sarah would see this through. She would pass the test.

"But a quick cup would be fine." Sarah pointed toward a coffee shop at the end of the street, casting around to see if any G-2 men were in sight.

As they slid into the red benches in a booth, Sarah noticed they were the only customers in the shop, which made her feel conspicuous. She stole anxious glances out the window to the street as her former neighbor filled her in about the inconvenient roadwork two blocks from Sarah's old house, the neighbors who had transformed their flower beds into victory gardens to alleviate wartime shortages, and the mongrel of the new residents in Sarah's old house.

Boston life seemed eons ago. Sarah didn't care about the neighborhood when she lived there. She cared even less now. She sipped her coffee slowly to collect her thoughts. She must come up with something plausible to tell Eleanor.

"Well, enough about me," Eleanor said. "What's happened to you and your dear family?"

Eleanor's monologue had given Sarah time to concoct what she hoped was a viable story. "Kurt is working out by Puye Cliff, the site you visited. It's called *Puye*, not *Pooh*. He works with archeologists there on a method to tell how old the ruins are through chemical analyses." She was shocked at how easily she lied and synthesized snippets she'd overheard during a picnic at Puye Cliff a month ago. She had only half listened to Kurt and his colleagues talk about ways that scientists might use carbon to date ruins. "Anyway, Kurt finds the work very—how do you say it?—stimulating, and we live up there. It's very basic, isolated. I get to Santa Fe only once in a while to shop. This is why I was in such a quickness—no, how you say it?—such a rush, when I saw you." Sarah smiled, proud of herself.

"Sounds fascinating. Amazing that with his scientific skill, your husband is doing archeology and not war work." Eleanor seemed to scan Sarah's face like searchlights.

Was Eleanor truly baffled? Or was this part of a ploy to trap Sarah?

"He does what he can, where he finds a job," Sarah said indignantly. Then she said a polite goodbye, excused herself, and bustled away. As she left the coffee shop, she noticed the G-2 man who had followed her earlier standing across the street. He faced away from her, so it wasn't clear if he had seen her. She walked back to Dorothy's office, increasing her pace as anxiety mounted. Despite the cold, she arrived sweating and pounded on the door.

"Sarah, what's the matter?"

Out of breath, Sarah grabbed Dorothy's upper arms. "I have to confess to security. I have to file a report. Oh, God, help me."

"I'll get you a glass of water. Calm down, dear. What happened?"

Between sips of water and blowing her nose, Sarah described her encounter with Eleanor and the fabrications about Kurt's work.

"Now, now. Everything will be all right." Dorothy patted Sarah's arm.

When Sarah regained her composure, Dorothy excused herself and returned in a few minutes. "You are not to go back with the rest of the convoy. We will let it be known there are some bureaucratic matters that need attention, and we'll get you a separate escort back tonight."

Her tone was calm, reassuring; she didn't seem angry or worried.

"I've just had a word with security," Dorothy continued. "You will have to fill out a report of exactly what happened. But, Sarah, you did fine." Dorothy patted Sarah's arm and gave it a gentle squeeze. "You didn't give anything away. G-2 couldn't have come up with a better cover story."

Sarah went to the bathroom to wash her face. She did not like the terrified woman who stared back at her in the mirror.

CHAPTER 11
CHRISTINE

December 1943

Thomas came up behind Christine and swept her hair to the side to kiss her on the nape. He wrapped his arms around her waist and moved with her to the Andrews Sisters' "Boogie Woogie Bugle Boy" pulsating from the radio.

"I love Sunday mornings," he said, pressing against her.

She leaned into him for a moment, then poured the eggs she had frothed for an omelet into the pan.

"Hmm, such good smells." He nuzzled into her neck, and she rested her head on his chest to hold on to the moment of casual affection, rare in recent months, before turning her attention back to her cooking.

"Look at the snow," she said. "The ski slopes should be perfect. Good of you to wake up."

"Mmm. Making up for lost time. It was the week from hell."

"What happened?" She folded the omelet into itself.

"Whatever could go wrong, went wrong." He stretched and sat at the table. "What's that?" he asked, noticing the pots Christine had pulled out earlier in the morning from the closet.

"Some pottery I picked up in San Ildefonso." Christine slipped the omelet onto his plate. "What do you think?"

He shrugged. "Not my taste."

She slammed the plate in front of him with more force than either of them expected. He looked up at her, nonplussed. She glared at him. "But what do I know?" he added.

Christine served herself the rest of the eggs and sat down, scraping her chair noisily.

"You really don't know," Christine muttered. Since meeting Maria a month earlier, Christine had visited the potter two more times, once to watch a firing of the vases and once to join her when she dug for clay.

"Boy, no one makes an omelet like you do," Thomas said in that cheerful tone he used to placate her when he didn't know what he'd done to annoy her. "So, what's this with the pots?"

Christine was shocked that he didn't know. Could he be so wrapped up in his work that he hadn't noticed? Or was it just that he stayed at the lab so late that by the time he got home she was fast asleep, so there was never a time to fill him in about her days? With his attention on her now, she told him about San Ildefonso, Maria, and a letter she had sent to Samantha with some sketches of the pots. "I thought I might send one of the vases to your mother for her birthday," Christine said. Angelica, a collector of Victorian bone china cups and art nouveau, was just the sort of client Christine wanted to attract. She did not add that her mother-in-law always seemed to insinuate that despite Christine's training at London's Royal Academy of Art, her humble origins could never quite match the artistic discernment acquired by osmosis from good breeding. "She's a good test case. If she likes it, I'd know there's a real market for this kind of work."

"I don't know what she'll think, hon. And I don't like the idea of your wandering around in the desert alone."

"I've been doing it for weeks now, borrowing Oppie's horse. He said I could. Actually, the first time I rode out to Maria's, it was to see if I could find a pot to replace the one that got broken at that party.

Thought I'd give Oppie one for the holidays—to fix things between us." Christine wasn't sure if she meant fixing things between the Sharps and Oppie or fixing matters between herself and Thomas, who hadn't ever mentioned the incident at the party, but still, somehow, seemed to hold it against her.

"Getting a replacement was a good idea. But I still don't like it—you're going out there by yourself."

"How long do you think I can sit at home, twiddling my thumbs and cleaning the house?" she said, setting two cups of coffee on the table.

"Aren't you in that theater group?"

"Amateur theater does not make a life."

"Why are you raising your voice?"

"I'm not."

"Well, you sound angry or something."

"Why would I be angry? I haven't seen you all week, and when I do, you tell me I have silly ideas."

"The theater group is a perfectly good idea," said Thomas.

"The theater group was your idea, not mine. I'm talking about selling Indian pottery."

He shrugged. "Do what suits you. You always do."

She was so angry she could barely swallow. The eggs felt like soggy cardboard in her mouth. When was the last time she had done what she wanted? It was he who always did what suited him. She was left to cope with the consequences. They ate in silence. Her cutlery scratched the plate, a counterpoint to the jingling Christmas songs on the radio. She was still raging silently when the news came on.

"Reports from the Italian front indicate that the Allied port stronghold of Bari has been attacked by German bombers. More than twenty cargo and transport ships in the harbor were reportedly destroyed. Among the vessels hit were two ammunition ships, setting off explosions, which shattered windows seven miles away, according to local reports. In addition, a bulk

petrol pipeline on a quay was destroyed, and gushing fuel has spread over
much of Bari harbor, igniting and engulfing many ships."

"Damn Germans," Christine muttered. She smacked her fork on
the plate, rose, and turned off the radio. "How long are we going to be
stuck here because of them? How long before we know what is going
to happen with our lives?"

She cleared the plates and pointed her question directly at him. "Are
we ever going to win this war?" It was silly to act like it was Thomas's
personal responsibility to bring the war to an end, but she was so angry
at him. "This uncertainty, this sense of life on hold, I hate it. How long
will it go on? And you think I should just act in amateur plays until
it's over?"

"Hey, it's Sunday. We can't make the war disappear, but let's make
it a great day." He raised his cup of coffee as if it were a wineglass and
he was offering a toast.

"Stop trying to mollify me. I'm not a child."

He put down his cup and gave her a look that mixed affection and
amusement. "Au contraire. You are my delectable better half."

She got up and took her plate to the sink, her annoyance at him
wavering at his obvious attempt at appeasement.

"Whadya say we first make up for those nights I missed—and then
head for the slopes?" he said, pulling her to him when she came back to
the table to finish clearing it.

She was glad to see him breezy and enthusiastic—the way he had
been for so much of their life together, a spirit he'd lacked in recent
months.

"It's past the right time. It won't work."

"It doesn't always have to be about a baby."

She looked at him to see if he meant it. For months, their lovemaking had been synonymous with the campaign to become parents.

"Really, it doesn't." He undid the belt on her morning robe, slipped
his arms inside, and leaned his head on her stomach. She ran her fingers
through his hair and held him. He rose and led her to the bedroom.

In bed, he kissed her neck and worked his way down, knowing exactly where to stop to make her soften—on the insides of her thighs, on the backs of her knees. He conducted her body as if it were an orchestra he was intent on rousing to a breathless crescendo. He laughed when she moaned in pleasure, and whispered "Ah, yes, that's my girl" as he entered her, sure now that her body would accept him. His movements were swift, confident in his knowledge of her, luring her to obey his body as it always did and releasing himself into her only when she fully surrendered to his touch. Later, he smiled and closed his eyes, and she lay and looked at his lean, strong body, at the fine light-brown hair on his chest, at the veins pulsing through the pale underside of his upper arms. Did he ever gaze at her as she did at him? Did he really see her anymore? She felt played, not loved. Why did she feel lonely after making love? She rose and went to shower. Soon Thomas joined her.

"I can tell this is going to be a magnificent day." He kissed her nose as she toweled off. "First having you, then the ski slopes. We're so lucky!"

She managed only half a smile back. She felt outwitted somehow.

A blast of cold air hit them as they walked out the door, but it did not dispel her inner ferment. Thomas was essentially indifferent to her passion for the pots and would at most tolerate her promoting them—as a concession—in hopes they would distract her so she would ask him fewer questions. Even though there were secrets he had to keep, he could surely tell her more than he did. She looked over at him, lugging their skies, poles, and leggings, and wondered what other, unseen burdens he carried. It was as if he made love to her so he wouldn't have to talk to her. The result was that she still had no idea what he had gone through the past few weeks. She dodged a snowball hurled by a child playing in the space between the barracks, then waved to Martha, who was building a snowman with her husband and their four kids. Did Martha have real conversations with her husband? Did anyone have real conversations with anyone here? Well, there was Gertie. Conversations with her seemed genuine.

Thomas flagged down a couple of lab technicians who had commandeered a military jeep to drive to the slopes. He and Christine piled in with their gear. When they reached their destination, bursts of laughter and lab-liberated cheer punctured the crisp air as they waited for the ski lift. The ski resort operated solely for residents of the Hill. When Thomas found a few colleagues, Christine suggested they continue to the top, while she'd get off on the intermediate slope. Even though she had grown up in Maine, Thomas was by far the better skier, having learned as a child from elite ski instructors when his family took winter vacation in fancy resorts in Colorado.

"I'll get off at the intermediate level," he said. "So we can ski together."

"I'll only hold you back."

"I don't mind," he said. "It's our time together." He leaned into her gently.

"No, go on. I know you love to ski from the top."

He smiled at her sheepishly. "You sure you don't mind?"

"Of course not." The very fact that he had offered to forgo the high slopes touched her. She knew how much he loved the challenge of the advanced runs, how competitive he was and how he always wanted the best of everything. It made her proud that he had chosen her, as if she, too, was the best of everything. She was sorry she had been so harsh with him earlier.

"Go on to the top with the others," she said. "I know you want to."

He squeezed her shoulder in thanks, and they each grabbed a chair, rising above the trees that glistened with ice so bright it was blinding. The blue-shadowed snow extended in all directions until it collided on the horizon with mountains and sky. As they slowed to the stop on the intermediate level, Christine spotted Gertie and Jimmy. She jumped off and waved to Thomas as he drifted up and away toward the experienced section, then lugged her skis and poles to the takeoff point.

"Watch me. Look, I'm getting good," Gertie greeted Christine, laughing as she pushed off. She wobbled for a moment, regained her balance, and slid away.

"Keep those skis parallel, legs together," Jimmy called after her as she curved out of shouting range.

"You're quite the instructor. Algebra, horseback riding, now skiing," Christine said to his back as she attached her skis.

His eyes trailed Gertie until she was out of sight. "She's got such dogged determination. It makes teaching her easy." He turned to Christine, blowing into his hands to keep them warm. "Never met anyone like her. She'll be a better skier than me in no time."

"Does that bother you?"

"The first day I went to tutor her in algebra, all I wanted was to get the job done, keep my promise to her father. I figured she'd just be some annoying kid."

"She is special, mature beyond her years."

"Yeah. So I've learned. Now I worry that once I teach her what I know—algebra, skiing, whatever—she'll get bored and leave me in the dust."

"You needn't think that way."

"She's so different from other people. She means what she says and says what she means. How many girls like that do you know?" He shook his head in amazement and stared down the hillside, as if he couldn't believe his good luck.

"Not many—girls or guys." Christine laughed.

"And she's so alive, so curious. It takes my breath away."

"Mine too." Christine smiled. "But don't let the pyrotechnics fool you. She wants what any woman wants—a warm, sane place to rest her head and her heart. With someone who's straight with her and really listens. Give any woman that, and chances are she'll stick around."

"You figure?" He turned to Christine, his face hopeful.

Christine stood, smiled down at him, and shoved off down the mountain. "You've got a good chance," she called back.

She swerved, the wind whipping her face. The wet-wool scent of her coat and mittens mingled with the sharp smell of the pine trees. Below, plumes of powdery snow spewed from skiers ahead. She held her poles close to her chest, hurtling forward with a satisfying sense of coordination. Funny how she could feel so in control zooming down a mountain at God-only-knew what speed and so muddled in the rest of her life.

As she sped up, Christine shifted sharply to the right, narrowly missing a boulder that was mostly blanketed by snow. She'd noticed a naked bit of rock at the last moment and veered away. For the rest of the run, she cruised on the adrenaline from the near miss, pacing herself as she skied, letting her mind wander. She thought of Jimmy and Gertie on the slopes. Their excitement in each other's presence reminded her of her own courtship. She had been flattered that a person so sure of himself as Thomas should emphatically want her. It had not crossed her mind then to consider the possibility of refusing him. These days, she wondered what he had seen in her then and whether it was something he saw in her still— or wanted. Lately he seemed to abhor her ambition, something he had once admired, and to want her only to admire him. She had once found that easy to do—but her esteem for him was now mixed with resentment.

Christine slowed to the end of the run. Her cheeks tingled, the cold air against her warm body making her lightheaded. She caught the lift back up the mountain and watched the sun-tickled snow shimmer below her as she reached the summit.

After two hours of skiing, she joined Gertie and Jimmy at the lodge. But she felt in the way of their molten glances, so she caught a ride back to the base with some of Jimmy's mates. As she walked from their dorms to her home, her mood sank with the sun. Despite the invigorating day, she felt a longing for something out of reach. It had been a while since she had been around people as smitten with each other as Gertie and Jimmy—shy, teasing, then shy again. That kind of love couldn't last any longer than the sunset, which was smoldering its last gasp of crimson as she climbed the stairs home and parked her skis on the porch. Was mature love intrinsically anemic? she wondered, as she opened the door and flicked on the lights. The house was cold. She lit the stove and headed to the kitchen to cook dinner. Thomas would be home soon, and he'd be hungry.

CHAPTER 12
CHRISTINE

December 1943

Christine was heading to the door of Fuller Lodge after rehearsal when Kurt approached her, bowed, and swept off his visor-rimmed beret, exposing a bald head.

"May I walk you home tonight, madam?"

She bowed back to match his playful chivalry. "I have become accustomed to being escorted home."

As they exited the lodge, they were greeted by a blast of cold wind.

"Fun, aren't they, these rehearsals?" she said.

"Indeed, and at least until the performance, they are an essential diversion . . . from everything else."

"You've had a bad week?" she asked.

"Yes, quite awful."

"Thomas has been tense these past weeks too. During the improv, you did rage and frustration so well—a real Gulliver tied down by the Lilliputians."

Kurt guffawed. She was taken aback to see him laugh wholeheartedly and pleased that she could amuse him.

"But you can't talk about it, of course. Right?"

"Right," he said.

"Well, I've actually had a good week," she said.

"Oh?"

"I've been learning about the pottery the Indians around here make, all the motifs, the different styles. I've been cataloging them. And a colleague in New York has agreed to let me send her some pieces with explanations: how they're made, their symbolism. She's going to try and sell them in her gallery—the one we used to run together—on the Upper East Side."

"The pottery is very beautiful. I saw a piece once at Oppie's," said Kurt.

"Yes, and it's fascinating to see all the stages it takes. Maria, the potter I've met, took me along with her once when she collected clay— from two different spots. She sifts some of it through a sieve and also collects volcanic ash—sort of bluish—which she adds to the sand to make her clay. I would love someday to do a chemical analysis of the mixture she uses, compare her clay with that used in ceramics in other parts of the world and in other times."

Christine's enthusiasm uncorked as she went on about her plans. "I hope I can develop a market for Maria's ceramics. She is willing, and I think we can work together well."

"How resourceful of you." He took her fully into his gaze. "Impressive."

"Why, thanks." If someone as formidable as Kurt believed she could make a go of it, maybe she could.

"I would buy a few pieces myself, but Sarah wouldn't want them. She likes things that remind her of Europe. Personally, I find their lines elegant."

"Yes, that's what attracted me at first too. But that's not the half of it."

"Oh?"

"The motifs are a world unto themselves. Serpents, bears, clouds, raging winds—all good luck. The Indians believe the most fearful forces are also the ones that bring good fortune."

"Fascinating. If only it were true," said Kurt, rearranging his scarf against the cold.

Christine threw him a puzzled look.

"Well, think about it. Do the most fearful forces bring good fortune?"

"I don't know." They walked on in silence. "What about the gadget?" she asked.

"What about it?"

She was relieved he hadn't shut her up. It was the first time anyone working on it had admitted in her presence that the gadget even existed.

"Isn't it a good force?"

"We don't know yet."

"You don't know if it works, or you don't know if it's good?"

"Both," he said.

The wind howled. An army jeep passed by, its headlights flooding their path for a moment before it drove on.

"What you are working on is good. Surely you believe that."

"What's good in the context of war can be bad in other contexts."

"Can we afford to think of other contexts right now?"

"I suppose not," he said. Their steps crunched the snow as they walked in sync in silence, Kurt apparently lost in thought. "I never imagined I would dedicate so much energy, so much of my life, to destruction. And that's what war is about, destroying. No one has to convince me that Hitler, Nazism, is bad. But we don't know how to destroy selectively. To destroy only the bad. It is not possible. There is always a price." He spoke more to the desert than to her, then seemed to catch himself. "I'm sorry. I did not mean to talk about this. My doubts, they must make me sound like a traitor. As if I am not convinced of the cause. I am, of course, committed, and yet it does not stop my wondering sometimes."

"We all wonder sometimes."

"Yes, well, I don't know if wondering does any good. Maybe it is best not to wonder too much. Maybe it is best to keep our thoughts to ourselves."

"Everyone here keeps their thoughts to themselves too much."

"Perhaps," Kurt said. They walked silently for a few paces. "So if we are to talk about important things, let us talk about your pots. I have an idea for you. I have a friend in Chicago, a refugee like myself, an anthropologist who specializes in the beliefs of polytheistic religions and cultures. I am sure he would want to hear about what you learn. I will bring you his address," said Kurt.

"I would appreciate that. Thanks," she said as they reached her house. It felt exhilarating to talk seriously about her work to someone.

"Thank *you*, madam." He bowed. "I sleep much better after our walks home."

"The night air does one good," Christine said.

"If I thought it was just the walk, I would walk every night."

"I'm glad you are sleeping better," she said evenly, hiding how flustered she felt.

He touched her sleeve.

She hadn't expected that. She patted his hand, still on her arm, as if he were a child.

"Good night," she said and pulled away toward home. As she walked, Kurt's words echoed in her mind. So, he needed someone to talk to. Everyone did. She shouldn't let it go to her head.

She reached home. Once inside, she switched on all the lights and drew together the curtains in the living room. As she filled the teakettle, she remembered the wistful way he touched her sleeve. Had she imagined that? Sipping her drink, she closed her eyes and reenacted the scene. What if she had touched his sleeve back, instead of just patting his hand?

She looked in the mirror at her naked reflection as she undressed for bed and wondered whether Kurt would think her beautiful. She was lanky and angular, her pale skin freckled from her shoulders to her arms. Her breasts were small. She was taller than Kurt. Would that bother him? She was crazy to be thinking this way. He must be at least fifteen years older than her. And yet, he was kinetic, open minded—not at all how Gertie described him. Talking to Kurt, she forgot he was Gertie's father. Thinking about him now, all of Gertie's complaints about him suddenly seemed misguided, even churlish. It was unrealistic to expect Gertie would understand her father was vulnerable and insightful; children always had a jaundiced view of their parents.

Readying for bed, Christine piled up her hair with both hands. Holding her elbows out, torso stretched, she looked at herself in the mirror again, then dropped her hands and let her hair fall. A faux femme fatale. And a barren one, whose body did the world no good. She put on her nightie and slipped in under the cold sheets. When would Thomas come home? She lay on her side, imagining herself in his arms. She twisted and turned until she fell asleep, but it was under the image of Kurt's face, cocked toward her with its attentive gaze.

CHAPTER 13
SARAH

December 1943

Sarah was ironing Kurt's shirts in the kitchen and listening for the third time to the radio news bulletin on the sinking of two British destroyers by German submarines off the coast of Algeria when she heard Gertie burst through the front door.

"*Liebchen!*" she called. It was more a reprimand at the ruckus than a greeting.

"Hi, Mama." Gertie dropped her books on the table and gave her mother a peck on the cheek.

"You are hungry?"

"No."

"I have made some cookies."

"I'm fine."

Sarah placed the iron upright on the ironing board and turned off the radio.

"Maybe a taste?" She took out three butter cookies from the gingerbread-house cookie jar on the counter and poured her daughter a glass of milk. Gertie sat down and took only a polite nibble. She was usually hungry these days. A teenager, as Americans would explain.

There was no such thing in Germany. There were children and there were adults. But Americans thought it was natural, the way Gertie behaved—hungry, moody, and noisy so much of the time. If she was not hungry now but in a good mood and late coming home from school, it could only mean she had stopped by at Christine Sharp's on the way and snacked there. It was good Gertie had a sensible older person to talk to, but Sarah wished her daughter would confide in her instead. She sighed and returned to her ironing. She sprayed Kurt's shirt with starch and was about to ask Gertie about her day. But before she could, Gertie posed her own question.

"Mama, what was it like, the first time you met Papa?"

The child had never shown the slightest interest in such matters.

"You want, maybe, to know if it is like the first time you met Jimmy?" Sarah tried to make her remark in that bantering American tone Gertie seemed to respond well to these days.

Gertie blushed and took another bite of the cookie. "Oh, Mama, really!"

"You are spending a lot of time with this young man, no?" Sarah sounded sterner than she intended. In fact, she did not disapprove of Jimmy. He was always polite to her, considerate of Gertie, and Kurt liked him. It was a pity he wasn't Jewish. But there weren't many suitable Jewish men in Los Alamos. And it was more important that Gertie be settled with someone solid and sensible than someone who was Jewish. Given anti-Semitism, maybe it was safer in the long term, even in a place like America where no one seemed to care what faith one followed—or didn't follow.

Gertie sipped her milk. "Yeah. I do like him a lot, but I'm not like you, and he's not like Papa, so that's got nothing to do with it."

"Really?"

"Christine asked me how you met, and I had no idea. So now I'm curious."

Sarah draped one shirt on a hanger and reached for another. Americans had a peculiar tendency to ask personal questions. Why should Christine be interested in the Koppels' family history? But Sarah did not want to dismiss her daughter's question. Should she tell her that it had not been love at first sight? Or second sight. Sarah had initially been certain that Kurt was far more interested in her sister, Hannah, who was not only the accomplished musician in the family but also far prettier and more vivacious.

Kurt, the son of a friend of a friend who had recommended he contact the family when he moved to Hamburg to do his doctorate in physics, had come to their home for Friday-night dinner. Sarah found it amusing that he arrived with wine, chocolates, and flowers. Three house gifts for one dinner seemed overzealous, but he otherwise showed no great anxiety and fit easily into conversation with her parents. She sat quietly by and helped finish preparing dinner while Hannah entertained the visiting young man with her piano playing. Kurt lavishly complimented Hannah, who responded flirtatiously throughout dinner. Sarah focused on serving the food and observing their guest: the way he meticulously cut his chicken and consumed it with efficient elegance, the wry anecdotes and apropos jokes with which he peppered the table talk, and the earnest way he answered Hannah's questions about his studies, his vacations, his family. Kurt had seemed to enjoy both the food and the feminine attention. As he left the table after dinner, he stopped a moment at the sideboard, where the Sabbath candles flickered in a set of heavy silver candlesticks.

"They remind me of home," he said.

"Their light always makes me think of Rembrandt's paintings," Sarah remarked as she followed his gaze. He looked at her then, as she cleared away the plates, as if noticing her for the first time.

"Indeed," he answered.

Weeks later, he would tell Sarah that he had always compared the light in his own parents' home to the warmth of Rembrandt's interiors. That moment after dinner was, she suspected, as close to falling in love with her as he would ever come. For her, it was enough that he chose her, not Hannah. She knew, too, that over the dinners in her parents'

home during the months that followed, he appreciated her assidu-
ousness in the kitchen, her uncomplaining ways, and her moderate
expectations of those around her. It was the latter, above all, which she
surmised drew him to her, the lack of pressure she put on him, a man
so ambitious he needed no prodding from others. After high school, she
had considered studying to be a bookkeeper (her father's suggestion) or
a librarian (her mother's suggestion) or apprenticing to be a hatmaker
(Hannah's suggestion), but she had no genuine interest in any of these
endeavors. It was difficult to explain to Gertie that Kurt had married
Sarah because she was a person who asked for nothing, expected little,
and had no ambitions other than to have a family. This did not seem
a particularly sterling quality, more an absence of personality than the
presence of character.

"There's not much to tell," Sarah said as she looked up from her
ironing. The sun flooding the room couldn't have been more different
from the milky light of her parents' parlor where her restrained romance
with Kurt had progressed.

"Oh, Mama, there must be."

Sarah hung the shirt on a hanger, gripping it as if to steady herself
against the wave of longing that assaulted her. She missed home so
much. She smiled sadly at Gertie's expectant face. "We met in my parents' home. Your father would come often for dinner. I think he was
lonely in Hamburg, and my mother was a good cook. He was studying
hard. He felt relaxed around me. I felt comfortable around him, secure."

"That's it? You just felt comfortable and secure around each other?"

"Yes, it is good to feel comfortable with another person." Sarah
spread out Gertie's flannel nightshirt on the board and began ironing it.

"What about love?" Gertie looked at her mother.

Sarah hunched over the ironing board. How to explain? She had
never expected more than comfort and security in marriage. In fact,
there had been little of either. Of course, Kurt had been right to take
them away from Germany. But he provided no comfort after that. Yes,
he bought her a piano in the house they rented in Rochester that first

winter. But neither she nor Kurt played piano, so it only served to remind Sarah how much she missed her sister's playing. Sarah wanted the house filled with music, but there was none she cared to listen to on the radio, which broadcast only pop tunes and advertising jingles. Desperate for something familiar, she had asked Kurt for a phonograph and a few classical records. And he bought her a record player and seemed genuinely glad she had asked, as if grateful that her request was so easy to fulfill. They spent many evenings that first year in America listening to static-riddled renditions of their favorite music: Strauss waltzes, Mozart concertos, Bach. But after a year, Kurt admitted that he hated the scratchy static and would listen with her no more. Besides, he was too busy for music. And after that, when she listened, she missed his presence more than she enjoyed the music. So she stopped listening too. But she had brought the phonograph with her to Los Alamos because it reminded her of how much Kurt had wanted to please her. She didn't want him to know how little it had helped.

"I mean, wasn't there a moment, a special moment, when you knew you were in love?" Gertie persisted.

Sarah wanted to tell her daughter to go do homework. It was painful to talk about the past, and she didn't have wisdom to impart to Gertie about romance. Kurt had been the only man who ever courted her.

"I can't remember a specific moment. It just seemed right," Sarah said finally. She looked back at the ironing basket still half-full of towels and underwear. In Germany, the servants ironed the underwear, and now, with no servants, she ironed it all herself. She suddenly had a heretical thought. No one saw underwear, so what did it matter? She would first iron the towels and decide about the whites later. Maybe she would just do Kurt's and Gertie's and not her own. Or maybe just Kurt's.

"There must have been something!" Gertie insisted.

Yes, there had been a moment, a Friday evening, when after dinner, she had been absorbed in cross-stitching a tablecloth and had looked up to see Kurt gazing at her with pleasure.

Sarah cleared her throat. "Well, I was quite pretty. In any case, your father thought so. He made me feel pretty. There was that."

"Yes, Mama, you were very pretty." Gertie smiled. "I can see that in the old photos. You still are pretty, you know."

Gertie was trying to be kind. Sarah didn't feel pretty these days. The dry air here was not good for her skin, and she had put on weight. She felt for a bobby pin in her hair and pushed back in place a strand that had strayed from her bun.

"What is that friend of yours, Christine, so curious about?"

"Everything. About our life in Germany."

"Oh? And what do you tell her? Do you remember much?"

"How could I forget? All those wonderful Sunday dinners at Oma and Opa's. And the walks we would take in the park afterwards. Remember how I saved bread all week to feed the pigeons and ducks?"

"I remember you once put the breadcrumbs on your head!" Sarah smiled at the memory.

"It was horrible! All of a sudden the birds landed on my head and started clawing me, and I cried. Opa batted them away and said to me: 'If you don't want pigeons to eat off your head, don't put breadcrumbs there.' It's just the wisest thing anyone has ever said, isn't it? I think about him any time I'm about to do something I'll be sorry about."

"And this you told Christine?" Sarah asked. It was strange to think of Gertie sharing her grandfather's wisdom with Christine Sharp, who did not strike Sarah as a woman in need of advice.

"Once I got going, I remembered lots of other things. How on the way from the park we would stop in front of the cathedral and buy chestnuts in winter and ice cream in summer. Do you remember how noisy we would be, how people would look at us because we talked and laughed so much? I didn't care that they stared at us. And I remember how Papa and Uncle Bernard argued a lot about leaving Germany. They never agreed about that, did they?"

"No, they didn't." Sarah sighed as she folded the last towel. She would try, just this once, to not iron anyone's underwear, not even Kurt's.

"Papa was right, wasn't he?" asked Gertie.

"Yes, he was," said Sarah.

"What has happened to them all, Mama?" Gertie asked softly, scanning Sarah's face intensely.

"Gertie, please stop asking. Please. I don't know." Sarah felt physically frozen, her jaw clenching. She put the laundry basket on the floor and dropped into the armchair. She grasped the arms. The blackness of the unknown threatened to swallow her.

CHAPTER 14
CHRISTINE

December 1943

"You must be the only person who joined the troupe for the food," Christine said to Owen as he gobbled down the meatballs in tomato sauce that she had brought from home. She had gotten into the habit over the weeks of sharing her cooking with him backstage during rehearsals while they waited for their scenes.

"I don't come *just* for the food. Also for a charming costar with whom to enjoy it." He smiled and slurped the meatballs up like a vacuum cleaner. "This is delicious."

Owen was a fun costar and a credible love interest in *You Can't Take It with You*. He played Tony, the boss's son. Christine, cast as Alice, falls in love with Tony and tries to shield him from her eccentric family, including her bomb-making grandfather, played by Kurt.

Christine could identify with Alice. To get into her part, she had only to remember how much she had dreaded introducing Thomas to her own family. It wasn't because Christine's parents were poor—there was no shame in that—but it was their lack of curiosity, their passivity, their fear and resentment of anything outside their immediate world that embarrassed her. Thomas had made the best of the visit, lavishly complimenting her mother's burnt cooking, ignoring her father's inebriated state, but they had never visited her parents together again. Christine tossed her head to dismiss the memories and focused on Owen and the food at hand.

Tall and muscular, Owen sported dark-blond hair that seemed to beg for a hand to sweep his front flop aside, the better to reveal big eyes that vacillated between innocence and insolence. There had been plenty of waiting time during their many rehearsals to talk and kid around, and Owen was a master at both. His background was not so different from hers, so there was an ease in their relationship that made him seem like a younger brother she'd never had.

Christine heard Kurt's voice on the stage, and Martha's. She had apparently stopped the scene being rehearsed to add some instruction.

From Fuller Lodge's main hall, she also heard the tune of a fiddle as couples do-si-doed—as usual on Wednesday evenings. From another room came the sound of a rehearsing barbershop quartet. So many people intent on having a good time, so keen, like herself, to forget where they were and why.

"You have no idea how much I love garlic," Owen said.

As they ate, she told him about the first time she ever cooked with garlic, when she was new to New York City and decided to try her hand at eggplant parmesan.

"I'd never eaten either garlic or eggplant before. I was so pleased with the way it tasted that, on the spot, I invited my neighbors—two NYU students—to join me for dinner. They brought a bottle of red wine, and I remember how thrilled I was, thinking that this was the life, cooking exotic meals and drinking wine with neighbors for no special reason."

The door on the stage side of the room opened.

"Oh, you are here," Kurt said as he walked into the room. His eyes glanced from Christine to Owen. He sniffed the air as if affronted.

"What's that smell?" he asked.

"And a good evening to you too," said Owen. "To your question, dinner. Meatballs in tomato sauce. Delicious. All gone." He wiped his mouth with his hand. During rehearsals, Owen seemed to forget that Kurt was one of the senior bosses. Or maybe disregarding hierarchy came naturally to him.

"Hello, Kurt. I should have thought to save you some," said Christine.

Kurt sat down on the worn sofa and shrugged. "No matter. I have eaten."

He looked gaunt under the single bare bulb that dangled from the ceiling by a wire. She wondered if there was some new trouble at work that was eating him or some disturbing news about his family in Europe. Sitting on the sofa, under a war poster that screamed **It Can Happen Here!** in bold red letters against a background of a bombed-out European city street, he seemed so small and vulnerable, and she wished she could flee with him to somewhere tranquil and beautiful.

"You don't know what you're missing," said Owen, cleaning the last drop of tomato sauce from his plate with a finger and licking it dramatically.

"I am not accustomed to tomato sauce eaten with meatballs," Kurt said, watching him. "In Germany, we eat meatloaf. With gravy. No garlic. No tomatoes."

"Sounds dull," said Owen, rising to take the plates from the table. He turned to the sink to wash them, his back to Christine and Kurt. Christine smiled apologetically to Kurt, as if she, not Owen, was the rude one.

Kurt looked at Owen and back at Christine.

"It's not dull," he said. "It's very tasty." His eyes flashed with anger for a moment, just long enough for Christine to wonder if he was resentful of her having shared a meal with Owen. He shouldn't be. There was no contest between the two men. Sure, Owen was fun, but Kurt was probing. With Owen she swapped anecdotes; with Kurt talk plunged headlong into fears, longings, and aspirations. He amazed her with his frankness and insights. She would rather have dinner with Kurt any day.

"I am sure meatballs are good also with gravy," Christine said. "I should try that next time." Her eyes lingered on Kurt, on his self-contained compactness, that bald round head. He was no one's definition of good looks. Yet, his large, ever-alert blue eyes were mesmerizing, especially when they bored into her, as they now did, with focused appreciation.

"You should. I am sure you will like it," Kurt said.

Christine glanced at Owen's back to make sure he hadn't noticed their exchanged glances and cleared her throat. "How did your scene go?"

"Martha's nervous. Hard to please," Kurt answered. "Seems worried we're not ready yet, with only a week more to rehearse."

Just then, Martha called for Owen and Christine to take the stage. Kurt accompanied them to the rehearsal room.

"Aren't you done for the evening?" Owen asked.

"I thought I would watch," said Kurt. "Stand in for you in case you need to be called away. The lab awaits you, rather urgently, no?"

Owen frowned and threw a what's-gotten-into-him look at Christine.

"I come here to not think about work for a few hours. That's allowed, isn't it?"

"Duty comes first."

"Sure. But there isn't only duty."

"You're too relaxed for your own good," Kurt said.

"You're too anxious for yours," said Owen.

Kurt's eyes again flashed with anger.

"Hey, take it easy. Both of you. Come, Owen, we're on," Christine said.

Owen's eyes trailed Kurt, who planted himself in a seat at the far end of the theater, obviously determined to stay and watch.

"What's his beef?" Owen murmured to Christine as they made their way to center stage.

"Tough day at the office, maybe," she answered.

"There's nothing but tough days at the office. For all of us."

All through the scene with Owen, Christine was grateful she was blinded by spotlights and couldn't see Kurt. Just the thought of him there was distracting, and Martha scolded her for inattention more than once. Owen, too, was edgy during much of their scene, glancing often at his watch. But for a different reason, Christine surmised. She knew by now that frequent glances at a watch were the telltale signs of a deadline on some experiment at the Tech Area, one that couldn't be talked about, of course, but one that Kurt was worried about too. Owen rushed the scene and fled as soon as his last line was done, not even bothering to say goodbye. As she descended the side stairs of the stage, she noticed that Kurt, too, was no longer in the theater.

On her way out, she picked up her coat, the last one in the backstage room, and noticed Kurt's plaid burgundy scarf under it. How could he go out on a cold night like this and not notice he was missing his scarf?! She picked it up, held it to her face, closed her eyes, and breathed in the smell of Kurt's cologne and the cherry tobacco he used in his pipe. She let herself conjure up his face and attentive eyes before folding the scarf into her clean empty pot. She'd give it to Gertie to return to her father. Christine put on her coat and headed toward the main room of the lodge. The square dancing was over for the night, and she could hear laughter, the clink of beer glasses and coffee cups, and Benny Goodman's "Taking a Chance on Love" blaring from the jukebox. The room itself smelled of sweat, burning embers of pinewood, popcorn, hot dogs, cocoa, marshmallows, beer, and whiskey. She was about to leave when she noticed Kurt at a small table near the exit, his beret visible behind a copy of the *Los Alamos Bulletin*, the Hill's daily paper. She wove her way through the crowd, stood before him, took the scarf from the pot, and laid it in front of him.

"You forgot this," she said.

He put down the newspaper and looked up at her.

He did not seem surprised, which in turn surprised her. Instead he smiled at her and took the scarf, and she suddenly wondered whether he had left it backstage for her to find.

"Aren't you going to thank me for bringing you the scarf—the one you left behind on purpose?" she tested him.

He suddenly looked like a child, caught out by a parent. "Ach, you are too clever for me."

Shouldn't he now invite her to sit down?

But he seemed confused, unsure of the lines for this scene that he had himself scripted. He stroked his chin, agitated, as if he was about to say something, and then dropped his hand as if thinking the better of it. She'd never seen him so hesitant, so at a loss for words.

"Perhaps I am too rash," he said.

She looked at him, puzzled.

"Rash, yes, I think that is the word. I should not have left my scarf. I should have not watched you rehearse. I should have just gone home."

There was an uncomfortable silence. He looked back at his paper, picked it up, put it back down, and picked it up again.

"Well, I'll be getting on then," she said. "Bye."

He nodded as she turned and left. She glanced back. He was buried in the newspaper. He could have asked her to have a cup of tea together. There would have been nothing wrong with that. She banged the door behind her. She walked a few paces and then stood still and closed her eyes, letting the quiet of the night wash over her. The cold air and the silence were a relief from the teeming lodge.

She heard the door of the lodge creak and, without opening her eyes, she knew he was standing behind her, waiting for her to turn.

"We are both ready to go home, yes?" he asked.

She nodded, and they walked in step. In the distance, a siren wailed from the Tech Area. Kurt sighed heavily at the sound.

"At this hour?" Christine said.

"A failed test, I'm afraid," said Kurt.

Christine had noticed that the alarms emitted from the Tech Area at different times did not all sound the same, but she only now realized that they were a code, with meaning for those in the know.

"Owen rushed out from the rehearsal."

"Yes, he will be disappointed," said Kurt.

The siren wound down, then fell silent. In the stillness a pack of coyotes howled.

"It's hard to believe that in less than a week, it will be over: the rehearsals, the play. One night and then nothing," Kurt said.

"I know. I'm a bit nervous. Do you think I'll do okay?" Christine asked.

"Here and there, there's a line you might do differently."

Kurt had never commented on her acting. She looked at him quizzically as they kept walking, curious to understand.

"Where you and Tony start to fall in love, you have a line about acting nonchalant," Kurt explained.

"You mean the scene where I say to him: 'Won't it be funny in the office tomorrow, seeing each other and just going on as if nothing has happened?'"

"Yes, that's the line. You say it very gaily, as if it is inconsequential that they have to hide their love."

"How do you think I should do it?"

"More regretfully," said Kurt. "Show that you understand you're getting into a complicated situation. It would give your character more depth. She's not a silly girl. Don't make her one."

"Martha's never told me to change the intonation there."

"It's just my opinion," said Kurt.

"That's why I'm listening," Christine said softly. She saw his point and wondered how many more chances there would be to hear his opinion. When the play ended, so would their walks. She blew out her breath, which puffed into a cloud in the cold. She always thought it was magic, the way that happened. She wanted to lift her hand to touch his cheek but stopped herself as the headlights of a jeep were suddenly visible over a hill, the vehicle approaching. Instead, she pointed toward the area it illuminated some two hundred feet away.

"Look, they've put up new fencing," she said, indicating the concertina barrier between them and the jeep.

"I think it's been there awhile," he said.

"Really? I never noticed," she said.

"There are lots of things you don't notice," he said.

She was startled at the anger in his voice. She was suddenly acutely aware of his physical presence, of the smell of his tweed coat.

The jeep drove by. They walked in silence until the sound of its motor was swallowed in the night.

Her eyes scanned beyond the perimeter fence where a new area had been cleared, the snow plowed to the side, a trailer park installed. The trailers were lined up like loaves of bread evenly spaced on a baker's tray. Only two had lights on. In a week or two, she imagined all would be lit at night. Los Alamos kept spreading, like butter melting in a pan. When she had first come here five months ago, there had been hundreds of families. Now there were thousands. How many exactly was never mentioned. Another military secret. For all anyone knew, if the war kept going, Los Alamos might stretch as far as Santa Fe.

Would these new residents feel as dislocated as she had when she'd arrived? And yet, looking at the trailers, she did not feel sorry for the inhabitants, just as she did not feel sorry for herself. Not anymore. There was Gertie, and there was the play, and yes, above all, there was Kurt. The idea of not seeing him was suddenly unbearable.

"I've been sleeping well for several weeks now," he said softly, "ever since our talks, our walks home."

He stopped and turned to her. "I'm starting to need you."

He clenched his gloved hands into fists and dug them into his pockets.

She longed to say "I need you too." But she didn't dare. Instead she concentrated on the rhythm of their feet on the pavement and the howling coyotes in the distance. They continued in silence until they reached the crossroad. They could split here and each walk home alone, or he could take a longer route by her home first before reaching his own. Recently they had taken the longer path, and he moved in its direction, but she put her hand on his sleeve and turned to him.

He took her in his arms and kissed her on the mouth—a kiss that was precise and quick, gentle, not sloppy or lingering.

"What are we doing?" she said, stepping back in shock.

"Trying to save ourselves."

"Is that what this is?"

"I think so, yes." He drew her back and kissed her again, this time more deeply but not for very long, then pulled away to look at her.

She thought she would faint—from desire or from horror, she was not sure. He reached to encircle her shoulders. She lowered his hands and held them in hers, then brushed a kiss on his lips.

"I want to walk home alone tonight," she said.

She felt his eyes on her as she walked away. With every crunch of her boots, she tried to obliterate the kiss from her mind, but it was as if she and Kurt were connected by a rubber band. Every step from him only made the bond tauter. She feared it would snap. She considered going back; he might still be standing at the junction in the road. No, she couldn't do that. He was Gertie's father. She was Thomas's wife. What was she doing, kissing him back? What if someone had seen them? Good that these rehearsals were ending soon. But he didn't belong to Gertie or to Sarah, and she didn't belong to Thomas. No one belonged to anyone.

The coyotes continued to howl as she walked home. Night after night, in every season, their wails punctured the air. She wanted to join them, howl loud, for Kurt, whom she imagined now reaching home, entering his house, quietly taking off his shoes so as not to wake his family.

She rewrapped her scarf to cover her ears, to muffle the sound of the coyotes, but she heard them nonetheless as she reached the Sundt units.

Going straight to the bedroom, she undressed and burrowed under the covers, as if by doing so she could hide from herself. She closed her eyes. All she wanted was to sleep. How could she have let matters get so out of hand?

Yet, nothing had happened, not really.

It was all reversible.

CHAPTER 15
CHRISTINE

December 1943

A week later, on Christmas morning, Christine woke early. She nestled into the down blanket, trying to recapture sleep. They had left the curtains open, and the morning light lashed the walls with dazzling white. She was struck by the stillness. No construction today. She closed her eyes and breathed in the soapy smell of the sheets, changed yesterday, mixed with the warmth of Thomas. He stirred, and they made love. She was attentive to him in ways she knew he liked, and he accepted her ministrations with a sense of entitlement that she found annoying even as she proffered them. He grunted his appreciation and lay still, spent. She trailed her fingers along the contours of his body, admiring, as she had so many times, his wide, almost concave chest, his muscular arms, the narrow curve of his hips, and wondered how different Kurt's naked body must be. Discomfited that such a thought should impose itself at this moment, she turned away from him, onto her back, letting the rays warm her stomach. Thomas was so perfect. Why was that a problem? She turned back, only to find him gazing at her.

"What are you thinking about?" she asked before he could ask her. She forced a look of interest while she remembered what it was like to kiss Kurt and that after tonight, after the play, there would be no more of those electrifying, furtive embraces they had allowed themselves on their way home in the last week of rehearsals.

"I'm wondering when we'll open our presents," Thomas said.

Christine smiled, grateful he could not read her mind. "You're such a kid." She slapped him playfully on the thigh. "You just can't wait to know what you got, can you?"

"No, no. I want to know whether you like what I got you."

"Liar! But now you've made me curious." She amazed herself at how well she could act the lighthearted, playful wife and was even more surprised to find that in doing so, she could quell thoughts of Kurt.

They put on their robes and exchanged gifts by their modest Christmas tree, decorated with popcorn strings and a few shiny ornaments acquired in Santa Fe. She had never liked the big, elaborate, compulsory Christmas gatherings with Thomas's family or the lackluster ones of her own family, so this was about the best Christmas she could imagine. Small and intimate. He'd bought her a reproduction of Cézanne's *The House with the Cracked Walls*. She was touched that he remembered the painting that had first brought them together and that he had taken what must have been considerable trouble to get his hands on this reproduction for her. Yet, the house in the painting, which she had once thought of as peaceful, now struck her as decrepit, the painting sadder than she remembered, or maybe it was just that she was sadder. She didn't much care for reproductions, always preferring a real painting of an unknown artist to a copy of one by someone famous. But Thomas didn't know that; he had so clearly made this effort to please her.

She smiled at him brightly. "It's lovely. Thank you. It will look perfect in the living room."

She kissed him and handed him his gift—snowshoes—which he wanted to try out immediately, so after a light breakfast they bundled up and went out. Thomas trekked through the snow in his snowshoes;

an unleashed mutt yapped and bounded behind him. Walking abreast of Thomas in her regular boots, Christine remained on the road.

The snow-lined main street was full of people: couples strolled arm in arm, clusters of fiercely cheerful single guys and gals plowed past, children panting with excitement and effort pulled their sleds and dodged snowballs hurled by older siblings. Smoke curled from the top of chimneys, punctuating the air with the smell of burning pine. It all seemed choreographed to accompany the Christmas carols crackling over the loudspeaker, direct from Los Alamos's radio station, KRS. In between songs, the station duty officer, sounding like a circus ringleader, offered holiday greetings, reminding one and all of the evening's theater performance at Fuller Lodge. Each time he mentioned it, Christine felt her pulse quicken in excitement and anxiety. She'd be fine tonight, wouldn't she? And it would be a relief when the play was over. Though she would miss Kurt, he would exit her life as he should.

As Christine continued to walk on the road, she exchanged holiday greetings with neighbors. She waved to Jimmy and Owen, who were walking together, their hands in the pockets of their parkas, their shoulders hunched against the cold. She joined a cluster of neighbors at the corner, consulting on last-minute arrangements for Christmas lunch. It was, of course, Martha, incurably vivacious and community minded, who had come up with the idea of going house to house for different courses within the Sundt barracks. And Christine had to admit that it was a great idea. They would all start at the Sharps' with soup. Martha was hosting the main course, with side dishes and salad provided by others. Dessert and coffee would be at a third home. By the time they finished eating, the actors among them would need to get ready for the evening's performance.

◆　◆　◆

During Christine's first moments onstage, she was supposed to play the role of a skittish and fluttery young woman. And on the night of the performance, that required no acting. She threw herself into the scene, releasing her preperformance nervousness and continuing on a wave of adrenaline. The thrill and rush of the moment carried her forward, her lines flowing without a need to think about them.

She hadn't counted on the laughter of the audience. After all those rehearsals, she had almost forgotten that *You Can't Take It with You*—a comedy about a madcap family building a bomb in the basement—was funny. The guffaws forced the actors to stop repeatedly, but Christine's mind, even as she acted, was elsewhere: This is it. The moment we have been working toward for weeks. Tomorrow it will be all over.

She couldn't wait; she had grown bored with repeating her lines over and over again, rehearsal after rehearsal, and with the dead times, waiting around while others practiced their scenes. Yet she'd miss that special energy of working intensely with others toward something defined and finite. In her last scenes onstage, she had to stop her mind from wandering to stay in character as naive, lovestruck Alice.

When the cast took its bows, Christine was blinded by the stage lights, unable to see the people calling out "bravo" with the excessive enthusiasm only an audience of friends and family can muster. As she bowed, she stole a look to her side, and when she caught Kurt's eye, he bowed even lower, as if he were taking final leave not only of the audience but also of her. Suddenly, she was eager to get to the dressing room and wipe off the stage makeup.

The storage room for musical instruments and stage props that served as the dressing room smelled stale and dusty. It had a bulb-framed makeup mirror, fully lit. Christine wiped the itchy makeup away with cold cream to reveal her imperfect, freckled face. It was good to get the gunk off, good that the play was over, good to go back to being herself, good to have no more rehearsals that fed her distracting thoughts about Kurt. She gave her forehead and lips a last wipe, discarded her costume, and changed into her dress—an emerald green, low-cut satin number with a fabric belt and full flounce.

Thomas was waiting for her in the dimly lit hall. He was so maddeningly well bred that even she could not tell whether his praise of her performance was genuine or only polite. He gave her a hug and a single red rose. Where in the world had he managed to buy a rose for her in the middle of winter? From the main room of the lodge, strains of a sax and trumpet piped the hit song "Never Let Your Left Hand Know What Your Right Hand's Doin'," punctured by laughter and the sound of chairs being cleared away as people quickly converted the impromptu theater into dancing space.

Kurt was down the hall at the entrance to the men's dressing room with Sarah, Gertie, and Jimmy. Surrounded by them, Kurt seemed diminished. He waved at her limply. Gertie, following his hand, turned and saw Christine and immediately broke away to rush over and hug her.

"You were smashing! You should be making movies with Clark Gable!"

Christine laughed, struck a pose with her hand holding the back of her head up, the tip of her toe pointed behind her on the floor. "Of course, darling," she said grandly, then dropped the stance and hugged Gertie back and mussed her hair. "You silly dilly! You liked it?"

Gertie nodded vigorously as her parents joined them.

"So, it is over. May I congratulate you on an excellent performance," Kurt said, bowing slightly. He looked sallow in the dim light, that essential vitality she usually felt in his presence muffled now.

"You as well," she said, bowing slightly back.

"Yes, Kurt, that was most impressive—I've always admired you as a scientist, now also as an actor," Thomas said.

"Thank you, very kind of you, Thomas," Kurt said. "My wife, Sarah," he said, his arm at his wife's elbow.

"Yes, of course, we've all met," Christine said, feeling the smile she brandished quivering with nervousness. She hoped Sarah would interpret it as postperformance excitement.

Sarah nodded but seemed at a loss for words. The foundation color of her eyes was sadness, spilling a darkness that seemed to leach into her surroundings. Christine wanted to escape its intensity and wondered if Kurt and Gertie ever did too.

Christine shifted away and looked Instead at Gertie. "Oh! Before I forget, I have a Christmas present for you."

"Christmas present? We do not celebrate Christian holidays. We do not accept presents for Noel," said Sarah.

"Of course, you're Jewish. I'm so sorry. It just didn't occur to me that a Christmas gift might not be appropriate. How silly of me. Stupid really. But still, a present. I didn't mean any harm. I just didn't think . . . ," Christine stammered.

"Please, Mama," begged Gertie, turning to Sarah.

"We can make an exception, Sarah, yes?" Kurt said, his question a statement.

"It's just a little present," Christine said apologetically to Sarah, who gave her husband a lost look, then shrugged.

Christine handed Gertie a small box. "Open it another time, whenever you want. It doesn't have to be today."

Gertie shook the box to guess the content, oblivious to the awkward silence of the adults around her. She started to undo the wrapping.

"It is not polite to open presents in front of people," Sarah said.

Christine looked at Sarah, surprised, then glanced at Kurt for an explanation. She had enjoyed choosing the present, a bracelet with a fish charm.

"This is the custom in Europe, to wait, to open things only afterwards, in private," said Kurt.

"Oh?" said Christine. Charm bracelets were all the rage these days. Gertie had been hankering for one for a long time, and Christine decided a fish was perfect—a reference to their swimming lessons, the start of their friendship, and Gertie's success in turning Christine into a passable, if not enthusiastic, swimmer.

"It is so the person giving the gift will not be disappointed if the person getting it does not like it," explained Sarah.

"But what if the receiver likes the gift? The giver won't see their joy," said Christine.

"True. But not to give offense, that is more important," said Kurt.

Thomas coughed and turned to Christine. "Shall we join the party?" She looked at him gratefully and nodded.

"You're welcome to join us," he said to Kurt and Sarah.

"I think we go home," said Sarah. "So many people, much noise, too warm." She pulled out a handkerchief from the sleeve of her flower-beaded pink cashmere cardigan and patted her forehead.

"Oh, Mama!" protested Gertie.

"Mrs. Koppel, could Gertie stay?" asked Jimmy.

Sarah looked at her husband.

"It is all right, Sarah. I will walk you home. I'll come back for Gertie later."

"No need. I can bring Gertie home," said Jimmy.

"I will come back after I escort Sarah. To see if you are a good enough dancer for my daughter," Kurt said. Jimmy looked confused, unsure if his boss was joking. But Kurt's eyes were twinkling.

"Come on, Jimmy." Gertie giggled, latched onto his arm, and led him away.

Sarah nodded goodbye to the Sharps and walked toward the door, Kurt following.

"Let's get a drink," Christine said to Thomas. She needed one after seeing Kurt with his wife. She didn't know what annoyed her more, the imperious way he acted with Sarah one moment or the empathy he showed his killjoy wife the next.

"Yes, let's. We could both use stiff ones after those heavies." Thomas put an arm around her. "It was nice of you to buy a gift for Gertie." He led her through the crowd to the bar in the central room of Fuller Lodge. The heat from the dancers added to that of the fire, crackling in the stone fireplace. The bodies and flames cast shadows against the wreath-studded walls. The sinewy music; the sweat and perfume; the smell of mulled wine, eggnog, burning logs, and a huge Christmas tree all converged into an inebriating sensuality. It dared some revelers to slip kisses on suspecting and unsuspecting lips. For others, it evoked memories of holidays in other times and other places. Christine stopped part way to the bar, overcome by the crowd. The music, the din of laughter, the tinkle of glasses made conversation almost impossible. Thomas signaled to her that he would go on ahead, she should wait, and he would bring their drinks. Most of the talk tonight was about the play, the food, the new drive to collect scrap metal. But there was also the news of Eisenhower being named the supreme Allied commander in Europe, speculation over why Roosevelt had not given the job to George Marshall, what it meant strategically, and assessments of how long the fighting would drag on.

Thomas emerged from the throng with their gin and tonics. They clinked and watched the dancers until the musicians took up Layton & Johnstone's version of "Lullaby of the Leaves." Thomas clasped Christine to him and led her in a slow foxtrot. Christine found her rhythm against him, comforted by how easily she could follow his lead, leaning into him, letting emotions seep out of her—the sadness and relief of the play being over, the image of Kurt following Sarah out of the hall. Muffled close to Thomas's chest, she hummed to the words, lulled by their wish for dreams. She clung to Thomas and to this moment, full of all these good, smart people with whom she shared her life, all striving for a sense of normalcy. And yet, it was illusory. There was nothing normal about thousands of people living in a place that was not supposed to exist, working on something they were not supposed to talk about, acting as if this fly-by-night community would endure when in fact they were waiting for the war and all this to end. Yes, even the friendships and even the parties. But Kurt was not momentary. He couldn't be. Yet he had to be.

She opened her eyes and saw Gertie and Jimmy dancing. Jimmy was smiling bravely at Gertie so she would not feel bad each time she stepped on his toes, which she did with remarkable regularity. Jimmy looked anxious for the music to end, but Christine knew Gertie would not give up before she conquered dancing completely, perfectly. So like her father.

The tempo of the music quickened as the band struck up "Boogie Woogie Came to Town." Thomas greeted colleagues as he danced with Christine.

"Got to hand it to you, you sure pulled one over on G-2," Thomas said over her head to Rich Feynman, who was standing at the edge of the dancers, drink in hand, grinning, but alone as always.

"Bunch of idiots, always interfering. They had it coming," Feynman answered, raising his glass to Thomas.

"That was a fine acting job, Christine," Feynman called out to her. "You're a lucky man, Thomas, to have your lovely wife with you this evening." Everyone knew Feynman's wife was kept off site at a sanitorium for her tuberculosis.

"Thanks, Rich. Send Arline our regards," Thomas answered.

"What was that about G-2 security?" Christine asked as Thomas twirled her around the floor.

"Nothing. Just an inside joke." Thomas kissed the top of her head.

Again, dismissive affection to stop her asking questions. It was hard to believe that a joke bantered around at a party was so top secret Thomas couldn't share it with her. But she didn't have a chance to linger on her annoyance as people stopped to compliment her acting. Thomas, looking simultaneously proud and bored, broke off to bring back another round of drinks. In his arms again, she felt cocooned; so many lovely people, overflowing with cheery goodwill. Nothing was required of her other than to smile and to keep moving with him in time to the music. What more did she want? What more could she want? She closed her eyes, leaning against Thomas's chest. She wanted to believe they would be okay. Even this new pottery business of hers was showing promise. Next week she would move Maria's pots into an abandoned toolshed. She had found an occasion amid all the holiday festivities to give Oppie a replacement vase. He had been surprised and pleased, and immediately acquiesced to her request for a place to store

Maria's work when she had told him of her plans to promote the pottery. With his help, she had been granted the use of a shed at the edge of the Hill. Its floor was matted with hay, but other than some stacked wood in one corner, it was empty—perfect for the pots, for organizing the pieces she would put together for a springtime show in Samantha's New York gallery.

The music stopped, and she noticed Kurt standing along the wall, talking to a cluster of colleagues and intermittently glancing at Gertie, who seemed to think the music demanded mashing her partner's toes every eighth beat. Christine caught Kurt's eye, and her heart lunged for him with an intensity that astounded her. Suddenly, Thomas's arm, hanging over her shoulder, felt suffocating. She tossed her hair and pulled free.

"I'm ready for another drink," Thomas said. "You?"

"No, thanks. I've had enough. I want to step outside for a few minutes."

"It's freezing out there."

"I know. But it's so hot here. I need some fresh air. Don't worry. I'll take my coat."

She found her parka and walked out. The cold air felt good. So did the silence of the night. She leaned against a tree and looked up at the sky, a tweed of stars. In the distance, the Tech Area was lit up. She felt sorry for the soldiers assigned guard duty tonight. In her coat pocket she fingered the key to the toolshed. She breathed in the clean, pure snow smell and heard steps behind her. She turned around as Kurt came close and stood alongside her, leaning against a tree next to hers.

"You really were spectacular tonight," he said.

"You as well." He had indeed outdone himself that evening. But he seemed to be spectacular at anything he undertook.

"I have always liked acting, ever since high school. It is a way to get out of myself, to dare to be someone else."

"Do you want to be someone else?" she asked.

"Not exactly, but to lose my self-consciousness, yes. To go deeply into what I know about myself—the good and the bad—and reconstitute it to become someone different. It is hard to imagine a part more different from who I am than the part I played tonight—someone who stops working to do what he pleases, doesn't act responsibly, ignores authority, believes only in love. Imagine!"

"Acting didn't do that for me," said Christine.

The trees were close enough that the steam of their breath mingled. Trying to keep warm, Christine curled her fingers into fists and plunged them deeper into her pockets.

"Maybe you are always already genuinely yourself," Kurt said gently.

"What does that even mean, to be genuinely oneself?"

"I don't know. All I know is that ever since I am in America, and especially here, I have felt like I am walking alone in a forest at night, afraid of what would jump at me from the trees," Kurt said, then paused. They heard laughter and music from the lodge. "Around you, the forest is peaceful, like now, here," he added quietly.

"I don't know what to say."

"I cannot stop myself from thinking of you. I need to see you," Kurt said.

Christine was quiet. Her mind was racing, but she didn't dare to look at Kurt as a thought formed in her mind, a crazy idea, which she hurried to dismiss. No good could come from it. She thought of Thomas, of how well they had danced this evening, but still the way he had just dismissed her when he hobnobbed with his colleagues gnawed at her.

"What happened between Rich Feynman and G-2?"

"Excuse me?"

"He breached security or something, didn't he?"

"Oh, that," Kurt said. "Feynman, he's very—how do you say—cocky, yes? We are all under orders to lock away our papers at night, against spies. If we don't, we are fined. Feynman left his out overnight last week and G-2 found them, brought him in for interrogation, wanted to fine him. But Feynman said the calculations on the papers were all wrong, and argued that he should be rewarded, because if a spy found the papers, the calculations would have helped to mislead the enemy. Told G-2 they should plant more false information rather than run around fining scientists." Kurt laughed. "He got them so confused, made such a fuss, they just let him go."

"I see," said Christine. Why was Thomas so intent on not sharing anything—not even an amusing anecdote like this one—with her? It was infuriating. Kurt didn't try to deliberately keep information from her for no reason. Not secrecy for the sake of bolstering his own importance.

"Why do you ask about Feynman?" Kurt asked.

She coughed and cleared her throat.

"I've been given a toolshed for storing my pottery. That old shed between the pond and the Tech Area. Do you know which one I'm talking about?" she asked, clutching the key to the shed in her pocket.

He looked up at the sky. "I'm glad for you. But, Christine, you are avoiding what I am trying to tell you. I want to still see you."

She did not move from the tree she was leaning on, her gaze like his, on the heavens.

"Meet me at the shed, on Thursday at eight o'clock."

CHAPTER 16
JIMMY

December 1943

Trekking from the dorm to the gym, Jimmy felt like a heap of rumpled laundry after last night's party. His toes still throbbed from Gertie's clumsy dancing, but the pain was worth it, the cost of being in her company, of making her happy. And he had a hangover from all the alcohol he'd consumed. Hopefully, a workout would clear his head. Opening the metal door of the gym, he was accosted by the smell of sweat and old exercise mats. The clank of dumbbells dropping to the floor drew his eyes to the far corner.

"So, you're not dead after all." Owen's voice echoed against the cement block walls. "Never known you to pass out like you did last night. Tried to wake you for breakfast, but it was a no go." He abandoned the dumbbells and made his way to the rowing machine.

A new war poster had been taped on the beige-painted wall above the equipment. **BACK THE ATTACK. BUY WAR BONDS!** it blared, featuring a helmeted soldier holding a .45-caliber submachine gun against a background of parachutes.

Jimmy took off his jacket by the wooden bleachers left over, like all else in the gym, from the Los Alamos boys' school. He picked up the dumbbells, still warm from Owen's touch.

"I guess I did have more than a bit."

"Bet you got more than a bit from the Koppel girl, heh." Owen puffed as his arms kept up a rhythmic rowing. "There's no gettin' too much of her." He guffawed.

Jimmy didn't respond, concentrating instead on lifting and lowering the dumbbells. In some ways Owen was right. There was no getting too much of Gertie—her big eyes that swallowed him with attention, her quirky observations of the partygoers whispered into his ear.

Jimmy added five pounds to the weights and started pumping again. Gertie made him feel competent when he taught her to foxtrot and waltz, dances he himself barely knew. And then there was the present she had given him—a Great Tantalizer Puzzle game, with four wooden cubes. It was just the sort of thing that intrigued him, figuring out how to place the cubes in a row so four colors showed on each side. She really had his number. He was grateful that she didn't seem to mind that he hadn't thought to get her a present. She had waved her hand dismissively when he apologized. "Teaching me how to dance, that's a great present," she said. Amazingly, she seemed to mean it, not getting all offended the way most women would. For the first time in his life, Jimmy had felt comfortable at a party because he was with her. He set down the weights and shook out his hands before starting a second set.

"Come on, man, you suddenly a mummy or something?" Owen asked as he continued rowing, his muscles rippling from stomach to chest to arms. "I'm your best guy, so give me the scoop. How far d'ya get with her?"

"Drop it," Jimmy said with a scowl intended to wipe away Owen's smirk.

"Oh, must be serious if you won't talk about it," Owen taunted, a glint in his eyes.

"Give me a break. I can't be working for Kurt Koppel and messing with his daughter at the same time."

To distract from the pain of his muscles as he lifted and lowered the weights, Jimmy concentrated on his friend. The light from the window glistened off Owen's rippled chest, smooth as the polished marble of a Greek statue. Jimmy was entranced by the sudden beauty of the moment, by the comfortable brotherhood of the two of them pumping iron in the still, cavernous gym, by the light reflecting like amber off the wooden floor. His eyes followed Owen, who had moved to the weight press and was pressing his legs together and apart, together and apart, while doing the same with his arms against the machine's resistance pads.

"What's working with Koppel got to do with holding off on Gertie?" Owen asked, extending arms and legs again, the equipment wires whizzing. "You think you're the first Joe to ever fall for the boss's daughter?"

"Koppel trusts me." Jimmy watched as Owen ramped up the set. Arms, legs, open, close, the weight press clanked with the regularity of a metronome.

"You're beginning to believe your own bull. Nothing wrong with a squeeze here and a rub there," Owen said.

"I don't know. It doesn't feel right." Jimmy moved to the rowing machine, grabbed the oars, and pulled them hard. A lot hadn't felt right. The machine thumped along with his thoughts. He'd felt confident in Gertie's company, all right; but when she'd pressed into him as they danced close, he had tried to keep a respectable few inches between them, only to have her move in on him until this, too, became a kind of dance: Gertie trying to rub up against him, him trying to keep her—and her feet—at bay. Sure, it was all flattering, yet inside he'd cringed. Even more when she suggested they step outside, just for a few minutes. He'd suspected that if they moved away from the party, she'd expect him to kiss her. She was too much to handle sometimes. With the excuse that he was thirsty, he'd peeled away to get them drinks, a ginger ale for her and a Manhattan for him. To avoid any more dancing, he'd guided her by the elbow to the overflowing buffet. Soon she was scarfing down the snacks. She was particularly keen on the piggies in a blanket, which she tried to pop in his mouth, giggling and trying to snuggle. He'd gone for a second Manhattan and then a third, bringing her back a ginger ale each time. With preposterous optimism, Gertie had tried to make conversation, but the room was far too noisy, so she'd shrugged and laughed and tried to pull him back toward the dance floor several times until he'd succumbed. He'd kept scanning the room for Kurt, whom he'd finally sighted along the wall, looking distracted and vaguely lost. Jimmy had guided Gertie to her father, and, ignoring the pools of disappointment in Gertie's eyes, took his leave of them.

"Beats me what you're waiting for." Owen interrupted Jimmy's reverie. "If Gertie was as hot for me as she is for you and stepping on my toes as much as she was killing yours last night, I'd definitely figure she was good and ripe to put out. From what I've seen, she's raring to go, and she's got a right nice little pair of rocket boosters to play with."

God, Owen could be so crude. "The way I was raised, you need to show a girl respect," Jimmy said as he stopped rowing and grabbed a towel to wipe the sweat from his face.

"What Gertie understands is that everyone talks respect and restraint. But you gotta be dumb to believe it and nuts to actually exercise it. Nobody does." Owen abandoned the weight bench and headed to the pair of knotted ropes dangling at the other end of the gym.

Did Owen think of women as anything other than sex dispensers? Jimmy watched him slither up one of the ropes with Tarzan-like competence. And Owen was a great guy, the best friend one could wish for. It was lucky they were still together. Owen had been gung ho to fight overseas and was devastated when he was turned down by the army for flat feet. It had been Jimmy who convinced him that joining the engineering corps would be just as important to the war effort. He'd lobbied his superiors, and Owen made it in.

But Owen could be so thick sometimes. Didn't he get that Jimmy was not going to steamroller his way with someone as delicate as Gertie? Sure, she was plucky and had more confidence than he could ever imagine having himself. He was still stunned, grateful, that she gave him the time of day. She was easy to talk to but also vulnerable—oblivious, it seemed, to the possibility that every feeling combusting in her might not be reciprocated. He feared that the happiness he felt in her presence might be wiped away by any move he made beyond what she so ardently believed she wanted. No way was he going to mess up what they had by putting the moves on her. It ticked him off that Owen didn't get that. He scowled at his friend, who was making his way up an exercise rope, but was suddenly struck again by how graceful Owen looked, legs wrapped around the rope, arm muscles snaking with effort as he gripped his way to the top with perfect control.

Appreciation of Owen's supple body trickled from Jimmy's eyes to his groin. Flustered by his rising member, he turned his back to the ropes. It must be the hangover and all this musing about Gertie. He felt trapped. His eyes darted around the room, scouting out the equipment. What next? No, not the weight bench. Not the pommel horse. He felt his penis slacken. Thank God!

His eyes lit on the punching bag. Its soft, stained leather, battered by generations of testosterone-driven adolescents, invited contact. He socked the bag with relish, releasing tight packets of confusion with each *whomp*. What was he going to do with Gertie? Take that and that and that, he muttered under his breath, not knowing exactly who it was that he wanted to bash. He moved around the bag, hitting it each time from a different angle. Owen came into view at the other end of the room, and again there was this stirring in his groin.

It was not the first time he had felt an urge rise in him when he was with Owen. It had happened at times when Owen would come back late and, finding Jimmy reading in bed, would tell him—in excruciating detail—just how far he had gotten with the evening's date. Jimmy would watch Owen undress, imagining him through the girl's eyes, taking in his smooth body, aroused by the descriptions of sex, even after Owen switched off the lights and soon snored softly.

Jimmy hit the bag hard to punch away the memory. If he hit the bag intently enough, surely the whisking in his stomach would go away. He fought with all he had, pummeling it, the bag swinging back at him harder each time. He dodged and thwacked, working himself into a frenzy until he felt he was going to explode. And then, in the midst of a mislaid punch that almost crushed his wrist came a flash of clarity: he had no desire to do with Gertie what men did with women. He wanted the Owen from those dreams. He went at the bag even harder then, furious at the insight. Take that. No way. And that. Ridiculous. What a stupid thought! He fought as if he could expunge the realization by hitting the bag hard enough. But his mind kept racing to how many times he had wanted to touch Owen and hold his face in his hands. To how he marveled at the muscled backsides of his dorm mates when they emerged from the shower. To a surreptitious French kiss that Spencer, a classmate no one liked at his high school, had once planted on his lips. Although he had spurned Spencer, he had thought about that kiss often. Spent, he stopped and glanced toward Owen, worried that his thoughts had seeped across the room. Owen, slithering down the rope now, caught Jimmy's eye and smiled.

Jimmy's lips trembled as he tried to smile back. His eyes followed Owen, who pulled out a mat and began a set of sit-ups. Bathed in sunlight, Owen's stomach contracted, his lambent chest muscles quivering with effort. Jimmy hugged the bag, which smelled of sweat and leather. His heart beat like a trapped bird, desire whirring through him. He closed his eyes, hoping to dispel all sensation. When he opened them, he systematically hit the bag but couldn't stop himself from stealing glances across the room at Owen. The sepia light from the grated windows shimmered on his hairless skin. Mortified at hardening, Jimmy forced himself to turn back to the bag. He had to make this curse go away. He swung at the bag, trying to pulverize the fear and desire that stuck in his gut like jagged sheets of glass. He batted the leather harder and harder until his body shattered in release. Limp with shame, he hugged the punching bag and dared a peek at Owen, who continued his workout—oblivious. Thank goodness for that, at least. Then he walked to the bleachers, wiped his neck with a towel, and put on his leather flight jacket over his T-shirt.

"Hey, where you going? How about a beer and a burger at the lodge?" Owen called across the room.

"No," said Jimmy. "I'm beat." As he headed out of the gym, he noticed, tacked on the door, a new war poster of a blonde snuggling up to a soldier. TELL NOBODY. NOT EVEN HER. LOOSE LIPS COST LIVES. Jimmy slammed down the push bar handle and kicked the door open. The frosty air hit him, and the warm wetness on his thigh tingled with the cold under his jogging pants. He pulled up the sheep's wool collar of the jacket, dug his hands into the pockets, and trudged toward the dorm, but the thought of running into his dorm mates was more than he could face. He headed to the perimeter fence, the tamped snow creaking under his feet. A woodpecker knocked at an electricity pole, *tap-tap-tapping* like the thoughts in his head. How would he ever look Owen in the eye? But this was just an accident; it wouldn't happen again. Surely it was the hangover and thinking of Gertie while looking at Owen. Somehow his body had gotten things all mixed up. There was nothing wrong with him.

Yet, this stirring had not been unfamiliar. It was as if he had happened upon something long misplaced and forgotten. His roommates in that private boarding school he had attended for a year had sometimes given him a hard-on. He'd told Gertie he'd left the private boys' school because he'd been homesick, which was true. But it wasn't the only reason. Men got sexed up about men if they were young and kept at close quarters. Isn't that what they said about inmates in prisons? It just happened. It didn't mean anything, did it? But he'd felt mortified and frightened in a way he couldn't explain, so he had asked to leave Exeter and return home. The red-winged woodpecker streaked by, showing its bright underwing against a background of the mountains in the distance. Usually Jimmy thought the mountains majestic, but today they seemed like bared teeth, raring to rise up and tear him apart.

CHAPTER 17
CHRISTINE

December 1943

What should she wear—slacks? A dress? What does one wear to meet a lover for the first time in a shed? Not the sort of question that *Woman's Home Companion*, lying on Christine's night table, was likely to answer. The editors of that magazine would only castigate her for what she was about to do. And just weeks ago, she would have resoundingly agreed. She knew it wasn't fair to Thomas or to Sarah. And that Gertie, too, would be hurt if she—or any of them—found out. But they didn't have to know. And Christine was sure that if she did not go ahead with this, she would never forgive herself. The few days without seeing Kurt had been excruciating. She simply could not run away from this man who had touched her so deeply. She now realized that she had never experienced true passion. She had to allow herself this. Just thinking of Kurt, she felt her nipples tingle. To calm her body, she turned her attention back to the issue of her clothes.

Unable to settle on slacks or a dress, she put off the decision; she plucked her eyebrows, applied lipstick, then wiped it off. What if it left telltale signs? In any case, he would not see her lipstick in the dark. Back to the clothes. She settled for a skirt and knee-high socks rather than stockings. And a blouse with buttons down the front—but skipped a bra. Bras were complicated to undo, and she did not want to make this more complicated than it already was. Her nipples tingled again as she put on her coat, hardening painfully when the cold air hit her as she left the house. The rhythm of her boots as she walked seemed to echo "you're doing this, you're really doing this." Her mind emptied of everything else but the moment, noting every tree she passed. She nodded to the few people who crossed her path on their way to evening bridge games or to music practice at Fuller Lodge or coming home from the Tech Area. Closer to the shed, at the edge of the Hill, there was only the hooting of owls. Her bare hand, deep in her pocket, clutched the shed key as she walked, bracing herself against a wind gathering strength with the night. She felt like a spy on a mission against herself. The shed creaked from the wind as she unlocked the door, which gusted open, almost throwing her back. She stepped into the darkness, slammed the resistant door behind her, lit the flashlight, and checked her watch—7:52 p.m. She unrolled the sleeping bag she had brought to the hut the previous day and spread it on the hay floor, then took out the down blanket and wondered what to do next. She considered sitting on the blanket to wait, but that was awkward with a coat on. Should she undress and get under the covers? Too forward, even for the audacious woman Kurt imagined her to be. Still unsure of the best pose for meeting him, she took off a boot. There was a rustling. Then another sound, and the door opened. Kurt poked his head in, seeing her with one boot off and one on. She felt his amused smile more than saw it as he closed the door behind him.

"You came," he said softly.

"You too," she answered as she pulled off her second boot.

He joined her by removing his shoes. At a loss for words, she wiggled her toe on his stockinged foot. He wiggled a toe back, then faced her, stripped her first of her coat, then his own. He took her hand and kissed the palm, then the spaces between her fingers. She couldn't believe such a simple act could make her weak with desire. He felt her quiver and pulled her toward him. He smothered her hair with kisses and murmured her name, inhaling her, then stepped back. "Let me believe you are here."

She stood before him and opened her blouse, button by button, as he watched. He lowered the blouse off her shoulders to reveal her breasts. Her nipples were hard, but she wondered if her small pert breasts could possibly compare favorably with the voluptuousness of his better-endowed wife. Rather than wait for a verdict, she led his hand to the zipper of her skirt.

"Wait," he whispered.

"What?"

"I brought a precaution. A moment." He stuck his hand in his pocket.

She wanted to laugh. Someone worrying about getting her pregnant. All she and Thomas had been doing for three years now was worry about why she wasn't getting pregnant.

"There's no need," she said.

"You have taken care?"

In response, she kissed him and guided his hand back to her skirt. This time he did not hesitate, unzipping it in a single motion. The skirt crumpled to the ground, and he gently slipped both his hands into her underwear, around her buttocks, and drew her to him with a gentle decisiveness. She unclipped his bow tie and then unbuttoned his shirt. They became a tangle of quickly discarded clothes, conscious not only of the cold but also of their limited time together and the need to keep quiet. Once under the comforter, he kissed her long and hard. More than the taste of his tongue, which gently probed her mouth, she was overcome by his smell. It was not the traces of cologne she was used to from his scarf—more like the odor of a new book, but pungent like nutmeg. Blending with the scent of the hay on the shed floor, it intoxicated her as he held her head in his hands. She glided him into her. It felt as if he sank not only his wanting into her but his fear of wanting, all his waiting and the release from waiting, which intermingled with her own.

She was surprised at how light his body was on top of hers compared to Thomas's—and immediately tried to banish the comparison. Kurt's lighter weight made it easier for her to move under him freely, allowed her to lift her hips toward him, to sway with him rather than feeling pinned down as she was when making love to Thomas. She wanted to cry out her mounting pleasure, but the need to not make any noise only intensified sensation and focused it inward, so that it flowed throughout her body like lava, lapping her, silently erupting over and over, until she was sapped. Afterward, she held him and stroked his bald head.

"Christine . . . ," he began.

"Shhh," she said. "Sleep a bit."

While he did, she stared at the ceiling, letting her mind and body slowly separate and reassemble. She looked up at the pots on the shelves. Her eyes, accustomed now to the dark, took pleasure in the beauty of their rounded shapes, each beautiful but different. From coils, Maria's deft hands created this perfection, like Kokyangwuti, the Hopi mythical spider woman Maria told her created all living creatures, including humans, from earth and saliva. Kokyangwuti created this world after earlier worlds had failed and been destroyed. The pots, the primitiveness of the shed, the pungent hay, Kurt's need for her—so without prelude, artifice, or romance—these were the materials of her own re-creation, making her feel centered within herself, new and whole. The Hopi creation myth of Kokyangwuti allowed for second and third and fourth chances at creation and re-creation. Maybe there was something to that. We re-create ourselves over and over, trying to get it right. She lay in the stillness and let the silence and perfection of the moment wash over her.

She almost drifted into sleep herself, but the sounds of revving jeeps and laughter brought her back to the moment. Then the wind gusted, rattling the door. Kurt jerked awake.

"Who . . ." He lifted his head.

She pulled him back toward her breast. "Shhh, it's just a patrol," she whispered. The door continued to shake from the wind as if it would burst open. It didn't have a lock on the inside. The jeep moved closer. They could see its headlights through the crack at the bottom of the door. She felt Kurt hold his breath and realized she was holding hers too.

The jeeps seemed to pass them, although it was hard to tell with the howling wind and the creaking shed.

"It never ends for you, does it?" she said when the wind waned and their steady breathing returned.

"What?"

"The worry."

"Here, with you, for a few moments, it goes away. It did. It most definitely did." He propped himself up on his elbow and looked down at her, stroked her face with his other hand, and let it rest under her chin.

"You are so beautiful," he said.

"Thanks, but I don't think of myself that way. And I wouldn't have thought beauty mattered to you—a man who lives so much with ideas, so much in his mind."

"Look around," he said, his eyes roving to the pots. "The making of beautiful things, the appreciation of beauty, of course it matters, even more so in an ugly world."

She gazed at the shadow of the pots around her. Their unique shine was visible even in the dim light. Touched that he considered the pots integral to a better world, she rubbed her fingers down Kurt's cheek. According to Thomas, the pottery was a waste of time with little chance of success. She dropped her hand from Kurt's face. She must stop thinking of Thomas, of how hurt he would be.

She propped herself on her elbow to face Kurt. She wondered if he, too, had forced himself to dismiss thoughts of Sarah. "You have no regrets—about us?" she asked.

"No," he said. "You?"

"I don't want to hurt anyone. We won't, will we?" she asked.

"Of course not. We will be discreet."

"One has a right to do what is good for one, doesn't one?"

CHAPTER 18
SARAH

January 1944

Sunday morning started out like most. Sarah and Kurt were lingering over their tea, nibbling on toast with marmalade, when Gertie pranced in and kissed each of them on the forehead, a sure sign she was off to do something that had nothing to do with her parents. The child was dressed most unattractively in loose jeans that stopped midway down her calves and a red sweater—one of the few Sarah had not made for her—droopy from wear and dotted with lint balls. The fish charm on her bracelet tinkled when Gertie opened the fridge to get herself milk.

"Come sit with us," Sarah said.

"Yes, we are discussing Roosevelt's State of the Union address. Most interesting. So forward looking. Proposing a new bill of rights to assure economic well-being for all citizens. Visionary. What a president this country has!" Kurt said.

"I'm late. Going skating on Ashley Pond."

"Are you sure it's frozen over all the way to the middle?" Kurt asked.

Gertie rolled her eyes. "Guys have been playing ice hockey on it all week already." She gulped down the milk and swiped away the white mustache it left above her lips.

"Gertie, please, a napkin," Kurt said.

"You are going to wear that bracelet on the ice?" Sarah asked.

"I know, it's too fancy for skating, but I love it. I couldn't bear to take it off," Gertie said, giving it a little shake so that the fish charm quivered.

"I don't know what that Christine was thinking, giving you a present—for Noel. And doesn't she know that only family gives jewelry as a present?"

"Oh, Mom, not that again! What's the big deal? People give presents on Christmas. Even me. You should have seen how happy Jimmy was with the one I got him."

"You gave Jimmy a Christmas present?" Sarah was shocked.

"Yeah, why not? Bye!" Gertie fled the kitchen for the hallway, grabbed her coat, and slammed the door behind her.

Sarah shook her head.

"Relax." Kurt patted her hand.

She withdrew it. "Relax? How? She will forget we are Jews. And I face her alone, no help from you. It was humiliating at the Christmas party. It still hurts me, the way you took her side—in front of every-one—and let her accept that gift. What I think doesn't matter, not to you and not to her."

"What would have been the point of turning down the gift? It would only have offended Christine. And Gertie loves it."

"Loves what? A fish on a bracelet around her wrist? Who gives a bracelet with a fish to a Jewish child? I know my high school Greek as well as you do. Fish—*ichthys*—the acronym for *Iesous Christos Theou Yios Soter*—Jesus Christ, God's son, savior. Is she trying to convert our child?"

The mantel cuckoo clock in the living room, a parting gift from Sarah's parents, chirped nine times. Kurt looked hard at her, his eyes narrowing.

"Christine meant no harm. It was an act of friendship. I am sure the thought of the significance of fish in Christianity never crossed her mind," Kurt said.

"You have suddenly become an expert reader of Christine's mind?" Sarah retorted.

Kurt looked down and closed his eyes for a moment, as if trying to collect his thoughts.

"Apparently a better mind reader of her thoughts than of yours," he said coldly. "How did you come up with such a crazy idea? Christine trying to convert Gertie? *Abartig! Total verrückt!* There is nothing wrong with Christine. Gertie is lucky to have her as a friend."

Sarah didn't know what bothered her more, that she had spoken harshly to her husband or that he seemed to take the side of this woman they barely knew, this Christine. Both she and Kurt were changing, becoming people she did not recognize in a world that was scarier and more unrecognizable by the day.

"The world is *abartig, total verrückt*, not me. Warped and out to get us. Or has this place at the end of the world made you to lose your memory?" Sarah shot back at Kurt. "Have you forgotten what landed us here? What do we know of this Christine? Why, even, is she spending time with a sixteen-year-old? She has nothing better to do?"

"You're just jealous that Gertie talks to Christine," Kurt said. "What sort of mother is jealous of her child? Gertie was so unhappy when she came here. You should be glad that she has made friends with Christine, with Jimmy." He glared at her with derision, then took a large, decisive bite of his toast.

Sarah felt punched in the stomach.

"Christine, Jimmy, they are so unlike us. How could they possibly understand Gertie?"

He refilled his cup from the teapot on the table. "Obviously she thinks they understand her fine."

It felt like another blow below the belt, the insinuation that they understood Gertie better than she did. Maybe they did. That hurt the most. She looked at Kurt, but he avoided her gaze, quickly finishing his tea and rising from the table. He put his own dishes in the sink, something he rarely did. As if he wanted to be busy with anything but her.

"She is forgetting where we come from, who we are."

"She's not forgetting. She's adjusting. That's a good thing, Sarah. You need to adjust too."

Sarah burst into tears. "How? I go 'poof, poof' and I become someone new, who does not think about Germany, about our family, what is happening to them? Suddenly I don't miss the friends I have known from childhood, the countryside around Hamburg, the parks, the concerts, the lovely things our home was filled with? This is good? This is a possible thing?"

Kurt looked at her in exasperation, then touched her gently on the shoulder.

Sarah could not stop the tears streaming down her face. "Gertie will forget all we have endured."

"Don't cry. I'm sorry. I was harsh. You mustn't take everything so hard. We are safe here. Gertie is safe here. America is good for her. It is good to us."

"I miss everyone so much. I miss understanding what people are saying, what people mean when they talk. Everyone here is so strange. Even Gertie, even you." She pulled a handkerchief out of the pocket of her morning gown, dried her eyes, and blew her nose.

"I cannot help you, Sarah. You must find your way. I cannot find it for you." He kissed her on the top of her head and left the kitchen. She heard him in the bedroom, rummaging around, dressing, she imagined.

She sat in the kitchen, wringing the handkerchief in her lap. How could Kurt pretend not to understand? She was jealous that Gertie confided in others, and she envied Christine and Jimmy and all those people here who did not live under an interminable cloud of darkness and anxiety. The morning sunlight flecked the counters of the kitchen, but the brightness only made her head pound.

She heard the front door click as Kurt closed it behind him. He hadn't asked her to come with him. It seemed her unhappiness was a stench he wanted to escape. She stumbled to the bedroom and dove into the rumpled bed, burrowing under the duvet. If only she could stay there forever.

Her head felt heavy, feverish. Twisting and turning in bed, she wilted when her eyes fell on the pearl necklace that drooped off the ledge of the dresser. The memory of how she had clutched at the pearls when she had entered the office of her old classmate, Jurgen, at the Department of Internal Affairs in Hamburg seven years ago rushed back to her with a wave of nausea.

She asked to see Jurgen, hopeful he would make it easier to obtain a tax clearance certificate from the Internal Ministry, necessary as part of the paperwork for a visa for herself, Kurt, and Gertie, her parents and Hannah. Even though her parents said they did not want to leave Germany, she was convinced that if she moved along the paperwork, they would in the end seize the chance to join them in America. And so she reminisced with Jurgen about school and daintily consumed the ginger cookies and tea he pressed on her as they sat on the sofa in his office, which was bulging with red satin pillows and the bulk of his muscular thighs.

He finished his tea before her, and then set his cup in its saucer and looked up at her.

"So, what can I do for you?" He peered at her, smiling.

He must have noticed how she'd drawn in her breath, seeking courage. "Well, in these difficult times . . . my husband and I have applied for a tax clearance certificate. I did not want to trouble you. I know you have important matters to attend to. But everything, it takes so long. My husband, he applied many months ago. And my parents, my sister, we would like them to come with us. So I would like to start the process for them as well."

"You wish to leave the Reich?"

"As you know it is not easy, especially for . . . for, people like us."

"Ah, yes. With your looks, I forget. You are not Aryan."

"That has its difficulties these days," she said.

"So it is the clearance certificates you are after?"

"I was hoping, perhaps, you might be good enough to help us. We have of course paid our taxes. We have the stamp from the tax authorities. But we need the certificate from your department. It would be so kind of you."

"I can help you. It's simple. I only have to sign the form and you will be all set. But you must help me too." He spoke in a low voice and smiled at her slowly.

"Me?"

"Yes. I have fond memories of you. And you have remained attractive. I should very much like to kiss you." The smirk on his face merged into a lecherous glint in his eyes.

"Kiss me?" She clutched her pearls then as if they were a shield that could protect her.

"Does that surprise you? It shouldn't. Did you not have a certain interest in me, back in high school?"

"No. I mean yes," she stammered. "I thought you very handsome."

"I am no longer handsome in your eyes?" He leaned back, his arms out, as if inviting her to challenge his self-perceived good looks.

"Oh no, you are still very handsome. But, Jurgen, it has been so many years. We are married."

"Ah, my dear, you are as innocent as always. Charming the way you remain so easy to shock. Do you remember the time I left a dead rabbit on your desk? My, how you did scream." He laughed at the recollection, still pleased with himself.

"I do remember. A frightening moment."

"Well, let me apologize now." He rose and bowed before her.

That was more like it, what she would expect from a gentleman. She smiled at his back as he made his way to the polished wood desk at the other end of the room, then opened the cupboard inside where liquor was stored. He poured himself a shot of brandy.

"I was a mischievous boy. I still am," he said and laughed again, taking a sip of his drink and setting it down on the coffee table, along with one for her, before sitting down on the sofa. "And admit it, you liked my pranks. Well, maybe not that one. But most of the time you laughed with the others."

"I suppose I did," Sarah said. That was not the way she'd remembered it, but this was hardly the time to argue. "Your daring always shocked me a bit."

"I hope that is not still so," he said, slipping a hand along the back of the sofa and letting it drop onto her shoulder. "I do so much want to help you," he continued, taking the teacup from her hands, placing it on the table, and moving the hand that had held the cup onto his knee.

She felt the warmth of his skin through his pants. He guided her hand up his thigh, and she pulled away. "We are married," she repeated.

"We are. But I am who I am. I am giving you an opportunity, for the good of your family." He drew her toward him.

She smelled the polish of his leather boots, the wool of his uniform. He squeezed her.

"You are an intelligent woman, Sarah. It is not good to let opportunities slip by. Especially in these complicated times."

She noticed the vase on his desk with a drooping pink rose in it. "You aren't going to help us."

"Sarah, haven't you been listening? I want to help you. But for nothing in return? That wouldn't be fair, would it? You need to be fair."

She pulled away from him and went to the window, angry at herself. What had she expected? And yet, Jurgen was a fair man, and she knew if she gave him what he wanted, there was a chance he would keep his word and help get her family through the paperwork required for visas. She wanted those visas more than she had wanted anything in her life. She stood at the window with her back to him, fingering her necklace. How bad would it be to give in to him? Compared to all the horrible things happening around them—the beatings, the arrests, the sense of impending doom—how hard would it be to succumb to Jurgen, who was not a stranger after all but someone she had liked and joked with, not a brute even if he was a Nazi? It would be over in minutes, and she would emerge with what she needed.

"I don't have all day, Sarah. I am a busy man." He walked over then and clutched her from behind. "Come, frightened little bird. Jurgen can make things all better. That is why you asked to see me, no? So I will make everything all better?" She felt him harden into her. His hand had slipped up her leg. "Come, little bird. Make Jurgen feel good, and he will make everything all right."

She looked down at the off-white pearls still in her hand. A gift from Kurt, who had no illusions about the cruelties of the world but who trusted her and protected her.

She wanted to do the right thing. But what was it? She was going to vomit. Jurgen's hand continued to creep up her leg, his other hand now cupped her groin. She recoiled. Out the window in the street below, people walked briskly in and out of the building. A bus passed by, and she had a momentary flash of herself riding it home, the certificate in hand, knowing how she had obtained it. She would have to live for the rest of her life with the secret of what Jurgen was going to do to her if she let this go on.

She jabbed Jurgen with her elbow. "Stop!"

"You are not serious, little bird."

She jabbed him harder, twisting and wrenching. Then faced him. "Jurgen, you are better than this. Please don't do this," she'd said steadily.

Jurgen pulled away, jerked his neck as if he had a kink in it, puffy pink skin twisting and brimming over the collar of his uniform. He returned to his desk. He took a pen and twirled it around in his fingers. "So vermin stick to vermin. Is that it? You are a simpleminded fool. You do not know what opportunity you have just thrown away. Get out of my office. You will not get your damn tax clearance certificate."

He nodded toward the door. "Out," he said, then turned his full attention to his papers.

She was too shocked to cry as she stumbled out of his office.

Remembering the humiliation now, Sarah burrowed deeper under the down comforter, which emitted the cherry-tobacco scent of Kurt's pipe and the lavender potpourri that she stored in her sheets. She had only considered then the secret she would bear if she succumbed to him, not the secret she would bear forever by refusing him.

She closed her eyes remembering how, a week after her visit to Jurgen's office, Kurt received notice that the tax clearance application had been rejected, and they would have to apply all over again. They had lost their chance for a legal visa. Three days later Kurt was arrested on suspicion of tax evasion. He was held for a week, then told he would be released because the allegations were groundless. She was summoned to pick him up at the Internal Ministry after his release. When Kurt handed in the final paperwork to the clerk, she saw Jurgen emerge from his office behind the reception area. He stood by his door, arms crossed over his chest. When their eyes met, he looked at her coldly and stepped back into his office. Just in case she had any doubts this trouble had been his doing. Or needed a warning that he could do worse.

It had taken many additional weeks and much of their savings to obtain false visas. And there had been no further talk of bringing along her parents and Hannah.

The thought of her family now made her throw off the comforter. Anxiety over their unknown fate poked her like a woodpecker boring into a tree. She never told Kurt about the meeting with Jurgen. She had made things so much worse. Had Jurgen taken further revenge on her family after she left Germany? Unable to stand her thoughts any longer, she fumbled for her clothes. No good to brood all day. Maybe she should make soup. And after that, she could polish the silver again. Not that it mattered. Not that anyone noticed.

CHAPTER 19
GERTIE

January 1944

Rounding the bend to the pond, Gertie smiled at the scattering of skaters and waved to schoolmates. She noticed a clutch of WACs huddled together, chatting and blowing into their hands near a bonfire at the edge of the pond. At the far end, Jimmy and Owen were shuffling a puck between them with hockey sticks. It had been hard to get Jimmy's attention recently. Once or twice, he came by the house after a work shift, eager to catch up. But as soon as she launched into an answer to his questions, he seemed distracted, almost mournful. And then he'd go away for days. No sign of life. What was she doing wrong? Or was it work? Around here, who knew? If it was work, he wouldn't tell her. Of course. Secrets, secrets, secrets. She had tried to ask her chemistry teacher about the heavy water Jimmy mentioned months ago, but hadn't understood the explanation—something about how it slowed down uranium in a reactor, whatever that meant. She was sick of all the not knowing in her life—not knowing why she was here and for how long, not knowing what people working here were really doing, not knowing if Jimmy really cared for her.

She tugged defiantly on her skate laces, hoping Jimmy would notice her. But he didn't. At least she was a good skater, able to skate backward and pirouette. That should impress him!

The ice was bumpier than she expected. Nevertheless, she circled around, then skated backward, crossing leg over leg. She skittered among the skaters, past Jimmy, waved at him and Owen, and called out, "Hi, guys." They stopped their game long enough to look up at her. She wound her way back toward shore, the wind blowing. Then she hit a bump and went flying. A cracking pain went through her wrist when she braced her fall with a hand. Sprawled on the ice, she quivered with humiliation. She had so longed to show Jimmy she was good at something, and now all she wanted to do was cry. She felt so stupid, and her wrist hurt like hell.

In a moment, Jimmy was at her side, along with Owen.

"Hey, are you okay?" Jimmy asked.

She wanted to assure him she was, but the pain searing through her limp hand and her throbbing bum were impossible to ignore. "I don't know," she whimpered.

"Let me help you up," he said.

"I can get up myself." She wasn't actually certain she could, not if she had broken her wrist.

"Sure you can, but let me help you anyway." He turned to Owen. "Gertie doesn't need both of us here."

"Whoa, man, I know she's your girl, but let's make sure she's okay," Owen said.

"I'm okay," Gertie said. But she wasn't getting up.

"She's okay," Jimmy said firmly to Owen.

"Sure. Have it your way." Owen backed away, his hands up as if in surrender.

Were they fighting over her? Even through the pain, she couldn't help but notice that Jimmy was claiming her as his.

"I'll catch you later," Jimmy said to Owen in a conciliatory tone. "We need to go over those concentration figures you were asking me about before we get to the lab tomorrow. You'll be around, right?"

"We'll see. There are people to meet," Owen said cheekily, rubbing his gloved hands together and looking toward the WACs, still by the bonfire at the other end of the pond. "See you," Owen said to both of them and skated off.

Gertie was shaking, whether from cold or pain or embarrassment or all three wasn't clear. She gave her good hand to Jimmy's outstretched one, and he pulled her toward him. Her wrist throbbed and so did her bum, but it felt so good to lean in on him. She wished they could stay this way forever, a sculpture on the ice.

"We better get you looked at," he said gently.

"I'm sure I'll be okay," she murmured into his coat.

His gloved hand stroked her head, then held her injured hand gently. She winced as he tried to straighten it. Even she could tell it was bent out of shape. He took her good hand in his, and they skated to the edge of the pond and a big log that served as a bench. Jimmy tenderly removed Gertie's skates. His conscientiousness was endearing. He followed her instructions on where to find her boots and maneuvered them onto her feet.

"Come, Cinderella, let's get you to the clinic," he said, giving her foot a final pat.

"Yes, my prince." She smiled, the pain momentarily forgotten as she hooked her good arm through his. She could see in his eyes that he approved of her not crying or complaining. He stroked her hair and kissed her forehead.

"My brave Gertie," he murmured and held her close. "Keep your elbow bent with your hand facing up. You don't want all the blood rushing to your wrist," he said.

"How do you know these things?" she asked.

"Trust me."

"I do, Jimmy." She burrowed into him. "There's no one I trust more."

He turned toward her, and she wrapped her throbbing arm around him, the wrist hanging limp. He looked down at her.

"Thank you," he said.

"Thank you?"

"I want so much to be worthy of your trust."

Before she could answer or ask what he meant, he kissed her on the mouth, fully. The fervor of it took her breath away. She felt his warm lips on hers, his tongue in her mouth. The wetness alarmed her, and for an instant, she expected to be disgusted but instead was surprised at how wonderful it felt to have him explore her this way. So, this was what real kissing was like. She was about to respond in kind, but before she could, he pulled back and kissed her again and again lightly on the lips, closed his eyes, and burrowed his face into her neck, then kissed it and moved back to her lips. A dozen little kisses that seemed to beg her to kiss him back. She complied, covering his nose, his eyes, his cheeks, and his lips with little pecks, like a hungry bird.

"Oh, Gertie," he whispered. "Oh, Gertie," he moaned. It felt like a supplication.

CHAPTER 20
CHRISTINE

March 1944

Christine was typing up the catalog copy on Maria's pottery for the upcoming exhibition at Samantha's gallery, deep in a description of Zia, the Hopi sun symbol, when Gertie bounded up the stairs, belting out "This Land Is Your Land."

Christine resented the interruption but also looked forward to it. She hoped Gertie would offer some scraps of information about Kurt that she could mull over in the interludes between their trysts.

"What a pleasant surprise!" She turned off the radio, reporting on the Allied bombing of Berlin, to give the teen her full attention.

Gertie kissed her cheek. "I'm starving."

"We'll see what we can do about that," said Christine, laughing. "But first take off those muddy boots."

Gertie kicked off her galoshes and set them in a corner before flopping onto a kitchen chair.

The child was a mess. She had matured beyond her clothes and was bursting out of her blouse, a white cotton affair with frills down the front and a big bow at the top. Christine would have to find a way to explain to Gertie that frills did not suit her. Nor did the wide belt that she wore on her wool plaid skirt, an attempt perhaps to be fashionable but one that only accentuated Gertie's short waist.

Christine set out some chocolate pudding.

Gertie mmm'd away.

"You sure love chocolate," said Christine. Did Kurt share his daughter's taste in sweets? She did not know the most basic things about him, yet he told her that she understood him better than anyone ever had.

"Is it possible *not* to love chocolate?"

Christine laughed. She hadn't ever considered bringing Kurt a treat; eating would steal time from lovemaking, which was always rushed, limited by her having to return home by 10:30 p.m., when she told Thomas bridge club was over. Maybe she would bring Kurt some pudding tonight.

Even with Gertie sitting in front of her, Christine couldn't stop thinking about Kurt's touch, the way he turned her insides instantly liquid. With him, her body swirled out of itself, wildly, recklessly, peaking breathlessly in minutes. Afterward, she would lie in his arms, surrounded by the pots until her body surged again with the urgency of a gushing river and rose to meet his and they lay exhausted, awed at their own insatiability.

"Can I have more?" Gertie asked, interrupting Christine's reverie.

If she gave Gertie more pudding, there would be none for Kurt.

"How about an apple? It's healthier."

Gertie grimaced but grabbed a piece of fruit from the basket on the table and sank her teeth into it.

How confused, hurt, and angry Gertie would be if she knew what the adults in her life were up to. Christine grew up believing that telling the truth was always good, however hard sometimes. But there was needless pain in truth. Sometimes deception was kindness, she'd come to realize. Christine knew she should feel guilty for being with Kurt. But she didn't. After her encounters with Kurt, she always found it easier to be with Thomas, more tolerant of the distance he had created between them, more accepting of his lack of attention to her. Fulfilled by Kurt, she demanded less of her husband so that rather than weakening her marriage, this affair seemed to be strengthening it.

She knew she should consider the potential for destruction the affair held. But her heart defied this; she had never felt so gloriously alive. It was as if the world had once been a pale watercolor painting magically transformed into vibrant oils. She only felt guilty for not feeling guilty. And never more conflicted about this than when she was with Gertie, enjoying her exuberance and fresh observations.

"What's new?" Christine asked.

"Well, there was a war-bond gala in New York, where Frank Sinatra auctioned off his shirt for five hundred dollars! Can you imagine having Frank Sinatra's shirt? I mean, it's ridiculous—what would one do with it really? But it would be swell to have, wouldn't it?"

Christine laughed. "Only if it sings as wonderfully as he does. I heard about that gala too. His belt went for three hundred and fifty dollars. But that's not what I meant. What's new with you?"

"Not much," Gertie answered.

"How's debate team?"

"Who cares about debate team?"

"I thought you did. I certainly don't care if you don't." Christine took a bite of an apple herself. Darn good apples. She'd been lucky to get to the commissary this morning just as they were being unpacked and had grabbed a dozen before the supply ran out.

"Ah well," said Gertie. Christine had never noticed that Gertie used that expression, like her father, when she was avoiding a topic.

"So what's up?" Christine asked, adding in a singsong voice: "There's something you're not telling me."

"What's up with you?" Gertie asked.

"The exhibit. Other than that, the usual. What could possibly be up?"

They stared at each other and burst out laughing.

"I can't hide anything from you, can I?" said Gertie.

"Why would you?"

Gertie looked down at her lap. "I got into trouble."

"Oh?" Christine tried to sound surprised.

"I snuck into Jimmy's dorm after hours."

"That doesn't sound like a federal crime." In fact, Christine knew all about Gertie's infiltration of Jimmy's barracks. Kurt had fumed about it so much during their last time together, they barely had time to make love. He'd been summoned to the Hill's military police headquarters two days earlier to find Gertie in custody. The police let her go only when Kurt promised that the incident would not be repeated. Gertie was becoming too wild, Kurt seethed. Matters were getting entirely out of hand. Why had he let this business with Jimmy go on for so long? No good would come of it.

Lying in his arms, Christine assured him that it was natural for a sixteen-year-old to be in love. He should be thankful Gertie was foisting her attention on such a gentle and kind young man. "Go easy on her," Christine had counseled. "She's strongheaded. Be too tough on her, and she'll rebel. Jimmy's good for her, good to her. Let them be."

Now, as Christine took down the laundry from the line on the balcony and folded clothes in the kitchen, Gertie prattled on about how she hadn't seen Jimmy for days and, worried that he was angry at her, had gone to the barracks to find him.

"Jimmy was furious. His friends were sneering at us. Then the police swooped in. They handcuffed me! I tried to tell them that my wrist was still weak from that sprain. But they ignored me. It hurt. I screamed with pain, so they uncuffed me. But it was horrible! What was even worse was that Jimmy didn't seem happy to see me. We've been together for almost six months. I wonder if he's tired of me."

Gertie paused to contemplate the matter for a moment, taking two huge bites of the apple to polish it off and picking up a second apple from the bowl. She sank her teeth into that one and munched it before continuing.

"And then they called Papa, and he came to fetch me. And he told me I was never, ever to see Jimmy again. He spoke in that quiet voice he uses when he won't be argued with. Honestly, I thought I was going to curl up and die. But three days later Papa changed his mind, said he was okay with my seeing Jimmy. Can you believe it? He never changes his mind! He said I could see Jimmy as long as I never go to the barracks. Fine by me. I never want to see that dorm again. It's so stinky and crowded."

"I'm sure it is." Christine laughed. So, Kurt had taken her advice. "Well, that worked out." Christine patted the folded sheets and clean clothes in a laundry basket.

"I guess. But I still don't know what Jimmy *really* is feeling and why he's been so distant."

As Christine cleared and washed the pudding dish, Gertie jabbered on, dissecting Jimmy's every utterance for innuendo.

"So, don't you think it's strange?" Gertie asked, trailing behind Christine, who took the basket of folded laundry into the bedroom.

"What's strange?" asked Christine, not really paying attention as she deposited the clothing in its proper drawers.

"The way Jimmy gets angry when I want him to kiss me," Gertie said.

"Men like to take the initiative." Christine closed Thomas's underwear-and-socks drawer.

"Why do you think that is?"

How different the child was from her father, who said so much with so few words. Kurt rarely spoke after they made love. He usually rose before her, and she would watch from under the covers, still dazed from their lovemaking, as he transformed himself from naked lover to respectable scientist, adjusting his bow tie, putting on his coat and hat, which he would tip to her. She would linger for a few more minutes after he left, longing already for the week to pass so they could meet again.

Christine pulled herself away from thoughts of Kurt. "I don't know. You are young and inexperienced, so he's cautious. Considerate. Or maybe he's not so experienced himself."

"How am I ever going to become experienced if he doesn't want to try harder to become experienced together?" She leaned on the side of the dresser.

"Don't worry. These things sort themselves out. Jimmy will come around when the time's right." Christine opened the top drawer to put away her underwear.

"Hey, what's that? A bow tie in your underthings?" Gertie giggled.

Christine had forgotten about the bow tie Kurt had left in the shed a month ago. She had retrieved it, stuffed it in a drawer, meaning to give it back.

"Papa has one just like it."

"I guess, I . . . they're pretty common, aren't they? It's, it's Thomas's." Christine slammed the drawer shut.

"I've never seen Thomas wear a bow tie," said Gertie.

"He doesn't." Her mind raced. "I mean he doesn't here. He used to wear them back in New York. It's so informal here, so he doesn't use it. But he has one." Christine walked out of the bedroom, Gertie following her.

"I bet he looks great in a bow tie. He's so handsome!" Gertie said.

God, how could she have been so careless to forget Kurt's bow tie was in that drawer?

"Yes, he always looks good, in whatever he wears," Christine said. Her heart pounded. She hoped it didn't show. She had to get rid of Gertie. "Honey, I need to work on my notes for the exhibition in New York," she said, sinking into a kitchen chair. "I promised to mail the catalog text this week."

"Oh okay," said Gertie, clearly disappointed.

Christine would have to remember to give Kurt back his bow tie tonight.

"Are you okay? You don't look well," Gertie said.

"I guess I'm anxious. The writing's been going slow. The pottery has not sold well so far. And a few of the most recent pieces I sent to New York arrived broken."

"Can I help, organize things, pack some pottery?"

"Thanks. No. I'm not sure there's much of a future in this little business of mine. I wish I could convey to art lovers just how amazing the Pueblo pots are. But it's hard—the pottery is so different from the sort of wares, the china, that most collectors are used to. And it's not old, like antiques that other collectors go for. If this exhibit doesn't succeed, I don't know what to do next." Christine suddenly realized that she was talking mostly to herself and turned her attention back to Gertie. "Sorry, honey, I didn't mean to bore you."

"I don't mind. I like it when you tell me your problems. You know, like a grown-up friend."

Christine smiled, not daring to dwell on the irony of all she would never reveal to Gertie. Then she remembered: "Listen. I do have some news. I've put in a job application here. They need a research librarian in the Tech Library."

"Inside the Tech Area?"

"Yes."

"You'll be working in the Tech Area? Wow, you may actually see the gadget!"

"I doubt that." Christine laughed.

"I imagine it sometimes, like a big balloon, filled with water in a huge room in the basement," said Gertie.

Christine laughed. "I'm sure it's nothing like that."

"Well, Jimmy said once they were using heavy water."

"He did?"

"Yes. What does it mean?"

"That he's talking more than he should." Christine sat down in front of her typewriter, sifting absentmindedly through photos of Pueblo pottery.

"God, you're as bad as everyone else around here."

Christine looked at her quizzically.

"Hush, hush, hush," Gertie said in her most sardonic tone. "Let's not talk about why we are here. This place is so full of itself for having so many secrets. I'm sick of it."

"Gertie, we're not talking about an Easter treasure hunt."

"What's happened? You used to be as eager as me to find out what's going on around here." Gertie put her hands on her hips and frowned at Christine. "You're different these days."

"Don't be silly. Of course I'm curious. As curious as you are. But there are reasons for secrets. Now go along, you must have homework to do."

CHAPTER 21
CHRISTINE

March 1944

Maria, in red sneakers and a full brown skirt, poked stakes into the ground of her newly turned vegetable garden. She straightened when Christine rode up on Odysseus and dismounted, causing the chickens to scatter and cluck in disapproval. Christine kissed Maria's cheek. It smelled as sun drenched as a fresh tomato.

"What brings you out here?"

"You and the gorgeous weather."

Maria laughed. "The weather, I understand. But me?"

Christine needed a biographical note on Maria for the exhibit. But there was another reason. Life had felt like a whirlwind recently—finishing the catalog, filling out the job application for librarian, navigating the roller coaster of feelings that Kurt stirred in her. Being around Maria, reticent and commonsensical, always seemed to help ground Christine.

"The person organizing the exhibit of your work in New York sent me some questions about how you learned pottery, about your life, and I couldn't answer them. I realized we haven't talked much about you!"

Maria smiled. "No need," she said as she sat down on a low flat boulder, her thick wool skirt fanning out around her. "The pottery. It must speak for itself."

"Yes, of course. And it does, but people are curious about artists."

"Why? It does not matter who makes something, only if it is beautiful, if it is good, created with a pure heart."

"It is out of respect and awe at the results that people want to understand how an artist comes to create their work."

Maria shrugged. "It's not something that can be explained."

Christine sat beside her and took in the view of the yard. "Still. Maybe you can tell me how you got started."

"What gets anyone started on anything?"

"I don't know," said Christine.

"What got you started, coming out here and buying my stuff and asking me questions like you are now?"

"Honestly?"

Maria nodded, her eyes on Christine. "Two things: Their beauty. My boredom."

Maria laughed. "That's my answer too."

The two women watched the chickens scrounging the ground.

"When I was young, I worked for an archeologist out on a dig, a bit west of here," Maria began, turning her body toward the west and looking out on the desert in that direction for a few moments before shifting back to face Christine. "I was always good at making pots. Long time, I make them. My tia Nicolasa used to do pots all the time, and I would go to her place and work with her, when I could. I liked being with her better than being at home where it was noisy and I was the oldest, so my mother always wanted me to help out. Making pots with my aunt was better than cleaning. Better than cooking too. And sometimes, my tia Nicolasa goes to Santa Fe and sells some pinch pots. Then she gives me some money from the ones I make. My tia passed away, and I stopped. But when an archeologist come to these parts, and my husband worked for him, they needed someone to make copies of things from the dig, so he hired me." Maria stopped; her mind seemed far away.

Christine let her own silence be her next question, the one that really needed answering, the matter of inspiration and motivation. She was learning to be patient and still, like Maria. She watched the chickens pecking the ground until Maria was ready to answer.

"The stuff they find at the site was by my ancestors," Maria said finally. "The pots, they speak to me. It seemed they asked me to make their beauty known again after they were buried for so many years."

Maria got up, went back to her garden, and put the rest of the stakes into the ground as Christine watched.

"I try to take the spirit of the pots and carry it on. My pots are different. Some people don't like that. I don't know what my ancestors think. I hope they understand, and it's always in my head. I remember those old pots."

Christine turned her face to the sun and lay back on the boulder, the cold stone under her, the warm sun covering her. Maria stood and picked up an empty watering can. "You want lunch?"

"I'd love some!"

Maria started toward the house.

"Wait, I have this for you." She handed Maria an envelope. "Some money from the pots."

Without opening it, Maria tucked the envelope into the pocket of her skirt.

"Don't you want to know how much there is?"

"It won't turn into more or less if I count it later or now, will it?" said Maria, opening the door and ushering Christine in.

Unlike her pottery with its clean, simple lines, Maria's home was cluttered, stuffed with knickknacks. The kitchen, living room, and dining room were all one area, dominated by a large wood dining room table and a fireplace. Maria took out two pink store-bought bowls and ladled the chili simmering on the fire. She set the bowls and two squares of corn bread on the table.

"Eat up," she said.

The chili was spicy. Christine stifled a desire to sneeze.

"You have children?" Christine asked, groping for conversation.

"Five. Four alive, one passed on as a baby. Three of the boys are in the army, overseas."

A baby who died. Christine couldn't imagine the pain behind that simple fact. And yet, four live children. That was something. She stifled her envy. "You must be proud of your boys."

Maria shrugged. "Never meant to raise them to fight white men's wars."

"What do you mean?"

"Uncle Sam is happy to take them from here to fight his wars. Says they're fighting for freedom, for democracy. But does he let them vote here in the USA? Does he let me vote? No ma'am."

"What do you mean?"

"Indian Nation. Doesn't have the right to vote."

"I had no idea."

"There's lots of things white folks have no idea about." Maria said it quietly, without anger, a statement of fact.

"It must have been hard sending them off."

"That's the truth."

Christine couldn't think of anything more to say, suddenly uncomfortable. There was so little she knew about Maria, even less that she understood. Asking questions about her life felt like walking through territory better left undisturbed. Sometimes relations could best be nurtured by keeping some distance, by knowing about a person only what they wanted you to know. She was unsure what Maria really thought of her, or of white folks, as she called them.

"How's Robert?" Maria asked, putting two glasses of herbal tea on the table and sitting herself down.

The change of topic seemed like an offer to return to neutral, common ground.

"Oppie? I don't know. Don't see him around much. He's busy." There were more and more people at Los Alamos, the Saturday night parties consequently had become bigger and more dispersed, so Oppie no longer indulged in idle chat with someone like Christine, whose ego it was not essential he tamp or stroke, whose output at work he did not need to worry about or praise.

"What you all doing up there?"

Christine shrugged. "Don't ask me. It's got to do with the war. But what, I don't know. Maybe I'll know more soon. I've applied for a job."

"Doing what?"

"Research librarian."

"What's that mean you'll do?"

"Well, when someone needs information about something, they ask me to find it for them instead of looking for it themselves."

"Hmm. How do you know where to look?"

"It's mostly scientific stuff, in journals."

"I guess everything's about the war these days," said Maria.

"Things seem pretty tranquil around here, as if nothing much changes."

"Bring you to me, didn't it?"

"But that's good, no?"

Maria smiled. "You're a good woman. I like it, you coming to see me. You take an interest in the pots. You still going to come here if you have yourself a fancy job?"

Christine looked around Maria's house, with its scent of drying herbs and corn bread, its eclectic array of dishes and rugs, and its thick enveloping walls.

"Absolutely! On the weekends if there's no other time."

CHAPTER 22
CHRISTINE

March 1944

Christine changed clothes five times for the job interview, so she was late and out of breath when she finally flew through the door of the administration building. Here was her chance to be part of the victory effort, to be an integral part of whatever Los Alamos was really about, and she may have blown it already.

In her rush, Christine almost missed Office 105E. She knocked. A woman with a thin face opened the door a sliver.

"I'm here for a job interview with Sergeant Lee."

The door opened a few more inches. The WAC looked her up and down. "You're late."

"Just a little." Christine smiled weakly. "Sorry."

The WAC sighed and moved aside. "Sit down," she ordered and nodded toward a straight-backed chair. Her block-heeled brown oxfords clicked as she returned to her desk.

Christine noticed the phone on the receptionist's desk. She hadn't seen one since her orientation in Dorothy's Santa Fe office the day they arrived in Los Alamos eight months ago. Maybe her job would come with a phone. Pathetic that the idea of talking to people somewhere else seemed exciting. Her eyes roamed above the desk to a recruitment poster of a WAC with dark curly hair in front of a flag. **ARE YOU A GIRL WITH A STAR-SPANGLED HEART?** Christine contemplated the question, reaching no definitive conclusion before another WAC appeared from the inner office to take her to the interview. They wound their way through a space the size of a football field, past dozens of scattered desks. The click of typewriter keys pulsed through the room, interspersed with the *ping* and grind of the roller whenever a typist started a new line. The WAC led her to a glassed-off cubicle along the wall at the end of the expanse where the sergeant sat, engrossed in a file on her desk. Private McDougal pointed Christine toward a chair in front of the desk, coughed to catch the sergeant's attention, and turned back toward the reception area.

Sergeant Lee, her brown hair swept into a tidy French bun, looked up at Christine and emitted a tight smile through fire truck red lipstick. She motioned her to sit down and turned back to the document. She seemed about Christine's age. Her polished fingernails, which matched her lipstick exactly, ran along the text she was reading, sometimes doubling back. Was she perusing Christine's personnel file? Why was she rereading certain lines? Christine tried to calm her nerves by surveying the space, noting the file cabinets lining every wall, the absence of windows, the glare of the no-nonsense fluorescent lights. She envied the purposefulness of the women in khaki uniforms, typing furiously or filing.

"Quite an operation you have here," Christine said.

Sergeant Lee looked up and closed the file. The golden WAC insignia on her lapels glittered with authority.

"Indeed," she said, pride evident in her tone. "So, Christine Sharp, what can you tell me about yourself?"

Christine felt the sergeant's gaze lingering on her pastel yellow swing skirt, which suddenly seemed frivolous. She should have chosen her straight navy skirt.

Christine explained her chemistry background and elaborated on the employment form she had already filled out in triplicate. She reiterated her precollege work experience shelving books at a public library and explained her PhD topic—food preservation.

"I didn't get far into my doctorate," she added. "My husband's professional opportunities took me away from my studies."

"Of course." The sergeant smiled understandingly. This response annoyed Christine, although she couldn't say why.

"Our opening is for a research librarian. That's quite different from shelving library books. You have insufficient relevant experience as far as I can see, don't you?" The sergeant's tone was kinder than the question.

Christine shot her a look of confidence that belied her desperation.

"Well, I'm not actually privy to what relevant experience might be, so it's a difficult question to answer."

Oh fudge! She was being snippy when she wanted to make a good impression. She clasped her hands in her lap and tried again.

"I think my chemistry background is relevant," she said. "More important than experience as a librarian. I know a lot of scientific terms. That's sure to be useful to find relevant material. And I've conducted research myself. I know the leading scientific journals—in chemistry at least—and what areas they tend to cover, or don't. Surely that's important."

She felt her voice rising like that of an insistent child and lowered the register to sound mature. She paused to consider what she might say next. She wanted the job, but if she seemed too knowledgeable, she just might blow it. Since Oppie's cocktail party, when he hinted her article was censored because it mentioned atoms, she had been speculating about what was being built at Los Alamos. She was sure the gadget used ions of some kind. Back in grad school, she had considered specializing in irradiated food. But it was too difficult to obtain radium for the process. And there were concerns that while irradiation killed microbes and bacteria, it might also be harmful to humans. So, she had worked on artificial pectin instead. But here at Los Alamos, scientists were sure to get whatever rare isotope they needed. And as for creating something unhealthy for human beings, well, that's exactly what weapons were supposed to do.

"I'm sure I could get the hang of the logistics once I get started."

Before the sergeant could interject any objections, Christine leaned forward and continued. "I've always been a fast learner. I'm hardworking and very precise," she added, as if she were revealing some deep but true secret about herself.

"General Groves won't like it, taking on personnel not fully qualified." Sergeant Lee folded her arms across her substantial chest and looked at Christine as if appraising a sofa for purchase. After what felt like forever, the sergeant smiled.

"He'll just have to suck it up, won't he?" she said, slapping her hands on her desk. "The library's a mess. When can you start?"

"Yesterday." Christine laughed with relief.

"Hold your horses. Security haven't had their say yet. They'll need time to clear you."

"I'm ready when they are." Christine couldn't believe how peppy she sounded. She didn't care if the job meant giving up the freedom to go riding into the desert or having less time to promote Maria's pots. Her eyes gleamed at the idea of being part of the buzz around her, doing something to help the war effort, working close to Kurt and, yes, close to Thomas too. Especially if it rekindled the kind of stimulating conversations she used to have with her husband before the move to Los Alamos. He would no longer be able to lord it over her about secret this and secret that. As a research librarian, she might even learn more than he knew, because she would presumably help scientists in different areas of expertise find information about a wide range of issues related to the gadget. And she imagined that Kurt's admiration for her would only grow if she could show him that her knowledge extended far beyond the arts. She almost skipped with joy as she returned to the reception area, imagining herself being useful, part of the effort that had brought them all here to Los Alamos. On her way out, she glanced at the recruitment poster over the reception desk. She didn't know what the heck a star-spangled heart was, but she was pretty sure she had one.

CHAPTER 23
JIMMY

March 1944

Even after Jimmy tinkered for days, adjusting the neutron reflector and checking over Kurt's calculations, the experiment had not yielded the reaction they needed with the last bit of enriched plutonium the lab still had available. They'd have to wait for a new batch to arrive. If they didn't improve their outcomes, Oppie might decide to put all bets on the team working with uranium, and phase out the testing in Koppel's lab. It wasn't just the loss of prestige that worried Jimmy. He was sure they were so close to getting the results they needed, it would be a huge loss if they weren't given the chance to prove plutonium would work just fine. When he left the Tech Area, Jimmy was still trying to figure out what materials might better stimulate the subcritical reaction they needed and how to calculate the amounts. He was drained but too agitated to go back to the dorm—and too hungry, so he headed to Fuller Lodge.

Moonlit shadows of oak branches splattered patterns on the asphalt path. The scent of pines and the breeze, which no longer bore the bite of winter, helped him unwind. Strains of fiddle music cajoling square dancers to do-si-do beckoned even before he entered the log-and-stone lodge. Inside, he was immediately enveloped by the smell of beer and sweat. He ordered a burger and a beer, then slid into the only available chair in a corner of the dining area. A couple stood in front of him, blocking his view. The guy was bent like a pry bar over his girlfriend. She curved into him, her skirt swaying into his groin. Jimmy tried to look away, but they were so close there was nowhere else to gaze. The guy's muscles, tanned under his white T-shirt, tensed and flexed as he squeezed the girl in his arms. His thumb worked its way up her ribs and under her breast while his trim buttocks circled into her. Jimmy took a gulp of beer and hunkered into his burger. He could not stop looking at the man's butt, in front of his face and blocking his view, doing what should be done in darkened rooms. Jimmy grew hard, tried to glance away, but was drawn back to the man's gyrating. He guzzled down his beer and lurched away from the dancing—and the couple's grinding—and out of the lodge.

He inhaled the smell of wet grass, glad to be back in the calming night, but he was even less ready for sleep now. The guy's face, with that satisfied grin, kept rising in his mind. He had never felt like that man seemed to feel, holding that woman. Every day he thanked his lucky stars to be in Los Alamos and part of the most exciting research he could imagine. But he had never experienced the contentment he saw on that man's face. He sometimes watched the guys in the dorm ogle girlie magazines, full of women with breasts so big they looked like zeppelins, about to lift and fly away. The guys joshed about how much they wanted to bury their faces in all that flesh. To him, the idea seemed vaguely repugnant. Of course, he was a regular guy, just a bit shy when it came to women.

Suddenly, he heard a cry from the direction of the perimeter fence and noticed a shack, its outline barely discernible. It looked like a large toolshed. Was a coyote trapped inside? There was a gasp and a moan. The sound was human. He felt himself blush. He heard murmuring. He stopped and listened. More murmuring. A woman laughing.

Owen said he should accept that lust lurked at every turn. Hearing the human voices, Jimmy had to acknowledge that normal people did things he found hard to fathom. Who was in the shed? None of his business. Besides, he should get to bed. It was late. But he didn't move. He leaned against the tree and waited.

There was a smell in the air he couldn't identify. Jasmine or honeysuckle perhaps. Something sweet that reminded him of the shampoo smell of Gertie's hair. He smiled at the thought of her. She would approve of his eavesdropping. She was curious about everything and often annoyed him with all her questions. Yet, he felt lighter when he told her things he didn't even know he thought, stuff he had never considered before, like why he liked physics more than math, or why he didn't think he'd ever go back and live on Cape Cod, or how he would spend $10,000 if he had a week to live.

From the shed came muffled sounds. It wasn't right to eavesdrop. On the other hand, maybe it was time to show Owen he wasn't so naive. Hang around long enough to find out who was in the shed.

Waiting, he shivered. He blew into his hands and reassessed the latest lab tests to get his mind off the cold. Lost in thought about increasing beryllium to reach supercritical mass, he was startled when the door of the shed creaked open. The bereted head of the figure who emerged was unmistakable. Only Kurt wore such a hat. Only his boss stuck his hands in his pockets in that peculiar, determined way. What was Kurt doing here, walking quickly down the path a mere twenty yards away? His first thought was not generous; it was of treason. Jimmy did not know he had it in him to doubt Kurt, but he was, after all, German. There were so many warnings about spies, all those posters admonishing people to be careful, to trust no one. But Kurt was Jewish. It made no sense that he'd be a spy. Besides, that would not account for the moaning. It was almost more of a comfort to think of Kurt as a spy, tapping away in Morse code, than to imagine him cavorting. Or maybe he was with his wife, and they were both spies, and this was their cover. Also preposterous. Jimmy's head was spinning. He should leave now, but he didn't move.

Beyond the perimeter fence, spotlights illuminated the latest trailer park constructed in recent weeks on a low ridge below the Hill for the families of the growing maintenance crew. The trailers, their windows dark, were scattered like children's blocks, sheltering hardworking folks who would be up at dawn. Or were they cavorting too? The whole world was up to no good. Himself included, hiding behind a tree, waiting . . . for what? He should go to the dorm, go to sleep.

While he deliberated, the door squeaked, and a woman came out. She padlocked the door, then slipped the key in her pocket. She wrapped a shawl around her shoulders with a graceful move, then threw her head back, loosening her hair. In a flash he knew it was Christine Sharp: lithe and light on her feet. As she walked away, he leaned into the tree to absorb the shock. He tried to come up with some reasonable explanation, but there was none. Owen always said people were doing such things, cheating on their spouses, looking for adventure with someone new. Jimmy could believe it about Christine Sharp. She'd struck him as unconventional. But Kurt? Jimmy had never admired anyone as much as he did his boss. Jimmy found Kurt's German rigidity, that insistence on doing the right thing and doing it well, endearing. Kurt put such store in being upstanding, exacting. He looked down on those who didn't take life seriously. How would Jimmy face his boss tomorrow and the next day? How would he face Gertie?

CHAPTER 24
CHRISTINE

March 1944

Although it was past midnight, Christine forced herself to stay up for Thomas, due home after two days in the desert, testing God knows what. She rarely slept well when he was away, worried that whatever he was testing might blow up in his face. Maybe he had escaped the danger of combat, but if he and his colleagues were dealing with atoms and atomic energy—as she surmised—their work entailed isotopes, radioactive materials, dangerous stuff.

She opened the living room window to calm her nerves. The streetlight at the end of the common yard buzzed as if it, too, was anxiously awaiting Thomas's arrival. All the hobby groups—the folk dance club, the barbershop quartet, the jazz ensemble—had disbanded for the night, so the road was empty and silent.

She wanted Thomas safe at home, and she looked forward to telling him about the research-librarian job. Before the interview, she'd considered her chances of getting the position so slim—given her lack of training—that she hadn't mentioned it to him. She didn't want him to pity her if her hopes for a job were dashed. But now that all had seemingly gone well with Sergeant Lee yesterday, she was eager to tell him.

Kurt reassured her when they met last night. "Of course, they couldn't say no to you. You are so competent. In everything," he said, slipping a hand between her legs, kneading her gently. With Thomas away for the field test, they had the luxury of more time to talk, to make love slowly. Her body, responding to Kurt's attentions, rocked gently in his arms. Kurt made her feel so beautiful and sexy, instilled in her a sense of vitality that spilled into lust also for Thomas, so that she knew she would greet her husband with open arms when he returned. The truth was she wanted to—and believed she could—have it all: Thomas, Kurt, and entrance into the inner sanctum at Los Alamos.

"I hope I'm not being unrealistic, but I can't wait to become part of the real action in this place," she told Kurt during their latest rendezvous. "I'm so fed up with living only in a parallel universe of civilian life, when it's so beside the point."

"Normal everyday life is not beside the point. It's what the war is about after all, no? For the right to a decent life, to live in a free society, to enjoy our children, and play music, create art, think our thoughts, to love. You and I, we are part of this normal world, this parallel universe as you call it. It is not beside the point, is it?" Kurt said.

"If I get the job, the two worlds will merge," she said.

"Perhaps it will be necessary for me to send my assistants to the library, and not come myself. We will have to be discreet."

She had been so focused on wanting to be part of whatever was happening at Los Alamos, she hadn't fully considered how awkward it might be. She had assumed a librarian received written requests for articles and sent the articles to the correct lab. Did Kurt and Thomas just pop by the library whenever they needed something? In her eagerness for the job, she hadn't thought this through: What if they showed up at the same time?

"You go to the library a lot?"

"Yes, almost everyone does—and sometimes Oppie holds meetings in the conference room so we can find references quickly and check the literature as we discuss matters."

It was just as she'd hoped. The job would give her the chance to be at the very center of things.

"We will have to be good actors—much better than we were in the play. I do not know if I am a good enough actor to see you and seem indifferent." He smiled at her, affection mixing with apprehension in his gaze.

"We'll be good actors. We already are, no?" She stroked his cheek.

"It will be difficult."

"So, you don't think I should take the job?" She wanted the job more than ever now, but Kurt was right. Discretion would be difficult.

"I didn't say that."

He cupped his hand around her muff.

Her body surged at his touch.

"Of course, it will be wonderful to see you more. And finally, I will be able to talk, really talk, about work. If you are part of the team, I can tell you everything. Without fear of G-2."

She felt him hardening as he spoke, and he pressed his lips on hers. It thrilled her that just the thought of being able to share his work with her aroused him.

She remembered the tenderness of their lovemaking now as she closed the window in the living room. Restless, she mixed herself a gin and tonic and sat down on the green gabardine sofa. She flipped aimlessly through the latest Sears and Roebuck catalog, looking at clothes she did not need, then tossed it onto the coffee table. Not yet ready to retire to bed, she curled up with a book, the latest by Harry Emerson Fosdick—a gift from Samantha, who touchingly remembered how Christine used to consume the preacher's advice books. Christine turned to the title page of this latest bestseller, *On Being a Real Person*. How young and naive she had been in New York to think one could improve oneself following rules from a book. Like road maps, rules only went so far. How was one to know how to be good and real—whatever that meant—in the uncharted territory she was treading now? The move to Los Alamos had forced her to become a contortionist, bending in unexpected ways to cope. The good preacher Fosdick would say she was sinning, but her time with Kurt made her marriage better. She could tell Kurt what was in her heart and share her dreams of making Maria's pottery famous. The result was that she was far less annoyed when Thomas showed no interest in her day. Yet, there was still much that held her to Thomas: his dashing confidence that made her feel part of his privileged world, his sense of fun, his rueful humor, their shared history, and their desire to be parents together. It was all so confusing. She was growing groggy, and the book slipped from her hand.

Christine awoke to Thomas's kiss on her forehead. While she got her bearings, he picked up the book from the floor. She slid over to make room for him on the sofa. "Man is the only creature who can consciously create itself," he read aloud from the book. "Interesting," he said and set it aside.

Christine sat up and looked at her watch. It was 2:00 a.m. "How did the tests go?"

She knew from the way he tightened his lips that they must have gone badly.

"That bad?" she asked.

"Yes, that bad."

"What happened?"

"Christine, you know I can't talk about it."

"Can't or won't?"

"I'm too tired to answer that. I'm going to bed."

"Wait. Have some dinner. I made your favorite stew—and pecan pie."

"I'm too tired to eat."

"We need to talk."

"Now? Can't it wait until tomorrow?"

She knew it would be better to wait until tomorrow, until he was more receptive to her news. But she resented being put off.

"It can wait. Can I get you something to eat, drink?"

But he was already heading to the bedroom and didn't answer.

At dawn, she awoke to Thomas fondling her from behind. She slithered toward him, and he slipped into her, releasing himself into her with a satisfied groan, as if sex was relieving, like a badly needed piss. When he was done, she turned to face him. The long lines of his face were discernible even in the dim light. His sandy hair, tousled, made him look mischievous.

"It's good to be home," he grinned at her and stroked her cheek.

Being married meant convenient sex. She knew that. She stroked his cheek back, felt the stubble on his strong jaw.

"Can we talk now?" she asked.

"Sure. Shoot."

As the sun began to rise, she told him about the interview, how it had started out badly and ended well. "Sergeant Lee pretty much said the job's mine. Imagine, if I get it, we'll get to talk the way we used to."

"You? A research librarian? I thought you were selling that black pottery." He reached for the pack of cigarettes by the bed, sat up, and lit one. Smoking was a new habit he had started a few months ago.

"I will do that as a sideline, or stop selling them if I have to." She sat up, too, beside him, and waved away the smoke.

Thomas took another puff, exhaling slowly, the smoke dancing in the early morning light. "Honey, you keep fluttering from thing to thing. Chemistry, art restoration, pots. Now a research librarian. I don't get it," he said, putting the cigarette in the ashtray on his night table and lying back down to face her. He twiddled with a strand of her hair and swept it gently behind her ear. "You were furious at me for not taking you seriously about the pots. And now, presto, you are ready to drop them?"

She tossed her head away from his hand. "I want to be part of your world."

"But it's dangerous. It could hurt our chances of having a baby."

"Dangerous? In the library?"

"Working in the Tech Area. What do you think we're making there? Cookies?" He sat back up, flicked the cigarette in the ashtray, and resumed smoking.

"I figured out a long time ago that what you are doing is dangerous. Don't forget, there was a time when I was going to specialize in food radiation. I know radiation is bad."

"Why are you bringing that up?"

"Come on, Thomas, I have some notion of what you are up to. Certainly isotopes, radiation of some kind, bombarding atoms. I wasn't born yesterday. I studied some of that stuff. Or have you completely forgotten? But if there's a danger, it's in the lab, not the library. I think you're afraid of my taking the job. I don't know why. But it's got nothing to do with having a baby. No one tells the WACs not to work in the Tech Area because it's dangerous."

"The WACs are army. They don't have a choice. You do. You need to take care of yourself. You have it good. Pottery. Horseback riding. Nice social life. Enough food coupons to make wonderful meals. Why get a boring job as a librarian when you don't have to?"

How had she dared to imagine the job would restore the foundations on which their relationship had started?

"I want to be useful." Why couldn't he understand that? She felt like crying.

"There are the drives all the time—for metal, rubber, war bonds. You could get more involved in those. Why a job that will lead you to neglect duties at home?" He crushed out the cigarette in the ashtray.

"Where is the man who used to say we would one day be Dr. and Dr.?"

"Things change. The world changes." He lifted her chin and kissed her nose. "How about a piece of that pecan pie for breakfast?"

As she reached for her slippers, she wanted to throw the pie in his face.

CHAPTER 25
SARAH

April 1944

Sarah did not see Gertie off to school these days because of the headaches, which pierced her from the moment she awoke. In any case, it was better to stay away from the child and avoid spreading that dark cloud enveloping her. From bed, buried under the too-heavy comforter, Sarah listened to Gertie and Kurt preparing breakfast in the kitchen, chatting against the din of the morning news on the radio. With Kurt working late every day, breakfast was the only time father and daughter spent together. Sarah smelled the oatmeal, heard the clatter of spoons and dishes as Gertie served Kurt. This was as it should be, without Sarah ruining the atmosphere.

Soon enough they left, Gertie to school and Kurt to work. Sarah fumbled for her slippers, donned a morning gown, and headed to the kitchen. She filled the kettle and listened to the only station with international news. This morning, like most, reception was fuzzy. Snippets of the correspondents' reports faded in and out, the airwaves of a competing channel flitting through with a commodities report on corn feed and an expected rise in meat prices. The main news was of Soviet advances in Crimea and the latest in the struggle at Monte Cassino, a place she and Kurt had visited on their honeymoon in Italy. Then the local weather report: another perfect day. And the sadness she could not shake.

She remembered the view from the Monte Cassino monastery, bombed to ruins weeks ago but still a battleground between the Nazis and Allies, according to today's report. She and Kurt had lunched on the patio there with cheese sandwiches, tomatoes, apples, and a bottle of wine, overlooking the lush hills and valley, and they'd kissed in front of a passing young priest. They had been amused by his discomfort, had laughed and kissed some more, elated by their own lighthearted indulgence in pleasures the cleric would never know. The priest might well be dead now. There were so many people whose fate she could not guess. As far as she could tell—her fears reflected in the newsletters she received periodically from the Emergency Committee to Save the Jewish People of Europe—it was reasonable to assume that most of her family in Germany was dead. The most recent newsletter estimated the number of Jews killed by the Nazis at three million. What were the chances her family was not among them? The not knowing made her feel hollow. Yet, none of it seemed real here, where the only intimation of war was the never-explained, ever-present "gadget," while daily life revolved around whether there was milk at the commissary or enough gas coupons for a ride in the mountains on Sundays.

She dipped into the oatmeal Gertie had left for her, gooey and lukewarm. She considered how sharp Kurt had been with her for mentioning Monte Cassino, when, exceptionally, he came home yesterday before she fell asleep.

"What a beautiful place it was. What a beautiful day we had there. Horrible to think of it all now rubble," she said as they settled into bed.

He picked up a scientific journal on his night table and looked at her with the pity one would extend to a stray cat one has no intention of feeding. "I do not wish to dwell on it."

"How can you not?"

"I must concentrate on the here and now. On my work, on our lives."

"Do you want to forget everything about there? About our past? Even beautiful Monte Cassino?"

"I haven't forgotten. But you are back in the old country all the time. You are not with us, not with me, not with Gertie."

He sounded angry. The hurt must have shown on her face because he softened his tone, laid aside the journal, and took her hand in his.

"It is unhealthy, for all of us, the way you are, *liebling*. I do not want to be swallowed by sadness. We must save Gertie from our worries too. Save yourself. In these times, do what you must to move forward." He patted her hand.

"How does one save oneself?"

He looked down at their interlocked hands. "Everyone finds their own way." He turned off the light and curled away from her in bed.

Replaying the scene as she ate her breakfast, Sarah could not erase from her mind Kurt's furtive expression, so different from his usual stern manner when he imparted advice. Yesterday, he had glanced away. And he had switched off the light rather than finish the journal article, that shifty look still on his face. In a flash, she understood: it was a look of guilt. How had he put it? He was saving himself. Suddenly everything made sense: Kurt's change of mood these past months, the way he slept soundly at night. His cheerfulness. His distance. The absence of intimacy, which, although it had never been frequent or passionate between them, had been consistent. That undershirt of his, inexplicably torn, in the laundry last week, which he insisted had ripped because it was old and worn. The bow tie he inexplicably misplaced. As clear as a knife gleaming in the sun before it was plunged into flesh, the knowledge flashed into her mind. He was saving himself with a woman.

Sarah lurched to the sink with the half-empty bowl of oatmeal, overcome with nausea. Was this what jealousy felt like? No, she was not jealous, not even angry. For so long, despair and loneliness had clung to her, layer upon layer of it, until she could almost smell it. What use was she to anyone? Clearly none to Kurt. Not even to Gertie, who had found her way here. Leaning against the counter, she thought she might faint. She felt buried under a mound of earth. Kurt had ventured elsewhere not because he was a bad man but because he did not want to suffocate with her. The one part of her life that had felt solid, her marriage, was suddenly stripped bare. The unspoken pact between her and Kurt to do right by each other, to face the cruelties of the world together, had collapsed.

Sarah filled a glass with water and shuffled back to her chair. At least there was Gertie, strong and ambitious, not like Sarah, who wanted to consume as little space as possible. But Gertie would grow up and go away. And Kurt would leave, of course, if he had found a woman with whom he could forget all that Sarah never could. Without leaving, he had already abandoned her.

She returned to the bedroom, intending to dress, and noticed her pearl necklace on the dresser. The one Kurt had given her on the morning after their wedding night. It was these pearls she had clutched when she refused Jurgen's advance. She grasped them, their gentle paleness now a promise broken. It was the most beautiful gift he had ever given her. She remembered how tenderly he had put them on her, closing the clasp on her nape while they were still in bed that wedding morning. He had smiled, his eyes full of wonder at her body. He had touched the pearls, then dropped his finger to her breast. "So delicate. So lustrous. Pearls for my pearl," he had said, his eyes meeting hers.

She choked at the memory, picked up the necklace and twisted it, pulling until it tore apart. The pearls bounced and scattered on the floor. Tears streaming down her face, she sank into the bed. How fervently she had believed in the sanctity of her marriage that day with Kurt and later when she pleaded with Jurgen. How silly she had been to think she was virtuous in resisting Jurgen's advances. She should have been practical then, like Kurt. If she had been less sanctimonious, she might have saved her parents and her sister. Abasing herself, rather than fleeing Jurgen's office without the tax clearance document, would have been far less destructive than the guilt that had consumed her ever since. She could see now that saving others, saving even oneself, outweighed marriage vows. Of course, Kurt must save himself. Even if it meant saving himself from her. And yet, how could he do it? She cried until she escaped to sleep.

When she awoke, the sun was already high in the sky. Her eyes fell on the oak valet dressing rack on Kurt's side of the bed, a wedding gift from her father. For years, he had carefully planned the next day's attire, putting the cuff links in the dressing-rack drawer, matching the tie with the shirt and suit he planned to wear. He no longer used it, perhaps because he no longer wore jackets to work in Los Alamos's informal environment, or because he had abandoned as futile the habit of planning for the next day. And she? How was she to plan for the next day? And the day after that? There was a bottomless black pit lurking at every turn, waiting for her to fall in. Had it ever not been a part of her? Surely there were times when darkness receded to the edge of her consciousness—when Gertie was young, when caring for her child lightened the darkness. Back then, there was also Kurt's gentle attention and the company of Mama and Papa and Hannah. Sarah's head throbbed. She just wanted to sleep. Forever.

CHAPTER 26
CHRISTINE

May 1944

The doorbell rang as Christine was reading a letter from Samantha, full of good news about the exhibit of Maria's pots, the positive critique in the art-dealer magazine *Gallery*, and a mention in the *New York Times*.

Certain it was Martha coming to gossip, Christine reluctantly turned from the letter, girding herself to be neighborly. But when she opened the door, a short, stocky man filled the entrance, a G-2 agent, judging by the fedora and pointed shoes. Finally, that routine security check for the librarian job. Christine smiled at him, but he did not smile back.

"May I come in, ma'am?" He slipped his foot in the door, leaving no option of closing it.

"And you are?"

"Duncan Edwards. G-2." He lifted his fedora briefly, revealing slicked-back hair.

"Yes, of course. I've been waiting to hear from you."

He smelled of cigars as he slid past her into the living room.

"Please, have a seat."

He didn't sit down.

She sat down on the sofa. "Make yourself comfortable," she said, pointing toward the straight-backed chairs that faced the sofa.

He ignored this too. His eyes swept the room, pointedly stopping to take in the empty whiskey glass on the coffee table. She wanted to explain that the glass was from last night, not this morning. And she'd only had one drink. And nothing stronger than a gin and tonic.

"I'll get right to the point. You have been involved in unauthorized activity." He planted his arms on his hip, as if trying to fill the room with his importance.

"Excuse me?"

His lewd look clued her in that this was not about the job.

"Your tramp-like behavior."

"What are you talking about?"

He picked up the empty whiskey glass, sniffed it, set it back, then glanced at the open book splayed on the coffee table. He picked it up and read the title out loud. "*On Being a Real Person.*" He snorted, then snapped the book shut and turned to her.

She wanted to snatch the book from him.

"Your moral turpitude. It is unauthorized."

"What?"

"Don't think we don't know."

Good God, this was about Kurt.

"Moral turpitude? Since when is G-2 in the morality business? I understood there would be a security check, not a morality check!"

"It is intolerable for Los Alamos residents to participate in disreputable behavior of any kind."

"My personal behavior—and it isn't disreputable—isn't any of your business."

"You are quite wrong about that, ma'am."

Her heart beat furiously. "This is outrageous!"

"Let me repeat myself, it is intolerable for Los Alamos residents to participate in disreputable behavior of any kind."

"I haven't."

"Really?" He cocked his head, his eyes radiating contempt and ridicule.

"Really." She narrowed her eyes at him, trying to appear more self-assured than she felt.

He looked her up and down, as if mentally undressing her.

"Let me be clear. If you do not desist from your treacherous behavior, we will have to make certain facts known to your husband."

She needed to breathe. The curtains in the living room were closed. She rose and flung them to the side, then opened the window. She could feel the man following her with his eyes. There was no one in the yard, no one to witness this humiliation. She turned back from the window. He reminded her of a hunting dog, the kind that picked up the scent of fear and ran with it. The first rule with dogs was not to let them know one was scared.

"Facts." She laughed in his face. "The fact is you don't know the facts."

"The fact is that we have information about you that would certainly not please a husband."

"And sharing any information you think you have would serve what purpose, exactly? National security? The development of the gadget?" She let him see only her anger. "The fact is that you are threatening me, for no good reason and to no good purpose."

"Mrs. Sharp, I suggest you sit down," Edwards said.

"I'm fine," she replied. She wished she had a cigarette even though she didn't smoke.

"Sit," he ordered, pointing her toward the sofa.

She concentrated on appearing unflustered as she obeyed him.

"The security of the project could be compromised if key personnel conduct activities that leave them open to blackmail. Nor can we tolerate destabilizing factors: divorce, marital tension, that sort of thing." Edwards glared at her.

She sat back, taking him in. "Even G-2 cannot control divorce and marital tension."

Edwards smiled smugly, which riled her more, but she kept her voice steady.

"You have matters backwards. The only one threatening blackmail is you. Divorce, marital tension—they're more likely to occur if you reveal behavior best left discreet."

Christine was surprised at her own calm. She would not let them sense how much it terrified her that they would indeed reveal the affair to Thomas. Would they really dare? They were such numbskulls! Couldn't they see that it would do far more harm to the project than good to divulge her infidelity to Thomas? If G-2 knew of Kurt's anxiety, his insomnia, the relief she brought him, they should thank her.

Edwards's eyes narrowed. "Have you no shame at all?"

"None," she retorted. She wanted to tell him there was no shame in love. Certainty balled up inside Christine like a rock, the truth of what she felt for Kurt lodging itself resolutely. What she had with Kurt was good and pure. And it wasn't doing her marriage any harm. "Get out of my house."

Edwards did not budge. Instead, he coughed. "I don't think you understand the complexity of the situation, ma'am."

"Oh?"

"You have applied for the position of research librarian in the Tech Area. Given your moral turpitude, you're not going to get security clearance. People will likely ask questions. We might have to show them your file."

"You're bluffing." Christine's eyes scanned his face, looking for hints that she might be right.

"Don't try us." Edwards glared back. "If you do not wish your behavior revealed, then you must desist completely and immediately. In any case, you will not receive authorization to work as a research librarian. If people ask questions, we will need to explain that it is due to your immoral behavior, which makes you a high security risk. Better to not have such questions raised. I am sure you will figure out a convincing explanation of why you've changed your mind about taking the job. If you withdraw your application for the job, we will not have to reveal your security file. It's as simple as that."

Christine glanced down at her feet. Her head was spinning.

Edwards coughed to draw her attention. "This conversation must remain strictly between us. No one is to know what we have on them in their file. If you reveal any of this conversation to Dr. Koppel or anyone else, we will consider that a further breach of security. Have I made myself clear?"

What could they do to her? To Kurt? To Thomas? What did any of this have to do with security? Or with the gadget? It was all about power. And they had more of it than she did. They always would.

"I'll be on my way, ma'am. No need to show me out."

Molten with anger, Christine barely noticed the click of the door. She would defy G-2. She would not abandon Kurt. But how could she stay with him? If G-2 told Thomas of her affair, he would never understand that she had meant him no harm and still cared for him very much. If they reported the affair to Oppie, Kurt would fall apart. If these G-2 men and their superiors had a modicum of common sense, they would keep her secret.

The doorbell rang again. That G-2 man returning with new threats? She must not let him see how defeated she was. She smoothed her hair. "Come in," she called without rising from the sofa.

Martha poked her head in the doorway, a red turban over her curlers, all smiles. "Hi! Good morning. Just wanted to let you know they had a delivery of eggs at the PX this morning. If you want some, you'd best get over there on the double."

"Thanks for letting me know." The only thing Christine could think of doing with eggs right now was pelting them at the G-2 man and maybe saving one or two to hurl at Martha.

"Is everything okay? Saw you had some company this morning?" Martha's cheery eyes brimmed with curiosity.

"Yes, yes. You know how security is around here. There's always some silly thing G-2 wants to check up on."

"They are a bit creepy, aren't they?" Martha giggled conspiratori- ally. "But heck, I guess it's cause we're all so important here, right? Oh, have you heard? Word is that the men are not coming home for dinner tonight. They have meetings with some brass that showed up unexpect- edly from DC to rake them over the coals."

"I hadn't heard."

Martha stood at the door a moment as if waiting for an invitation to come in.

"You okay?"

"Yes, of course. Just about to do some cleaning."

"Okey dokey." Martha flitted her fingers in a little wave and closed the door behind her.

Christine got a dustcloth, taking out her fury on the particles coat- ing the furniture. She couldn't decide if she was angrier at Edwards's attempts to make her feel like a tramp or at G-2's audacity in denying her a job she could do so well. Thank goodness Thomas wouldn't be home for dinner so she could think matters through. Dust puffs, stirred up by her broad strokes, danced in the sunlight. The dust and sand never went away. They merely redistributed themselves until the next time she took a swipe at them. She looked out at the blue sky. A perfect day to go riding. And why not? A ride might help clear her mind.

She changed into jeans and riding boots. As she buttoned her blouse, she caught sight of herself in the mirror and tried on the label "a woman of moral turpitude." Ridiculous, outrageous, but then why was she trembling?

She slammed the door behind her. The shaking subsided as she walked, but she was still seething. Overhead crows cawed noisily. No matter what Edwards said, she felt neither guilt nor remorse. *Honesta turpitudo est con causa bona.* "Turpitude is honest in a good cause." The phrase popped into her head from some long-forgotten Latin class, part of the requirement for chemistry doctoral students. Someone famous once said that. She couldn't remember whom. Kurt would probably know. He was so erudite. There wasn't a subject she could think of that he didn't know something about. And he was insightful. When she had dared once to ask him what was the main problem holding up the gadget, he did not respond with the usual admonishment about the need for secrecy. He had thought about her question. She could see he struggled with how to answer, even to himself. She had loved how, without giving away anything he shouldn't, he had made her understand for the first time the exasperation that trickled through Los Alamos like a foul-smelling stream no one wanted to acknowledge. "It's as if we've all been rushed to an elaborate kitchen to cater a huge event, but no one is telling us how much food will be delivered for us to cook, or how many people to expect at the event, or whether the event will happen at all." She had felt his relief in being able to express his own frustration in a way that made it concrete. She remembered his grateful gaze. Her love was good for him, for both of them.

She entered the familiar barn, its warm dankness like a bed with a sleeping lover. She passed bales of hay near the entrance to the stall where Oppie stabled Odysseus. But the horse was already being harnessed by someone hidden from view on the other side. All she could see were legs, and then the figure emerged: Jimmy. When he saw her, he backed away as if he wanted to bolt.

"Hi! What are you doing here?" Christine asked.

"I could ask you the same question."

"You're taking Odysseus out?" she asked.

"I'm on duty later tonight. Oppie told me I could ride him whenever I want."

"He's told me the same thing."

"Well then, you take him. He's ready. There are plenty of horses that need exercise."

"You sure you don't mind saddling up another horse?"

Jimmy shrugged, looked to the ground.

"So, you come here often?"

He nodded, his head still down, handed her the reins, and walked out of the stall.

"Do you want to ride together?" she asked. The G-2 man had unsettled her. Jimmy's reassuring presence would help restore her balance.

Jimmy stopped in his tracks, his back to her.

"We don't have to, if you want to be alone," she said.

A horse neighed, and Odysseus stomped a hoof.

"I suppose we could go together," Jimmy said without enthusiasm as he continued to the neighboring stall of a filly.

Christine sensed his reluctance. "Are you sure?"

"Yeah, fine." He shrugged and busied himself with saddling the filly.

"I'll wait for you outside, then." Why was Jimmy so circumspect? Was it because Gertie had broken up with him? She didn't blame Jimmy for the breakup. If anything, she'd fought in his corner when Gertie had reported self-righteously that she'd left him because he held back too much, not only about his work but even more about his feelings, as if he didn't trust her. Gertie was young enough to believe that people who loved one another had to tell each other everything. She had yet to understand that there was intimacy in giving a partner space, that this took greater trust than prying into every nook and cranny of a loved one's mind.

Christine mounted Odysseus and breathed in his malt-like smell. The horse pranced with pent-up energy; she held him on a tight rein and let him walk back and forth in front of the barn, promising him softly that they would soon be on their way. She was feeling better already. Deciding how to handle Edwards's threats would wait until after she rode and cleared her head.

When Jimmy emerged, they made for the perimeter fence.

"I was planning to head towards Española," Jimmy called back to her.

"Sure." Strange that he had not asked her where she might want to go. He was usually so diffident. He seemed more reticent than ever. Maybe he really wasn't right for someone as high-spirited as Gertie. They left the perimeter road and the desert spread out in front of them. The hills looked like open books with curved pages spreading to the horizon. Christine dug her heels into Odysseus, nudging him alongside Jimmy's horse.

"How've you been?" she asked.

"Busy. Working. Licking my wounds over Gertie. Let's gallop." He took off without waiting for an answer.

Odysseus let rip. Christine felt her ponytail flap on her back, her blouse whipped by the wind as she hunkered into the horse's rhythm, squeezing her knees into his flank. Whirls of sky and clouds and sand flung past like paint across a canvas. When the horses were winded, they slowed to a trot.

"God, that felt good." She noticed Jimmy's frown. "Are you okay?"

He seemed annoyed by the question. "Not really."

"You miss Gertie?"

"Yes. You will too."

"Me? What do you mean?" asked Christine. Was Kurt being transferred? Was G-2 going to vent its vengeance on him too? Surely, he would have told her if he was leaving.

The dirt road was wide enough for both horses, so she maneuvered hers alongside Jimmy's. The midday sun soaked the desert in a golden sheen, the mountains clear in the distance.

"What's going on?" Christine asked.

"Gertie broke up with me for not telling her things. In the end, she'll break with you too." Jimmy took a slug of water from his canteen. Christine hadn't thought to bring water. Jimmy didn't offer her any.

"What do you mean?"

He capped the canteen silently. "Never mind. I should keep my trap shut. It's none of my business."

"What?"

"Nothing."

"No, there's something. What's the matter?"

"Never mind. Let's just go on."

"Jimmy, have I done something?"

"How do you live with yourself?" He scowled and looked out beyond the cliff, which overlooked a canopy of trees in young green indicating a watering hole.

Christine felt her stomach drop. She cocked her head.

"Don't act like you don't know what I'm talking about." He still avoided looking at her.

"What?"

"You and Kurt Koppel."

What was happening? Had G-2 deceived her? Were they trying to publicly shame her despite Edwards's promise her affair with Kurt would remain a secret if she ended it? But surely if it was public, she would have heard, and not from Jimmy.

"He said something?"

"No, of course not."

"So . . ."

"I just know." This time he faced her, his eyes daggers of pain and anger.

"How?"

"Does it matter?"

"Have you . . . told anyone?"

"How can you betray your husband? How can you betray Gertie?"

The horses snorted as if they had no patience for human nonsense.

"It has nothing to do with Gertie."

Jimmy looked straight ahead, concentrating on the landscape as if to remove himself from his statements of the facts.

"It does," Jimmy said, looking at her in disgust. "I couldn't handle it. I couldn't face Gertie knowing what I know and not tell her. She thinks she broke up with me, but I raised a fuss about nothing, I got her angry so she'd break up with me."

"You broke up with Gertie because of Kurt and me?"

The rustle of beetles scurrying across the sand was suddenly audible in the silence around them. Christine could feel sand in her mouth, grinding between her teeth, scratching her throat.

"Gertie kept going on and on about how you are her best friend, the only person who is honest and open with her—and accusing me of being secretive and not confiding in her."

This was a consequence Christine had never imagined: that she would be the cause of a rift between Jimmy and Gertie. She found it deeply unsettling that Jimmy had taken such a drastic measure. How could he do that to Gertie? What else had he done?

The squeak of saddle leather and the slapping of stirrups against the horses' flanks syncopated in the vastness of the space around them as the horses picked their way along the trail.

"How long have you known?"

"Too long."

"Did you report me? Kurt?"

"Is that all that matters to you?"

His look of exasperation made her feel she must explain herself. "I don't want to hurt anyone."

"As long as no one knows, there is no hurt, no deception?"

"Deception, yes, certainly. But if no one knows, then there is no hurt."

Jimmy's silence was his condemnation. "Maybe I should have, but I didn't report you."

"Don't you think I'm good for Kurt? You work with him every day. Don't you see that he's been a different man in recent months?"

"He's been terrifically creative and productive recently. Probably more than when we first arrived."

"Don't you realize it's because of me?"

His eyes turned glacial, and he looked back out over the desert. "I have no idea." He shrugged. "And it's no justification."

"If I leave Kurt, it will affect his work, *your* work."

They rode on for a few minutes, until they reached a small oasis of reeds concealing a marsh. They eased the reins to let the horses drink.

"You have an exaggerated sense of your importance," Jimmy said. "Kurt had a world-class reputation, long before this hanky-panky of yours. He may feel sad if you break up—believe me, I know how that feels—but he won't suddenly stop being a brilliant scientist."

Christine tossed her head. She listened to Odysseus slurping water. Kurt had sought her out in desperation, wanted her in a way that thrilled her. Jimmy just didn't understand.

Jimmy patted his horse on the nape.

"Come on, Brownie," he said, pulling the reins, but the horse resisted, eager for more water. He let Brownie have her way and looked up at Christine. "It's just plain wrong, what you're doing. It's that simple," he said.

She tugged at Odysseus. Enough water. They spurred their horses, continuing toward Española.

"So, where you come from, there is no 'hanky-panky,' as you call it?" Christine asked. "Everyone is faithful and loyal?"

"Don't know. I'm from a small town on Cape Cod. I never paid attention to that kind of stuff. But it wasn't Sodom."

"I'm not from Sodom either. Grew up in Maine. Small, provincial, quick to condemn." She wanted him to understand her, not judge her. He had always seemed such a compassionate person.

"All I know is that it's a sin. It's wrong. Not what God intends."

Jimmy saw life as a matter of good and evil. She used to think that way too. But life was so much more complicated than that. "Who's to say what God intends? Does God intend this war? And all the innocents that are killed? Do you really have faith in God's intentions? Or if God is not in control, then why do we care what he intended if he leaves the world to its chaos?" The strain of the morning's encounter suddenly overcame her. "I want to turn back," she said.

She pulled her horse around, and Jimmy followed. Sensing they were headed home, the horses kept up a fast clip. The clouds trailed across the sky, seeming to accompany them. They stopped for a drink. This time, Jimmy handed her the canteen. Their disagreement lay between them.

"Whatever you think about God, it's still wrong. Shouldn't you be thinking about your husband? What about Kurt's wife? And Gertie?"

"Kurt's a wonderful man. I don't have to explain that to you. There's nothing wrong with Thomas. Or with Sarah Koppel. It's not about them." She handed back his canteen.

"Think of all the lives you are going to ruin. Including yours." He capped the canteen and fastened it on his belt and did not wait for her response.

As they urged the horses toward the stables, Christine tried not to think of what a mess her life was. Or all she would have to do to fix it.

CHAPTER 27
GERTIE

June 1944

"I thought a dog might make a good companion now that the school year is about to end," Papa said to Gertie at breakfast. "I've asked Jimmy to find a kennel and drive us there on Sunday." He smiled, clearly pleased with himself, and watched for her reaction as he sipped his tea. As usual, it was just the two of them, Mama still in bed.

Could he tell from her face that she was not only surprised but also puzzled? Despite her pleas for a dog, from as far back as she could remember, her parents had never agreed to a pet. But Papa had been unpredictable lately, remote and gruffer than usual, and then suddenly indulgent. Typical of him not to notice that she hadn't seen Jimmy for weeks.

"A dog? That's great. But why go with Jimmy?"

"Why not? You are fond of him, yes? And someone must drive us. He will borrow a car."

"I'm not seeing Jimmy anymore."

"What happened?" Papa set down his teacup and gave her his full attention.

"Nothing."

"If it was nothing, you would still be with him, no?"

"Well, I'm not." She cracked the top of the soft-boiled egg with a spoon and picked off the smashed shell bits to create a hole. "Why don't I ask Christine if she and Thomas can take us? I'm sure they can find a car to borrow. Instead of Jimmy. We could make a nice day of it."

"No!" Her father banged his fist on the table, then grabbed it with his other hand as if he was trying to control his initial anger.

What was wrong with him? It was just a suggestion. He always had to have things his way. Did she even want a dog anymore? In another year she'd be off to college. Still, a puppy would be fun.

He rose and picked up his dishes. His hands trembled as he took them to the sink. He usually left it to her to clear the table. He hadn't even finished his toast. What was it with him? All nerves and as impossible as ever.

He sat down again, dabbed his forehead with a handkerchief, straightened his bow tie as if to collect himself, and reached for her hand. "What happened with Jimmy?"

She fought back tears. Papa really did care, which was sweet. But she didn't want to tell him. In fact, she wasn't sure she could explain it herself. "Nothing you would understand."

"He is a proper gentleman, yes?"

Gertie rolled her eyes. If only he knew how rarely Jimmy even kissed her. "It's not what you think."

"So, what is it?"

"He got angry at me."

"Really? He is usually so even tempered."

Papa was right—Jimmy was rarely riled. And he was also kind and attentive, and funny sometimes. But what was the point when he clammed up so often? Was it unreasonable of her to want to go for a romantic walk along the perimeter fence after a movie at Fuller Lodge? He had reacted abruptly, insisting he didn't want to go for a walk. When she asked why, he had flown into a rage. He was tired of her prying, of her attempts to make him talk about topics she knew perfectly well were barred. She regretted now having walked away in a huff. But truly, didn't a girl have the right to want her boyfriend to confide in her? And why should she feel guilty for wanting to take a walk, maybe stopping to smooch?

She popped a spoonful of soft-boiled egg into her mouth, looked up, and met Papa's stare.

"I thought you don't like dogs," Gertie said.

"And I thought you liked them very much. At first, I planned to surprise you, so I asked Jimmy to go with me to pick one out. But he said you'd be more attached to a dog you chose yourself and offered to drive us both to see some."

So, this was Jimmy's doing, the idea of riding all together to the kennel. Maybe he missed her and wanted to get back together. She hoped so, even though it was she who had broken up with him. His goodness was like a smell that she wanted to inhale for the rest of her life. She missed his earnestness and the way he made her feel brave and daring and interesting. But too often he would begin to talk and suddenly go silent. She'd only go steady with him again if he was ready to share with her all that was in his heart and mind. She wanted to experience the world with him, to share all her impressions, to know what he was thinking every day, forever. Wasn't that what love was about? Not just caring, which he clearly did. But also sharing?

Now, about this trip on Sunday to find a dog: What should she wear?

Gertie was looking out the window when Jimmy pulled up in front of the house in a dust-encrusted green sedan. Her heart leaped when she caught sight of that curly black hair she loved running her fingers through. When he emerged from the car, her stomach remembered with a jolt his sturdy chest, the way she'd leaned into it so comfortably. His pale-blue T-shirt was the color of his eyes. She imagined his exposed muscled arms curled around her. He stood by the car as if weighing whether to come to the door or wait for her and Papa. He saw her in the window, smiled, and waved. What could she do but wave back?

"He's here," she called to Papa.

"Shhh," Papa said, emerging from the bedroom in an open-necked plaid shirt. No bow tie today. "Mama's still sleeping."

Papa led the way out, and Jimmy busied himself with opening the front car door for him, leaving Gertie to enter the back seat on her own.

"So kind of you to do this on your day off," Papa said.

"Glad to help out," Jimmy answered, smiling at Papa and continuing to ignore her as he settled into the driver's seat.

Was she just some charity case? Maybe he'd only thought of her as some poor thing who needed help with math, and horseback riding, and skiing—all those things he knew how to do. He was just being kind because he admired Papa, as if Papa were God. She wanted to get out of the car right now, burrow in her bed, and forget about Jimmy. But they were already driving away.

"You all set back there?" Her eyes met Jimmy's in the rearview mirror. His fluttered away, then skittered back to her, as if he was trying to gauge her mood.

"Yes, I'm fine," she said, setting her floppy hat on the back seat and looking out the window in order not to return his glance.

They drove past the water tower at the center of the base, skirted a baseball field where a game was in full swing. In an empty lot between units, a group of children weeded and watered victory gardens. Jimmy waved at small clusters of his dorm mates, dressed up and walking to or from Fuller Lodge, where there were church services on Sunday mornings. Families, too, headed back and forth. Jimmy had explained to her how the Catholics went first and then the Protestants.

"I hope our little outing didn't take you away from church today," Papa said to Jimmy.

"No, I don't go. I figure God can't help us much with what we need. Groves can if he would get his other boys to move faster."

Gertie's ears picked up. Groves was the general in Washington, DC, in charge of everything at Los Alamos. He was even Oppie's boss.

"So there's none left?" Papa asked Jimmy.

"None since Thursday. We can keep calculating, but that's not good enough at this point. Nothing to do until we get a new shipment."

"A shipment of what?" Gertie asked.

Papa looked back at her. "Nothing."

Of course they wouldn't tell her. If she had kept quiet, maybe they would have continued talking. Making oneself invisible seemed the only way to find out things around here.

"Why don't you two just leave me at the gate," Gertie said. "Go on without me."

"Why?" Papa asked.

"I don't feel well."

"You seemed fine this morning."

"Gertie, we won't talk about things we can't talk to you about, I promise," Jimmy said, continuing to drive to the gate. "It's beautiful out, Ed and Martha have let me use their car for the whole day. Let's make the most of it. It's been so long since I've driven a car. How long since you rode out of here in one?"

He understood exactly what bothered her. And annoyingly, his diversionary tactic was working. She found herself calculating when she had last been outside Los Alamos. Probably three months ago to go skiing. With him. By the time they approached the gate and halted before the military guards, she was glad she hadn't let her initial annoyance get the better of her. As the guards finished inspecting their passes and the back of the station wagon before waving them out, she found herself looking forward to the trip. And indeed, when they drove off, it seemed like a heavy blanket had lifted off them.

"So where are you taking us, young man?" Papa asked jovially.

"I heard about a farmer about thirty miles from here who raises dogs."

They were descending the mesa, past peaks that cast shadows on the crater floor. The intensity of Los Alamos receded with every mile, and Gertie felt her spirits rise.

Jimmy switched on the radio, and they listened to a saxophone whining the recent hit "My Heart Tells Me (Should I Believe My Heart?)" and Eugenie Baird's sinewy voice singing of her fear that her beloved does not love her.

Then came the ten o'clock news:

"Masses of Allied air- and seaborne troops have landed on the coast of France and have been fighting their way inland across a hundred-mile stretch between Cherbourg and Le Havre, in the long-awaited invasion of Hitler's Europe. The Allied High Command disclosed that more than one thousand troop-carrying aircraft, including gliders, have been taking part in the gigantic operation in what was termed 'an unexpected success.' Two US cruisers and the battleship Nevada *shelled German defenses in support of the landings."*

"It sounds like that big invasion military analysts have been predicting for weeks is finally happening," Jimmy remarked.

"Victory in Italy, Allied advances all over the place, and still the war goes on. Do you think we're ever going to leave Los Alamos?" Gertie asked. "Will this war ever end?"

Papa threw her a horrified look. "You must not speak that way; the war will be over soon, especially now with this invasion."

"What do you think, Jimmy?" Gertie pressed.

He switched off the radio.

"Haven't a clue. I'd guess more than a year but less than five."

"Five years? I'll practically be out of college by then."

"Really, dear, you must not think about these things," Papa interjected.

"I like to think about the future. What may happen and what the world will be like. I've started reading science fiction. It's fun."

"I used to read it, too, when I had more time. *Frankenstein*. And *Twenty Thousand Leagues Under the Sea*. What are you reading?" Jimmy asked.

Was he really interested, or was he just trying to make conversation?

"A really great book, by H. G. Wells, written a long time ago. Christine gave it to me a few weeks ago. *The World Set Free*. It's hard, and there are parts I have to read twice to understand. Do you know it?"

"No," said Jimmy. "What's it about?"

"Christine gave it to you?" Papa said, shaking his head disapprovingly. "If I thought you should read it, *I* would have given it to you."

"So you've read it?" asked Gertie.

"Yes, of course, years ago, when I was at university." He seemed annoyed. She was tired of his grumpiness.

"You'd really like it," she said to Jimmy.

"Why's that?"

"It talks about how humanity developed; how there was steam around for many years before anyone thought to make a steam engine, and how there was electricity—like lightning storms—around forever before anyone thought electricity could run things. Then it talks about the future, how there are atoms that have been always around, but one day scientists will know how to make them disintegrate and explode and create limitless power that will change the world—forever!"

Jimmy took his eyes off the road and looked at Papa askance. "You said you know this book?" The car swerved almost out of control.

"Yes, yes," said Papa, his hand stretched out to buttress himself against the sudden movement.

"Sorry. You okay?" Jimmy asked.

Papa straightened himself and nodded. "So what were we talking about? Oh yes, that book. It's science fiction. Wishful thinking, really. There's a terrible war using this power, and it is so terrible that the nations of the world set up an international government that rules the use of atomic power, and everyone's lives are better than they ever imagined they could be. As I said, science fiction." Papa shrugged.

"But it's a great book!" said Gertie. "And isn't it amazing that Wells predicted the war so many years ago? He even said it would be against Germany!"

"He did?" Jimmy seemed impressed.

Gertie felt encouraged to press on. "Christine gave me the book for a reason, didn't she? It's got something to do with what you all are doing here, right? The gadget, no?"

Papa was shaking his head, his eyebrows raising and lowering, looking out the window. He seemed exasperated. He muttered under his breath in German.

"Remember, we weren't going to talk about such things," Jimmy said but kept glancing at Kurt, who continued looking out the window and mumbling.

"Aha! So I'm right. Christine's right. It does have to do with your work. She's smart to have figured it out!"

"I know she's your friend, Gertie. But she's a troublemaker," Jimmy said.

"I thought you liked her. She always says nice things about you."

"She doesn't understand limits. Don't be like her."

Gertie had never heard Jimmy sound so stern.

Papa, his hands on his lap, kept pounding a fist into his open hand, like a baseball pitcher pounding a ball, and murmuring, "*Wie konnte sie das tun?*"

"Papa, are you okay?"

Jimmy glanced at Papa, who ignored him as if in another world.

"What's he saying?" Jimmy asked, catching Gertie's eye in the backview mirror.

"He keeps saying, 'Why did she do that, what was she thinking?'"

Jimmy nodded and pursed his lips. They sat in uncomfortable silence as the car drove past the undulating flat desert, rolling to the horizon in shades of beige and copper red. As they passed huge cacti, their ugly, bulbous yellow flowers in full bloom, Gertie wished everyone would stop acting so strangely and hoped she hadn't gotten Christine into trouble somehow.

"Look at the cloud over there," Jimmy called out, pointing to some wispy clouds in the distance. "When I was a kid, we always made up what the clouds looked like on family outings—that one looks like the cloak of a magician, don't you think?"

Papa looked at the sky where Jimmy pointed, as if coming back from a trance.

"And we always sang songs."

Jimmy was so obviously trying to lighten things up. The least she could do was help him.

"What songs?" Gertie asked.

"'Home on the Range,' 'Oh! Susanna.'"

"Don't know them," Gertie said.

"Really? Then I'll teach you."

They all seemed eager to dispel the heaviness that had settled into the car. Papa and Gertie agreed that "Home on the Range" was a lovely song, but neither saw the point of "Oh! Susanna."

"You are lucky to enjoy silly things," said Papa.

"It's actually a love song," said Jimmy.

"All the more reason for it to make no sense, no?" said Papa as a sign for the kennel came into view.

CHAPTER 28
JIMMY

June 1944

Jimmy turned into Taylor's Top-Breed Mutts. From the oxymoronic sign he wagered they'd probably find more mutts than top breeds. He rounded the dirt driveway to the ranch-style home, its color the same bland beige as the yard, littered with car parts, washing machine cranks, and rusty lawn mowers. Jimmy tooted the horn, which brought out a bald farmer. The screen door banged behind him. The laces of his black army-style boots were untied and snapped like nervous garter snakes around his feet as he walked toward them.

"Jake Taylor," he said, extending a rough hand to each of them as they emerged from the car. "What can I do you for?"

"We're looking for a dachshund," said Kurt.

Where did that come from? Kurt had not mentioned wanting a dachshund. His boss was full of surprises, on matters big but also small.

Taylor laughed. "Not much demand for them around these parts. They don't do well in winter snow with those little legs. You'll be wanting a bigger dog, I should think." They trudged behind him to the kennels in the back.

Gertie headed straight for a cage where a German shepherd was suckling three puppies.

"Please, Gertie, not that kind of dog," said Kurt.

"Why not?"

"They are guard dogs, police dogs," Kurt said.

"Oh, Papa. You and Mama are always thinking of over there. Here normal people have German shepherds."

"It will upset your mother."

How odd that Kurt should worry about upsetting his wife over a German shepherd when he had acted in ways that would have concerned her so much more, if she knew. When Jimmy discovered the boss he idolized could stray so completely, his world fell apart. For weeks, he hadn't been able to look Kurt straight in the eyes. But after a while, Kurt had seemed so despondent. Jimmy figured that either Christine had broken up with him or Sarah had found out, or both. When Kurt asked him a week ago whether dogs made good companions, saying he was thinking of getting a puppy for Gertie, Jimmy wondered if his boss was trying to fill a hole in his own life, one left perhaps by Christine. Jimmy knew about such holes; he missed Gertie more than he had expected.

Gertie meandered among the cages, looking at the various alternatives. "How big do those grow to be?" she asked, pointing to a cage of medium-size dogs.

"They're mixtures of cocker spaniel and Labrador," said Taylor. "They'll be smaller than a German shepherd, but they won't be so small you'll be trippin' over them as you would a terrier."

Gertie entered the kennel, sat on the straw-strewn ground, and reached out toward a puppy, who dropped the sock it was chewing to sniff her with interest. She gingerly picked up the soft ball of fur, which wiggled in her arms as she laughed, hugging and nuzzling it.

Jimmy had forgotten what a hearty laugh she had. Would she have him back? From the drive this morning, it seemed there was a chance. When he found himself aroused by Owen, he forced himself to conjure up Gertie's smiling eyes, the sun glistening off her dark hair, and her seductively glossy lips. Maybe it was the strain of the work or the radioactivity of the materials they were testing that stirred up those strange urges, that mixed Owen with Gertie and Gertie with Owen. Who knew what effects being around all that radioactive material might have? Maybe that was what had affected Kurt too. All those poisonous materials, bending his mind, twisting everyone's minds. After the war, these aberrations would end, he told himself. Things would be normal.

"We'll take him," Gertie said, emerging from the cage, the puppy in her arms.

"You don't want to look around some more?" Kurt asked.

"When I see what I like, I know it."

So like Gertie to be decisive.

"I'll call him Buddy."

"That's a silly name," said Kurt.

"Papa, it's okay for a dog to have a silly name."

"What do you think, Jimmy?" Kurt asked.

The last thing Jimmy wanted was to take sides.

"Well, first of all, I think the pup's a she, not a he."

Gertie looked down at the pup. "Hmm, I hadn't thought about that."

"What about Susanna?" Jimmy suggested.

"Like the love song, the one you taught us." Gertie looked down at the dog. "Do you want to be Susanna?" She nuzzled the dog's stomach with her nose.

"It will remind us of this lovely day," said Kurt.

"Susanna it is," said Gertie.

Taylor and Kurt headed toward the barn so that Kurt could pay for the dog and be briefed on its care. While waiting for them to return, Jimmy watched Gertie cuddle the dog.

"We're going to be great friends, Susanna, aren't we?" Gertie said to the pup as it squiggled out of her arms. Jimmy watched her twirl the sock above the puppy's head. Susanna leaped for it, yelping with excitement.

Jimmy suddenly knew that he wanted to watch Gertie all his life. Watch her play, watch her laugh. In a few years, she'd be a woman but still her spunky self. He could imagine figuring out life together, facing whatever fate served up with her at his side.

"I've missed you, Gertie," he blurted out.

Gertie looked up from the dog. "Me too."

"So?"

"So? What? Is anything going to be different?" Gertie asked.

"Maybe."

Gertie fussed over Susanna. She stood up and looked at him.

"Here, hold her." She handed the puppy to Jimmy.

Susanna licked his face. Gertie brought the leash that had been hooked onto the cage, clipped it to the pup's collar, and put Susanna on the ground.

"Well, *she* seems to think I'm okay," Jimmy said, trying to sound lighthearted.

Gertie stood and faced him. "I think you're okay, too, Jimmy. Much more than okay. But I need to know, will there be no secrets between us?"

"I can't promise there won't be any secrets. But fewer secrets. I think I can promise that."

"Good," she said. She brushed up against him, her breasts soft, alive, like the pair of guinea pigs he had once had as a child and was leery of touching, put off by their raw paws on his hand, afraid they might bite him. Her breasts were not guinea pigs; it wouldn't hurt to touch them. He stilled the desire to pull back his hand, forced himself to stroke a breast lightly, once. It moved but only slightly, less than a guinea pig. She murmured in ripe willingness and wriggled closer. He dropped his hand. She lifted her face for him to kiss. Love was all about attention. He was terrified that he couldn't give her what she deserved. He pulled back and coughed.

"Your father will be back any moment now."

"He wants us to be together."

He raked her hair from her forehead. "But he wouldn't want me to take advantage."

He stooped down to Susanna, who had been yapping at their feet, and petted her.

"Why do you think Papa suddenly decided I could get a dog?"

Jimmy shrugged, but he had some idea. If Kurt's affair with Christine was over, which was likely, judging by his mood recently, he might be looking for an excuse to go for long walks to reminisce. Or maybe he was looking for some new object on which to foist his emotions. Jimmy tried to dispel those thoughts and concentrate on Gertie, who was running her fingers through the dog's fur the same way she used to comb them through his hair. He had forgotten how physical she was and how uncomfortable that felt. He would have to get used to it again if they were back together. But he loved how she smelled of the sun and sweat and lollipops, how he had missed her sweetness.

"I've wanted a dog for such a long time, but Papa's always been so against the idea, I stopped asking. Strange that he's suddenly changed his mind."

"Indeed," said Jimmy. He hated having to admit to himself that by his reticence he was already breaking his promise to be less secretive.

CHAPTER 29
SARAH

July 1944

Sarah clattered the dishes into the sink, annoyed at Susanna's doleful stare. She was incensed that Kurt had bought the dog without so much as asking her. In the past, they had agreed that a dog would be too much trouble and make a mess. And then, out of the blue, a month ago, he'd come home with a dog, a fait accompli. It made her want to kick him, or Susanna, or the world, or all three.

Instead, she reached for the cookie jar, took out a gingersnap, and bit into it hard. The cookie was underdone, doughy; it stuck to her teeth. She still could never tell how long to bake anything here. A Black Beauty, Dorothy had called the oven, praising this purportedly wonderful feature of their home when they first arrived. In fact, its heat was inconsistent. This, in addition to the havoc that the high altitude played on recipes, turned her baking, which had once been a source of joy and pride, into an uncertain and often failed undertaking.

She munched the too-soft cookie so as not to waste it. If Kurt bought the dog for Gertie, why did he not insist the child take care of the pet? How would Gertie learn discipline and responsibility if Kurt was the one who fed Susanna and took her for walks whenever he was home?

"You spend more time with the dog than with me," she said when he crawled into bed at midnight after a long walk with the dog.

"She is affectionate," he replied.

Even in her half-sleep stupor, she sensed the condemnation in his tone. But drowsy from a sleeping pill, she had drifted off before she could summon a response. Now in the light of day, she was needled by the despair in his voice. Why the need of affection from a dog? Months ago, she had suspected a mistress. But now it hit her. No mistress. A wife so unaffectionate that he had gotten a dog? This was far more insulting than philandering. And yet, was he wrong? When had she last kissed him, taken his hand? When had he last taken hers? Although she had never known passion, there had been years of companionability, a meeting of each other's expectations. She did not know when or how, but America had drained them of each other.

Sarah sat down hard, swaying back and forth in the chair. The glass bottle of sleeping pills jingled in her dressing gown. What was she to anyone? She took out the bottle and eyed it. Her hand quaking, she took out a pill and dropped it into her coffee, stirring thoroughly. The pill made the coffee bitter. She gagged, then forced herself to gulp it down. Drowsiness made her forget, helped her to stop thinking.

She closed her eyes and remembered her sister, Hannah, playing a Chopin nocturne. Los Alamos was an arid cage, entrapping and protecting her; she was wasting away, looking at the beautiful views while losing, day by day, everything dear. The Chopin piece rose in her mind. She tried to suppress the melody and yet longed to hear it. Evidence of Hitler's murder of Jews was emerging with ever-greater frequency. More than a year ago there had been reports in all the newspapers of hundreds of thousands deported to an extermination camp after an uprising in the Warsaw Ghetto. The latest headlines were that all the Jews of Budapest had been forced into a ghetto, their homes pillaged, their possessions taken. As a child, she had spent an enchanted week in

Budapest with her parents and Hannah. They had walked by its rivers, visited distant cousins her age and aunts and uncles, whom she had never met before. Now all those with whom she had enjoyed that week were most likely dead. Although there were reports of Allied advances, who knew if it was just propaganda? Hitler seemed invincible. Just this week, he had squashed a military coup by the Wehrmacht. Kurt argued that the officers rebelled because Hitler was losing. Whether Germany lost or won, there was no one for them to go back to, as far as she knew. And after all the hate that had surfaced in Germany from under that veneer of culture and civilization she had so loved, she could not imagine returning there. But unlike her, Kurt did not seem to mind that they would live forever in the unbearable cheerfulness of America.

Gertie, too, was lost to her, rarely home. In no time, she would leave for college. Gertie was bright, ambitious, and, above all, fearless. She was made for America. She was being formed by America. She no longer belonged to Sarah, if she ever had.

Sarah went to the living room, dug out a recording of the nocturne, turned on the phonograph, closed her eyes, and let its cosmic yearning suffuse her. Hannah used to play the piece often. Sarah hadn't thought of it as melancholy, only beautiful. But now its sadness overwhelmed her. She longed for the smell of the chamomile that Hannah put on her hair to lighten it, for the touch of her mother's hand on her brow, for the clove-scented tobacco curling out of her father's pipe from behind his newspaper.

What was left for her now? Jovial people enervated her. They seemed like martians from another planet emitting a poison that weakened her slowly. Or more accurately, she was the martian, stranded on a strange planet. She envied those already dead, who no longer faced the grueling effort of living. No one to chide them to try harder, to endure, to change. She pulled the pills from her housecoat, took out two, gulped them down, and put the bottle back in her pocket.

Sarah wrapped her housecoat around her, suddenly cold despite the heat seeping into the house with the advancing day. She longed for the dark of the bedroom, with its drawn curtains and soft bed. She lifted the needle from the record. She ought to put it away before it collected dust. She should water the plants. They were wilting from neglect. Instead, she shuffled toward the bedroom and lay down. The pill bottle dug into her hip, so she pulled it out and set it on the night table. Ending this existence was the only thought that did not exhaust her.

CHAPTER 30
CHRISTINE

July 1944

Christine was deep into an archeology book, *Indians of the Rio Grande Valley*, which she had recently managed to obtain through her new contacts at Santa Fe's Museum of New Mexico, when Gertie bounded up the stairs, screaming.

"You have to come. It's Mama!"

"What happened?"

"She won't wake up! I can't get her to wake up!"

Christine rushed down, and they dashed across the yard, Gertie sobbing. Some boys playing stickball in the yard stopped to stare. Hand in hand, Christine and Gertie raced along the road, which was oddly empty. No jeep or car to flag down, just the dusty road shimmering ahead in the heat. Martha walked toward them from the distance, weighed down with grocery bags. Her smile froze when she registered Christine's grim expression and Gertie's cheeks, streaked with tears crusting dry from the heat.

"What's the matter?" Martha asked.

"We don't know," blubbered Gertie. "Mama, she's . . ."

"Apparently unconscious." Christine completed the sentence. "Please let them know at the clinic. Get them to send an ambulance to the Koppels'."

"Oh my! I'll go right away." She bustled past them, the grocery bags slapping at her legs.

"Kurt needs to be told," Christine called to Martha.

"Of course," she answered.

As they continued at a trot toward the Koppels', Christine tried to think of something reassuring to say, but only clichés came to mind. She had no idea how to handle this emergency. Best to keep silent. She pressed Gertie's hand as reassurance.

They bolted through the front door, and Susanna yapped at their feet, almost tripping Christine as they lurched into the bedroom. The brocade curtains were drawn shut. Their eyes needed time to adjust to the dark. The smell of Kurt's pipe, mixed with that of a woman's cloying perfume, infused the airless room. Gertie flicked on the night table light as Christine approached the bed. Sarah lay on her back, dressed in a blue-and-white-checkered housedress, the bedsheet twisted around her lower body. Her face showed no sign of pain. Christine sat on the bed and bent down, relieved to hear Sarah's heart and see her chest move.

"She's breathing," Christine declared.

Gertie tried to shake her mother. "Mama, wake up! Wake up!"

But nothing happened.

"Let's try cold water. Go get a cloth to wash her face," Christine said.

While Gertie fetched the water, trailed by the puppy, Christine scanned the room, uncertain what she was looking for. She spied a pill bottle on the night table, picked it up, and read the label: Nembutal. The bottle was empty. She put the bottle back, then turned to Sarah, who looked peaceful, even though her hair, usually in a bun, was spread across the pillow. When awake, Sarah was so unassuming that Christine had never noticed the well-proportioned features, the pert nose that lifted at the tip like a child's, and the plush mouth, now half-open, as if about to ask a question. She could easily imagine that Sarah inspired a desire in men to protect her and how that might have once attracted Kurt. Until now, Christine had thought of Sarah as a washed-out canvas, but stroking Sarah's forehead and tidying her dark-blonde hair, she felt a surge of compassion, a sense that this was a woman whose innocence had been violated. Sarah reminded her of the simple milkmaid in a Vermeer painting overlayed with Picasso's *Guernica*. That was the way of this world. It wasn't Christine's fault, or Kurt's, or anyone's. Surely the affair had nothing to do with this. After all, it had been over for more than two months. No reason to think Sarah had suspected anything. Still, as she pulled up the blanket to cover Sarah's arms and shoulders, her eyes swept the room, scanning for a suicide note.

Gertie returned and opened the curtains, then knelt by the bed with a tin bowl to wash her mother's face. But Sarah didn't stir. The dog settled in a corner, her eyes gloomy, and whimpered.

"We better get some things together," Christine said. "Where does your mother keep her undies and nighties?"

Gertie pointed to the dark wood dresser topped with framed pictures.

Christine rummaged through the drawers. The first held Kurt's underwear, meticulously ironed, folded, and stacked in neat rows. She slammed it shut, surprised at how intrusive it felt to view them. The second drawer was full of Sarah's underwear, equally tidy. She extracted two pairs of sturdy white cotton underpants. In the bottom drawer she found Sarah's nighties, sorted by season: flannel in one pile, cotton in another. From the summer pile, Christine pulled out a modest pink cotton affair, embroidered with tiny roses. Closing the drawer, she glanced at the photos on the dresser top. There was the requisite wedding picture: Kurt when he still had hair—brown but already thinning—and a trim beard. He was younger than she was now, an earnest distant look in his ever-alert eyes and in Sarah's placid ones. A sweet couple. She wanted to linger on the other photos, no doubt of the family in Germany, but instead told Gertie to get her mother's toothbrush and slippers. Meanwhile, Christine returned to the bedside to wash down Sarah's arms, pale and flaccid as tapioca pudding.

When the ambulance drove up, Gertie met the two attendants. She was remarkably calm as she led them to the bedroom.

"What do we have here?" asked one of them, a large-built man with quick, sure movements that inspired confidence. He felt Sarah's pulse and wrapped a blood pressure sleeve around her arm.

"I found this." Christine showed him the bottle of Nembutal.

He read the label. "That'll do it," he said ruefully, shaking his head. He held the dark bottle to the light and jiggled it, confirming it was empty. "Any idea how full it was before?"

Christine and Gertie shook their heads.

"What will it do?" Gertie asked.

The attendant gazed at Gertie as if he had just registered how young she was. He stumbled over an answer. "Um, well, it sort of . . . I mean it does . . . it puts you in a deep sleep," he said, busying himself with shifting Sarah onto the gurney, helped by his partner. When the men loaded Sarah into the vehicle, Christine tried to put an arm around Gertie's shoulder, but Gertie pushed it off and moved away, as if she had to face this alone, unprotected.

Outside, the attendant clicked shut the back door of the ambulance. "We'll meet you at the clinic. The nurse there will deal with the paperwork."

"I don't have a car," Christine said.

"No room in the ambulance. You'll have to walk, but it's not far. We'll get her settled. Who's the husband?"

"Kurt Koppel. Works in the Tech Area," Christine said.

The attendant wrote the name down on a clipboard. "The clinic will notify him." He headed for the driver's seat.

The ambulance zoomed off, lights flashing. Christine and Gertie followed the vehicle on foot.

"Will Mama be okay?"

Christine's throat was dry. The unrelenting sun still throbbed. So now, too, did Christine's head.

"Probably. Yes. Because you found her."

They rushed by a building site where dozens of workers were hammering dry boards into place and continued past bulldozers clearing land for more housing units. Two jeeps roared past, ignoring Christine's attempt to flag them down, leaving them coughing, their eyes tearing in a cloud of dust.

"She was trying to kill herself, wasn't she? That's why people take a bottleful of pills, isn't it?" Gertie choked as she spoke, still trying to clear the dust from her throat.

"Shouldn't be more than ten minutes to the clinic," Christine said, staring down the road at the jeeps disappearing in the distance.

"She wanted to be dead, didn't she?" Gertie persisted.

How could she answer Gertie's questions? They needed to move faster. Christine took off at a sprint. Gertie followed after her. Hawks cawed overhead as if urging them on their way.

The clinic, now ahead, was as unremarkable as all the other buildings on the Hill, a one-floor unpainted concrete block set in a dirt lot. A few cars were parked in front, and the ambulance stood at the side door by a ramp to the building.

They dashed past a plaque that read No APPOINTMENT NECESSARY and were immediately hit by a blast of cool air as they entered the clinic. Christine hadn't been in an air-conditioned place since going to the movies in New York City. Her head was swirling with thoughts of how to help Gertie and what to do next, but, God, that cold air felt good.

A nurse sat beside a radio at the reception desk, taking notes. The news announcer was reporting the latest changes in ration coupons.

"Excuse me," Christine said.

The nurse looked up at them, distracted. She nodded but turned back to the broadcast. The pin on her lapel indicated she was an army corps nurse.

"Please, it's important!" Christine interrupted.

The nurse sighed and lowered the volume on the radio.

"We're here about Sarah Koppel, the woman the ambulance just brought in. This is her daughter," Christine indicated Gertie. "And I believe her husband is on his way."

"And you are?" the nurse asked.

"She's my friend," piped up Gertie. The nurse, peering through grim wire-rimmed glasses that seemed more suitable for an older woman, looked from one to the other, seemingly unconvinced by their age difference.

"A family friend," Christine explained.

This seemed to quell the receptionist's skepticism, and she directed them to the empty waiting area, offered to bring them water, then turned the radio volume up just as the newscaster announced a new war-bond issue.

As they sat on the straight-backed chairs in the waiting area, Christine took Gertie's hand. To avoid talking, Christine closed her eyes, trying to calm herself by listening to the barely audible radio announcer. But it didn't help.

"Mama was trying to kill herself, wasn't she?" Gertie asked again.

Christine kept her eyes closed. How was she supposed to know Sarah's pain? She didn't want to consider whether she may have played a part in any overdose.

"Don't do this to me, Christine. Don't try to protect me. You're the one person who levels with me."

It was as if Gertie had punched her in the stomach. How long could she hope Gertie would trust their relationship?

"I need to know. I need to understand," Gertie said.

The poor kid. She hadn't a clue how much worse knowing would be.

"I don't know your mother well, so I can't say. She may have made a mistake and taken one pill too many, just to sleep better."

"You don't believe that. You're just trying to make me feel better. But it makes me feel worse. You are treating me like a child." Gertie burst into tears.

"Gertie, please calm down."

What could she tell Gertie? Why didn't the receptionist bring the promised water? And where the heck was Kurt?

"Level with me. Someone must. If you won't, no one will." Gertie was sobbing.

"I don't know what your mother did or why. That's the truth. But it is also true that if someone takes an overdose—if that's what happened—it's because they are very unhappy. They may want to die. Or they may just want someone to find them before they do, like you did."

"I know Mama's unhappy."

"It's hard to know what goes on in a person's head."

"The family in Europe. That's what goes on in *her* head. It makes her crazy, not knowing what's happened to everyone. She only talks about it some of the time, but I know she thinks about them all the time. But killing herself? How would that help them? How can she do that? Don't I matter to her?"

"Of course, you matter."

"I know I'm not good all the time. But I try. I really do."

"I'm sure you do." Christine took Gertie's hand. "I'm sure it has nothing to do with you. Like you said, what's happening in Europe is horrendous, and not knowing the fate of relatives—that could drive a person mad." Christine turned to Gertie and wiped away the tears with her free hand, sorry she had no handkerchief. "Your Mama needs you to be brave."

Gertie took a deep breath and nodded somberly; she'd try.

The receptionist-nurse came with water, glancing at Gertie's tear-streaked face as she handed them the glasses. Christine tried to glean from the nurse's face some inkling of Sarah's state, but the woman was carefully neutral.

"What's happening with my mama?" Gertie asked.

"I'm not sure, dear. We'll tell you as soon as we know something," she said.

Christine and Gertie gulped down the room temperature water.

"It's my fault, isn't it? I'm cheeky to her, a lot. She hates that," Gertie said.

Christine held up Gertie's face to meet her eyes. "Listen to me. You mustn't think that. Ever. I don't know why your mother did what she did. We don't even know exactly what she did. But you were the person who found her. You got help. And if she's sad, it's not because of you. Believe me."

Christine let go of Gertie, sat back, and closed her eyes again. When would Kurt get here? One look at him and she would know if he had confessed to Sarah. A useless, stupid thing to do, if he had. Coming clean to expunge the past was an illusion, a cop-out. She had herself considered the possibility of confessing to Thomas but decided against it. It took greater courage to carry alone the burden of past actions—and move on. The G-2's pressure to end the relationship with Kurt had made her reconsider what she would lose if the affair became public. She would be bereft without Thomas. Kurt had made her feel admired and vital in a way she had never felt before, had given her a sense that she could soar. But those feelings didn't surmount the incompatibility in their ages, or their dreams, or her shared past with Thomas. In their hearts, she and Kurt had known their liaison was doomed from the start. Perhaps it was precisely what had also made it perfect, that once-a-week sanctum, where they could bare themselves, suspend time, live in the moment. The intensity had sparked in her the memory of early days with Thomas. Passion at the start of a relationship was easy. Perhaps she had ended the love story of her marriage prematurely. Had she hankered for the romance of beginnings? There was a quiet heroism to the sustained emotional mettle it took to love someone whose faults were intimately familiar. Thomas was a good man. Married love ultimately required investing in keeping passion alive—and she was determined to do so. This is what she had told Kurt when she broke up with him. At first, she had said it only to comply with the demands of G-2, but later she realized she believed it.

The sound of the receptionist's typing and the click of closing metal file cabinets jangled her nerves. Maybe she should go now, before Kurt arrived. Just as she was standing to leave, she saw through the window a copper-colored Ford station wagon roaring into the lot. Before the car came to a full stop, Kurt jumped out of the passenger side and swooped into the clinic with an agility and economy of movement that made Christine's heart quicken.

He stopped in his tracks when he noticed Christine in the waiting area, pointedly ignored her, and reached out to Gertie, pulling her out of the chair with both hands to embrace her. She was taller than he was, so, although he tried to put a protective arm around her, it was Gertie who hovered over him, to the discomfort of both, until he moved clumsily away. He stroked her cheek.

"My dear child, I'm so sorry. This is not something you should . . ." He could not finish the thought. He took her head in both hands, bent it down until her forehead reached his lips, and kissed it.

Christine remembered the feel of his lips on hers. She hated how her body remembered what her mind wanted to forget.

Kurt turned to Christine, looked away, then back at her, as if simultaneously repulsed and reassured by her presence. "Where's the doctor? The nurse?"

"I don't know. Now that you're here, I should go." Christine stood up.

"Go? No, wait. Where's the doctor?"

"I'll see if I can find someone."

As Christine walked away, she heard Gertie sobbing. "Why did Mama do it? How could she do this?"

Christine was too far down the corridor to hear Kurt's answers. When she returned with the doctor, Kurt was holding Gertie's hand, patting it, his lips pursed. Christine wanted to go but was rooted to the spot, unable to take her eyes off Kurt and wishing at the same time to flee. Realizing it would be awkward to leave before they were briefed by the doctor, she took a seat at the other end of the waiting room.

"Mrs. Koppel is going to be okay," Dr. Pines said.

Both Kurt and Gertie let out long relieved breaths.

"Can I see her?" Kurt asked. He looked like a deflated balloon, his face pale and lined, next to the implausibly young, pink doctor.

"In a little while. We've given her liquids to flush out all she has taken. We're not sure how much she had in her."

"Did she say why she took all those pills?" Gertie asked.

"She is not well enough to talk. Please keep that in mind when you go in to see her. The nurse will tell you when," he explained, then left.

Kurt's eyes, when they inadvertently met Christine's, seemed vacant, but her stomach still lurched at his glance. She clamped her hands on her knees, feeling as if her body would drift toward him if she did not hold it down. Her mind flitted back to their lovemaking, his smooth body on hers. She searched her heart as if patting the inner pockets of a flak jacket for a hitherto hidden packet of guilt or a vial of shame and found none. She had no regrets about what she and Kurt had been for each other. Did Kurt feel the same way? Had he told Sarah about the affair? Sarah seemed to be one of those women whose greatest strength is their weakness. Kurt had clearly not been immune to her weakness in the past. He would likely not be immune to it now either.

"I should be getting home," she said.

"Gertie should go with you."

"Papa! I'm staying here."

"You'll see Mama later. This is not a place for a child."

"I'm not a child!" cried Gertie. "Stop treating me like one!" She started to sob.

"Kurt, this whole situation is not for a child. Gertie's been here for the hard part." Oh God, she shouldn't have used such a familiar tone. But Gertie did not seem to notice her careless intimacy.

"She should go home." Kurt paced back and forth in the waiting room.

The phone at the reception desk rang incessantly. No one answered it.

"I'm not going home, Papa."

"She needs to see her mother," said Christine.

"I don't like it," said Kurt.

"Gertie needs to stay with you."

"That is not for you to say."

Kurt's eyes darted from Christine to Gertie and back again. There was a coldness in them Kurt had never directed at her before.

"And yet, I'm saying it." She met his cold eyes with a coldness of her own. "It's the right thing to do. Let her stay."

Gertie looked at Christine with admiration. She was clearly not used to anyone answering her father in this way. Kurt caught Gertie's look and scowled, turned to the window, and stared out, away from them both.

"Fine," he murmured barely audibly.

Gertie hugged Christine goodbye.

"Take care," Christine said to Kurt's back as she left.

Walking away from the clinic, Christine felt his eyes on her from the window. Did Kurt blame himself or her for Sarah? Would guilt turn what had been beautiful between them into something denied and best forgotten? The sight of him had stirred her, but she no longer needed his presence to retain a sense of worth. He remained with her the way the sun is burnished inside closed eyes long after one has stopped staring at it.

Caught up in her thoughts, she passed the turnoff to home and instead continued straight to the dorms. Her feet were smarter than her brain. A thin young man directed her to Jimmy through swinging doors to a long line of bunks. She'd never been to the dorms. The place smelled of dirty socks, ammonia, and fried food. The walls, unpainted drywall, were flimsy and reeked of maleness.

She found Jimmy sitting over a chessboard on his bed, watching his opponent, Owen, contemplate a move, affection and amusement playing on his face as he munched chips, looking relaxed. When he saw her, he stopped in midbite.

"Christine! What brings you here?"

Owen looked up from the board. "Hey, Christine. Good to see you. It's been a while."

Christine smiled distractedly at Owen and directed her attention to Jimmy. "Can I speak to you in private?" she asked him.

"Why? What's up?"

"You have a moment?"

"I have a shift in twenty minutes. I actually need to leave now." He indicated with his head that she could follow him.

She walked him to work, telling him about Sarah on the way.

"This is all because of you, isn't it?" he said softly.

If he had punched her in the stomach, she would have felt better.

"Unlikely. We ended it two months ago."

"Sarah must have found out." He pinned his identity tag on his shirt as they approached the Tech Area. "Don't they say the wife's always the last to know?"

Christine shrugged. "Sometimes the wife hasn't a clue. And there's no need for a wife to know, especially if it has no bearing on the present or the future. I'd appreciate it if you'd keep it that way. And that's not what's important right now. It's Gertie I'm worried about."

"I bet Sarah figured it out." Jimmy stuck his hands in his pockets and pulled slightly ahead of Christine.

Men streaming out of the Tech Area passed them; many smiled or nodded at Jimmy. Some, who knew Christine, nodded at her or cast perplexed glances at the sight of her straining to keep pace with Jimmy.

She kept her voice low. "The point is Gertie needs you now. So does Kurt."

They reached the Tech Area gate.

"Ma'am. You can't be here," said a military policeman, looking up from checking a briefcase and noticing she had no badge.

"I can count on you to comfort Gertie, can't I?" she called to Jimmy as he headed away.

"Of course," he said, sounding more like his usual kind self. "I'll find Gertie tomorrow as soon as I get off the night shift."

"Good. That's all I'm asking."

Christine headed home, her mind still whirling from the day. She glanced at her watch. Thomas had promised to come home tonight for dinner for the first time in weeks, and she was determined to make sure he was glad he did. She had been making a concerted effort not to complain—not about how busy Thomas was, not about missing New York, not about the muddy roads at Los Alamos or the frequent water stoppages. And although the chances seemed so dim, she still hoped for a baby. Maybe her positive attitude would help. And tonight was an optimal time to try. She'd planned a fancy dinner, had even bought some candles this morning. In a peculiar way, the affair with Kurt had improved her marriage. Continuous adoration of the kind Kurt has shown could become cloying, like too much icing on a cake. Romantic moments, like the one she hoped for this evening, were enjoyable because they were occasional. In truth, she was a lucky person: lucky she had met Thomas, lucky he had wanted to marry her, lucky to have known Kurt's love, lucky the affair had ended before their love led to irreparable damage. The only bit of her life that was unlucky was her barrenness. She would never let a child down the way Sarah had. Christine was sure she'd be a fantastic mother and Thomas would be a fun dad. Maybe they'd still be lucky that way. She had to focus on tonight, on making it special, despite the upsetting afternoon. She had done what she could to help out; it was time to leave the matter of the overdose to Kurt and Jimmy, and to Sarah herself.

Once home, Christine took a shower and put on her favorite sundress, white, and a blue sapphire necklace Thomas had given her for her birthday. She applied lipstick and, for good measure, a dab of Shocking, the perfume Samantha had bought her as a going-away present when she left the gallery, knowing Christine would love not only the scent but also the curved bottle design inspired by Mae West's figure.

In the kitchen, she unwrapped okra, bought fresh this morning from Martha's maid. Christine and Thomas had discovered okra since coming to Los Alamos; they both loved it. She'd simmer the okra for only a few minutes, then mix it with meatballs in tomatoes. As in life, the secret to avoiding a slimy mess was to turn off the heat in time and avoid overcooking.

CHAPTER 31
GERTIE

July 1944

Gertie slipped into the living room where Papa told her Jimmy was waiting, just off from his night shift. When he looked up from the sofa, she smiled faintly.

"What happened?" he asked.

She couldn't put into words the confusion, the exhaustion, the sadness that had seeped into her and into every corner of the room. She stood frozen; her silence was marked by the pendulum swinging on the mantel clock. "What do you think happened?" she said finally, bitterly, slinking down next to him and wrapping her arms around herself.

Her mother didn't want to live. The doctor had said that it was only because she had been brought to the clinic in time that she was alive. Gertie hadn't slept all night, twisting and turning, her stomach curdling with undigestible anger, guilt, and shock. So she had saved her mother, but she still was not sure whether she had contributed to her mother's death wish.

Now Papa came into the living room. "I must go. You will stay home today, yes?" he addressed Gertie. "You will see to it that Mama drinks, maybe eats, yes? You must ask someone to fetch me if there is a problem."

Gertie nodded, still curled into herself.

Papa hesitated at the door, then came back into the room, smoothed her hair, stooped, and planted a clumsy kiss on the top of her head. It felt like an apology—she wasn't sure for what.

He glanced at Jimmy. "How did it go yesterday? Did the test give the results we expected?"

"We're not there yet," Jimmy said.

What was *there*? Gertie wondered. Would they ever get to it? Would Los Alamos ever end?

"I suppose we must all recalculate," Papa sighed. "You'll take care of my daughter, yes?"

"I'll do my best." He smiled weakly at his boss, then cast a worried glance at Gertie.

The front door clicked behind Papa.

Gertie reached for Jimmy's hand—big, strong, encircling hers completely. He didn't prod her to talk, and she was grateful. She didn't want to think about what had happened. Instead, she stared at the chandelier, noting how it threw rainbow colors on the wall. It struck her that people, like light, were different wavelengths.

"Mama hasn't spoken to me except to ask for water," Gertie said, staring ahead.

"I'm so sorry." He squeezed her hand.

"I keep wondering what I did to make her want to kill herself."

"I'm sure it has nothing to do with you."

"Most mothers don't try to end their lives. Most mothers care enough about their children to want to be around for them, don't they?" Gertie drew back her hand from his and crossed her arms over her chest. "So, what's wrong with me that she doesn't want to stick around?"

Jimmy tried to take her into his arms. She did not unclench her fists. He kissed her forehead. "There's nothing wrong with you. You're the best reason to be alive."

"Then why?"

"It's not about you."

"How do you know?"

"I just do. You're an easy person to love."

She leaned into him, into the comfort he offered. He never said things like this. Despite her low spirits, pleasure fluttered through her for a moment. It was the closest he'd ever come to saying he loved her.

"It doesn't explain Mama."

"Gertie, you must believe me. This was not about you." He said it softly, kissing the top of her head.

"Christine said the same thing."

"Well, there you have it," he said, moving away to face her, as if he wanted to sound more authoritative. "Two people who know a bit more than you do about life."

Gertie was silent for a few minutes, listening to the clock pendulum click back and forth, her gaze falling on the pot of violets on the living room table that Mama tended so carefully. "I was mean to Mama."

He held both her arms, one with each of his hands, facing her. "I wasn't always kind to my parents when I was your age. It's part of growing up. I'm sure she understands that."

"Does she? I'm sure she was never mean to anyone."

"But you told me yourself, loads of times, how worried and sad she was about your family in Europe. Who wouldn't be?"

"Why is her family in Germany more important than Papa and me?"

"It might be other things too."

"Like what?"

"I don't know. Sometimes things can make a person so sad they can't take life anymore. People are different that way." He stood up and paced the room, suddenly agitated. "Gertie, you need to accept that you may never know what it is. Sometimes it's better not to know—whether it's about what we're all doing here, or what may have motivated your mother. We all have secrets, sometimes from others, sometimes even from ourselves."

Gertie was surprised by his outburst. What was he trying to tell her? What did any of Mama's actions have to do with secrets? Had she found out something about Los Alamos she couldn't live with? Still, no matter what, Gertie could not imagine choosing to be dead.

"If Mama felt she was falling apart, why didn't she talk to Papa or to me, or to someone? I always feel better when I talk about things with you. Don't you?"

"Sometimes it feels impossible," said Jimmy.

"Personal things, not about work?"

Jimmy nodded.

"Like what?"

"There are things . . ."

"What things?"

Jimmy paced back and forth, mashing one fist into the open palm of the other hand. She had never seen him so restless. Finally, they seemed to be having a conversation that felt like a heart-to-heart, or at least an attempt at one.

"Whatever it is, you can tell me."

"I don't even know how to explain." He stood in front of her, then paced again. "I worry that I don't know how to be with you, that maybe I limit you. I wonder if I should let you go." Jimmy turned back toward her, ran his fingers through his curls. "There is something in me that makes me unable to give you all of me, in the way you deserve." The sound of two birds calling to each other flitted in from outside, filling the silence. She tried to make sense of his words.

People said sixteen was too young to make decisions about the future, but people were wrong. She knew Jimmy was meant for her. She loved the way he cared about doing the right thing, his modesty, how he looked now as the morning sun flecked his blue eyes with gold. The fact that he worried about limiting her was exactly what made her want to be with him.

She stood up and wrapped her arms around him, touched his nose with hers, then his cheeks, rough and stubbled after the night shift.

She kissed him fully on the mouth. "You taste so good. Jimmy, kiss me." She snuggled against his chest. It felt as if she was melting into him. Her body wanted him more than she had ever wanted anything. He kissed her on the lips. She opened her mouth to him; his tongue explored her mouth for a moment. She felt she was swirling in one of those kaleidoscopes in movies when couples kissed. She wanted the moment to last forever. But Jimmy pulled back, pecked her cheek, and caressed her shoulder.

"Shouldn't you check on your mother?"

"Oh God! Only you could make me forget about Mama." She smoothed her hair. "I'm hungry. You must be too. Why don't you make us some breakfast while I check on her?"

Mama was sleeping, sprawled on her back, arms flung out and up as if in surrender, murmuring. Gertie wanted to kiss her but was afraid to wake her. So she sat in the chair next to the bed, trying to make sense of the words. Mama had always been so fragile. She looked even more delicate now, tossing about, battling who knew what demons. Gertie had never considered how hard and draining it was to always be afraid that no matter what she did, Mama would still be sad. Did it wear down Papa too? Jimmy wouldn't have to worry about her that way, nor she about him. He lived with such a strong sense that all was well in the world, and if it wasn't right now, it soon would be. She wanted to live in his world.

"Get better, Mama, please," Gertie whispered. She couldn't imagine coming home from school without Mama's carefully laid out cookies and milk there to greet her, without Mama asking her about school, commenting on her clothes, or trying to stop her squabbles with Papa. Until today, that had all seemed trivial. She kissed Mama on the forehead before leaving the room.

She stood in the doorway to the kitchen. Jimmy had set out cereal and milk and was crooning to the radio, which made Gertie smile as she watched him open cabinet after cabinet until he found the bowls, poured the cereal, and pulled two spoons from the cutlery drawer. He was so intent on the words, he didn't notice her as he continued singing, totally out of tune, that he would not complain, no matter what, as long as he had his heartthrob by his side.

"You talking about me?" teased Gertie, joining him in the kitchen.

He smiled with sheepish embarrassment for an instant before turning serious. "How's your mother?"

"Still sleeping."

"Is that good? Bad?"

Gertie shrugged. "I don't know. The doctor said to let her sleep. And to make sure she drinks a lot when she's awake." She dug into the cereal. "I can't believe how hungry I am."

They munched silently, the radio faintly broadcasting "Swinging on a Star." Gertie turned it off.

"I still don't understand why she did it."

"I guess it's about finding happiness in the day to day. I don't know if your mother knows how to do that."

Gertie nodded slowly, then put her hand on Jimmy's. "You have that, you know."

"What?"

"That ability to look at the world and see good. Mama doesn't. Neither does Papa. They think that if they imagine all the possible bad things that could happen, they can prevent them."

"What about you? What do you believe?" Jimmy asked.

"I don't know. What do *you* think? Am I more like you or more like them?"

"That's not something one can know about another person. But there's a folktale my grandma told me once. It's about a guy who has a hot dog stand—makes great hot dogs, with lots of relish and nice big buns—and he has loads of customers. But then he starts worrying about bad times coming, so he skimps on the relish, uses smaller buns, and then he stops providing napkins and buys cheaper, poorer-quality meat. Fewer and fewer people come to his stand because the hot dogs aren't as good as they used to be, and he makes less and less money. And he feels proud that he prepared for bad economic times. My grandma calls that a self-fulfilling prophecy."

Gertie shrugged. "There's a difference between running a hot dog stand and figuring out early enough how bad things could get under Hitler. If my parents hadn't imagined all the bad that could happen, we never would have left Germany. Was that a self-fulfilling prophecy? I don't think so. The trick is to know when imagining the bad can save you and when imagining the bad gets in the way of making things good." She stirred her cereal.

Jimmy stared at her and then nodded slowly. He took her hand across the table, and she smiled at him.

"I probably do have a capacity for happiness, although it's hard to see or feel it right now," she said.

"No one would expect you to now, what with your mother and all. But on balance . . ."

"Yes, on balance, I'm different from them. More like you, and I could work on it, couldn't I? With you?"

"Definitely."

A moan sounded from the depths of the house.

"It's Mama. I have to go." Gertie pulled away, leaving Jimmy to finish breakfast alone and let himself out of the house.

CHAPTER 32
CHRISTINE

August 1944

A trip to Maria was long overdue. Christine had money to give her from recent sales and hoped to bring home a new supply of pots, in demand since the successful exhibition at Samantha's gallery. But this was not why Christine dug her heels into Odysseus's flank, eager to get to San Ildefonso. She needed to get away from Los Alamos, escape the images that kept haunting her of Sarah's wan face and disheveled body strewn on the Koppel bed.

Christine urged the horse into a gallop, the movement of their synchronized bodies and the countryside whipping past her finally dispelling that constant nagging in the corner of her mind . . . *What if Gertie had not found her mother in time?* She turned on the path toward the village, past the landmark black basalt volcanic mound at its end that shimmered like a mirage in the midday heat. She found Maria near home, placing patties of dry dung around her kiln. The kiln itself was a delicate balance of pieces of sheet metal—carefully placed over pots about to be fired—about the size of a large open umbrella.

Maria stopped her preparations and gripped both Christine's hands in greeting. "It's long time."

"Too long. At least two months. I see you're busy."

"Not so much. The morning was quiet, so good for firing. Now there is too much wind. With wind, the pots don't fire good. So we can have quiet time."

She ushered Christine inside and went to fetch them water.

Christine looked around. The house looked different. She wasn't sure why.

"Not much quiet time these days," Maria said, setting two cups of water on the long dining room table.

"Oh?"

"My mind is busy."

"Busy how?"

"People, they see you come to buy the pots, and you bring money. And I buy a stove." She pointed proudly to the new stove in her kitchen.

"Congratulations," said Christine, casting an admiring eye, realizing that this was what had changed about the house. They sat on a bench at the dining table. The area was an open continuum with the kitchen.

"It's a fine stove. And now, the women, they want to make pots, too, to get money for stoves. I teach them to polish the pots, and the ones that are good with their hands, I show them how to make the pots. So there are more pots. Maybe there are also more people who want to buy them. My daughter-in-law, she thinks we can sell the pots for people to buy them here, and also sell sundries and dried goods that people in the village need."

"Do a lot of people come and visit the village, looking for your pottery?"

"Not a lot, but some. On weekends, mostly. And if gasoline rationing ends—it will someday—there'll be more folks coming, I expect," Maria said.

Christine liked the idea of Maria gaining a wider distribution of her wares. The more her pottery became known, the more there would be a market for them, and the more Christine herself could sell.

"You think a store is a good idea?" Maria asked.

"It might be," said Christine. But if pots made by other women were of a lesser quality than Maria's, the market value of all the pots would go down. "You should sign your name on the bottom of your pots. And any woman who makes a pot should sign her name on hers. So people won't be confused about who made what."

Maria furrowed her brow. "Why my name? Many women polish, prepare my pots for firing. And my daughter-in-law, she makes the decorations, now that Julian is gone."

"Still, if you make the pot, you should sign it. People will want to know it was your hands that formed the pot, not someone else's."

"Why does it matter?"

How could she explain to Maria that she had been working hard to brand the pots, linking them closely to Maria and her biography in the catalog that accompanied the show in Samantha's gallery and in articles she had been writing for specialized journals? And it was unclear whether the other women Maria was teaching would be as deft or have her eye for pleasing proportions.

"It makes it more personal, if you have your name on it. And you can pass on whatever part of that money you think others should get."

"White folks . . ." She shook her head. "They don't know me, so why?"

"Well, I've written about the pots and how you make them, how you started out with an archeologist and working with your aunt— everything you told me. And now people associate the pots with you, so they like it when the pots have your name on it."

"But the others, they help. It's not just me."

"Yes, but you are the one who guides them, the one who leads the way, the one the customers know."

"We work together; I don't think of the pots as just mine. My name shouldn't matter."

Christine smiled to herself. Maybe if Rembrandt or Michelangelo or other famous artists with bevies of underlings working for them had thought like Maria, the art world would be different.

"Trust me. People will pay more for them when the name is there," Christine said, pulling out a wad of cash from her pocket. "Here's the money from the last batch. I'll be able to bring you a lot more in the future if the pieces are signed."

Maria took the rolled bundle of bills from Christine. As was her habit, she did not count the money in her presence. She stuffed the wad in the pocket of her apron with a finality that indicated she accepted Christine's point, and the subject was closed. "You want some more water?" she asked.

"I'm fine. It's good to be here, to see you, to get away from home."

"Why you want to be away from home?"

"Sometimes sad things happen there."

"Sad things happen everywhere."

"Yes, but when I'm here, I don't think about them."

Maria was silent, busying herself with shucking corn in the adjoining kitchen.

"There's a woman, she tried to kill herself," Christine blurted out, surprising herself that she would mention this.

"You know why?" Maria asked, her eyes on her work, her nimble fingers picking away strands of corn silk clinging to the ears.

"Not really. Maybe because she's a sad person. Maybe because she misses her relatives who are in Europe and probably dead there."

Maria sighed and continued to prepare food. "People got their reasons. Sometimes lots of reasons." Only the sound of Maria chopping vegetables filled the room for a few moments.

"Maybe she thought I was taking her husband away from her. But I'm not." Christine wondered if there was some sort of truth potion in the air. How had she dared to say this?!

"Ah. She thinks her husband doesn't love her. That he loves you?" Maria turned from her work to face Christine.

"Maybe." There was no going back now.

"*Do* you love her husband?" Maria sat down on the bench next to Christine and looked into her eyes. The directness of the question made it impossible not to answer.

"I do." She sighed. "But I love my husband too." She looked at Maria, hoping for understanding. "I want to be a good wife."

"Then you will be." She patted Christine's thigh. "It's up to you. The right way is always the best way." Maria got up and resumed her kitchen chores.

"You make it sound easy."

"It is. Imagine if your husband just disappeared one day, like my Julian did. Went out for a walk and never come back. Found dead in the wilderness after four days. How'd you feel? Would you be sorry?" Maria's voice was flat, betraying little emotion as she gathered up the debris from the corn.

"Of course, I would."

Maria came back to the dining area, stood over Christine. "So be glad for every day you have him." She started toward the door. "Now come, I'll show you some of my new pieces."

CHAPTER 33
SARAH

October 1944

Sarah was awoken by Kurt's rustling near the bed, and she fumbled for the light on the night table. "What are you doing?"

"There's been an accident."

"What time is it?"

"Three thirty. A guard came to tell me. Someone in the lab has been hurt."

"Gott im himmel!" She saw his fingers shake as he tied his shoes.

"Yes, my worst nightmare." He finished dressing and brushed her forehead with his lips as if he were fortifying himself for what lay ahead.

She heard the door close behind him. A few months ago, Kurt would not have kissed her, would not have even told her why he was dashing out in the middle of the night. But things had changed in the three months since *"die pille vorfall"*—the pill incident. Kurt had become attentive like never before, not even in the early months of their marriage. In the immediate days after the incident, he beseeched her to explain what had prompted her action. It took time for her to believe that he really wanted to know or trust that he might understand her desperation. But he had persisted with a quiet intensity she had seen him devote in the past only to his scientific research. She hardly knew where to begin: the worry about the family, her irrelevance to Gertie, the suspicions of a mistress, the motivation for the dog. These all gnawed away at her like a motor rumbling louder every day and all the time. Did she have intuition, or was she suffering from paranoia?

They had walked to Ashley Pond at twilight when she was steady enough on her feet to go out, two days after she came home from the clinic. They had stood by the water and watched the last sunbeams of the day sweep the horizon and the floodlights switch on around the Tech Area. A breeze had rustled through the reeds at the far end of the pond.

"It's the dog," she had blurted out into the quiet.

"Susanna?" He had looked at Sarah as if she were a stranger.

How could she explain? He had looked like he really wanted to understand.

"You bought her without asking me. You didn't even tell me you wanted a dog. Why a dog? Then you take so much care of her. So much love should be first for human beings, no? For me. For Gertie. You take the dog for walks, but until tonight, you never suggest a walk with me. You feed the dog, but never offer to prepare me even a cup of tea. You pet the dog, but don't touch me. It is so *beschämend* to feel less loved than a dog."

Kurt, his brows furrowed, had been so contrite she was sure that there had been not just a dog, but also a woman. She had not asked. She'd just wanted Kurt to be fully with her, like he was in that moment.

"I do love you, Sarah," he had said, facing the water, not her. A chorus of frogs had croaked in the pond like booing soccer fans.

"You say it like you might say it's going to rain today, with no emotion in it. Something you are used to saying, without really thinking about it."

The conversation had its effect. He had taken her hand, kissed it. Kurt had become solicitous, gone back to little habits that meant so much to her—chatting while he held a skein of wool for her to roll into a ball for her knitting, listening together to records on the phonograph. He came home for dinner almost every day now, and they took frequent strolls in the evenings, hand in hand. She even suggested, with time, that they bring Susanna along. Sometimes Kurt was too preoccupied with work to talk, but she didn't care. Perfunctory sex, too, had returned to their lives, which was all sex between them had ever been, and Sarah found comfort, if not any particular pleasure, in its regularity. Of course, the worry about the family in Europe only intensified. The frequency of news reports on concentration and death camps had increased. Still, it was easier to focus on the present when Kurt was so attentive. Paris had been liberated, Belgium and Luxembourg and Greece as well, so there was hope that this *schrecklich* war might end soon. When she thought about the incident, she was glad that Gertie had found her in time.

Sarah tried to return to sleep, but she was too awake now. She went to the kitchen and prepared herself a cup of tea, which she brought back to bed. She wondered what sort of accident Kurt was dealing with. She hoped no one was hurt severely. And that there were others there to help him. Particularly Jimmy, whom Kurt held in such high esteem.

Gertie, too, seemed attached to the young man. She was spending most of her time with him, and he appeared serious about her. Gertie was so high spirited; it was best for her to be tethered to a sensible man sooner rather than later. If Gertie ended up marrying Jimmy, their children would be safer in the world—only half Jews, not full Jews. Safety was important, more than anything else. Kurt believed Jimmy was destined for a great career. Jimmy was certainly kind and eager enough to please. He was not cultured, apparently from a simple family. But that did not matter in America. What was that expression they used? To pull yourself up by your bootstraps. She was not sure what bootstraps were, but Jimmy apparently was pulling them high. Gertie's heart was settled on him. The comfort in that, and in Kurt's recent attentiveness, along with the medication prescribed by the doctor, kept at bay the darkness that had so long overwhelmed Sarah.

But when would Kurt come home? Poor man. It had been a late night—he had come with her to see *Casablanca* at Fuller Lodge earlier that evening because he knew how much she loved Ingrid Bergman. Now he was up and about, dealing with who knew what sort of accident. She replayed the film's final scene in her mind as she fell asleep, until Kurt woke her.

"Everything is okay, yes?"

"No. It's Jimmy. He's been hurt."

"What happened?"

Kurt waved the question away, sat on the edge of the bed, then covered his eyes with his hands as if he had a headache.

Sarah knew better than to press him. She lay by his side and rested her hand on his thigh until he was ready to say more. The early light of day seeped like skim milk through a crack in the curtains.

"Jimmy touched some material he shouldn't have. Dangerous material. I don't know how it happened. He did not follow regulations." Kurt bit his lip, not moving otherwise. She had never seen him so close to crying.

"He will get better, yes?"

"No. He is not going to get better," he whispered. He sighed and stroked her hand absentmindedly. "May you be spared what I have seen."

"*Mein Gott*, the poor boy! What happened to him?"

Kurt shook his head and pursed his lips. "You cannot talk about this to anyone, you understand, yes?" He let go of her hand and slipped into bed beside her.

"What will you tell Gertie?" Sarah asked.

"Gertie?"

"Where is Jimmy?"

"They took him to the hospital. In Santa Fe."

"She will want to see him."

"No one must know what happened. Not Gertie, not anyone outside the lab. I probably should not have told you."

"*Verschwinden?* He cannot simply vanish," said Sarah.

"He must. It will be terrible for morale if people see what has happened, if they see what effects there can be from our work, from the gadget. We must make it seem that he has simply been called away."

How long did Kurt plan to lie to Gertie? How could he seem so comfortable with doing that to her? It meant Sarah would have to lie too. She didn't like the idea one bit. It wouldn't make sense to Gertie that Jimmy would be called away and not tell her.

"Called away? For what?"

Kurt moaned. "In the morning I will think of something."

CHAPTER 34
CHRISTINE

October 1944

Christine was wrapping up a new shipment of pots to send to Samantha when she heard the firm knock on the door. She glanced at her watch—11:00 a.m. She opened the door to find Kurt, dressed impeccably as always, his mouth twitching uncharacteristically. Her stomach surged with familiar longing superseded by dread. She had not seen him since he'd raced to the clinic about Sarah, more than two months ago.

Her eyes darted around beyond him. What if someone saw him at her door?

"Can I come in?" He pushed his way in before she could reply.

She closed the door.

His brows were furrowed. His eyes flitted, distracted, almost as if he didn't see her.

She resisted the desire to touch his arm.

"What's wrong? Is it Sarah?"

He headed for the living room and sat down emphatically on the edge of the sofa, cracked the knuckles of one hand, then the other. "There's been a terrible accident."

"Sarah?"

Kurt shook his head.

"Oh my goodness, Gertie? What happened?"

"It's Jimmy."

"Jimmy? Hasn't he been sent on some special mission? In the Pacific, no? Thomas mentioned something about it yesterday."

"Yes, that is what everyone has been told. But it's not true." Kurt hesitated, searched Christine's face as if assuring himself he could trust her. He looked down at his hands, then back at her. "Jimmy touched something lethal. He has been in hospital for the past two days."

What was Kurt telling her? It must have been something radioactive. Stuff that could eat up a human body. Everyone knew that, ever since Madame Curie died of anemia from years of exposure to radium and polonium, her laboratory notebooks so dangerously radioactive they were sealed away in lead-lined boxes in France.

"You mean he's here, not on his way to the Pacific?"

"He's in a hospital in Santa Fe."

"How bad is it?"

He leaned his head back on the sofa and closed his eyes, deflated.

"Can the doctors do anything for him?"

He shook his head, his eyes still closed. Christine wanted to hold his hand, limp at his side.

"How dreadful!"

"You have no idea. He's in terrible pain."

Outside, the wind howled, a sandstorm in the making. Why was he telling her this? Surely all this was top secret if even Thomas had been purposely misinformed.

Kurt opened his eyes and stared out the window at the swirls of sand dancing like dervishes in the wind. "I need your help."

"Me? What can I do?"

"Do you have a drink?"

"A drink?"

"Yes, bourbon, scotch, something."

She'd never seen Kurt with anything more than a glass of red wine.

"Bourbon okay?"

He nodded, and she got ice cubes from the fridge and poured them drinks, setting a bottle of Walker's DeLuxe bourbon on the table. He wouldn't be telling her about the accident without permission from higher up. What did they want from her? she wondered as she handed Kurt his drink.

He took two gulps. "Gertie is so upset that Jimmy left without saying goodbye. She is hoping he will write to her. She must get a letter."

Of course, Gertie would be beside herself. She had left a note on the kitchen table yesterday when Christine was out, saying she needed to talk. It had been near dinner when Christine saw the note, and she figured Gertie would show up after school today.

"You must help me." He set the drink on the coffee table and fished for a piece of paper in the breast pocket of his jacket. "I wrote a letter—as if from Jimmy—but I don't think it is good enough to convince her."

"Really? Is this necessary?" But she was curious, and, of course, she did want to help. She took the paper and read it to herself while Kurt downed the rest of his bourbon:

> Dear Gertie,
>
> Please accept my apologies for leaving so suddenly without saying goodbye but I was rushed off on a mission I cannot discuss and was not given time to do anything more than collect what I needed for the trip which apparently will be for some time, maybe until the war is over.
>
> Sincerely,
> Jimmy

"You make a terrible twenty-three-year-old boyfriend." Christine couldn't help a wry smile.

"That is why I need your help."

"You want me to write a letter from Jimmy?"

Kurt nodded gravely. "I have received special permission from Oppie to ask you to help. He convinced G-2 that you were the best person for this. You are Gertie's closest friend, and you know Jimmy. You can write a much better letter than I or G-2 can."

It was good to know that Oppie trusted her. She wondered if he knew about her affair with Kurt and suspected that if he did, he wouldn't let that stand in the way of recruiting her help. But how long did they think they could protect Gertie? It wasn't fair to Gertie or to Jimmy. Shouldn't they be allowed to see each other? Especially if Jimmy was in bad shape.

"This is crazy!"

Kurt looked at Christine. He looked haunted. And exhausted. "It's not going to come out. Not now. Not soon. Not as long as the war is going on. Those are the orders from above. G-2 insists. It would be terrible for morale. I need you to be discreet. I need your help."

"It seems so wrong." She felt bad protesting when he was so troubled, but she had to say it. What were they really doing here in Los Alamos? She'd never considered how seriously Thomas, Kurt, all of them, or any of them might be irradiated. She took a slurp of bourbon.

"G-2 has ordered me to spread that story about Jimmy being on a special mission to the Pacific."

"Are there no limits to their deceptions?" she sighed. Those horrible guys from G-2. Why keep this accident secret from Jimmy's colleagues? They surely knew the dangers. To ignore those dangers for fear of a loss of morale? A lousy reason. It was infuriating.

"G-2 insisted."

"They always do, don't they?" She emptied her glass and slammed it on the coffee table. "They're convinced they have the right to decide our lives. I wouldn't put it past them to never let us out of here, just because it's for the best."

"Christine, are you going to help?" Anger mixed with desperation in his eyes, like those of an animal snared in a trap, hoping for mercy and resenting the need to ask for it.

"Sorry, I was ranting." She patted his arm, then rose to get a piece of paper and pen from a drawer in the kitchen and a book on which to write.

She returned to the sofa and poured another drink for herself from the bottle on the coffee table. As she penned the letter, she felt Kurt's relief. Even as he stood up and paced the room in agitation, his gratitude was palpable. He was oblivious to her worn dungarees and uncombed hair. She had forgotten how much she missed the way he made her feel smart and competent and beautiful. She took a few sips of bourbon and closed her eyes, conjuring up Jimmy and remembering the cadence of his voice, imagining what he might write to Gertie. She wished the wind would stop howling, wished she could believe that this was the right thing to do, that this was for Gertie's good.

When she finished, she held the letter out to Kurt, but he continued to pace.

"It is odd, I always thought only about the goal. About winning, how important, how vital it is to win," Kurt said, his back to her, facing the window.

"You can't possibly have imagined we could win the war without causing pain."

He turned to face her. "Of course, in theory. But seeing the pain, so close up . . . it is horrendous, unconscionable."

"I can't even imagine what it must be for you to see Jimmy suffer so. But inflicting pain on the enemy, it is necessary, unavoidable, no? You must know that." Christine searched his face. He looked so lost.

He sank onto the sofa next to her. "To reach a goal, one must focus, not think of anything but how to succeed. There is so much pressure. So much fear that the other side is trying just as hard." His eyes roamed the room, looking without success for a place to rest. "We know that, so we work harder to get there first. We find solutions to one problem after another, not thinking about the human consequences."

What could she say? That Kurt had no choice? That he couldn't have been so naive?

She refilled his glass, handing it to him with one hand and stroking his cheek with the other. He blinked, acknowledging the touch, but as if it had distracted him as a fly might.

"Certainly, what happened to Jimmy has not led you to forget what the Nazis have done to our boys in Europe, to all those relatives you told me about when we first met—twenty-three relatives, was it? I remember because the number struck me then—all killed, you believe."

He only looked more miserable.

"Better for the deaths to be on their side than on ours, no?" she said, but Kurt looked down at the carpet as if he was no longer sure. Of anything.

"Come, look at the letter." He peered over her shoulder as she read out loud:

> Dearest Gertie,
>
> I have been sent on a secret mission (although I can say it is in the Pacific). So sorry I didn't have a chance to say goodbye to you in the rush to leave. Feel really bad about that. Please understand and forgive me.
>
> I'm working hard at something important (sorry I can't say more) and have to stay here and not come back to Los Alamos for some time—I don't know how long. You can imagine how sorry I am about that. But still, what I do is important, and that matters. I know it matters not just to me, but also to you. We all need to make sacrifices, right? Not much time to write. I miss you like crazy already and can't wait to see you again.
>
> S.W.A.K.,
> Jimmy

"What are those initials?" Kurt asked.

"Sealed with a kiss. It's what young people write these days."

"Hmm, sounds a bit forward, no? Keep it the way I had it—'Sincerely.'"

"Jimmy would never write 'sincerely' to Gertie. It's not what one writes to a girlfriend."

"Perhaps. But cross out that last line about seeing her again."

"It's what Jimmy would write."

"Jimmy will never see Gertie again." He threw back his head and gulped down the bourbon.

"Never?"

"He's dying—the most horrible, awful death."

"Maybe the doctors will be able to do something for him."

"If you saw him, you would know—he is not going to live, and if he does, he will be in such pain, he is better off dead. The smell of his body, it is terrible. I cannot say more."

He didn't need to. Maybe it was better, after all, that Gertie be kept in ignorance.

"Still, 'can't wait to see you again' *is* what Jimmy would write," Christine said.

Kurt sighed. "It is too much of a lie."

"The whole letter is a lie."

"The letter is a necessary lie. Telling Gertie he can't wait to see her—it's one lie too many."

"Is there such a thing?" Christine laughed bitterly.

"Some lies are necessary. Some are not."

Christine nodded, rewrote the letter without the last line, and handed it to him. "You will have this sent?" She knew she had written a good letter—but it only put off the inevitable. At some point, Gertie would have to learn that Jimmy was dead, and Christine knew already how impossible it would be to console her.

"Yes. G-2 will take care of it." Kurt closed his eyes. Christine let him rest. She put away the book on which she had written the letter, returned the pen to the drawer.

"I have missed you so much," Kurt said softly from the sofa, his eyes still closed.

Christine sat down next to him. She touched his cheek.

"I promised myself . . . ," he began.

She put her two fingers on his lips to silence him. "You don't need to explain."

"I am trying to be a good husband."

"Me too. A good wife. But I think of you all the time."

"Do you?" Kurt opened his eyes slowly. They still were filled with pain, but there was a flash of hope, like a drowning man who suddenly sees a floating lifesaver ring.

"Yes, I miss everything." She was not surprised when he kissed her, tentatively at first, sending a charge through her, every pore of her skin remembering what his body could do to hers. Who was to say that what had happened to Jimmy wouldn't happen to Kurt, or to Thomas? She did not resist when he began to unbutton her blouse, when he buried his head in her breasts. One had to cleave to life, to suck all one could of it. Kurt's tongue was in her mouth now, as if her thoughts had fused into his. Her body throbbing, she led Kurt to the bedroom, where, for the first time, they made love in a bed. Their bodies ripped through each other, transporting them away from the horror of the day, colliding into pure sensation, to warmth, to intoxicating dankness. Thigh intwined thigh; her body melted and arched to meet his. She offered him her soft, wet, gasping mouth, to restore him, to restore herself. They consumed each other to feel the force and pull of life, to blot out death. He was in her, and she gushed wetness to greet his rhythmic plunges. She dissolved into gasps and moans, her body quaking, writhing, until they were both spent. They lay breathless for minutes, stunned by what they had just done yet reluctant to leave the moment's intensity.

Slowly, sound filtered into the bedroom, back into consciousness: laundry whipped in the wind in the courtyard, horns honked on the main road, and flocks of birds called to each other as they flew south for the winter.

"This will not happen again." He stroked her cheek and the length of her neck with a finger, letting his hand rest around her nape. She tilted her head to meet his cradling hand.

"It shouldn't." She tried to imprint in her mind his huge, sad eyes, his pale skin, his shiny bald forehead that she found so inexplicably alluring.

She could already feel her body aching to do this all over again, but he rose, showered, and dressed. He placed his hand on her shoulder to go. "Thank you," he said and left the bedroom, stopping in the living room to take the letter before letting himself out the door.

She showered, using his discarded towel to dry herself, then stripped the bed, burying her face in the sheets, the smell of Kurt mingling with that of Thomas. She burst into tears, over Jimmy, over wanting Kurt and Thomas and knowing she could not have both.

CHAPTER 35
CHRISTINE

October 1944

The smell of ammonia assaulted Christine when she entered Jimmy's hospital room. His eyes were covered with white bandages, and his groans were so loud he did not hear her. Kurt had said that the accident blinded Jimmy, so it was not his bandaged eyes but the rest of his body that shocked her. He was swathed in gauze, some parts stained with the mustard color of oozing pus. His elbow and lips, his only exposed features, were deep purple red. It seemed rude to interrupt his moaning, like disturbing a person praying. So, she sat and waited for him to notice her. She wanted to cry, looking at his body, at this near corpse. What could she possibly say? Why had she even agreed to come? She should have spared herself this. But G-2 thought she might be good for his spirits. She was among the few who knew he was in the hospital, and her time, unlike that of essential personnel, could be spared for a visit. They had written down the false name under which he had been admitted—Jimmy Cameron. They had not given her the choice of saying no. She had no idea how she might lift his mood. Outside, a bird twirped as if alarmed by Jimmy's groans, which morphed into a low howl that seemed unlikely to ever stop. Finally, she coughed.

"Who's there?" Jimmy asked. His voice was hoarse, weak, unrecognizable.

"It's me. Christine. I've been here awhile."

"Christine?"

"Yes, special privileges. I'm from the cheer-you-up brigade." She tried to be light, but it fell flat.

"It doesn't get worse than this." He wheezed like he was a hundred years old.

"Yes, it's absolutely ghastly."

"Ah, Christine. Thank you." He gasped. "You don't pretty up things." She could barely hear the words. He seemed to try to say more but it came out an indecipherable gurgle. Then he lapsed into silence. She let a few minutes pass. Laughter filtered into the room from the nurse's station down the hall, and she wondered if Jimmy heard it too. Or perhaps, he had fallen asleep.

"Everyone else tries to make me feel better." He started to move to face her but groaned instead, the movement apparently too painful to complete. So, he remained on his back, his bandaged face to the ceiling.

"That only makes me feel worse," he rasped. He was silent for a moment, perhaps gathering strength to go on. She wished she were anywhere but in this room.

"No one admits it. But I know. I'm going to die. So much radiation."

He was right, of course. He was probably radioactive. Might even be endangering her or anyone who came near him. She mustn't think about that; there were so many unknowns with the gadget. She didn't know which lethal materials were being used to make it; there was no point wondering, not now, not here. She must focus on Jimmy. But what could she do for him? Should she open a window? She wasn't sure the air would do him any good, but maybe she would feel less like she was suffocating. She flung the window open with a grunt.

"Does that feel better?" she asked, immediately embarrassed by the stupidity of her question.

"It's eating me alive," he wheezed. She was startled, then realized he hadn't heard her, that he had meant the radiation, not air from the open window. Maybe the only thing she could do for him was let him tell her of his pain.

"I can't imagine what that must feel like," she said.

"My skin, it burns. Also my eyes, where they used to be," he whispered.

Tears welled as she remembered his kind blue eyes, how he had gently suggested she might come to like Los Alamos that first day when she reeled at the brackish water. Those eyes that gazed in self-doubt and awe as Gertie whizzed away from them both on the ski slopes less than a year ago. Those lively eyes that revealed an innate gratitude and eagerness to please. Gone. She mustn't cry. She coughed and wiped her tears with a handkerchief.

"I've brought you a letter from Gertie."

"From Gertie? She knows?"

"No, Kurt and I sent her a letter, as if from you. We told her you were called away on a special mission to the Pacific. And she wrote back. The letter was intercepted. Oppie thought it might comfort you. Kurt didn't want to read it to you himself. Embarrassed, I guess. They decided to send me."

"I think of her. I cry, even without eyes. For Gertie, and for Owen too. What does it mean? That I think of Owen. I am crazy, going crazy."

Again, she could feel tears welling. Maybe he was indeed out of his mind, hallucinating. They must have him on all kinds of medications. And then the radiation itself. Who knew what it did to one's brain?

Jimmy continued. "When the pain is worst, when my skin corrodes, eats itself, it is Owen I cling to. Through the pain. To try and make it less." He paused, gasping for breath. "That's wrong, isn't it? Not normal, is it?" he whispered.

What was he doing? Sitting in judgment on himself now? He'd always ridden securely on his moral high horse. He owed himself some latitude.

"This whole situation is not normal," Christine said.

"Remember when we went horseback riding and you said no one really knows what God intended for us? I am trying to make sense of things. Wondering if he intended this end for me." A yellow-green liquid oozed from his mouth. He sputtered, insisting on going on. "Maybe this is because of the way I think about Owen. It's a sin."

It amazed Christine that despite his pain, he remembered their conversation. He was lucid yet confused.

"I'm sinful. Bad," he said softly.

She suddenly felt angry at Jimmy for putting himself through torture now, in this place, in his state. What was he trying to tell her? Was he gay? He didn't seem like some of the homosexuals she had known in the art world in New York. But then one never knew everything about anyone.

"What's bad and wrong is that you are lying here blind and in pain."

"I brought this on myself. I'm a walking sin. I was meant to die."

She wanted to shake him, rattle his bed. She paced at its foot to calm herself. Suddenly, Gertie's complaints that Jimmy shied away from kissing made sense. Christine had always attributed Jimmy's sexual reticence to shyness or inexperience. But why was Jimmy practically engaged to Gertie if he danced at the other end of the ballroom? Maybe he thought Gertie could fix him. Maybe he was right. What did she know? The homosexuals she had met—artists, gallery owners, art collectors—had been witty and smart and sensitive. Yet it seemed repulsive, men with men. She didn't want to think about it. And it was totally beside the point now.

"Jimmy, stop this. You were meant to live. And to love. We all are. In our different and imperfect ways. No one's perfect. Including me, as you have made clear to me in no uncertain terms. For goodness' sake, give yourself a break."

"I'm in so much pain," he wheezed. "It's easier to believe I deserve the pain. That there's a reason."

"Jimmy, you mustn't think that. It was an accident. You didn't do this to yourself, did you?"

"No. I was just an idiot. Lost my concentration for a minute. Dropped something. That's all it takes. A second of not paying attention. But I deserve it."

"You don't!"

The late-afternoon sun sliced into the room, reflecting off the pale-green walls and illuminating the wooden cross over Jimmy's bed.

"If this isn't a punishment, then I would be better off dead. That would be better, yes, to be dead. In any case, I will die, in days, in weeks. So why suffer this pain? Why wait?"

"Don't say that!" Christine wanted to tell him he had every reason to live, that the pain would lessen, and he would get better. But it would be a lie. She couldn't imagine what his future would be like. She knew enough about radiation to understand that what awaited him was the ever-more painful disintegration of his body. And probably in continued isolation. It was unbearable to think about.

"Do you want to hear Gertie's letter?"

"Yes."

Christine opened her purse, the envelope with the letter already sliced neatly open by the censor's knife. She cleared her throat. In the hallway, the soft-soled tread of chatting nurses could be heard making rounds with a squeaky medicine cart. Christine waited until they passed by, heading for other rooms.

> Dear Jimmy,
> I was so glad to get your letter. I admit, I was very hurt when I heard you left without a word to me, but now that you have explained, I understand, and of course I

am not angry at you. It must be frustrating to be away, unable to finish what you have been working on so hard.

School has started, and I love being a senior. You can tell the teachers think of us differently. It's as if they know they will not be able to control us for much longer, so they are beginning to free the reins (like you say, it is best to do that with horses and I guess with people too!). We get to spend a lot of time planning our senior research project. I am thinking of doing mine on the relation between the Bureau of Indian Affairs and the Indians around here. Do you think that's a good subject? Christine said she'd help me. She's really interested because of the pots she gets from her friend in San Ildefonso.

Everyone is beginning to talk about college, and I have to figure out where I want to go next year. Any advice? It's all so confusing, and my parents, of course, are no help. My grades are good (you do remember that I had some excellent tutoring in math—along with a few extra-credit lessons in kissing!), so I can go most any place that lets in immigrants and Jews. If you are going back to MIT after the war, maybe I should study in Boston so we can be near each other. I would like to be in a city, and I like Boston. What do you think?

Mama is better these days. Papa is in a foul mood. He needs you to cheer him up. I'm hopeless at it, it seems. I think he misses you almost as much as I do.

What do you do with your days? Tell me everything (no secrets, remember . . .)

I miss you gobs.

S.W.A.K.,

Gertie

Christine was surprised that Gertie, who usually wore her emotions on her sleeve, had managed such a cheerful letter. She had clearly tried to sound upbeat for Jimmy's sake. In fact, Gertie came to Christine's every day to moan about missing Jimmy, how she regretted not appreciating him enough, how nothing seemed to matter with him gone. All typical teenage stuff, her melodramatic longing natural—and understandable. Christine dreaded to think how much deeper Gertie's pain would yet become.

Jimmy was silent. In the corridor, the cart with squeaky wheels passed by again. Did they not stop by Jimmy's room because they had nothing effective to give him?

"Gertie is so sweet. How are you going to answer her?" he whispered.

"I don't know yet. What would you want me to tell her? Otherwise, Kurt and I will have to think of something."

"You and Kurt," he said and whimpered. Jimmy was moaning now, louder than before. Was it because of the thought of them in cahoots, his lingering anger at the affair?

"The pain. It's really bad. Please call the nurse. I need more painkillers. Right away. To knock me out," he groaned.

"I'm sorry, I must have tired you."

"No. You haven't. The pain makes me crazy. Get the nurse. Go now. But come again. Promise you'll come again," he whispered.

She tried to promise by patting his bandaged hand, but he yelped in pain at her touch.

CHAPTER 36
JIMMY

October 1944

Most of all, Jimmy missed water: its coolness coursing down his throat when he scooped it up along the shores of the Frijoles River after a horseback ride. Or water from the faucet in the barracks, tepid and tinged with brown, quickly used to wash off sleep and the night before the precious liquid ran out. And there was the glittering surface of Ashley Pond, where he and Gertie had gone so often to argue and reconcile.

Now, all liquid entered his body with an intravenous tube. The only water was the daily sloshing in a bucket when the orderly washed the floors, killing or redistributing the germs on the ward with the swish of his mop and leaving behind the stench of ammonia. Afterward, the squeaking of the nurses' shoes on the wet linoleum penetrated through the pain of the burns.

His body felt like cracked desert soil, bubbling and bursting from the heat, as though he was sunburned both inside and out. When the nurses changed his bandages every few days, he could sense layers of his skin coming off, encrusted with pus and sticking to the gauze, leaving a lower layer of skin that continued to sear. The last time they removed the bandages, he had a new sensation of a bare head, and he felt the nurse's hand remove loose tufts of his hair.

In recent days, nausea had overcome him, a seasickness worse than he could have ever imagined on his father's fishing boat. Often, he vomited, although he had nothing to vomit. His arms and legs were swelling. He heard the medical staff discuss his malfunctioning urinary tract and how to eliminate liquid from his body. Periodically, a doctor would question him about how he was feeling. Often, he was too groggy to answer, but once or twice he had asked about his prognosis, and the answer was always: "We're doing our best." So he stopped asking; he drifted in and out of consciousness. At times, when the painkillers gave him some slight relief, Gertie hovered in his mind like an unreachable cloud, her smile a formation that changed in the breeze. He wanted to touch her, but his arms were smoldering weights. Thoughts of Owen sizzled him with pain and pleasure. At first, he tried to will Owen's image away, but not since Christine's visit. Let Owen be the pain and the relief from pain. He no longer cared. He just wanted the pain to end. He wanted to join Gertie in the clouds. Or be a wave in the sea off the coast of Cape Cod on a misty day, a cool day, which wouldn't burn like his scourged skin. He was parched all the time. If he were a wave, maybe he wouldn't be so thirsty, maybe he could escape this interminable pain.

He had only himself to blame, the carelessness of a moment that had caused the accident, this slow, excruciating dying. He had been so excited when Kurt told him they had finally received a plutonium core—a smooth, shiny ball of the stuff about three inches in diameter—to use for experiments. He couldn't wait to see if the calculations he and Owen had been poring over for months would prove accurate. Owen had been concentrating on the use of beryllium as a nuclear reflector, Jimmy on tungsten carbide. How much tungsten was the right amount to position around the core to heighten neutron activity, just below critical mass? A quiet night shift, the perfect time to find out.

He was sure it would be no less than four bricks, so he started with that, and the meter had clicked just the way it should, indicating greater activity but not yet near critical mass. He added a fifth brick, which made the meter rise more—those neutrons were streaming back fast now toward the core. Mesmerized, his heart racing, he had dared to add a sixth brick, but it made the meter dip into the red zone, dangerously close to critical mass. He rushed to pluck the brick off. Too quickly. It slipped out of his hand, falling into the center of the assembly. It glowed a most eerie blue. He swiped the brick off the assembly, immediately feeling his hand tingling as the brick thumped to the floor. He ran to the security booth at the Tech Area entrance for help. By the time he reached the gate, his hand was burning with pain, turning black.

Now he was damned, lying here, his life over. He seethed at himself in whatever recesses of his body the radiation hadn't yet touched. His body curled and separated itself from life, layer by layer, and through it all, under the gauze, seeped an antiseptic smell that never left. He heard some lucky bastard snoring at the end of the hall. He wondered if it was day or night.

At first there had been visitors: Oppie and Kurt had come when Jimmy had been too drugged to speak, so they hadn't exchanged a single word with him. He wanted to tell them how sorry he was that the core would have to be retested now, to see if it was still usable. Sorry that he had been so careless. Sorry that they had given him a chance to make something of himself and he had blown it. But he couldn't speak, his mouth dry, parched. He had not even managed a groan. They assumed he was not conscious when they stood around while he was checked for radiation. He heard a technician read off the meter, "Still radiating at five hundred ten rems."

"Amazing he's still alive," Oppie said.

"How long can he possibly last with so much in him?" Kurt asked.

"Days, weeks. I can't imagine more than that," Oppie answered.

Jimmy understood their curiosity. He also resented it, the feeling that he was an unexpected experiment. In the end, he would die. But he couldn't muster words. He lay mum, then slipped from consciousness. They were gone by the time he came back to himself. How long ago had that visit been? A few days? Weeks? In any case, too long ago. Why was he still alive?

There were others who came at times, although he couldn't identify their voices. The words *hopeless* and *unfathomable* were whispered in his room. No one told him what was happening. They seemed to think he was delusional. Not surprising, really. Sometimes he howled in pain, talked gibberish. He could feel his mind slipping. He felt his digestive tract consuming itself. He smelled his own decay. The snap of the rubber gloves the nurses and doctors put on served as a warning of the pain that would surge through his body the moment they touched him.

Often the nurses left the door open so that he heard the radio from their station, catching only occasional headlines.

"The German city of Aachen is now fully encircled by the American army. The taut battle line stretches fifty miles between Aachen and the Maas River in Holland . . ."

He wished they would close the door so he wouldn't have to hear any more. He was so tired of it all. And yet, sometimes he found comfort in the thought that life was continuing, that there was a world beyond his bandages and pain.

Of course, they had not let Gertie come. He was grateful she would not see him like this, bandaged from head to foot. He cried—yes, he was still capable of tears—when he thought of the dreams he had once had of a family: a wife, children. He had believed that with Gertie he could do anything, even come to love her as a man should. He thought, too, less frequently, of his parents. He had never thanked them properly for bringing him up with a strong sense of duty, a commitment to purpose, and a work ethic that had served him well. He doubted they had been informed of the accident. Would probably never know the truth. He hoped they thought he had been shipped to the Pacific, died there, was missing in action. At least they would be proud of him. Finally. A real hero. The irony brought on a new bout of retching. Jimmy knew the army. He was being kept alive for observation, so the doctors could learn about the effect of radiation, of the bomb he had been so honored to work on. He would never know if it worked. In the end, his only contribution to science would be a greater understanding of the various ways radiation could destroy a human body. How much more of this was he expected to take? How long had he endured it already? It felt as if the pain had been forever.

CHAPTER 37
CHRISTINE

November 1944

Ten days after her first visit, Christine stepped into Christus St. Vincent Hospital in Santa Fe again. The smell of ammonia, as strong as on her first visit, hit her the moment she walked inside. Her steps echoed as she climbed the stairs to the second floor and walked down the long corridor to Jimmy's room. This time, she knocked first to avoid catching him in midmoan and entered only when he responded.

"Christine?"

"Yes, Jimmy."

"Ah, good."

Then he was silent, just like the last time. She did not know what to do with herself. Had he slipped into sleep or lost consciousness? She tiptoed to the chair at the foot of his bed and sat down to wait. A flock of chickadees swooped into the cottonwood below the window, chirping in the afternoon sun, their black-capped heads disappearing into leaves so lushly yellow they seemed on fire.

"Christine, is it?"

"Yes, Jimmy. It's me."

"Good."

Kurt had told her Jimmy kept insisting on seeing her, obsessively telling the doctors, the nurses, anyone who would listen that he had to speak to her. And Oppie had obtained G-2's authorization. She had been warned that Jimmy might not be lucid. His body emitted a putrid smell that competed with a telltale wisp of antiseptics. She was glad he could not see her scrunch her nose at the stench. She opened the window, but the room still reeked. She heard the swish of nurses' uniforms passing the room.

"Please, close the door," Jimmy said.

Christine obliged and then returned to the chair near the window.

"How's Gertie?" he rasped.

"Doing well, other than missing you. Preoccupied with exams and with choosing a college, busy with debate club. She's taken up tennis. I've asked her to horseback ride with me, but she won't go. Says it makes her miss you too much." Christine felt her response petering out like a windup toy losing power.

"I'm glad she's well."

What could Christine add? It was ludicrous to ask Jimmy how he was doing. The stench of pus, of urine, of blood told her. She was surprised he had the presence of mind to ask about Gertie. He was more lucid than she had expected.

"I don't have . . . I don't have much time . . . to talk," he gasped. "The painkillers . . . don't work . . . for long. So listen. Closely."

She came to his bedside. "What is it?"

"Help me," he whispered.

"Help you?" What could she possibly do for him?

"End this. Please. You must . . . end this."

"What are you talking about? You're not making sense."

"Don't!" he groaned. "Don't pretend. Listen." His hoarse voice cracked. "Listen, please!"

He was crying. She still wasn't sure how he could without eyes, but she could hear the choked emotions from his throat.

"Okay, calm down. I'm listening."

He breathed deeply as if summoning all his energy to speak.

"I'm no good. To anyone. Not myself . . . not the project . . . not Gertie." He gasped between words, groaned, then persisted. "All there is, is pain, worse all the time."

She felt his heavy breathing, as if he was trying again to gather the wherewithal to keep speaking.

"If you think this isn't a punishment. If you believe all this has nothing to do with the sin of who I am, then end it," he croaked. "How much pain am I supposed to endure?" It came out as a whisper.

Christine looked away to the wooden crucifix over his bed, to the chirping chickadees outside, to the green walls of the room, to the black and white tiles of the floor.

"Have you spoken to the doctor?"

"You believe I don't deserve this pain. That's what you said. If this is my punishment, so be it. But if you believe what you said . . . then end the pain. You have the guts. No one else has the guts . . . only you . . ."

"Me?" He had asked for her because he thought she had guts? He expected her to end this, somehow? *How?* He couldn't really believe she would do anything so drastic? So illegal? So risky? So—did she dare say it?—so immoral. That's why he had asked her here. He considered her the most immoral person he knew. It was hardly flattering, even if now he called it guts.

"You do believe I don't deserve this, don't you? Your saying so eased my mind. So now . . . please . . . end the pain," he whispered. "You know it is the right thing to do. You have . . . guts."

"That's why you asked to see me?"

"Yes." He groaned, then his body shuddered.

Christine glanced out the window at the bruise-colored mountains in the distance. True, she had been haunted since her first visit by Jimmy's impotence over the pain of his every waking moment. Certainly, she had wondered when it would end and how. Yet what he was asking her to do was abominable. How could he even ask? And yet how could he not? She was the one who had tried to assure him the pain was not punishment for the sin of desiring Owen. It seemed he would believe her only if she killed him. If she were Jimmy, she would want to be dead. Jimmy, his body wrapped in bandages, blind, was unable to carry out his wishes himself. Yet, who was she to take this on herself? How could she? How could he have imagined her capable of this? She had no clue how to even do what he was asking her to do! Kill. Murder. Mercy killing. There, she had said the words to herself, called it by its name.

"I know only two people with guts," Jimmy whispered. "Gertie . . . Gertie . . . and you." He breathed heavily, determined to finish the thought he was trying to express. "I can't ask Gertie. You understand . . . you don't follow the rules. You don't do what's expected . . . look at me." His voice cracked, then was silent for a minute, as if giving her time to consider his plight. Finally, he whispered hoarsely: "You have to end this. Please."

"I don't know what to say."

"Say nothing . . . just do it."

"If anyone should do something, it's the doctor."

"He won't. They want to keep me alive—I'm an experiment. They don't care about the pain."

"They warned me you talk crazy sometimes."

"Christine, you have compassion . . . I know . . . so kill me. Please."

"Jimmy, this is crazy talk."

"It's not crazy."

"It's taking a life. No one has the right."

"Someday you will make a life. You will have a baby."

"Me, a baby?" Christine laughed bitterly. "Now I know you're crazy."

"You'll have one. I'm sure."

"Jimmy, stop this talk."

"End this pain. You can, only you."

"You're asking me to commit a crime."

"Every day, in war, people are killing people. Killing children, women, the elderly. When they call it war, it's not a crime. How can it be a crime to end my pain?"

"Please, stop. You're muddled, confused." Why wasn't she flying out the door, calling for a doctor to sedate him? She must be as crazy as Jimmy.

"Everyone on the project, we are all killers," Jimmy whispered, as though to no one. Then he seemed to remember she was in the room. He called out, his voice momentarily strong with conviction. "Join the crowd, Christine. Do your bit for humankind—do your bit for me."

"You're mad. You're not making sense."

"Christine, there is no other out for me . . . from the pain. I'll help as much as I can. I won't resist, I promise. No one will suspect you. No one will know. My life signs will end. No surprise to anyone. Free me."

"I don't know, Jimmy." She looked around the room. Free him. He wanted her to free him. How? Were there pills she could give him? Could she stop the various feeds going into and out of him? Certainly not. All of that left too many traces. Was she thinking like a murderer already, considering how to kill without being detected? Could she really do this? It was convenient to think that Jimmy was deranged. It was uncomfortable to admit that he was right to question why it was criminal to put him out of his pain while soldiers who killed were considered heroes.

She moved to the window. Her sudden appearance startled the birds in the cottonwood. They cried and flew away toward the sun, which was streaking the sky pink with the coming sunset. Surveying the room again, she turned back to Jimmy.

"I can't see you, but I know you are listening," he rasped, then coughed. "I can feel you looking at the pillow."

She hadn't been looking at his pillow, but now she did.

"I promise I won't change my mind," he croaked. "I won't cry out. I won't struggle. I will make it easy. I can't see you, but I can feel you. I can tell you're looking at the extra pillow at the foot of the bed."

Her eyes swung to the extra pillow. He was guiding her. He had thought this through. Christine was silent. She felt numb.

"You know what I say makes sense. It's not crazy talk," he whispered.

Jimmy's words rattled in her head. She could not accept them and could not dismiss them. Chatter from the nurses' station filtered in through the closed door. Her eyes lingered on the pillow at the foot of his bed. She fingered it, clutched it, then relaxed her hand. Could it be that easy?

"Good, Christine. I can hear your hands on the pillowcase. Amazing what small sounds a blind man hears." His voice was strong, the thought of dying already a balm.

"Yes, good, you're holding it with both hands. I can tell. Come close. Ah. Ouch! Oh, a kiss on the forehead. Sweet of you. But it hurts. Every touch hurts. Even a kiss. Now you must work quickly." His voice was so seductive suddenly, sinewy.

Christine gazed at him. She wanted him to stop talking, stop insisting. Kissing him had felt like kissing a mummy. She wanted to flee. Why had she come? She glanced at the closed door. It would be so easy to just drop the pillow back at the foot of the bed and leave.

"Don't cop out, Christine," Jimmy whispered. "I promise not to yell. No regrets. Do it."

The pillow smelled of Ivory soap. She nuzzled it to her face and felt her tears wet the fabric. She wished he would stop begging. She wanted to make him better. The squeaky wheels of the medicine tray sounded outside, stopped outside Jimmy's room. There was a knock on the door, and the nurse opened it without waiting for an answer.

"Everything okay?" she asked.

Christine nodded and smiled weakly, her heart beating wildly. What if the nurse had come in while she was smothering him? Why was she even considering doing this? She was as crazy as Jimmy.

"He asked for another pillow," Christine said, fluffing the one in her hand, her head nodding toward Jimmy.

"I'll get that for you," the nurse said, taking the extra pillow, giving it a pat, and delicately moving it under Jimmy's head.

"Ouch. No. That hurts," Jimmy moaned. "Take it back. It doesn't help."

The nurse shrugged, gently removed the pillow, and put it back at the foot of the bed. "It's hard to know what to do for him," she said to Christine as if Jimmy wasn't in the room.

"Yes, it is," said Christine. "Is any of that for him?" Her head indicated the tray of medicines out in the hall.

"No, he's set till dinnertime." The nurse returned to the tray and continued down the hall.

Christine closed the door and turned to Jimmy. She didn't believe in divine intervention, but wasn't the nurse's sudden appearance a sign, warning her against this folly?

"Please," he whispered. There was a white residue at the edge of his mouth; his lips were cracked and dry. He seemed so sure he wanted her to act. He did not deserve so much pain. There was no hope. She was unlikely to get caught. The nurse had just left without a reason to return soon. And yes, Christine knew how to keep her mouth shut. Could she really live with a secret this size? She looked down at Jimmy, at his face, only the mouth visible among the bandages.

"Please, please, please."

It sounded like a prayer.

She felt her arms tremble and move as if of their own accord. Her heart pounded in her ears. She retrieved the pillow from the foot of the bed and pushed it down on his face with all her strength. He had promised not to struggle, but after a few seconds there was an involuntary kick of his leg. She almost pulled the pillow back. Maybe he was having second thoughts. Then she felt him still. He had not changed his mind. She pushed down harder. She counted to one hundred. Then to two hundred. She kept her eye on the door, terrified a nurse might enter. She started to gag, forced herself to take deep breaths and look around the room, calm herself. She heard the birds outside, a different flock, with a guttural warble, soothing, peaceful. Late-afternoon shadows fell on the plant by his bedside. She closed her eyes and kept counting—to three hundred. Then pulled back the pillow, not sure he was dead. She kissed him on his bandage-covered forehead again. He did not moan in pain this time. He was dead. But she pushed down with the pillow again. Just to be sure. She counted to one hundred again, slowly. Then she smoothed the pillow, turned it over, placed it back at the foot of the bed, and left the room.

She walked steadily down the hall, past the nurses' station, nodded at the nurse—a different one than earlier—who nodded back at her. Then she ran down the stairs as fast as she could, dashed into the parking lot, and got into the Packard sedan she had borrowed from Martha.

She wanted to sit and absorb what she had done but was overcome with the need to flee from the hospital. She stopped at a nearby gas station to use the fuel-rationing coupon G-2 had given her for the trip to the hospital. She watched the gas attendant to see if he saw anything amiss. Could he tell she was distraught, a criminal? He was young, high school age maybe, with freckles even more abundant than hers. He offered to wash the window; she nodded and gave him two quarters. His eyes lit up at the size of the tip, and he thanked her profusely. She hadn't meant to give him so much. Two quarters? Well, at least she had made his day. She had to be careful. Had to act normal. What would she do after a visit to a patient at the hospital on a normal day? She'd go into Santa Fe for Christmas shopping. So that's what she ought to do. Now. Act normal. If only her heart would stop pounding. If only her hands on the steering wheel didn't feel so clammy and cold as she drove to the center of town and parked.

She walked up Otero Street, turned onto Marcy, her feet carrying her on to Lincoln in a daze, barely noticing the shops, oblivious to the traffic. As if by instinct, she circled back onto Palace Avenue, stopping finally at a record shop. As she flitted through the records sitting in the bins, her fingers twitched. If only she didn't keep feeling Jimmy flinch under the pillow as she picked up a gramophone record of Lawrence Welk for her parents. If only she didn't remember Jimmy's voice croaking "please, please" as she picked out a recording of a live concert of *Madame Butterfly* featuring Licia Albanese for Thomas's parents. She hoped her in-laws, particularly her mother-in-law, would like the record. Angelica was always hard to please—and the one person, Christine wagered, who would not be surprised if she were apprehended for murdering Jimmy. Why was she even letting herself think this way? She must stop. She set her mind to finding something for Gertie, settling on an album of songs from the Broadway musical *Oklahoma!*

She had already ordered a new set of skis for Thomas, so she did not need a gift for him. They had cost a small fortune, but she had thrown caution to the wind and purchased them anyway. Thomas had so few pleasures these days, and skiing was one of them. He'd been using the same skis since college. He deserved a new pair. Maybe he deserved a new wife, a better one, who did not cheat on him, did not go around murdering people. If the truth ever came to light, would he stand by her? Would he visit her in prison? Would he understand why she had smothered Jimmy? Would he understand the spell Jimmy had cast on her with his whispered commands, with his pleas? All that, maybe yes. But Thomas would never understand why she had cheated on him.

As she stowed her packages in the trunk, her attention was drawn to Saint Francis Cathedral across the street. She felt outside her own body, watching herself from afar, going through motions she could not account for. Although she had no desire to confess, she found herself walking into the church anyway. Would remorse overcome her there? It was cold inside. She turned right to the votive stand, flickering with candles, and lit one for Jimmy. Maybe now the feeling would come, some sense of regret, but it did not. Her eyes welled with tears of sorrow that he was dead. She lit another candle; she did not know for whom. Maybe for herself. For the person she once was. She had never felt more herself and less herself than she did standing before these winking candles. There would be lies ahead. She might be questioned by the police. After all, she was the last person to see Jimmy alive. Would she confess to anyone? To Kurt? To Thomas? No, this was a burden she would carry alone. That is what Jimmy expected.

She felt the presence of someone standing behind her. A priest. He was young, so smooth skinned she wondered if he was old enough to shave. His thin, pale hands fingered his rope belt nervously. "The confession booths are available for your use," he said. "Just so you know."

"Thank you." She wondered with horror if he had been reading her thoughts, then looked around and noticed she was the only person in the church. "I'm fine." She smiled and left, closing the heavy wood door behind her.

On the drive back to Los Alamos, the desert unrolled before her, the light dripping on rock formations like maple syrup on a stack of pancakes that stretched below her to the horizon. Shifting gears as she climbed the hairpin curves, she felt glad to be alive, to be going home. She was suddenly ravenously hungry. Beyond that, she did not feel anything. It was as if she had fused with the landscape. She could not recall the hospital room, what Jimmy had said, or how she had responded, only that he had twitched at the last moment.

She passed the security check at the entrance gate of Los Alamos, pulled up in front of her fourplex, unloaded the gifts from the trunk, and returned the car keys to Martha. Once home, she took a long shower and washed her hair, even though it wasn't dirty. Afterward, she rubbed herself with body lotion, slowly massaging it in, as if this attention to her body could unlock her numbness. She kept expecting her reflection in the mirror to show her new status as a murderer, but it didn't. When she had lost her virginity, she had also studied herself, expecting to look different. Perhaps seismic changes did not always leave a visible trace.

CHAPTER 38
SARAH

November 1944

The grave was the deepest Sarah had ever seen—a good three meters down in the sand, in the middle of nowhere. Why so deep? But this was not the only odd aspect of Jimmy's funeral. It was also the smallest Sarah had ever attended. Just Oppie; his wife, Kitty; Owen; Kurt; and herself at the gravesite. She had been surprised when Kurt asked her to join him, even more to find both Oppenheimers there. Oppie looked as genteel as ever in a camel hair coat and matching porkpie hat. Kitty, chain-smoking cigarettes, wore wide-legged black pants and a fur jacket, which seemed far warmer and more likely to keep out the wind than Sarah's cashmere coat. She shivered not only from the cold; the fact that G-2 would allow wives to attend was alarming. Especially since this was clearly top secret, without even a chaplain, pallbearers, or Jimmy's parents present. She could think of only one explanation: Jimmy's death had so unraveled Kurt and Oppie that despite the obsession with secrecy, G-2 decided wives were essential emotional support. Terrifying. And true.

Ever since the accident, Kurt seemed to be falling apart. All light had drained from his eyes, his walk was heavy, he muttered to himself frequently. These days, drawing him into a conversation felt like groping behind a heavy curtain.

Now, Kurt was weeping silent tears, his body shuddering. In twenty years of marriage, she had never seen him cry. Not when he was forced from his job for being a Jew, not when they wrenched themselves from Germany, not when his mother passed away and he could not attend her funeral. She gave him a handkerchief, which he accepted without looking up. He didn't seem to notice the cold or the fact that the steady wind was drying his streaked face, crusting his skin.

Kurt's tears somehow prevented her own. His weakness made her stronger. Her thoughts gravitated to all their relatives, to the thousands, millions of civilians, to the Jews who had been killed and never honored with funerals and the soldiers who were scattered on the battlefields of Europe, North Africa, and Asia. So much loss. Standing by the pit where Jimmy was about to be buried reified for her the destruction in so many corners of the world. Yet this burial of one human soul paradoxically instilled a deep belief in the world, one she had not ever felt. The juxtaposition of the deep pit of a grave and the exquisite sapphire sky above them, the desert stretching out to the horizon, gave her an eerie sense of comfort that the world would go on, no matter who died, no matter what happened. And with it came an epiphany, a desire that took her by surprise; she wanted to be part of the future, and the sadness within her that just months ago had led her to want only death had itself died.

She glanced at Kurt, who was still weeping. Why had Jimmy's death broken him? Sure, Kurt had a deep affection for the young man. But there must be something more. Did he blame himself? But Kurt hadn't been in the lab when the accident happened. If Kurt had done something wrong, there would have been hell to pay to Oppie, to G-2, to the army brass. And no one seemed to blame Kurt. It had clearly been an accident, maybe even Jimmy's fault.

She looked around at the small group. Oppie, always thin, seemed swallowed up in the burgundy scarf wrapped many times around his long neck, his face gaunt, almost ghostlike, his usually twinkling eyes as listless as Kurt's, which were barely visible under a black sheepskin cossack hat. Although Oppie's willowy frame loomed over Kitty, he seemed to need her help to stay upright.

"Come, honey," Kitty murmured to Oppie, guiding him, almost as if he were blind.

At the edge of the grave, three G-2 men eased the plain wood coffin into the ground. G-2 had not entrusted the pallbearing to others, clearly taking severe measures to ensure only a few people were in the know. What was G-2 so afraid of?

Oppie stared into the grave.

"You wanted to say a few words, dear, didn't you?" Kitty nudged him.

He looked at her blankly.

"Dear, talk." She smiled up at him, disentangling him from her arm.

He startled, as if just woken, and peered at the group. He held Kurt's eyes, perhaps looking for Kurt to save him. But Kurt was still brimming with tears. There was no solace there.

"I suppose I should say a few words." Oppie fumbled for a handkerchief to dab his face and returned it to his coat pocket. He coughed, closed his eyes for a long moment, put the fingers of both hands to his temples as if trying to gather his thoughts, then let his hands fall to his sides and addressed the mourners.

"It is written in the Bhagavad Gita, 'Nothing is lost or wasted in this life.' We must believe that this is true in the passing of Jimmy Campbell, a conscientious scientist, our only casualty to date. We have tried to ensure the safety of all who work here, but through no lack of effort on our part, we have lost him. We honor him today. He will always be part of our success."

There was silence. Sarah wished someone would play music or say a prayer or read a poem. No one seemed to know what to do next.

Oppie coughed. "Does anyone wish to add anything?"

Kurt stepped forward, swallowed, and searched for words. "Jimmy was an outstanding young man—thorough, meticulous, and talented in his work. He was also kind and gentle. I will miss him, as will everyone privileged to know him. There are lessons in accidents. His has led us to hard truths, which give me no rest."

Sarah did not understand what Kurt meant but noticed that he was frowning at Oppie, who looked away. The tension between them was tangible.

Kitty must have noticed it too. She linked a protective arm through her husband's. "Are you okay, dear?" she asked Oppie, who looked up and cast a hard glance at Kurt before lowering his head to Kitty and nodding.

Owen coughed to draw attention to himself. "May I say a few words?"

Kurt and Oppie both nodded and stepped aside to let him near the open pit. For this occasion, he had worn a tie, its knot peeking out under a simple wool plaid coat. He took out a piece of paper from its pocket, coughed, and read:

"Jimmy was my best friend. We always looked out for each other, ever since we met in college. Without him, I would never have gotten to Los Alamos. Both of us considered it the greatest privilege of our lives to be here, to work here." Owen's bare rough hands trembled, the paper shaking. He sounded like he was choking, and he looked cold.

"Jimmy was the diligent one, pulling me away when we went drinking at Fuller Lodge so that we would get a proper night's sleep, never letting me slack off. His earnestness made me a better version of myself. He will not have the chance to taste so much of what he wanted in life." Owen looked up for a moment from his notes. The wind, which was picking up, whipped his hair. He swallowed hard several times, stared back at the speech in his hand, as if he could not find his place.

"He found love here, hoped to marry the young woman who captured his heart—Gertie—to have children, to succeed as a scientist. He deeply believed in our work and in its success. I, for one, will keep soldiering on, for both of us."

With that, Owen abruptly shoved the paper deep in his pocket and grabbed the large shovel near the grave. He quickly dumped a shovelful of sand into the open pit. He repeated this several times and slammed the shovel back in the pile of sand. Each of the others followed suit, the sand thudding onto the coffin.

Then it was over. They were back in the cars, the Oppenheimers in their own black sedan, Sarah, Kurt, and Owen in a second sedan, driven by a G-2 agent. As the small party drove away, Sarah saw the two remaining agents were filling the grave. Would the site be marked? She had so many questions for Kurt, but she knew better than to ask now in the dense silence and in the presence of the agent.

While making a cup of tea for herself in the kitchen, Sarah noticed the letter Gertie had left on the table to be mailed to Jimmy. He had been buried three months ago. How long could they pretend that he was alive? What was G-2 planning? Sarah glanced at the snowcapped mountains shimmering in the distance. She sliced open the letter with a knife. She was not one to pry, but under the circumstances she felt she had to gauge whether her daughter was adjusting to the absence of Jimmy and perhaps glean how she might help her if she wasn't. Sarah smoothed the pages and allowed herself a moment of pride at Gertie's careful penmanship. So like her daughter to write in perfect straight lines.

Dear Jimmy,
Thanks for your last letter. I hope you are well. Life here goes on as usual, except that somehow everything is different. I can't explain it. No one is acting themselves. Papa these days is withdrawn and sad, barely talks, and is more absentminded than ever. He doesn't even ask me about my grades or tests, if you can

imagine such a thing!! Maybe it's because he misses you like I do!!! And Mama now wakes up early in the morning, fusses and prepares breakfast for us, and gets Papa up. It's almost as if she has to coax Papa to go to work. It's so strange. She makes his favorite foods all the time and insists that he come home for dinner. She barely mentions the relatives back in Europe these days. It's as if she's so worried about Papa, she no longer worries about anything else. Seems like in our family, there always has to be at least one sad person!!

It's supposed to snow again this week. Every time I ski, I can hear you telling me to keep my legs parallel. Remember what a good time we had on the slopes last year? Oh well, maybe next year. You never answered my question about applying to schools in Boston. Christine is all for Mount Holyoke. That's just a few hours from Boston. And I've been thinking about Simmons, which is in Boston and would be even closer to you. Answer me or I will be insulted! I need to figure this out soon. It is hard to decide from so far away. I wish I could visit the colleges, but of course, that's not allowed. I guess I should be grateful I will be let out of here to go to college at all! At least my grades are good. Papa says I can go anywhere I want.

Miss you and can't wait to see you.

Write to me soon.

S.W.A.K.,

Gertie

Sarah folded the letter back into the envelope, stroked it as tenderly as if it were Gertie's hand. The child understood so much without knowing anything. Gertie's description made Sarah see how they had all changed. Indeed, Kurt was the center of her concern. Ever since Jimmy's accident, Sarah felt as if she were trying to hold back an avalanche of Kurt's out-of-control feelings. One day he was agitated over the failure of a lab test, the next day distraught when the work went well, as if he wanted it to fail. Just last night, he had sighed so deeply when he came to bed, letting his shoes fall with such a heavy thud, that she had been startled.

"Another difficult day, yes?" she asked.

"The work, it is progressing."

"So?"

"I have no fight in me." He sat at the edge of the bed and ran his fingers on the top of his bald head.

"Ah, with your colleagues, problems."

"No. I just don't care about the war anymore." He shrugged as if surprised at himself and shook his head. "I don't see what success will look like."

Sarah pulled herself up to sitting position to better see his face. "What, Hitler is suddenly not an enemy?"

He unclipped his bow tie and started to unbutton his shirt, preparing for bed. "Of course, he is. But so many people are being killed. So many more will die. Terrible, horrible deaths. Painful, tortured deaths. Like Jimmy's. I don't want to be part of it." He reached for his pajamas, under his pillow.

"How can you not be part of it? How can you not want to fight for our family, for our friends, for all those Hitler wants to destroy?"

He rose to undress. "The reports from Europe. There are more of them every day, of mass graves. Ghetto uprisings suppressed. What does that mean, *suppressed*? That everyone has been killed, no? One does not need a wild imagination to know the truth. One must draw the logical conclusion." He folded his clothes and put on his pajamas. "And now, reports also from a few prisoners who escaped from concentration camps. They try to tell the world what the Nazis have done with people in those camps. Winning the war will not save the victims. What's the point?" He got into bed, covered himself, but stayed sitting, leaning against his pillow.

Sarah slipped her hand into his. "Maybe the reports are exaggerated."

"You do not believe that," he said dismissively.

He was right. She didn't; if anything, she suspected the reports in major newspapers might be minimizing the destruction. She received occasional newsletters from the Emergency Committee to Save the Jewish People of Europe, a fringe organization with informants in Europe. It painted a far more dire picture. "The only way to know the truth is to win the war. Surely not everyone is dead."

He lifted his hand in desperation and let it flop down. "I do not have the will. I do not know how to get myself up in the morning." He was so agitated that he got up and began pacing back and forth at the foot of the bed.

Sarah watched him. His restlessness, it made her nervous. She must reassure him, whatever her own doubts. "If we win the war, some of those Hitler wants to kill will be saved."

"And how many will die until then?" He kept pacing.

"The Allies are advancing. The Battle of the Bulge. The Allies won it. And then the Yalta Conference. The end of the war is near." She followed him with her eyes. "Kurt, this is not a time to be discouraged."

He stopped for a moment and turned to her. "I am tired," he said in a quiet, defeated voice.

"You have been this way since Jimmy died."

"Yes."

"If he were alive, Jimmy would want you to keep working."

Kurt started pacing again. "Maybe, I am not so sure. Not if he knew what death would look like."

"Death is death."

Kurt stopped and looked at her. "Deaths are not all the same. His was terrible."

"You have never told me."

"No. I don't want to. And I can't. But it has taken away my motivation."

"Kurt, come here. Come to bed. You must rest, you must go on. You must believe. We cannot leave here."

"I don't know. Maybe we can. Maybe we should." He started to pace again, faster now, even more agitated.

"You don't mean that. I'm sure you don't. Come to bed. Come warm my feet."

But Kurt had shaken his head, gone to the living room for a while. When he did come to bed later, he'd kicked and twisted in his sleep and awoken in the middle of the night—as he often did—in a sweat. His restlessness had woken her, and he confessed to having yet another nightmare about Jimmy. Kurt did not give her details, but she understood that Jimmy's last days had been difficult.

Now, she took her empty cup to the sink and turned on the water, relieved when the faucet sputtered to action, indicating there would be enough water to wash the breakfast dishes. She turned on the radio and tried to understand the gardening advice being proffered by local station KRS. *"Plant seeds inside now—tomatoes, peppers, zucchini, and melons are particularly recommended. Then, in two months, replant them outdoors for this year's victory garden."* She turned off the radio. Hopefully, by the time the vegetables were ripe in a victory garden, the war would be over, and they would have moved on—to where, she was not sure. She wiped the dishes, then found a new envelope for Gertie's letter and carefully copied Jimmy's address to mail it later.

She tried to write a shopping list but couldn't concentrate. These letters between Jimmy and Gertie needed to end. It was wrong to let Gertie continue to weigh studying in Boston to be close to Jimmy, to lead her to believe she would see him again. Kurt said G-2 demanded he keep making up letters from Jimmy. He was, apparently, remarkably good at them, given how convinced Gertie was that the letters she received were indeed from Jimmy. Sarah wondered if it was truly G-2 pushing to continue the correspondence or whether Kurt was reluctant to stop, to accept that Jimmy was dead.

Sarah took out a recipe for Glory Buns, which Martha had clipped for her from *Family Circle* magazine some months ago. The buns were reminiscent of the rolls of her childhood. Kurt liked them, so she made some often, now that she had learned by trial and error to adapt the recipe to Los Alamos's high altitude and the vagaries of her Black Beauty oven. Baked goods not only needed to cook longer here, but she also had to decrease the baking soda and increase the liquids.

As she mixed the ingredients and kneaded the dough, she considered how to ease Gertie into the truth about Jimmy. Gertie could not be told everything, but she must be told something. In fact, all those who had been led to believe Jimmy had shipped out for a special mission in the Pacific needed a newer story, closer to the truth. Kurt said that at the right moment, G-2 would plant a credible story in the *Los Alamos Bulletin*. Kurt and Sarah would be notified in advance so that they could tell Gertie just as the newspaper issue was circulated. It would seem natural, as if they read the news in the paper and were sharing it with her. When Kurt told Sarah of these plans, he concluded by saying: "I need you to tell Gertie. I simply cannot."

Sarah was pleased Kurt considered her capable of this task. Not that she had any idea how she would carry out his wishes.

CHAPTER 39
CHRISTINE

February 1945

Tonight, Christine would tell Thomas she was pregnant. To celebrate their eighth anniversary, they would dine at the Otowi restaurant. Located ten miles east of Los Alamos, it was the only place cleared for residents of the Hill seeking rest and relaxation and was thus booked months ahead of time. Thomas had secured a coveted reservation. For the first time since their arrival on the Hill, they would be going off site for dinner. Until now, she had planned to tell Thomas the news when they came back—in bed, with the lights off. But giving herself a final inspection in the mirror and smoothing a hand over her still-lithe figure, she changed her mind. She must find the wherewithal to look into his eyes and tell him they were going to have a baby—without revealing her doubts that he was the father. In front of the mirror, she practiced. She tried a coy, shy face, eyes lowered, and murmured, "Thomas, our prayers have been answered." Sappy, not like her at all. She looked up gayly, added a glint to her eyes, and tried: "We have more to celebrate than you think." Yes, she liked that. She practiced it again, this time with an imagined glass of wine in hand, then powdered her nose and cheeks, almost completely concealing her freckles.

As she hung up the three dresses she had tried and discarded, she remembered how the pregnancy had surprised her. She hadn't felt sick or noticed any change in her body. It was only when her period, erratic in the best of times, was three weeks late that it dawned on her to make an appointment with a doctor. But with a spate of post-Christmas pneumonia and whooping cough ripping through the Hill, she had to wait weeks for an appointment. In the meantime, she broke off all contact with Kurt. Despite their good intentions to be faithful to their respective spouses, they proved unable to keep their hands off each other when they met to concoct letters from Jimmy. If the doctor confirmed she was pregnant, she did not want to tell Kurt. The best way to ensure that was to not see him. She let him know she would not produce any more letters. It was high time G-2 figured out a better way to account for Jimmy's ongoing absence.

When the doctor confirmed her pregnancy, she was giddy. She was a proper woman after all. For so long, she had felt a curse on her marriage for not giving Thomas the child they so wanted. Carefully scheduled sex with him had become a ritual, one without fervor, like a lapsed Catholic continuing to go to communion in order not to admit to a loss of faith. She wanted the baby to be Thomas's. If she told herself the baby was his often enough, it would be true. She had to make sure Kurt did not for a moment think the baby was his. She smoothed out her stomach. There was no bump yet.

Since leaving the doctor's office last week, her sense of the rightness of the world had grown along with the fetus inside her. Jimmy had prophesied she would have a child in their last conversation. The pregnancy seemed heavenly acquiescence of her decision to help him and brought her as close to believing in God as she had ever come. Thomas was away the day of her visit to the doctor and for the next three days, off to another one of those infernal field tests that so exhausted him. When he came home, he had gone to sleep, then rushed to the lab, came home, and slept some more, and so they had not really spoken. He had not noticed her buoyant mood, and there never seemed to be the right moment to tell him the news. Still, the pregnancy focused her, made her feel in charge of her life, prodding her to consider how a baby would change everything.

Although a part of her would always love Kurt, she found him off-puttingly morose since Jimmy's death. Gloominess clung to him like mold that she was unable to dispel. The pregnancy had crystallized the rightness of holding onto Thomas with all her might. A baby would finally cement her place in his world of assumed and effortless success. His sense of privilege and grace had awed her from the moment she met him, and she had been breathing its aura ever since, but until she produced an heir, she could never feel secure within its constellation.

She could imagine Thomas lifting a toddler to his broad shoulders and pretending to giddyap like a horse or splashing with a child in the sea. She remembered that the first thing Gertie ever told her about Kurt was that he had taught her to swim by throwing her into a pool when she was four—sink or swim. Christine suspected Kurt still thought this was the best way to teach a child to swim. He was so stern. Thomas would make the better father.

As she took her pearls from the jewelry box on the dresser, her eyes fell on her wedding picture. She was surprised to feel a connection, lost when she first came to Los Alamos, with the younger version of herself in the photograph: confident and optimistic, wearing the same necklace now in her hand. She closed the clasp at the back and thought how hopeful the future looked. Given the recent declarations of Roosevelt, Churchill, and Stalin in Yalta, it seemed the Allies were going to win this damn war after all. She and Thomas might leave soon. Maybe their child would not even be born at Los Alamos.

She waited in the living room for Thomas, glancing at her watch. It was unlike him to be late. And yet he was. By half an hour already. She tried to still the panic that rose in her throat. Ever since Jimmy's accident, she had been scared that others might also get hurt, that something might happen to Thomas. She shook with anxiety. Fate was not going to grab Thomas from her just when she had finally conceived, just when she realized her marriage suited her. This couldn't be happening. She had to control herself. If she didn't calm down, she might lose the baby. Thomas had to be okay. Why was he late? What would she do if something happened to him? Would she insist Kurt was the father? No, never. If she had to, she would raise a child alone. Why was she thinking such thoughts? Did pregnancy make you crazy?

Outside, a horn honked, and a car door slammed. She rushed to the window and saw Thomas parking Oppie's familiar black Buick, borrowed for the evening. As he stepped out of the car, she grabbed her coat and flew down the stairs into his arms.

"Wow. What's the matter? Are you okay?" he asked.

"I was so worried. You're late."

She looked up at him. He was smiling weakly. His cheeks were hollow, his skin sallow. He looked so worn. Clearly, he needed this time away from the Hill more than she did.

"It's been a tough day. Things took longer than they should." He gave her a peck on the cheek and murmured in her ear, "But you look delectable." He held the car door open for her.

"I'm so happy you're here," she said as she sat and swung her legs into the car.

Thomas looked at her quizzically and started the engine. She rolled down her window, breathing in the smell of earth, patches of it visible amid the last vestiges of snow.

Thomas pulled away from the house. "Here's to a wonderful evening," he said.

"Here's to a wonderful life." She smiled at him.

CHAPTER 40
GERTIE

March 1945

Gertie closed her eyes and released the application packets to Simmons and Mount Holyoke into the post office mailbox. They thudded at the bottom, prompting Susanna to bark. Gertie stooped to cup the dog's face in her hands. "Wish me luck. I'm going to get out of here soon!" Susanna yapped in agreement.

Gertie figured one of the two colleges, maybe even both, would accept her, and then she would be near Jimmy again, come autumn. In Boston or near Boston. Maybe by then the war would be over, although it was hard to tell. There were reports of dreadful casualties at Iwo Jima. She checked the family mailbox, but it was empty. She hadn't had a word from Jimmy for a month, not even on Valentine's Day. Maybe his card was late. Or was he forgetting her?

Susanna pulled her along until they reached Fuller Lodge. Even before entering, Gertie smelled hot cocoa and burning pine logs. Inside, a fire crackled in the hearth, and laughter resounded off the thick walls. Owen was sprawled at a table with three WACs. They burst into gales of laughter, apparently at one of his jokes. When she got a hot chocolate and turned from the counter, she found Owen staring at her, amusement draining from his face. She made her way to him.

"Hi! Haven't seen you around much," she said.

"Been busy, hard times." He seemed surly.

"Have you heard from Jimmy?"

"Ah, no. No. Not recently."

He didn't introduce her to the WACs or ask her to join them. Well, who needed him and his doting WACs?

"I'll be getting on then. Have a nice time." She hoped the hurt was not evident in her voice. Owen didn't even pretend to be nice to her when Jimmy wasn't around; he obviously didn't consider her worth the time of day since she was off limits for flirting. As she threaded her way to the only unoccupied table and chair, a newspaper boy came in and left a stack of the *Los Alamos Bulletin*. She picked up a paper and read it as she sipped her drink, pretending her interest in the news was the reason she sat alone. There was a review, full of praise, of course, for the latest amateur-theater play, *Arsenic and Old Lace*. A photograph of the actors dominated the front page. And there was a notice about a new choir, looking for altos. Then her eyes fell on a one-paragraph item:

Former Hill Technician Perishes at Iwo Jima

Jimmy Campbell, one-time technician on the Hill, was lost at sea during operations at Iwo Jima. The only son of Linda and Tony Campbell, he is survived by his parents.

She read the item again. It couldn't be true. There wasn't even a picture. Didn't obituaries always carry a picture of the deceased, always smilingly unaware of their fate? Jimmy couldn't be dead if there was no picture. She read the item again. The word *dead* wasn't there. Lost at sea? It didn't have to mean dead. Maybe he had swum to shore and would write to her soon. Of course, he would. He'd jumped off whatever ship they stuck him on because he got seasick. He hated being on boats; she knew that. So he had swum to shore. Hadn't he? She read the announcement a third time. Like steeping tea slowly changing the color of tepid water, the printed words filtered into her mind, and with them the swirling, dizzying realization that she might never see Jimmy again. She looked over at Owen, laughing with the WACs. How could Jimmy be dead if Owen was laughing? It didn't make sense. She lurched toward him, then shoved the paper in front of him.

"What's this? Do you know anything about it?"

The WACs stopped their chatter.

"Um, no, well, yes, tragic. I knew something had happened. It wasn't clear what."

"You knew Jimmy is missing, presumed dead, in Iwo Jima? And you didn't think this was something you should tell me?"

"Me? I didn't know . . . it's not my place," Owen protested. "Your father, your mother . . . I was sure they would . . ."

"Would what?"

"I don't know . . . talk to you . . . something . . . I really don't know."

Owen squirmed; his eyes kept darting at her and then away.

"My parents? They know?"

"Didn't they tell you anything?"

"About what? This?"

"Gertie, I don't know . . . I mean, yes, I know Jimmy died . . . I thought you knew . . ."

"How would I know? The newspaper is just out now."

"I guess . . ."

He seemed so uncomfortable, as if he wished she would disappear, so that he could go on amusing the WACs, who were all staring at her now.

Then it struck her. "You knew before it was in the newspaper, didn't you?" Her eyes began to brim with tears. He didn't seem the slightest bit sad. Wasn't Jimmy his best friend?

"Mmm, yes, I heard. Something. There were rumors . . . I don't know."

Why was he being so shifty? As if he was hiding something. "And my father, he heard . . . the rumors?"

"I don't know. Probably . . . it's not for me to say."

"You keep saying that."

Owen sighed. "Gertie, I don't know what to say. It's sad. Horrible. Don't think I don't miss him. I do. Terribly."

"You could have fooled me! You don't seem sad at all!"

Owen looked down at his hands. Then up at Gertie again. "You don't know how I feel or how hard this is for me. Believe me, I'm plenty sad. I'll never have a friend like Jimmy again."

Gertie rushed out of the lodge, the door slamming behind her. The cold air hit her in the face and with it the realization that Owen had spoken the truth. She, too, would never again have a friend like Jimmy. Her stomach seized up so violently, she felt she might collapse. Why had Jimmy been sent to Iwo Jima? What did it have to do with his work at Los Alamos? He got seasick easily and never mentioned being on the sea in his letters to her. Nothing made sense. Gertie ran, not knowing where she was going, only that she had to flee this news. Susanna ran behind her, yapping and nipping her feet.

She turned on the dog. "Oh stop it, Susanna."

The puppy looked up and started toward home, beckoning to Gertie to follow.

"It can't be true, Susanna," Gertie sobbed, picking up the leash and following the dog.

"Gertie, wait a minute," Owen called out. He came up to her, panting, his coat and hers in his hands. She could see his breath in the cold air. He looked frightened.

"You forgot your coat."

"How can you be in there flirting with a bunch of WACs when your best friend just died?"

"He didn't just die, Gertie. It happened last month. His death is awful. I thought your parents were going to tell you—before it got into the *Bulletin*."

"You mean they know?"

He shrugged. "Maybe I've got it wrong. Ask them."

Gertie shook her head, unable to speak. She turned from Owen, her feet like weights.

"You shouldn't have found out this way. None of it should've happened this way."

Gertie shuffled away from Owen, aware only of the cold and the need to escape what he was telling her.

He grabbed her arm. "Gertie, listen." He pulled her around. "Jimmy really loved you, Gertie. He'd want you to know that. I was his best friend—I know. He loved you."

Tears welled in her eyes. The *rat-tat-tat* of woodpeckers boring holes into nearby trees seemed to hammer "no, no, no" through her head, chasing out any thought.

"Let me walk you home?"

Her head was pounding. "Go back to your WACs."

"Are you going to be okay?"

"No. But you can't do anything to help that."

Owen ran his fingers through his hair and took a step back, as if acknowledging he had nothing more in the way of comfort to offer her.

She turned from him and trudged home. No secrets. Wasn't that what Jimmy had promised? And now he was dead, and no one had told her. Jimmy was her world, and no one had bothered to let her know that it had shattered. Her parents, who were supposed to care for her, hadn't thought she should know. How long were they going to hide things from her? And why? She stamped the slush from her boots when she reached home and stomped in, failing to shed them as she should by the mat. The house smelled of something baking.

"Gertie, I've been waiting for you," Sarah called out.

Gertie walked into the kitchen, leaned against the door, and watched as her mother slipped cookies off a baking sheet. "Sit down, *schatz*, we must talk." Mama never said sentences like that. Talk? Mama wanting to talk? What had Owen said about asking her parents?

"I know already," Gertie said.

Sarah set the pan on the counter. "I wanted to talk to you about Jimmy."

"I said I already know."

"Know? Know what?"

"That he's dead. It was in the paper," Gertie said, pulling out the broadsheet. "Here."

"*Mein Gott!* Where did you get that?"

"What do you mean? Where everyone gets the paper. I stopped at Fuller Lodge after I mailed my applications."

"*Liebchen*, I was going to tell you, today, before the newspaper."

"It's not true, is it?" More than anything, she wanted Mama to say they hadn't told her anything because it wasn't true.

"Such a tragedy. I know how much you care for Jimmy, *liebchen*." Sarah tried to hug Gertie, but she pulled away.

"How long have you known? Why didn't you tell me?"

"*Liebchen.*"

"Damn your *liebchen, liebchen*. Stop pretending I can live in a child's paradise when the world is falling apart!" She ran out the door.

Where could she go? She stumbled toward Christine's. Tomorrow and every tomorrow after that would never feel like yesterday, when the future held the promise of Jimmy. No one would ever look at her like that again. She tripped up the stairs to Christine's house, burst through the door, and called her name.

Christine emerged from the bathroom. "Gertie! What is it? Not your mother, again?" She dropped to the sofa.

"My mother? Damn her! And my father! Have you heard?"

"What?"

"Jimmy. He's dead. At Iwo Jima."

"At Iwo Jima?"

"Yes, it's in the *Bulletin*." Gertie thrust the newspaper at her.

Christine stared at it, then heaved and sprinted toward the bathroom.

Gertie followed her.

Christine heaved a few times as if she was about to retch, but nothing came up. She looked at Gertie. "I have to sit down. I feel like I'm going to faint."

"It's enough to make anyone sick, isn't it?"

Christine sank onto the sofa. "Please, Gertie, get us both some water. I don't think I can make it to the kitchen."

Gertie brought Christine a glass of water and flopped down beside her on the sofa. Christine was the only person who seemed as sickened by the news of Jimmy's death as she was. She was so pale, she seemed more affected even than Gertie. At least Christine understood, felt the pain, Gertie thought, as tears streamed down her face again.

"He was my whole life," she blubbered.

"I know."

"He's so sweet. Always kind. *Was* so sweet." Her crying intensified as she corrected herself to past tense.

Christine took Gertie into her arms, stroked her hair, and handed Gertie a tissue. "This is so hard."

Gertie nodded as she blew her nose.

"Papa and Mama knew. And they didn't say anything. Why didn't they tell me? Why did I have to read it in a newspaper? It's so humiliating. As if I have no right to know. As if it's none of my business."

"I'm sure they just wanted to protect you."

"From what? Life?"

"They knew it would be hard for you."

"It's not right!" Gertie said. "Nothing's right."

Christine just held her. Kissed her hair. Didn't say anything. Gertie was grateful. She didn't want pity. She just wanted someone to absorb her sadness. Gertie let herself be comforted by Christine's spare body, let herself be hugged until she had no more tears, until she felt the shock wearing away slowly.

There was an insistent banging on the door.

"Hon, let me go get that." Christine extracted herself from Gertie to open the door.

Papa filled the doorway.

"Christine!" he cried. He stepped toward Christine. She stepped away.

"You must be worried about Gertie. She's here."

"She is? Sarah contacted me to say Gertie had run off. She was so worried. I thought, maybe you'd know . . ."

Christine moved aside.

Papa stepped into the living room, looked from Christine at the door to Gertie on the sofa.

Gertie stared at him. He seemed confused. For all his culture, his intellect, his fatherly love, he was a coward, an emotional amoeba.

"I hate you," she said. She had never said such words to her father. She had never vaguely felt the rage that welled in her now.

He stepped toward her.

"How long have you known? How long?"

"Gertie, please." He touched her shoulder.

"Tell me." She shook him off.

He dropped his hands to his side in defeat. "Not long." His eyebrows furrowed as if he were in pain. "Too long."

"I hate you." How could he have kept such information from her? Why did he think he had the right to protect her from what she needed to know?

Papa flinched. "Come home."

"I'm never coming home." If she had been a cat, she would have hissed at him.

"Gertie, please, come."

"I'm staying here."

Papa looked at Christine, still standing at the door. He looked like a small lost boy.

"Give her a little time," Christine said. "Let Gertie stay awhile."

CHAPTER 41
GERTIE

May 1945

The announcement came over the Hill's loudspeaker system, but at first Gertie and her classmates heard only a jumble of words through the closed school window. Then "God Bless America" blared, and Gertie stood up without permission and threw open a window.

"Something's happening, something important," she declared.

Other pupils followed her lead and opened the rest of the windows along the whole side of the room. The smell of jasmine accompanied the hot dusty air that billowed into the room. When the song ended, the voice of the WAC at the base's radio station rang out: *"It's over, folks. Germany has surrendered, unconditionally. V-E Day is here."*

It felt like a dream. Gertie watched the other kids whoop and hug each other, too stunned at first to join, overcome with an exhilarating sense of relief. But she was swept along as they all fled the room like puppies let out of a kennel, and their teacher joined the pack, all thronging to Fuller Lodge, instinctively understanding that everyone would converge there.

"Let's hear it for Uncle Sam," shouted one boy, and soon the rest of the class, including Gertie, joined in, kicking up clouds of sand and clapping in rhythm: "Let's hear it for Uncle Sam. Let's hear it for our boys."

From all sides, waves of residents spilled into the road: scientists from the Tech Area, still sporting lab coats, women pushing strollers or carrying groceries. Young children on tricycles pedaled furiously to keep up with their mothers. Engineering army corps soldiers in military jeeps, engines revving, roared past them, all headed in the same direction. By the time Gertie's class reached Fuller Lodge, the area in front of the building was already packed. "When the Lights Go on Again (All Over the World)" blasted over the speakers. Then the announcer repeated the news, adding bits of information: The surrender had taken place in Reims, France, two days before, the final surrender agreement signed just minutes ago in Berlin. Today was President Truman's birthday. "This is the best birthday present I can imagine," he had told reporters.

Then another song, "Der Fuehrer's Face." Here and there, a cluster of people sang the words.

Standing in the expanse in front of Fuller Lodge, Gertie caught sight of Owen walking toward her. Just seeing him reminded her of Jimmy, and suddenly she felt the familiar dark cloud of grief descend. How she wished it was Jimmy waving and threading his way toward her instead of Owen.

"What a day! Finally!" Owen stretched out his arms to embrace her in an exuberant hug.

She stiffened, took a step back. "Yes. I wish Jimmy had lived to see it."

"I do too." Owen, jostled by the crowd, kept bumping into her. They moved to the edge of the throng. "Don't think for a moment that I'm not thinking of Jimmy, that it's not only Roosevelt who didn't live to see this day. But still, we are allowed to be happy, aren't we?"

Could she blame him for having a sunny personality? Did she expect him never to laugh again because Jimmy was dead? Even she could not always be sad. She knew now that life went on, no matter who died. Even if she never loved anyone like she had loved Jimmy, her life would not be altogether without love or happiness forever. Still, at a time like this, a happy, important time, his absence jabbed her.

"I've been waiting to go off to college, to escape this place, but now it looks as if everyone will be leaving. The war will end, and there'll be no reason to stay."

"There are still the Japanese."

"How much longer can they hold out?"

"God Bless America" wafted from the speakers again, and it was hard to speak over the chorus of voices that sang along. But Gertie ignored the music and repeated her question.

Owen shrugged. "Who knows? The Japanese don't believe in surrender."

"Won't they surrender now that the Germans have?"

"I damn well hope not."

"You don't want them to surrender?"

"What would be the point of everything we've been doing here if they do?"

"You mean the gadget?"

Owen nodded, but before he could respond more, Gertie was squeezed around her waist from the back, and she turned to see Christine. Gertie hugged her back, feeling Christine's protruding belly against her own. Oppie, speaking through a squeaky microphone, begged for everyone's attention.

Christine ignored the appeal. "What a day! Can you believe it? My baby's going to be born in peacetime!"

"You think so? Owen doesn't think it's going to end so soon," Gertie said.

"Oh?" Christine seemed to just have noticed Owen was standing by Gertie. "Why not? The baby's due in September. Surely by then . . ."

Owen was about to answer, but Oppie began to speak.

"What a thrill it is to be gathered here, today with you, on this happy occasion. I am sure you are all as grateful as I am to have lived to see this day, one we have longed for," Oppie said.

The crowd cheered. Gertie scanned the throng for her parents. Although she had kept much to herself the past few months, ever since they admitted withholding the news of Jimmy's death from her, she wanted to share this moment with them, this end to their nightmares. But Oppie's ringing voice drew her back to his speech.

"Yet, we should not be sanguine. Germany's surrender is not the final act of this war." Oppie spoke from an impromptu platform in front of the lodge. "There are still battles raging in the Pacific, and American and Allied soldiers who cannot come home, who are fighting for their lives and our way of life. We must not forget Pearl Harbor. We must see this war to its end." Oppie paused and looked up at the brilliant blue sky for a moment before turning back to his audience. "Yes, this is a glorious day, but we must redouble our efforts to contribute to the end of this war. So, enjoy the victory that has been achieved, but remember that there are other victories not yet at hand. Enjoy this moment—and in an hour—everyone, back at work!"

The on-tap beer spout opened at the lodge. Strangely, the victory over the Germans made Gertie even sadder about Jimmy. How she would have loved to feel his arm around her today, sharing the moment, secure in the knowledge of a war-free future together. She wondered if others who had lost loved ones felt the same. Victory didn't justify the loss of lives or set matters right. Nothing did. Besides, Jimmy had died in the Pacific, where the war, as Owen pointed out, wasn't yet over.

Gertie's thoughts were interrupted by Mrs. Martin, trying to rally the seniors back to school, but the pupils ignored her. Other teachers, calling their charges, were having no better luck.

"She's dreaming if she thinks anyone is going back to class today," Gertie said to Christine. "I'm going to the post office. Maybe Mount Holyoke or Simmons have written."

"I'll come with you." They walked arm in arm. "Which will you choose if they both accept you?"

"Before, Simmons was my first choice. But without Jimmy, there's less incentive to be in Boston. So probably Mount Holyoke. It's got a gorgeous campus and a great reputation."

"I wonder where we'll end up," said Christine.

"Won't you go back to New York?"

"Who knows what's become of Thomas's lab or his department. Everything's up in the air. For everyone."

"I wonder where my parents will go." Did her father face similar uncertainty about returning to his job in Boston? She had never given much thought to where her parents might live after the war. Where were they? She had so much to ask them.

A cloud of dust caught by the wind swirled into them. Christine coughed up the sand in her throat. "It sure will be a relief to leave this godforsaken dust bowl."

"Where to, if not New York?"

"Anywhere that's not a desert!" Christine blinked furiously to squeeze out the grit irritating her eyes. "Thomas likes working with Enrico Fermi, so he'll probably want to follow him to Chicago."

"But what about Samantha and your business in New York?"

"There's not much of a business left. And Maria's ceramics might sell better in the Midwest. Besides, with the baby coming, Chicago makes sense. Thomas's family is there. If I give her a grandson, my mother-in-law might come to accept me, maybe even like me."

"How can anyone not like you?!" Gertie gave Christine a squeeze. "I just assumed everyone would go back to doing whatever they did before the war. But none of us are who we were before, are we?"

Christine placed a hand over her stomach. "I remember when we first met, you seemed so lost. I was, too, although I didn't wear it on my sleeve the way you did."

"I feel lost since Jimmy's gone. Papa and Mama still treat me like a child. Ever since I learned Papa knew about Jimmy—I don't even know for how long—I haven't been able to forgive him. I barely talk to him. I'm so angry. He never tells me anything about anything,"

"You must know by now, after living here for so long, sometimes secrets are secrets for good reason."

"I don't believe that."

"Then maybe you haven't changed much after all. Not as much as you should."

Gertie stopped to look at Christine. Were they having their first fight ever? It sure sounded like Christine was criticizing her. Gertie remembered the first time she had met Christine, how they had stayed at Ashley Pond until twilight, looking at the lit-up Tech Area and wondering what was going on there.

"I thought you always wanted to know everything about this place, just like me. It's why we became friends, isn't it?"

"It wasn't why for me. I thought you were a sweet kid, and an interesting one. And we both needed a friend. Besides, like you said, we've all been changed by this place. I know I have."

It was true—Christine was different these days, more guarded. Gertie attributed it to the pregnancy. Still, Christine was her best friend, the only person at Los Alamos she would miss.

"We'll stay in touch, won't we, if all this ends?" Gertie's eyes spanned the mesa, its ugly buildings scattered haphazardly and the majestic terra-cotta desert in the distance, both desolate and uplifting.

"Of course, we're like family." Christine squeezed Gertie's arm, looped through hers.

When they reached the post office, Christine checked the Sharps' box on the far right while Gertie went to the Koppels' box on the left. Gertie looked inside. Empty.

Christine joined her at the post office door, a Sears and Roebuck catalog clutched to her chest. "I wonder how much longer we'll need to be ordering everything through one of these." She thumped the catalog.

"Come, let's walk a bit. It'll do us both good. With the pregnancy, I've become lazy about getting exercise."

As they walked toward the water tower at the major crossroads of Los Alamos, Papa and Mama approached from the opposite direction.

"Here you are! We looked for you at the lodge," Papa said to Gertie. "To celebrate the wonderful news with you." He nodded at Christine, and Gertie saw his eyes wander to Christine's stomach. Mama's eyes followed his.

"You will have a baby soon?" Mama asked.

"Not so soon," said Christine.

The conversation was forced to a momentary halt by a convoy of jeeps that whizzed by, the drivers honking their horns in celebration, leaving the Koppels and Christine to bat away a swirl of dust.

"When?" asked Papa.

"When what?" asked Christine, her train of thought disrupted as she wiped sand off her cheek.

"When is the baby due?" asked Mama, explaining his question.

Christine stopped moving for a moment to gaze first at Mama and then at Papa before shifting back to Mama.

"They tell me October," she said.

"Having a baby, that is good," said Mama. She seemed pleased for Christine.

"I thought you said the baby is due in September," said Gertie.

"Did I? How silly of me!" Christine tittered. "It must have been the excitement of the moment. It's been such an emotional day!" Indeed, she seemed momentarily flustered. "Where do you think you will all be in October?"

Mama stared blankly at Papa, as if curious to know how he would answer. So did Gertie. He seemed distracted and remained silent.

Gertie filled the lull. "The war's not over yet. There is still Japan, right, Papa?"

"Yes. But it's not the same as fighting the Nazis."

"We're here to win the war, aren't we? To do whatever it takes to win it, no?" said Christine.

Papa frowned. "There are ways, and there are ways."

"Owen says you need to know if the gadget works," said Gertie.

Papa's frown deepened. He seemed angry. "Some people want to play with their toys, regardless of the consequences."

CHAPTER 42
KURT

June 1945

Kurt hadn't had a good night's sleep since the German surrender. He could not understand this, since the nightmare was over. Hitler was dead. And it seemed the Nazis had never developed an atom bomb after all.

Kurt looked at Sarah slumbering next to him. At least she was sleeping these days. He would wake her if he kept twisting and turning, so he rose, slipped a sweater over his pajamas, put on shoes, and quietly left the house. Perhaps he could walk off his anxiety.

He stared at the sky, at the firmament of stars, and considered all the Allied newsreels he had watched in the past few weeks. So many civilian corpses in Nazi camps. He had surmised for some time, from the bits of information buried in newspapers, that their dear ones in Germany were likely dead, but there had always been hope. Now, hope dimmed from day to day. He had requested information from the Red Cross but had received none so far.

Kurt glanced at the lights coming from the Tech Area. He no longer wanted to work there. Not since Jimmy's death. He had seen with his own eyes what a slight touch of radioactive material could do to one person. Now he couldn't stomach going to the lab, but it could not be avoided. Of course, he'd always known that radioactive material was dangerous on a theoretical level. But until he saw it eat up Jimmy, he had never fully faced the fact that an atomic bomb would not only mean instant death for those directly hit but excruciating, slow death for those merely exposed to its radiation. Thousands, maybe even tens of thousands. Before, he could dismiss the devastation because he believed that sometimes it is necessary to use evil to fight evil. But with the German surrender, it made no sense to him to continue to develop the two bombs—one with uranium and the other with plutonium.

Bathed in night lights, the Tech Area seemed a benign place. But in it, even now, his colleagues were working around the clock creating monsters. One creates a monster to kill a monster. But if the monster is dead, the revenge monster must be killed. The Allies would win the battles in Asia, although it could take time, would cost still more Allied soldiers' lives. But there was no serious doubt about the outcome. Eventually, the Japanese would surrender. Yet, Oppie kept pressing everyone forward frenetically to ready the gadgets against the Japanese. He did not often say so openly, but he wanted to try out the weapons before the Japanese surrendered—to see if they worked. Pure ego. This was science gone mad. Oppie was a brilliant man, and a good man, but he was precipitously shifting the goal of their work on the gadget. This was no longer about winning the war but about assuring American domination after the war over the Soviets, ostensibly allies now but considered unreliable in the future.

Kurt sighed and turned in the direction of Fuller Lodge. Even the intoxicating smell of pines that filled the air could not dispel his gloomy thoughts. He did not want to be part of the project any longer. Bombs against the Soviets were not what he'd signed up for. Neither had Oppie. Everyone here knew better than anyone else in the world the destructive capacity of the work. They should be standing together to stop the bombs.

Earlier in the week, Kurt had signed a petition against the use of the bomb on Japan, objecting to the precedent it would set for the postwar era, but he had been among a minority to sign. He feared it would be ignored by President Truman, to whom it was addressed.

Kurt had even considered tampering with the data in his lab, sabotaging the research. But he didn't have the courage to do it, too afraid of the consequences if discovered.

If only he could hide in some quiet place, return to pure science. He had become a physicist to be professionally awestruck by the majesty of the world. He wanted to be awestruck by beauty, not horror.

He would leave Los Alamos as soon as possible, although he did not know where he and Sarah would go. Not to the ashes of Europe. All that he had once loved about Germany—its adulation of beauty, its sophistication, the German language, even—now seemed vacuous, a refinement easily shunted aside by cruelty and evil. German culture was familiar, but he no longer wanted any part of it.

He knew Sarah dreamed of being surrounded again by Germany and the smells of her childhood, but even she knew that there was no going back. So, they were destined to remain foreigners, outsiders in this country that they would call home, although it would forever feel like temporary lodgings.

Kurt found himself standing by the tree where he and Christine had spoken on Christmas, after the play, when she had invited him to the shed. He leaned back and smiled at the memory. The only times he had felt at home in America had been in Christine's arms. There was something sheltering about her, alert yet nonjudgmental, and a resilience that allowed him to relax in her presence. He should have congratulated her when he saw her on V-E Day, pregnant. He had fleetingly considered the possibility he might be the father. But she said the baby was due in October, and he had calculated the last time they saw each other—and concluded the baby couldn't be his. On the other hand, she could be wrong about the due date. It had occurred to him that she might be hiding the truth from him. But they had made their choices—to live with the spouses they had and not with what they might have had together.

Kurt was at peace with the decision. Compatibility, shared history, or perhaps a certain emotional laziness had trumped passion.

Still, he wondered what he might have said to her on V-E Day if he could have spoken freely. He breathed in the early-summer air as if it were her perfume. He would have told her that he thought of her every day, that when he went to sleep, he imagined himself in her arms. He would have liked to spend the rest of his life in the aura of her unflinching competence and compassion, her keen and discerning mind, her veneration of the beautiful.

Kurt turned back and started toward home. He was bound to Sarah in an intimacy impossible to have with Christine. He and Sarah were of the same cloth. He did not soar with her as he did with Christine but was earthbound in the familiar, like a dog curling into his favorite corner after a long time away. With Christine, he had to explain everything yet could share anything. With Sarah, he needed to explain nothing, and for a very long time he had thought it unnecessary—even undesirable—to endeavor to share much of himself. She did not presume to ask, and Kurt had thought her uninterested and, truth be told, uninteresting. But after the pill incident, they had begun communicating on a new level. Although Sarah did not ask the sort of probing questions Christine did, she was curious in a quiet way. Kurt came to realize that he had starved Sarah, feeding her crumbs of himself because he thought she never hungered for more. But she was far more voracious than he imagined. And she surprised him at times. Just last week she had told him that she regularly tutored a neighbor's daughter in reading and was teaching the child also how to knit. She told him, too, of the guilt she felt for not succumbing to the seduction of her high school friend to try to get the family out of Germany. In this, at least, Kurt had been able to comfort her. The man might not have kept his word, and her parents, even if presented with exit visas, would probably not have agreed to use them. Sarah's refusal to confer sexual favors was its own kind of resistance, and Kurt had told her so. Sarah was a comfortable iteration of the familiar, with a subtle and intricate texture. He had done what his head said he must by staying with her, his heart only partially in agreement.

Kurt reached home. He looked at the stakes in the victory garden that he and Sarah had planted last week, even though they were unsure they would still be in Los Alamos by the time the vegetables were ready to harvest.

He looked out toward the mountains, their outlines only faintly visible in the dark. Sometimes the best way to hold on to someone, to the sacredness of moments together, was to let that person go. Opening the door to his house, he was simultaneously broken by and at peace with his choice.

CHAPTER 43
CHRISTINE

July 1945

Thomas jumped out of an army jeep and burst through the door. In the midday sun, he looked dusty as he hugged Christine and waltzed her around the living room. "This may be the happiest day in my life!" he whispered in her ear. "And I'm famished," he added, pulling away and beaming at her.

"Tell me—whatever you can, of course," she said as they walked into the kitchen. The sudden dancing had caused the baby to stir, stretching her abdomen from inside.

"The test. It worked. The gadget—we did it." He grabbed the toast with the marmalade left over from Christine's breakfast. "May I?" He bit into her toast without waiting for an answer and sat down. "It was beautiful. I just can't describe how stunning it was. I've never seen anything like it. Probably never will ever again. Just amazing!" He held the plate close to his face and wolfed down the rest of the toast.

"Wasn't it dangerous?" Since Jimmy's accident, she was certain they were fooling around with highly lethal levels of radiation.

"Not terribly. We took safety measures."

She doubted it was so simple. If only she could ask Kurt. But she couldn't. She must stop thinking of him.

She smiled at Thomas. "Good," she said, then cut two slices of bread, popped them into the toaster, and turned off the stove under the whistling kettle.

"So, if the gadget works, what happens next?" She retrieved the toasted bread and poured herself and Thomas some coffee. She was ready to go back to sleep until the baby was due—in two months. So much for the glow of pregnancy.

"I don't know." Thomas shrugged. "I'm just a scientist."

"Do they plan to use it?" Kurt's comments the day they learned of the Nazi surrender had discomfited her. Whatever it was they were doing here seemed less important.

"I suppose they will use the gadget, one way or another."

"Against the Japanese?"

"I guess. Who knows?" He shrugged and opened the kitchen window, letting in a warm breeze that whipped the kitchen curtains. Outside, dogs exchanged barks in the yard. The mountains were layered in hues of purple against a clear sky.

"Look at the gorgeous light, the shadows," he said.

Christine stared at Thomas. "There must have been some talk about it, no?"

"I don't get involved with that. I've been busy making sure the casings are a-okay."

"Do you ever think about the consequences?"

Thomas turned away slowly from the window as if reluctant to have his attention taken from the distant view of the mountains. "I was given a job to do. A tough job. I gave it my all. You know that as well as anyone. Day and night, six days a week, just like everyone else around here. And we did the job, and, it turns out, we did it well. I came home happy, proud even. Yes, proud. Can't you be happy with me, happy for me, for us, for America, even?" He spread marmalade on his second toast. "Cheers," he said ruefully, raising his coffee cup.

"Cheers," she said gently, raising her cup in return. "Of course, I'm proud of you, Thomas. But the grueling hours don't exempt you from thinking about the consequences."

"Look, I'm beat. I need a shower. Is there water?"

"I think so."

"Good. I'll go shower. Let's not fight. And I'm still hungry, could do with a second round of breakfast after I wash up. Let's make it a celebratory one, okay?"

She smiled and nodded, but after he left to clean up, she sighed. His intentions were good, and there she was, asking him unanswerable questions. The kind she thought it important to grapple with, not dismiss. She was being unrealistic. Thomas had his strengths; philosophizing and doubting were not among them. If she was hitching her future to him—and she was—she'd better come to terms with that. She remembered what Maria had told her so simply. She just had to do the right thing and remember to be grateful that he was well, and healthy, and present.

As she whisked some eggs for an omelet, she looked out the window. She would miss this view, with its palette of ochres and mauves, the jagged rocks and hidden caves in their endless variety. She would miss her trips to San Ildefonso and the conversations with Maria, who recently had proudly shown Christine her new shop, where she and her family were selling kerosene, dried goods, and tobacco to villagers, and pots to outsiders who ventured there in search of Maria's ceramics.

Christine was placing the breakfast plates on the table when Thomas walked in, smelling of pine aftershave. He hugged her from behind, nuzzling his still-wet hair into her neck and resting his hands on her stomach.

"I couldn't be happier," he said.

She closed her eyes and leaned into him. It always felt as if Thomas lived under the spell of a good fairy. Stay in his orbit and good fortune was assured. He deserved this moment of bliss. The gadget, the baby—everything going his way. And hers. When he pulled away and sat down, she passed him the salt and pepper before he asked for them.

"If the gadget works, your job here is done, or almost done, isn't it? The war will end sooner rather than later, don't you think?"

"It will be over soon. Time to move on. Won't you be glad?"

"I don't know. There are things I will miss."

"Will you? You resented coming here so much. But you've landed on your feet after all, just as I knew you would."

"It doesn't feel quite like that." For a moment she thought how cleansing it would feel to confess to someone—to Thomas or to Kurt—about Jimmy and what she had done. And perhaps be absolved. But it was too risky.

She forced a smile.

Thomas stopped eating and cocked his head at her. For a moment she feared he suspected all the things she didn't want to tell him.

"You know, you've changed," he said.

"Maybe. Or just become clearer about who I am."

"And who is that?"

"A person who does things her way, flouts convention, asks questions, even when they make her husband uncomfortable. Does that scare you?"

"A bit, maybe. But not much, if you still love me. Do you?" It surprised her that he felt a need to ask. Maybe he had sensed the distance between them more than she had given him credit for. She touched his bare shoulder and let her finger run down the front of his pale, strong rib cage. "I believe I do," she said.

CHAPTER 44
GERTIE

August 1945

Christine signaled to Gertie, who was babysitting Amalia, Martha's eight-year-old daughter, to come over to the bench at the edge of the playground.

"You swing on your own now," Gertie said to her charge and stopped pushing the swing.

"I can't touch the sky without you," Amalia retorted.

"I taught you to pump. Practice." Usually, Gertie was patient with the little girl and had been delighted when Martha offered her a summer job to babysit Amalia. But she was anxious to know why Christine had come looking for her. "You can keep the swing going on your own. I'll be watching you." Without giving Amalia time to protest, she joined Christine on the bench.

"What brings you way out here? It's a hot day to be walking around in your condition."

Christine put her hand on her belly as she sat down heavily. "It's hot all right. But I had to come and tell you. The gadget. They used it on Hiroshima. It's all over the news. It worked."

"Hiroshima. Who's that?"

"It's a city in Japan. They used the gadget on the Japanese. President Truman just made it public. The bomb was released overnight. The news was broadcast over the loudspeaker system. Truman even mentioned all the people who were involved in developing it. Everyone on the Hill is going crazy. Relieved, excited, making reservations for dinner in Santa Fe to celebrate and waiting to hear more details. I knew you wouldn't hear anything out here."

Above them, birds chirped in the aspens, and the breeze blew steadily, unperturbed.

"So the gadget was a bomb, just like we always thought?" Gertie said.

"Yes, an atomic bomb."

"What's that?"

"Powerful. More powerful than anything the world has ever seen. Truman said it was more powerful than twenty thousand tons of TNT. He didn't say anything about the casualties yet, but we'll hear of them soon enough, I suppose."

Gertie looked at Christine. "Was there a battle?"

"No. There wasn't any fighting. But there must be a lot of civilian casualties."

Gertie nodded, absorbing this information. "Aren't you happy that the gadget worked?"

"I want to be happy for Thomas, for your father, for everyone else here. But an atomic bomb means radiation." Christine stared at the horizon as if she were imagining that bomb. She sighed heavily and looked back to Gertie. "It doesn't just kill those it strikes. It poisons everything around it."

"It does?"

Christine looked at Gertie, then looked down and bit her lip several times, as if weighing whether to continue. Gertie had never seen Christine so distraught.

"Tell me," Gertie said.

Christine sighed deeply. "An atom bomb releasing as much energy as Truman indicated kills people by burning them from the inside, slowly and painfully, for days, for weeks, even for months." Her voice drifted off.

"Are you sure?"

"I studied chemistry, remember?"

Gertie glanced up at the sun and tried to imagine this bomb that burned people from the inside. She couldn't. People at Los Alamos were good. Papa, Oppie, all the others. They wouldn't want people to die the way Christine said. Maybe Christine was exaggerating. Gertie glanced over at her charge, who was pumping away, feet reaching for the sky.

"I should get back to Amalia," Gertie said.

"You should." Christine sighed and maneuvered her body, readying to get up. "Nothing we can do about the casualties but wait and hear how bad they are." She lifted herself off the bench. "I should go wash my hair and get ready for the festivities."

Gertie nodded and returned to Amalia. Suddenly everything seemed so fragile. Instead of feeling good about finally knowing what Jimmy and Papa and all the others had kept secret for so long, she felt confused. Did the bomb harm people the way Christine said? But wasn't that a good thing if it led the Japanese to surrender and saved American lives so that no more soldiers would die like Jimmy had? Amalia was wriggling off the swing.

"So did you reach the sky?"

Amalia smiled proudly. "Almost."

When the *Santa Fe Times* came out the day after the bombing, Gertie read every detail. Finally, it was in front of her, in black and white. All that Jimmy and Papa had been forbidden to tell her, now in bold capital letters in every newspaper in the world: FIRST ATOMIC BOMB DROPPED

ON JAPAN; MISSILE IS EQUAL TO 20,000 TONS OF TNT; TRUMAN WARNS FOE OF 'A RAIN OF RUIN'

In the following days, more information was released. 60 PERCENT OF HIROSHIMA REDUCED TO ASHES, and then the gory details: "Those outside burned to death, while those indoors were killed by indescribable heat and energy." The estimates of how many civilians were killed varied, but most reports estimated around one hundred thousand. And then there were reports about long-term effects and contamination of the city. Gertie was nauseated. She didn't know what to think. She couldn't talk to Christine, who was in the hospital in Santa Fe due to pregnancy-related bleeding. Her doctor had ordered inpatient bedrest until she went into labor.

Gertie noticed that there were many on the Hill who, like herself, had turned somber after the initial relief and raucous partying over the first bomb. And then two days later, Nagasaki was bombed.

Papa rarely went to the lab these days. He stayed in the bedroom, sleeping or with a cold compress on his head. Mama forbade Gertie from disturbing him and brought meals to his bedside on a tray. Gertie could hear the tone of their soft voices. Mama's was gently chiding. Papa's didn't sound like him; he was whiny, childlike, devoid of his usual assured authority.

Finally, she stopped him on his way back from the bathroom.

"I need to talk to you, Papa, please," she said.

"What is it, Gertie?"

"Please, sit with me, just for a few minutes."

"I don't want to sit and talk," he said.

"Please, Papa. I miss you."

He nodded and followed her to the kitchen. He seemed drained of life, like a dead man with eyes open.

Gertie sat herself opposite him at the breakfast table. "I need to understand. Why a second bomb, Papa?"

He shrugged. "Truman says the Japanese didn't surrender after the first one."

"He didn't give them much time to think about it, did he?"

Papa smiled the saddest smile she'd ever seen.

"You are smart, Gertie. Yes, he could have waited a bit. Given them more of a chance." Papa shrugged and sighed heavily. "But he didn't. Unfortunately."

"Why?"

"The bomb on Nagasaki was also an atomic bomb. But a different kind. Truman, the army, they wanted to make sure both kinds worked."

For the first time, Papa was not holding back information. In fact, he was volunteering it. That felt strange.

"And that's why tens of thousands of people were killed?" she asked.

Papa's mouth collapsed into itself. His fingers began shaking, and he entwined them to still them. "I'm afraid so," he said.

"Did you know?"

"That they were going to use the second bomb?"

"No, that people would burn to death from it."

Mama, back from shopping, came into the kitchen.

"Kurt, you are up."

He looked up at her with despondent eyes. "Yes, Gertie had some questions."

"Gertie, you mustn't bother your father. He's not well." She bustled about, stashing food in the fridge, while throwing worried glances at her husband. "Kurt, should I make you tea?" she asked gently.

He nodded.

"Go rest, I'll bring it to you. Gertie, don't bother Papa." Mama lit the stove under the kettle.

"Gertie, I'm tired," Papa said.

"Papa, answer me. It's the only question that really matters."

"Answer what? Gertie!" Mama sounded angry. "Stop."

Papa sighed. "Sarah, let her be. She is right to ask."

He turned to Gertie. His hands shook. His skin seemed pale and sickly, but it was his eyes that seemed timeworn, as if they could not see any more or did not want to.

"What did I know? The truth is, Gertie, I can't say."

"It's not complicated. Either you knew or you didn't."

Mama stopped in the middle of spooning sugar out for Papa's tea. "Gertie, how dare you talk to your father this way? Show some respect!"

Gertie ignored Mama, locking her eyes instead on Papa, the person she most admired in the world, even if grudgingly at times. He had always been her moral guide, but now he was deflated, like an old balloon.

"There are all kinds of knowing."

"That's not an answer, Papa." She hated to press him this way, but she had to understand.

"Gertie!" Mama shouted. Gertie was startled. Mama rarely shouted, and it was strange to see her act as Papa's protector when all her life it seemed that Papa was the one trying to protect them all. Suddenly, he seemed the vulnerable one.

"Let her be, Sarah." Papa searched Gertie's face, as if he was trying to judge whether he had a chance to gain a sympathetic hearing from her. "No one knew exactly how devastating the gadget, the bomb, might be. But yes, I knew it would be bad."

"Didn't that bother you? Worry you?"

Mama set the tea down in front of Papa. He blew on it. Silence filled the room except for Mama's unusually noisy movements as she put away the groceries from the commissary.

Papa sighed. "Against the Nazis, no, it didn't bother me. The big worry was that they were building a bomb like ours and would have it ready before we did. That's why we worked so hard. But when they surrendered, yes, I worried."

He sipped his tea, then set the cup down and continued. "I worked on a petition, with others. We wanted America to tell the Japanese about the bomb, explain its destructive power, give the Japanese a chance to surrender without hurting civilians. The petition was for Truman. But Oppie wouldn't let us send it around the Hill. He didn't permit us to deliver it to Truman, insisted our idea was already under consideration, so there was no need."

"Kurt, enough, you must not dwell. You did what you could. Go rest," Mama said.

Papa rose. He lifted up Gertie's chin. His fingers were cold despite the warm weather. "Do you understand? There were no easy choices. I must now live with mine." His eyes went dead again. He dropped his hand from her chin, took his tea, and shuffled to the bedroom.

Her eyes trailed after him. Papa had answered her questions, and she finally knew the secrets of this place. But there was no satisfaction in this, only the understanding that she still had so much more to comprehend.

CHAPTER 45
GERTIE

November 1948, South Hadley, Massachusetts

Owen had written to Gertie that he was coming east to a lecture at the University of Massachusetts, not far from Mount Holyoke College. Would she meet him while he was in the area?

What a question! Of course, she would, she answered.

Since she'd left Los Alamos for college a little over three years ago, they had stayed in touch with occasional postcards. Removing her hair curlers as she readied to meet him, she considered how well Owen had done for himself, on a tenure track to be a chemistry professor at the University of Chicago. No one she had known at Los Alamos lived there any longer. Christine, too, was in Chicago, where Thomas had also landed an endowed professorship at the University of Chicago, and she had opened her own gallery. Papa and Mama were back in Boston, Papa at MIT and Mama earning a degree as a nurse. When Mama had first announced her intention to study, Gertie was surprised, but the decision made perfect sense. Mama would be a fine nurse, lavishing the same gentle, persistent care on patients she'd always showered on the family. She and Mama would both graduate next year. Oppie was heading the Institute for Advanced Study in Princeton, New Jersey.

Although it was a prestigious position, he was being treated shabbily, she thought, no longer the hero he had been on the Hill. Instead, he was sidelined within the Atomic Energy Commission for objecting to US policy in the atomic arms race with the Soviets. Owen would likely have the latest on the politics of all that.

She buttoned a white blouse and tucked it into her plaid skirt, then combed her hair, which fell gracefully over her shoulders. Surveying herself in the mirror, she concluded that she looked much better than the last time Owen had seen her. The curves of her body were more comfortable with themselves, no longer surprising and disturbing as she had felt them to be when she was younger. Jimmy had always made her feel beautiful, even when she had not felt so herself. Now, as she applied her lipstick, she knew that although she did not turn heads, she was reasonably attractive.

Gertie still hadn't met anyone who made her as comfortable as Jimmy had, but she believed she would. Someday. Right now, she was focused on finishing her degree—a double major in chemistry and psychology—and applying for an advanced degree. She loved the intensity and challenge of academia, although she might one day want to apply her knowledge outside university walls.

It was 5:00 p.m. already, and Owen would be waiting. She gave herself a last once-over in the mirror and hurried down the winding staircase to the dorm lobby.

Owen was sitting in the corner of the wood-paneled reception area in a slightly frayed armchair. As she made her way to him, he looked up. That slightly mischievous grin she remembered slid across his face.

He stood. "My goodness, you are a sight for sore eyes!" He took her hand and twirled her around. "What a looker you've become!"

"And you look the same as before."

"I'll take that as a compliment." He laughed and proffered his arm. "Shall we go?"

She linked her arm with his. "There's a great burger joint down the block. But I thought we'd go for a walk first. The campus is beautiful, and I could use the exercise. I've been studying all afternoon."

They walked past pseudo-Gothic buildings. The air was brisk, hinting already at winter, and with twilight, the lights on the campus began to flicker.

She told him about her courses, how she was planning to go into neurology, a way to combine her interests in chemistry and psychology. He told her about his latest research in carbon dating and how it could be used to determine the age of anything organic at an archeological finding—mummies, parchment, seeds, or wooden implements. As they made their way from the campus to the diner in the center of town, a few blocks away, they talked about Oppie and the rumblings that he might be hauled before the House Un-American Activities Committee.

"Did you know that he never got top clearance even when he headed Los Alamos?" Owen asked. "Apparently, G-2 always suspected he was a Communist sympathizer, and now the powers that be keep him in the doghouse, cut him out of any high-level meeting, because he's trying to fend off an atomic arms race."

"Seems to me that's an honorable endeavor," said Gertie.

"But not practical. The Soviets aren't going to let up on arms, so why should we?" He asked it as a genuine question, without the cocky conviction Gertie remembered from their Los Alamos days.

"Hard to know the right thing to do. All I know is that Papa has never been the same since the bombs were dropped. He's convinced he should have done more to stop their being deployed on civilians, particularly on Nagasaki."

She paused, expecting Owen to defend the bombing, but he was silent. So she went on.

"Papa still teaches, but his heart isn't in it. He has lost not only his curiosity, but his zest for life. He doesn't even seem to care if I continue to study or not, just gets glum every time I mention pursuing a master's or even a doctorate."

Owen shoved his hands deep in his jacket pockets. "A lot of people who were at Los Alamos felt bad about it at the end." His somber tone hinted that he was not a stranger to self-flagellating conversations with former Los Alamos colleagues.

"What about you?"

"They say maybe a million Allied soldiers would have died if we hadn't bombed the Japs. They don't believe in surrender. It's their culture. The bomb stopped them in their tracks."

"I've heard that, but is it true?"

An eighteen-wheeler roared by, making conversation impossible until it passed.

"Lots of good things have come from the discoveries we made during the war. Carbon dating, radar to find lost ships, among other things. Science is neutral. It's not my personal responsibility—or your dad's—if politicians screw up what we've discovered."

Gertie thought to pursue the point. But surely opinions would always be divided, and she didn't know what she herself thought. Besides, they had reached Joe's Grill. A blast of warm air, smelling of burgers and fries, greeted them as they made their way to a booth.

"Have you stayed in touch with anyone from the Hill?" Owen asked after a waitress took their orders.

"I write to Christine occasionally, and to you, but that's it. Do you see her and Thomas often? You must work with him, no?"

"I do. He and Christine live up the block from me, so we're quite friendly. Christine's been very busy with her gallery. That potter friend of hers, Maria, has been winning all sorts of art prizes, and those black pots have taken off, big time. The connection with Maria really helped Christine establish herself and meet other Pueblo artists she now represents. Even though she's got a lot on her hands with little Jamie and the business, she found the time to throw me a birthday party last month." Reaching for his wallet, he pulled out a photo from the party and handed it to her. It showed Owen, Thomas, and Christine, who was holding their daughter, Jamie. Christine had put on a bit of weight, cut her hair, but still looked striking, her regal head cocked toward Jamie. Thomas looked as handsome as ever.

Owen reached for the photo to take it back.

"Can I keep it?" she asked.

He seemed to hesitate.

"Please?" she asked with an apologetic smile. "Christine's not good about sending pictures. And you can always snap another picture, the next time they invite you over."

"I suppose." He sounded inexplicably reluctant.

Gertie studied the picture again. "So that's what Jamie looks like. What a cutie! She must be three years old."

"Yeah, she is cute. Little ones always are. My theory is that it's nature's way of making parents put up with what a handful they are," he said ruefully.

"Said like a man not anxious to have any of his own," Gertie said, laughing. She was about to slip the photo into her purse, but something drew her back for another look. "Gosh, Jamie looks a lot like me when I was little."

"Little children all look kind of the same, don't they?" Owen shrugged, but he seemed suddenly less lighthearted.

"Do they?" Not as similar as this child looked like her.

Their cheeseburgers arrived, and she doused her fries with ketchup, as if in a trance, trying to overcome the sense of discomfort she had of seeing the double of herself at age three in Christine's arms. Jamie had a cowlick in the front that was just like Gertie's at the same age. And that smile—it was like hers in a photo Mama kept in the living room of the two of them back in Hamburg when Gertie was about Jamie's age.

"Hey, are you going to use up all the ketchup? Leave a little for me, okay?" Owen said.

"Oh, sorry. Here." She handed him the bottle.

"Are you okay? What's the matter?"

"Nothing. I'm okay." The photo lay between them. She couldn't stop staring at it.

"You sure?"

"It's just that Jamie, she looks so much like me. It's disconcerting." She took another look at the photo.

Owen shrugged but looked uncomfortable. "There are a lot of mysteries in life, a lot of unknowns. Sometimes it's better not to know."

"A strange thing for a man of science to say."

"Science is one thing. But human nature, I'm not sure about that."

"How can you make that distinction? Chemistry and neurology and psychology, they blend into each other. How can one be curious about one and not the other?"

"It was Jimmy's biggest complaint about you. How you always wanted to know everything about everything." He shoved fries into his mouth, oblivious to the impact of his words on Gertie. Even now, it hurt that Jimmy had considered her curiosity a fault rather than a virtue.

"He complained to you about me?" Were there other ways, too, in which he had found her wanting? Of course, the question was irrelevant, but still it mattered.

"Yeah, he always got hot around the collar with the way you pressed him to tell you things it was best not to know. He found that really hard." Owen kept a steady stream of fries moving from the plate to his mouth. His appetite clearly had not diminished with the years.

"I hated all that secrecy at Los Alamos." Gertie sighed. "Christine was the only one there who ever leveled with me."

Owen stopped midbite and gave her a strange look, one she could not decipher. In the next booth, a group of young women burst out laughing. The waitress came by and asked Owen and Gertie if everything was okay.

"We're fine, thanks," Gertie said, sipping her Coke through a straw. She looked again at Jamie, who had her fingers in her mother's mouth, and slipped the photo into her handbag.

"Why would Jamie look like me?"

"Beats me," he said with a shrug, then took a slug of beer and busied himself with fishing out some coins from his pocket and slipping them into the jukebox at their table. "Powder Your Face with Sunshine" came on, and the backup cooing "Smile, smile, smile" filled the diner.

She asked Owen about who else he was still in touch with from Los Alamos, his research and vacation plans, his recommendations on where to apply for graduate school, but her mind wasn't on his answers. She was thinking about Christine, how much she missed her, how peculiar it was that they were not in touch more and that Christine had never sent her a photo of Jamie. Gertie found it suddenly hard to swallow the hamburger. It felt dry. She couldn't finish it. No, she didn't want dessert, thanks, or coffee. They got the check, Owen slapped money on the table, and they left the diner.

They walked back to campus in silence, passing several gaggles of young collegiates on the street. Gertie barely noticed them, her thoughts still on the photograph, on that striking resemblance Jamie bore to her, on the lack of contact with Christine. Her mind ground slowly to make sense of it all.

Owen slowed as they approached the entrance gate to Mount Holyoke. "I should be getting to my hotel. My car's across the street."

"I'm glad you came."

"Are you? I feel I've upset you. Stirred things up. Maybe I shouldn't have come."

"No. It's good to see you. But that picture, of Jamie, yes, that threw me a bit."

"Maybe I shouldn't have shown it to you."

"Whyever not?"

They crossed the street to his car. He kissed her forehead. "Take care of yourself," he said. He unlocked the door, took a last glance at her before getting into the car. "My word of advice: secrets are secrets for a reason."

"I want to believe that the truth is important. Honesty is always the best."

He got in and turned on the engine. Then opened the window.

"Life is more complicated than that." He shifted into first gear and drove away.

Walking back to the dorm, she tried to swat away all the confused thoughts buzzing in her mind. How could she and Jamie look so much alike? Only relatives could look so similar. Had some covert genetic experiment been conducted at Los Alamos along with work on the gadget? Was that the secret Owen referred to? That didn't make sense. Ludicrous. But how else could Christine have a child that looked so much like a younger version of Gertie? She closed her eyes, holding back tears of frustration.

Suddenly it did make sense. The way Christine always defended Papa whenever Gertie complained about him. The way they had looked at each other, or rather avoided looking at each other, that awful day when Mama took too many pills. Had they had an affair? Was that why Mama took the pills? Gertie suddenly remembered that bow tie in Christine's drawer, the one that looked like Papa's, but which Christine had insisted belonged to Thomas. But did it?

The memories flooding back seemed so different now, filtered through the evidence of the photo in her purse. Papa and Christine? Had they been together? She felt she was going to be sick. Were they still in touch? Her parents seemed so close these days, it was unlikely. Did Papa know he had another daughter? No wonder Christine had never sent a photo of her child.

Gertie turned up her collar against the cold and headed back to the dorm. The lights on campus showed her the way. She wished Jimmy were alive so that she could admit to him that she understood now why he insisted that sometimes it was best not to know. She was unsure how to live with this new truth that was leaching into her, and yet she still wanted to know everything. Someday she would ask Papa whether he had loved Christine, and if so, why he had stayed with Mama. Someday she would ask Mama if she thought Papa had always been faithful to her, and find out if she knew about the affair, and whether that mattered now, seeing how devoted they were to each other. Someday she would forgive Christine for all the lies. And even if she did not do any of those things, have any of those conversations, someday she would go to Chicago. Someday, when she learned how to keep secrets, she would go meet Jamie. Maybe even soon.

AUTHOR'S NOTE ON HISTORICAL

BACKGROUND

Readers often wonder what is true in a historical novel and what was imagined by the author. All the main characters in this novel are purely fictional, yet people with similar biographies lived at Los Alamos, a highly diverse community that grew from several hundred people in 1943 to some six thousand people by the time World War II ended.

A real version of my fictional Sarah might not have been as lonely as suggested, for there were numerous Jewish refugee families from Germany and other European countries at Los Alamos. But she would indeed have felt older, since the average age of adults there was twenty-nine. A sixteen-year-old like Gertie may have had a few more playmates her age than I suggest, although most of the children at Los Alamos were indeed younger than Gertie, and boys predominated in the upper classes at Los Alamos's high school.

There were theater groups, musical ensembles, and many parties, where Robert Oppenheimer was known to display his skill at preparing martinis. Hiking, skiing, and horseback riding were all parts of life, although the skiing facility was not as developed in the winter of 1943 as it is described in the novel.

Cézanne's *The House with the Cracked Wall* can be found in the Metropolitan Museum of Art in New York City but was acquired by the museum years after I have Christine and Thomas viewing it.

Potter Maria Martinez lived in San Ildefonso, and her pottery was owned by Oppenheimer and others at Los Alamos. She was already well known by the 1940s, having been promoted in the 1920s by a number of people, prominent among them Alice Marriott, an entrepreneur and philanthropist, who, along with her husband, J. Willard Marriott, founded the Marriott hotel chain. The descriptions of Maria's early years, working with her aunt and archeologists, and the description of the death of her husband, Julian, are true to fact. Her pottery is highly treasured today, and I had the privilege of marveling over it at an extensive exhibit in 2017 at the National Museum of Women in the Arts in Washington, DC.

Dorothy McKibbin, Enrico and Laura Fermi, Richard (Rich) Feynman, and Kitty Oppenheimer, and the horse, Odysseus, are all true characters (and creature), although the Fermis are described at being at a party several months before they actually moved to Los Alamos.

Jimmy's Special Engineer Detachment arrived at Los Alamos in October 1943, three months after he greets the Sharps on their arrival at Lamy. His accident did occur much as described, although it happened after the bombs were dropped on Japan. I could not help but speculate how history might have been different if Oppenheimer and other scientists at Los Alamos had been forced to see firsthand—and on one of their own—the horrific burns and excruciating pain that a brush with radioactive material caused.

Some seventy scientists did sign a petition in July 1945 against use of atomic weapons on Japan, which Oppenheimer refused to deliver to President Harry Truman, but it was initiated by physicist Leo Szilard at Oak Ridge, Tennessee, another secret installation that was involved in enriching uranium to fuel the bomb being built at Los Alamos. Scientists at Los Alamos knew about the petition but did not have the opportunity to sign it.

For those interested in learning more about Los Alamos and its residents, please see the bibliography of sources that were useful in writing this book.

ACKNOWLEDGMENTS

The journey of writing this book started more than two decades ago in a chance conversation with American historian Aaron Berman, a close friend and professor at Hampshire College, who mentioned reading a paper that explored whether wives of scientists at Los Alamos during World War II were aware of the atomic bomb being created in their midst. This led me to think about concrete knowledge versus intuitive knowledge, about things we know and do but don't acknowledge or talk about. I began to conceive of a novel that would explore such personal tensions within the setting of Los Alamos, with its omnipresent, unspeakable secret. My deepest thanks to Aaron for that initial conversation and for so many stimulating and thoughtful ones over decades on topics far and wide.

I enrolled in an MA writing program at Bar-Ilan University in Israel, where the idea to write about Los Alamos morphed into interrelated short stories, only one of which has survived as a chapter in the novel. Nevertheless, the exchanges with fellow students—prominent among them Daniel Weizmann, Meira Meron, Bill Taeusch, and Sara Dayan—served as a prelude to writing the full novel. From among my fellow students, Rachel Karlin became a friend and close writing colleague who has read more iterations of *Hill of Secrets* than any other person, over more than a decade, providing both valuable suggestions and unflagging faith that this novel would be published. I am also grateful to her for introducing me to two excellent writing groups. I hope that this book inspires her to someday publish her own spectacular writing.

Special thanks are due to Evan Fallenberg, head of Bar-Ilan University's Shaindy Rudoff Graduate Program in Creative Writing, who became my thesis adviser at a critical moment, providing feedback and support when I most needed it. Authors Joan Leegant and the late Allen Hoffman, who taught in the program, also gave generously of their expertise and time.

To the longtime members of the Tel Aviv writing group—Judith Colp Rubin, Miryam Sivan, Michelle Orrelle, Anna Levine, and Michal O'Dwyer—your critique and camaraderie have been my lifeline. You gave me the courage to turn my full attention to completing the manuscript, and your insightful feedback over several years made *Hill of Secrets* an infinitely better book. Long may we write and share together! Past members of the group—Julie Zuckerman, Nicole Georgy, Natalie Shell, Sigal Kerem Goldstein, and Helen Motro—also provided valuable criticism.

Madelyn Kent's sense-writing classes were eye-opening experiences that deepened my sense of craft; writer/coach Barbara Kyle's cogent suggestions on the first chapters of the book led to a far more compelling manuscript.

Thanks are due to early readers of the full draft: Susan Kline vastly improved and polished the manuscript by ferreting out dull or imprecise language and asking thoughtful questions. Ellen Colburn and Kathy Wasiuk also painstakingly read every line, pointing out inconsistencies and errors. Dvorah Bushari and Don Futterman, fellow authors and trusted friends on matters of writing and life, provided insights and advice.

Friends whose enthusiasm for the manuscript helped to sustain my spirit when I despaired that *Hill of Secrets* would ever see the light of day include Maggie Bar-Tura, Margo Bloom, Heidi Haas, Roberto Marquez, Naomi Neustadter, Kit Patten, Steven Siegel, Barbara

Weinberg, Mandy Weiss, Nancy Wellins, and Connie Wilson. Judy Katz Charney and Galit Oren also encouraged me at critical moments.

I cannot express sufficiently my gratitude to Deborah Harris, long-time friend and colleague, who became my unwavering, wise agent, offering excellent suggestions and recruiting her talented team—Jessica Kasmer-Jacobs, Thomas Dayzie, and Geula Geurts—to improve the manuscript and to put it into the hands of Alexandra Torrealba, acquisitions editor at Amazon Publishing.

I feel extraordinarily lucky to have benefited from Alexandra's contagious enthusiasm from the moment she read the manuscript and from the professionalism of the Amazon Publishing team. Alexandra guided *Hill of Secrets* from manuscript to book with stunning efficiency, skill, grace, and intelligence. Among her many smart moves was to pair me with development editor Celia Johnson, whose excellent questions and suggestions left me feeling always in command while pushing me to go deeper into characters' heads and reminding me of what a reader might need to know. Such egoless, astute editing is an author's dream. I was equally fortunate to work with Megan Westberg, copyeditor extraordinaire, whose historical-fact sleuthing, stylistic suggestions, and scrupulous attention to detail left me in awe.

Finally, thanks are due to my family: My parents always encouraged me to write. My father, (the late) Benjamin Vromen, kept a special file labeled "Wunderkind Galina" (*wonderchild* in his native Dutch), containing anything I ever wrote that I shared with my parents. Only when I told him the subject of my novel did I learn that he had been approached as a chemist in the 1950s to work on an atomic weapons project—and refused. This was news to everyone in our family, including my mother. Talk about secrets in families!

My mother, Suzanne Vromen, has waited for years to see my name on a book cover. I appreciate her keeping the faith.

Knowing that my son, Adam Pely, is proud of my accomplishments means more to me than he could possibly imagine.

My husband, Doron Pely, gave me the space to pursue the dream of this novel, even when it seemed a never-ending undertaking with little prospect of success. He endured my bouts of frustration when the writing was not going well and suggested the title for the book. He provided feedback—when I finally dared to show him a late draft of the manuscript. Working up the courage to do so took me a long time because his opinion matters more to me than anyone else's. His love has sustained me in this endeavor, as it does in our life together.

BIBLIOGRAPHY

Anderson, Peter. *Maria Martinez, Pueblo Potter*. Chicago: Children's Press, 1992.

Bethe, H. A. *The Road from Los Alamos*. Woodbury, New York: AIP Press, 1991.

Bird, Kai, and Martin J. Sherwin. *American Prometheus: The Triumph and Tragedy of J. Robert Oppenheimer*. New York: Alfred A. Knopf, 2005.

Brode, Bernice. *Tales of Los Alamos: Life on the Mesa, 1943–1945*. Los Alamos: Los Alamos Historical Society, 1997.

Church, Peggy Pond. *The House at Otowi Bridge: The Story of Edith Warner and Los Alamos*. Albuquerque: The University of New Mexico Press, 1959.

Conant, Jennet. *109 East Palace: Robert Oppenheimer and the Secret City of Los Alamos*. New York: Simon & Schuster, 2006.

Fermi, Laura. *Atoms in the Family: My Life with Enrico Fermi*. Chicago: University of Chicago Press, 1954.

Feynman, Richard. *"Surely You're Joking, Mr. Feynman!": Adventures of a Curious Character*. New York: W. W. Norton & Company, 1985.

Gibson, Toni Michnovicz, and Jon Michnovicz. *Los Alamos: 1944–1947 (Images of America)*. Charleston, South Carolina: Arcadia Publishing, 2005.

Groves, Leslie M. *Now it Can Be Told: The Story of the Manhattan Project*. New York: Harper, 1962.

Hacker, Barton C. *The Dragon's Tail: Radiation Safety in the Manhattan Project, 1942–1946*. Berkeley, California: University of California Press, 1987.

Herken, Gregg. *Brotherhood of the Bomb: The Tangled Lives and Loyalties of Robert Oppenheimer, Ernest Lawrence, and Edward Teller*. New York: Henry Holt & Co., 2002.

Howes, Ruth H., and Caroline L. Herzenberg. *Their Day in the Sun: Women of the Manhattan Project*. Philadelphia: Temple University Press, 1999.

Hunner, Jon. *Inventing Los Alamos: The Growth of an Atomic Community*. Norman, Oklahoma: University of Oklahoma Press, 2004.

Jette, Eleanor. *Inside Box 1663*. Los Alamos: Los Alamos Historical Society, 2007.

Kelly, Cynthia C., ed. *The Manhattan Project: The Birth of the Atomic Bomb in the Words of Its Creators, Eyewitnesses, and Historians*. New York: Black Dog & Leventhal Publishers, 2007.

Litchman, Kristin Embry. *Secrets of a Los Alamos Kid, 1946–1953*. Los Alamos: Los Alamos Historical Society, 2001.

Malmgren, Peter, and Kay Matthews. *Los Alamos Revisited: A Workers' History*. El Prado, New Mexico: Wink Books, 2017.

Marriott, Alice. *María: The Potter of San Ildefonso*. Norman, Oklahoma: University of Oklahoma Press, 1948.

Mason, Katrina R. *Children of Los Alamos: An Oral History of the Town Where the Atomic Age Began*. New York: Twayne Publishers, 1995.

Nesbit, TaraShea. *The Wives of Los Alamos*. New York: Bloomsbury, 2014.

Peterson, Susan. *The Living Tradition of Maria Martinez*. Tokyo, Japan: Kodansha International Ltd., 1977 and 1989.

.Rhodes, Richard. *The Making of the Atomic Bomb*. New York: Simon & Schuster, 1986.

Rockwell, Theodore. *Creating the New World: Stories and Images from the Dawn of the Atomic Age*. Bloomington, Indiana: 1st Books Library, 2003.

Roensch, Eleanor Stone. *Life Within Limits*. Los Alamos: Los Alamos Historical Society, 1993.

Rosen, Terry L. *The Atomic City: A Firsthand Account by a Son of Los Alamos*. Austin, Texas: Sunbelt Eakin Press, 2002.

Sparks, Ralph C. *Twilight Time: A Soldier's Role in the Manhattan Project at Los Alamos*. Los Alamos: Los Alamos Historical Society, 2000.

Spivey, Richard L. *Maria*. Flagstaff, Arizona: Northland Press, 1979 (revised 1989).

Steeper, Nancy Cook. *Dorothy Scarritt McKibbin: Gatekeeper to Los Alamos*. Los Alamos: Los Alamos Historical Society, 2003.

Wilson, Jane S., and Charlotte Serber, eds. *Standing By and Making Do: Women of Wartime Los Alamos*. Los Alamos: Los Alamos Historical Society, 1997.

Yellin, Emily. *Our Mothers' War: American Women at Home and at the Front during World War II*. Free Press, 2004.

Online resources:

"Voices of the Manhattan Project." A public archive of oral histories of the project's veterans and their families, created by the Atomic Heritage Foundation and the Los Alamos Historical Society. https://ahf.nuclearmuseum.org/voices/.

Maria Martinez: Indian Pottery of San Ildefonso. Documentary filmed 1972 in San Ildefonso Pueblo, New Mexico. YouTube video from VHS, 26:46. https://www.youtube.com/watch?v=SkUGm87DE0k.

ABOUT THE AUTHOR

Photo © 2023 Johanna Resnick Rosen / Jo Rosen Photography

Galina Vromen began writing fiction after more than twenty years as an international journalist in Israel, England, the Netherlands, France, and Mexico. After a career with Reuters News Agency, she moved to the nonprofit sector as a director at the Harold Grinspoon Foundation.

Vromen launched and directed two reading readiness programs in Israel, one in Hebrew (Sifriyat Pijama, the Hebrew version of the foundation's PJ Library Program) and one in Arabic (Maktabat al-Fanoos). During her tenure, the two programs gifted twenty million books to young children and their families and were named US Library of Congress honorees for best practices in promoting literacy.

Vromen's stories have been performed on NPR's Selected Shorts program and appeared in magazines such as *American Way*, the *Adirondack Review*, *Tikkun*, and *Reform Judaism*. She has an MA in literature from Bar-Ilan University in Israel and a BA in media and anthropology from Hampshire College in Massachusetts.

Vromen and her husband divide their time between Israel and Massachusetts.